# COCKATOO CREEK

B. J. Scholefield

B. J. Scholefield

Cockatoo Creek
ISBN: 978-0-6485089-5-3 Paperback
Copyright © Baden James Scholefield 2019
First published 2019

Note found in a crack in the wall of an old house

.....'I'm goin off to do me bit

and kick the Kaisers bum.

I know I never prayed before,

but please look after mum.'


From the poem, 'This Old House'

By B.J. Scholefield

*For my wife Judy who gives me love*
*and lends me common sense*

# Contents

# PROLOGUE

*Derby District Hospital Clarendon Street, Derby*

*Western Australia 15th August 2008*

Sister Kathleen Murphy looked down at the name tag at the end of the white, wrought-iron bed. The words, Anna Cook had been hurriedly printed onto a piece of white cardboard and attached to the foot of the old woman's bed. The young Sister stood by the edge of the bed and spoke softly to the old Aboriginal woman who lay there. 'Hello, my dear, how are you today?'

The old woman did not reply but nodded her head in quiet acknowledgment. Outside, the urgent wail of an arriving ambulance broke the silence as it turned into the main gates.

The Sister smiled at the old woman and took her hand. 'I wonder if I could talk with you for a while?'

The old woman stared into Sister Murphy's eyes but remained silent.

'My name is Sister Kathleen Murphy. I am a teacher here in Derby at the Holy Rosary School. We are encouraging our students to take an interest in local history. Many of them are Aboriginal and one of them told me about you, and that you were here in the hospital.'

The old woman's expression remained unchanged, and the Sister began to wonder if she had understood her at all.

'The young girl who told me about you said that you lived out at Cockatoo Creek Station for most of your life. We were hoping you may have some interesting stories to tell us about the old days. If you were to agree, perhaps I could take some notes; that is, of course, if you don't mind.'

The old woman still did not answer, but Sister Murphy noticed that her eyes seemed to light up, if only for a second. The Sister stayed by the bed patiently waiting for a reply, but the old woman still remained silent.

'I'm sorry my dear, you're obviously very tired. Perhaps I could call again on another day. She smiled at the old woman. She knew she would not come again. She reached down and patted her hand. 'Goodbye, my dear and may God bless you.' She turned toward the door.

'So . . . you want to know about the old days?'

The sudden sound of the old woman's voice startled the young Sister. She smiled and returned to the bed.

'They were hard the old days, you know, much harder than now.' The old woman's voice was hushed and tremored with age.

'I am so glad you heard me, my dear. Would you mind if I sat on your bed, and we talked for a while? I promise we'll stop as soon as you get tired.'

The old Aboriginal woman's dark, noticeably oriental eyes seemed to come to life with memory. She lifted herself higher on her pillows and patted the bed for the Sister to sit close to her. 'If you really want to listen to my story, then I'll tell you. But, I warn you, some of it you will not believe, and some of it may make you angry, but I will tell you my story because I believe it should be told.'

The young Sister took out her exercise book and a brand-new ballpoint pen and waited while the old woman composed herself.

'They are all gone now, all of them from those days out at Cockatoo Creek,' she began.

Sister Murphy stroked the old woman's arm. 'Are you sure this is not too much for you, my dear?'

x

'I am old now, very old, and there is no one left for me. I am alone. But back then, I had many friends, good friends some of them are buried out there among the boab trees.'

'Please, go on, if it is not too painful for you,' the Sister replied. She stroked the old woman's arm again and opened her exercise book to its first page.

'I remember when the very first one of my friends was buried out there among the trees; it was one of the saddest days of them all.' The old woman stopped talking and closed her eyes for a few seconds before continuing. 'But there were good times at Cockatoo Creek and I remember them so clearly, even now. We worked hard in those days, but we were treated well by the station owners. There were bad times though, very bad times, and I wish I could forget them. God knows I've tried, but I know now they will stay with me until I die. So, if you wish to listen to an old woman's memories, then I will tell you my story.'

Sister Murphy nodded in agreement and began writing.

The old woman continued, 'I was born in a bush camp long ago, deep in the wild lands, you call the Kimberley. My name is Jiiarnna—'

'But—I thought your name was Anna,' the young Sister interrupted, and then apologized quickly. She looked back toward the foot of the bed where she'd seen the name tag.

The old woman smiled. 'My name is Jiiarnna. I am Aboriginal, but I am also part Makassar. My tribe is Ngarinyin and my people have belonged to this land since the beginning time.

B. J. Scholefield

# 1

# Blackfellas Boss

*Cockatoo Creek Station 320 kilometers northeast of Derby*

*North-Western Australia, Kimberley Country*

*15 October 1932 Late afternoon.*

A wedge-tailed eagle circled high above the first of the wet season's rain clouds that drifted slowly over the boab trees. The huge bird turned in an unseen column of warm air that rose up from the dusty plain below and gradually soared higher and higher in slow, graceful circles, its keen eyes searching the dry and dusty landscape that stretched away from horizon to horizon. Far below the magnificent bird, a small group of Aboriginals moved through the trees in a quiet, weary line. Their hard, calloused feet made soft crunching sounds on the dry leaves that even they were unable to silence. They were tired and hungry. For too long the weather had been harsh and unseasonable, and they had suffered with the passing of each dry and onerous month. Game had become difficult to stalk through the sparse grasses, and without cover, even they, with their prodigious skill with spear and boomerang, were finding it difficult to find enough to feed their hungry bellies. For many days, all they had eaten were a few lizards and an occasional handful of grubs, and now, water had become more of a problem than usual. The drying waterholes were farther and farther apart, many of them putrefied, contaminated by the rotting carcasses of the white man's starving cattle as they had weakened and bogged themselves in the mud of the shrinking pools. The rivers they knew of to the north were too far for them to travel at this time of the year, and perhaps even then, they would only be disappointed. They had never known it to be this dry. They were small in number now, only seven of them in total. Two of the old people had died in recent weeks and most of the young bucks had left them several weeks earlier, and headed in on the long walk to the tiny outback town of Derby. Once there, they hoped to find food and shelter in the rundown bush camp they'd been told of on the edge of that town. Perhaps then, the caring church people of that rough-and-ready cattle town would take pity on them. Many of the roaming Aboriginal tribespeople had made their way into the small outback towns that were scattered throughout the north-west to live in the ramshackle camps and survive on the scraps handed them by the white man.

This tiny group had travelled for many weeks from their traditional lands some distance to the north. The country there had become very dry, and the white man's huge herds of the red cattle had decimated the native grasses and most of the game the Aboriginal people traditionally hunted had either died or disappeared. They had travelled to the south in the hope the hunting would be better there.

However, as they travelled, it had become no better, and now, perhaps even worse. As they trekked through the parched savannah lands, they passed thousands of the white man's starving cattle, but all of them knew it was forbidden to kill them, for they'd been told of the slaughter of their people for eating the red beasts. Their tribe was Ngarinyin, one of several of the Kimberley tribes that called this vast northern land their home. The Ngarinyin were much smaller in numbers now, as were the Unambal people. The dry weather had forced them into small, fragmented groups as they hunted for food across their traditional lands.

Leprosy was rife throughout the tribes of the Kimberley, and in some areas, it had taken a terrible toll on their numbers. But because of their isolation, this small group had not had any suffer from that terrible deforming disease carried to their lands by strangers from other lands.

Even though the season had been harsh, the older members of their group wanted to stay in the bush. None of those who remained wished to follow the young bucks that had left them. The bush was their home, there they walked every day with their long-dead ancestors and sang to them around their campfires at night. It had been the land of their people since the beginning time. Since the 'Wandjina' had walked the land carving the rivers and pushing the stones together that would, in time, become the red and rocky hills of their sacred land.

Cautiously, the weary natives peered out from the shadows at the sprawl of station buildings. The quiet homestead with its sheltered veranda's, the long bunkhouse, the huge workshop, and the shady gardens that seemed incongruous in this harsh and difficult land. They saw the beautiful poinciana trees vibrant in the afternoon's fading light with their canopies of fiery red flowers. Cassia, heavy with pendulous bunches of brilliant yellow blossom and frangipani, their flowers, brilliant white in the afternoon's heat. Dogs were sleeping in the heavy shade beneath some of the trees, but the natives had approached the station carefully, the faint breeze in their faces, and the sleeping dogs were oblivious to their presence.

The stillness was suddenly broken by a loud noise from somewhere to the left of the weary group of natives. White cockatoos that had been sitting quietly in the treetops began to screech their annoyance at being disturbed. The natives turned toward the sound and watched a thin Aboriginal man dressed in the clothing of the white man step out from a nearby building. A dense cloud of bush flies followed him as he hitched up his dungarees and began pushing his arms through the sweat-stained braces that hung lopsidedly around his legs. With a weary gait, the Aboriginal man made his way toward one of the distant buildings.

The cockatoos, annoyed by the sudden clap of sound from the shutting of the outhouse door, rose from the treetops above the natives in a screeching cacophony of alarm. The Aboriginal stockman stopped, looked back and watched the dense flock of birds lift into the air and then begin to settle back in the treetops. In the fading afternoon light, their wings seemed to glow a brilliant white and their crests an incandescent yellow as they nodded their heads with annoyance and fought for position along the crowded branches of the massive boab trees. It was then that he saw the natives peering out at him from the shadows beneath the screeching birds. He kept walking—he had to force himself not to break into a run. He'd seen the spears and clubs that some of the natives were carrying. The Aboriginal stockman was suddenly afraid—very afraid. He made it to the manager's cottage, banged on the door and looked back at the boab trees. They were still there, watching him from the shadows.

Golly knew that attacks by bush natives were not uncommon in the Kimberley. He remembered some years before; the manager and a cook from a station farther north had been killed and butchered by a rogue group for no apparent reason, and he'd heard the stories about Jandamarra, the famous Aboriginal renegade who had roamed the wild Kimberley country some years earlier.

Jandamarra had at one time been a tracker for the Derby police but had turned against the white men who had employed him and led a band of Aboriginals on an attack of five stockmen droving cattle through Bunuba land, the land of his people. During the attack, two of the whites had been slaughtered.

As he stood by the door, waiting, Golly remembered the story in all its tragic detail. After several unsuccessful attempts to hunt down the renegade, Jandamarra, the police had recruited Micki, a famous Aboriginal black tracker from Broome. A man reputed to possess supernatural powers.

Mickie finally managed to hunt down the Bunuba man near his Tunnel Creek hideout in the Napier Ranges and had shot him to death. The police had later cut off Jandamarra's head and placed it in a jar of formaldehyde, and to comply with a request, it was sent to England to a firearms company as a gory exhibit illustrating the effectiveness of their weapons. Jandamarra's body was later buried in a hollow boab tree by his family somewhere in Bunuba country.

This had happened more than thirty years earlier, but Golly knew there were still wild natives roaming the Kimberley bush. The stockman was also aware that, to many aboriginals, Jandamarra was regarded as a hero, a legendary figure still held in high regard for standing up to the white man's seemingly unstoppable invasion of their traditional lands.

The stockman could hear the clatter of a knife and fork being put down impatiently inside the manager's cottage, and then the sound of footsteps. The door burst open, and the station manager, angry that he had been disturbed from his evening meal, looked down at him.

'What the hell do you want, Gollywog? It had better be bloody important,' Jan Muller snarled.

The station manager was a huge man, standing more than six and a half feet tall and built like one of the rugby forwards of his South African homeland. Jan Muller was a white Afrikaner. A man with a vicious nature and a fiery temper, and to make it worse for the Aboriginal stockman, he had no time at all for the coloured people of this world.

'Blackfellas, Boss, hundreds of 'em over there behind the shitter in the trees. They got spears and them killer boomerangs. Maybe we are all gonna get ourselves killed today,' Golly gabbled nervously.

Muller grunted and looked off in the direction Golly pointed, but he could see nothing, just the dark shadows cast by the boab trees and flashes of white from the cockatoos still shuffling about in the high branches above.

'Round up all the hands, and get them here as quick as you can, Golly—go on, get bloody moving.'

Golly turned and ran for the bunkhouse as fast as his skinny legs could carry him.

Jan Muller looked back at his table and his half-eaten plate of food and cursed. 'Damn blackfellas . . . !' He reached up and lifted down his old Rigby rifle from above the door and checked the magazine. It was fully loaded, as well he knew. He rested it against the wall and took down the holstered pistol that hung next to it and buckled it around his waist. The big Smith & Wesson revolver was loaded as well, but he slid it out of its holster, flipped it open, and spun the chamber out of sheer habit. Jan Muller knew only too well it paid to be ready for anything in the bush. His earlier life in Africa had taught him well. He holstered the pistol and walked across to a small cupboard near his desk and took out a box of Kynoch .350 calibre cartridges for the Rigby, tipped half of them into his left hand, and stuffed them into one of his trouser pockets. Then, with the Rigby comfortably in the crook of his left arm, he stepped out into the yard.

Most of the station workers were hurrying toward him now, carrying whatever weapons they could find. Some carried the old single-barrelled shotguns they used to hunt wild duck for the kitchen. One of them carried a military issue .303 Lee Enfield, while the rest carried knives or clubs, and one, the cook—an old Filipino, carried the well-worn axe he used for lopping the heads off chickens from the pen behind the bunkhouse.

Muller grunted at the stockmen as they approached him. 'Get in behind me and listen to what I say.' He threw the Rigby over his right shoulder. 'I want to get off the first shot, so wait for my signal—and watch out for the spears, the bastards can throw them more than a hundred yards. And someone—chain up those bloody dogs.'

One of the stockmen quickly rounded up the now yapping dogs and chained them, while the rest followed Muller toward the trees, most of them cautiously, watching this way and that, not really sure what was expected of them.

'I don't see them, Golly—where the hell are they?' the station manager hissed over his shoulder to the Aboriginal stockman following him.

'They must be back in the shadows a bit, Boss,'

Golly replied nervously.

Muller slammed a round into the chamber of the Rigby and increased his pace. The others followed his example, but anxiously and with much more caution.

In the trees, the hungry natives watched the group of men walking boldly toward them. Goonagulla, their leader, was an old man, and next to him was his granddaughter, Jiiarnna, and behind them both, the rest of their weary group. Goonagulla began to feel the first prickles of fear as he watched the approaching men.

He whispered a quiet command, and the natives laid their spears and weapons on the ground.

Goonagulla had seen many things in his long life, but only a few times had he seen pure evil, however, on this day, he saw it again as he watched the big white man leading the group of men walking toward him. This was a brutal, ruthless man, and the old man could sense a terrible evil that walked with him. He was suddenly afraid of what might now happen, but he fought off the urge to pick up the long spear at his feet and hurl it into the body of the big white man, and instead, forced himself to think only of his quest—to plead for food for his hungry people.

Goonagulla had helped white men in the past when he had found them lost and wandering aimlessly in the bush. He had fed them, given them water, and guided them safely back to their stations. The old man had done this many times, but he had never really trusted any of the white men he had come in contact with. To Goonagulla, they were a cruel race that did not really belong in this, the sacred land of his people.

Jan Muller had seen the old man in the shadows and knew instinctively he was their leader. He smiled and pushed the safety on his rifle forward to fire, ready to bring him down with his first shot. Less than fifty steps were all that separated them when he stopped and, with a steely look, lifted the Rigby to his shoulder.

Suddenly, the stockman, Golly jumped forward. 'Let me talk to 'em, Boss! Let me see what they want. They put them spears down on the ground nice and quiet you know, Boss—I don't reckon they're really bad buggers!'

'They look pretty bad to me, Gollywog, and I reckon I'm going to have me some shooting practice, so step the hell back out of my way, you useless bastard.'

Golly stepped back, fearful of what he knew was about to happen.

Just then the old Aboriginal headman stepped forward, his arms to his sides.

Jan Muller smiled and eased back the first pressure on the trigger, in readiness for the final squeeze and the impending recoil of the big rifle.

It was suddenly very quiet. The cockatoos that lined the branches of the trees above the natives now sat like alabaster statues watching the drama unfold below them.

The old Aboriginal headman slowly lifted his right hand and pointed his fingers into his mouth and then back to the small band of frightened natives standing behind him.

'They only want tucker, Boss—just tucker, that's all. No need to kill 'em today—no need at all, Boss,' Golly mumbled nervously. The other stockmen nodded in agreement and began to lower their weapons.

Jan Muller looked disappointed, but he kept the Rigby to his shoulder. He looked back at Golly and whispered, 'If you ever stick your black nose into my business again, I will cut your skinny throat. Do you understand me?'

Golly knew his boss only too well, and he knew instinctively that he meant every word. He replied quietly, 'Okay, Boss.'

Muller kept the Rigby aimed at the old Aboriginal man's chest, but now indecision began to creep into his mind. He saw a flicker of movement at the old man's side. He swung the Rigby to his right, hoping against all probability it would be a young buck with a spear raised. He readied himself for a quick shot. But it was a lubra, a young girl of no more than sixteen or seventeen years of age. The girl was attractive, very attractive. Muller lowered his rifle and studied her closely. The native girl was tall, bare-breasted and well-shaped. Her belly was flat and sleek and her dark skin shone like polished ebony in the evening light. A narrow string loincloth was all that covered her lower body and it seemed to accentuate her long legs and firm buttocks. Her hair was jet-black, long and sleek and slightly matted with the fine red dust of the bush. Muller noticed she had slanted, somewhat oriental eyes and much finer features than any of the others in her pathetic group.

Strangely, she reminded him of a tall Ethiopian woman he had once seen in a marketplace in Nairobi when he had visited with his parents when he was just a boy. However, that woman had not been a heathen like the one he was looking at now. She had been dressed in the traditional, Habesha Kemis of her people, and she had been truly beautiful, not at all like this naked, dust-covered bush native watching him from the shadows.

8

Muller remembered the brightly coloured cloth the tall Ethiopian woman wore and the colourful necklaces and bracelets that had adorned her slender, Nilotic arms and neck. It had been an almost forgotten memory that had suddenly reappeared as he stared at the native girl. In his mind, he saw again the tall African woman's beautiful smile as she showed him her hand-made wares in the shade of the flowering jacaranda trees that grew along that busy marketplace. He rested the Rigby in the crook of his left arm and bellowed back to Golly, 'Come here, you useless excuse for a stockman.'

Golly moved up and stood trembling at his boss's side. 'I hear you, Boss. Do you want me to tell these smelly black buggers to piss off or what?' he said quietly—nervously.

'I want you to tell this old black bastard that I'm going to give him some tucker. Can you do that?' Muller grunted.

'Yes, Boss, I reckon I can. He talks a different sorta language to me. But I can tell him okay.'

'Now listen carefully, Golly. This is what I want you to say. You're to tell him I will give him all the meat he can carry and potatoes he can put in his campfire coals as well. But he must leave that girl here with us. One more thing; tell him she will be looked after well. She will be given a job and a place to stay, and will live a long and happy life and will never go hungry again. Have you got all that?' Muller said in a lowered voice. He was nodding in the direction of the young Aboriginal girl as he spoke.

'Yes, I got it alright, Boss. You must be feeling a bit generous today,' the Aboriginal stockman replied nervously. He had just noticed a peculiar expression on his boss's face, and it made him feel uncomfortable.

'Just tell him what I said, and cut the prattle you stupid little black shit.'

Golly stepped forward and began speaking to the old man. The conversation seemed to take quite a while and the station manager was becoming impatient. However, it was a difficult task for the Aboriginal stockman; he had only a rudimentary knowledge of the old man's dialect, but he kept at it and eventually made Muller's demands clear to the old man.

'What did he say?' Muller grunted impatiently when the conversation finally came to an end.

'He said that his people are very hungry and more will die soon if they don't get some tucker, Boss,' the stockman answered nervously.

'Yes, yes—but what about the girl is he going to leave her here, or do I have to shoot the lot of them on the spot for spearing cattle?'

Golly looked confused. 'They ain't speared any cattle, Boss.'

Muller casually swung his rifle across his right shoulder and glared imperiously at the Aboriginal stockman. 'If I say they have—then they bloody well have,' he hissed. 'And you know the penalty for spearing cattle.'

'Don't matter anyway, Boss. He said the girl can stay if she is given tucker and looked after right.'

Muller looked back at the old Aboriginal head man and noticed he was nodding at him and smiling, as were the two older women standing behind him. The only other male in their group, a young buck, stood grim-faced watching the proceedings carefully from the shadows of the boab trees. The buck put Muller in mind of a sinewy black snake, coiled and ready to strike should anything happen to the old man.

'That's good, Golly—real good. Now, tell Santiago to get them some dried beef and all the kangaroo meat they can carry. The dogs will just have to go hungry until we get a few more. Tell him to give them a small bag of the worst of the potatoes as well. When he's done, he's to tell that bush nigger to clear the hell out of here right quick.'

'Okay, Boss, I'll tell him straight,' Golly replied nervously.

'And you tell them to stay well away from any cattle they come across, or I'll come looking for them.'

'Will do, Boss.' Golly turned back to speak to the old Aboriginal headman. But Muller continued.

'Tell old Santiago to take the girl over to the cook-house and give her a feed—as much as she can eat, and tell him to keep an eye on her, I don't want her running away—I've got plans for her.'

'Maybe she could work in the kitchen, Boss. She could help old Santiago. He sure needs some help, poor fella. He could teach her real good, and then she'll be a good cook just like him, Boss.'

'Just do what I told you to do, you skinny little black shit,' Muller grunted and turned to head back to his cottage—back to the remainder of his now-cold dinner.

'Okay, Boss will do,' Golly answered, relieved at last that the senseless slaughter of the bush natives had been avoided.

'One more thing Golly, tell old Santiago she can sleep in that little room next to his, and tell him he better lock her up each night until she gets used to the place. She can earn her keep helping him in the kitchen,' Muller yelled back over his shoulder as he trudged off toward his cottage.

After Golly had finished his conversation with the old man, he walked across to where Santiago was standing. The old cook was leaning on his axe, waiting for some sort of instruction.

'It's all over, Santiago,' Golly said to the old cook. He turned to the rest of the men who were milling about wondering what was expected of them. 'You boys can head on back to the bunkhouse. There's not gonna be any more trouble.' He turned back to Santiago. 'It looks like you finally got yourself a helper, Santiago, and a pretty one too.'

The old cook looked confused, but Golly went on to explain everything in detail to him. He told him the girl was to be given some food and where she was to sleep; and that she was to be locked in her new room just as soon as she had been fed. Santiago never replied but nodded his understanding to Golly.

The old cook went across to the group of natives. He put his hand out to the young girl and waited patiently while she spoke in her tongue to the old head man. Santiago was suddenly aware that most of the stockmen had started to wander back toward the bunkhouse and that he was alone with the bush natives. He began to feel nervous as he watched each of them step forward and stroke the young girl's arms in farewell and whisper their goodbyes. Only the young buck standing in the shadows stayed where he was and made no attempt to farewell the young girl. Instead, he suddenly reached down and picked up the spear at his feet and jabbered some sort of insult that Santiago could not understand. The old head man spun around and fixed his eyes on the young buck, and even though no command was given, Santiago watched him throw his spear to the ground in frustration.

Finally, hesitantly, the young girl stepped forward and took the old cook's hand. Santiago gave her a warm smile and at the same time, he nodded his respect to the others in her group and watched as all but the young buck smiled back apprehensively. Santiago continued trying to comfort the young girl as he led her away toward one of the distant buildings.

Jiiarnna could sense the kindness in the old man with the brown skin, and she walked cautiously but without fear by his side. After they had gone a short distance, she looked back at her people and, smiling nervously, lifted her free hand in an uncertain farewell.

Once they were inside the kitchen building with all its pots and pans, its huge wood-burning stove and its worn timber benches, Santiago poured the Aboriginal girl a cool glass of water, which she gulped down thirstily. Then, whispering soothing words to her, he led her out through the back door and across the narrow verandah to what was to become her new bedroom. He opened the simple wood-planked door to the small room and led her across to the narrow bunk bed. He motioned her to sit and patted her shoulder.

'What is your name, child—what are you called?'

The Aboriginal girl could not understand any of the words that Santiago said to her, but she realised by his tone that he was asking her a question.

The old cook tried again. This time he pointed to himself and said slowly, 'S-A-N-T-I-A-G-O.' Then, he pointed to the native girl and with an inquisitive look on his face, he asked. 'What is your name, child . . . ?' It took the old man a few more tries, before; finally, she seemed to understand.

'JIIARNNA,' she said slowly, smiling at the old cook. 'Jiiarnna . . .'

'Jiiarnna—is that your name?' Santiago asked, repeating the somewhat difficult word.

The native girl nodded eagerly and pointed to herself. 'Jiiarnna,' she replied shyly. 'Jiiarnna . . . Jiiarnna.'

Santiago thought for a few moments, and then he patted the native girl's arm. 'From now on, your name will be Anna, and because you will need a second name for the station records, your new name will be Anna Cook. The old man smiled at his clumsy attempt at humour and tapped himself on the chest. 'Me, Santiago Mendoza, and you—Anna Cook.'

They both began to laugh. But the old cook knew the young girl never really understood what he was saying.

'Now, Anna, you must stay here in this room until I come back for you,' he instructed. He smiled and went across to the door, left, and locked it.

Santiago went back to the kitchen and, with the help of one of the stockmen, gathered up the promised food for the natives waiting in the trees. A small hessian bag of potatoes, a large chunk of dried beef, and around twenty pounds of rather rank kangaroo meat were quickly put together. The old cook placed two loaves of stale bread that he had been keeping for making breadcrumbs in with the potatoes and instructed the stockman to take the bags of supplies across to the natives as quickly as possible and to make sure they left the area promptly before Jan Muller had a change of heart.

Jiiarnna sat quietly on the strange bed and looked around the tiny room. There was no window, just a set of three long wooden vents in the wall above her head. Next to the narrow iron cot with its thin kapok mattress was a worn wooden cabinet, and on it, a metal plate with a candle in its centre. She ran her hand across the chipped top of the bedside cabinet and absentmindedly picked up the candle and sniffed its faint perfume. She felt confined and uncomfortable. She put the greasy-feeling candle back on its metal plate. She was already missing her old grandfather and her people.

The young girl was still looking around the room when Santiago returned and unlocked the door. He gave her a smile to comfort her and led her back into the kitchen to the big wooden bench in the centre of the room. The Aboriginal girl stood close to the old man. She trusted him and felt comfortable with him and watched as he buttered her a thick slice of the bread he had baked earlier that day and spread sweet-smelling mango jam across it. When she had eaten her fill, Santiago led her back to her room and patted her head in a comforting gesture, encouraging her to swing her long legs up on the bed. Then the old man left the room, locked the door behind him, and went back to the kitchen to clean up the mess they had made.

\* \* \*

Jan Muller was watching from his cottage window as the natives, with their promised supplies, disappeared back into the trees and headed away from the homestead, which he knew could easily have been their killing ground. He shrugged his shoulders with disinterest and went back to his untidy desk and poured himself another glass of rum.

# 2

# A Good Scrubbing

Santiago had finished his cleaning and was preparing food in readiness for the following morning's breakfast when the kitchen door burst open and the massive bulk of Jan Muller entered the room.

'Where's the girl, Santiago?' Muller barked. 'Bring her in here. I'll be taking her back to my wash-house for a good scrubbing. Bloody bush niggers, they're dirty buggers. Get her up, man, and be quick about it.'

'I think she's sleeping, Boss. She was pretty buggered I reckon. She had a good feed and just went off to sleep.'

'Get her up, I said,' Muller hissed with an icy tone. 'And just you keep your mouth shut about this. I don't want any of the men to find out I've been washing blacks for a pastime. Do you understand me?'

'Okay, Boss. I won't say nothing—nothing at all. I'll go and get her now.' Santiago went back to the young girl's room, woke her, helped her to her feet and led her back into the kitchen to the impatient station manager. As they entered the room, Santiago felt the Aboriginal girl's hand tighten in his as she looked up at the huge figure of Jan Muller. The old man patted her shoulder in an attempt to calm her and tried to make her understand

15

there was nothing to fear by smiling and pointing to the station manager in a feeble attempt at communication.

'Her name is Anna, Boss. I gotta teach her to speak proper so she can understand us—poor bugger,' the old cook said nervously.

Jan Muller gave the young girl a forced and insincere smile and took her by the hand. 'She's about the same size as you, Santiago,' he said quietly. 'Get me a clean pair of your shorts and a fresh shirt, and just you keep your trap shut about this if you know what's good for you.'

'Will do, Boss,' Santiago replied. He quickly retrieved the clothing from his bedroom and passed the bundle to Muller. He nodded as he took the clothing and watched him lead the frightened girl out of the kitchen into the now-moonless night.

'She'll be back in an hour or so,' Muller grunted. 'When I bang on the door, you let her in and lock her back in her room. I reckon she'll need to get used to us for a bit longer yet.' He pulled on the native girl's hand, and they disappeared into the darkness.

Santiago sat down on the stool next to his wooden bench and looked at the bacon he had been slicing earlier. He felt unwell. The old cook hated the big South African. He was a brutal, violent man, and Santiago detested violence of any sort.

The station manager's cottage was quite a way from the kitchen building. It was situated next to the station owner's empty homestead and set among some of the bulbous boab trees that grew around the edge of the great clearing. With the native girl in one hand, Muller made his way across the clearing toward his cottage. They were almost there when several of the station dogs caught the young girl's unfamiliar scent. Two of the bigger male dogs stood up, shook the dirt from their hides and began to growl.

Muller snarled, 'Fuck off, mongrels.' The dogs backed off into the darkness, fearful of the big man they knew only too well.

Muller led the young girl up the narrow steps of his verandah to his wash-house and pushed open the door. The kerosene lamp was still burning bright, just as he had left it, and the bath, full of water, with a cake of cheap soap on the chair next to it. He led the Aboriginal girl inside, closed and locked the door.

16

Jiiarnna began to feel uncomfortable and suddenly very unsure of what was about to happen to her. She looked around the strange, windowless room and then at the galvanized metal bath brimming with water. She started to panic. Muller saw it in her eyes and gave her another of his insincere smiles and pointed to the bath-water.

'We're gonna get you cleaned up nice, and wash away all that dirt and nigger smell,' he said quietly, staring at the young girl's breasts. He patted her shoulder and reached down and undid the plaited loincloth that was the only clothing the young girl wore and tossed it aside. Then, as he stepped back to admire her naked body, he unbuttoned his shirt and threw it on the floor.

Jiiarnna shivered with sudden, unexpected fright. She had seen the markings on the big man's chest. The face of a snarling beast with evil yellow eyes, and below it, two crossed spears tipped with blood. Beneath the spears, was a word the young Aboriginal girl could not begin to understand, but it was a word Jan Muller had chosen very carefully when he had had the tattoo emblazoned across his chest in Johannesburg many years earlier, "*Ningesabi*," the Zulu word for, "No Fear."

The Aboriginal girl had never seen anything like it in all her young life. Panic started to overwhelm her.

Muller could see the distress in the young girl's eyes and sense her discomfort. He smiled again in an attempt to calm her and reached for her hand and passed it slowly across his chest, past the huge lion tattoo and the blood-tipped spears. He felt the native girl's hand tighten in his and her fingers tremble as he pressed them between the pale yellow eyes of the huge male lion.

'It's just a tattoo, beautiful,' he whispered. '*Simba*—my pretty one, *Simba*.'

Jiiarnna couldn't understand any of the big white man's words, but the soft whispering tone of his voice began to calm her. Then, she remembered, as a young girl, seeing the ancient paintings under a red cliff that her grandfather had shown her, paintings from the Dreamtime of strange people with white rings circling their heads.

'*Wandjina*,' her grandfather had told her, 'The ancient ones . . . The rain people.' She looked up at the big white man with the fearsome painting on his body. He was smiling at her. 'Just like the Dreamtime paintings,' she thought. She began to calm down. 'Just like the paintings under the red cliffs. . . '

Jiiarnna smiled nervously as the big white man's eyes passed slowly over her naked body.

The Aboriginal girl was tall, very tall, her breasts were full and well-shaped, and her nipples, the colour of the dark earth. She was indeed a beautiful woman. Jan Muller's eyes covered every inch of her ebony body and lingered at the small bush of silky hair that covered the mound between the native girl's thighs. He could feel the discomfort of his erection straining hard against his heavy dungarees. It had been many months since he had enjoyed the pleasure of a woman's body.

Jiiarnna held her head high as the big white man gazed at her nakedness, and for some strange reason, she was not afraid. Perhaps because he was smiling at her or perhaps because of the tender way he had held her hand as he had shown her the beast painting on his body. She was not sure, but he no longer seemed as fearsome as when she had first seen him. However, she was still unsure of what was about to happen to her.

Muller bent forward and picked up the native girl as if she were a child and not a fully-grown woman and lowered her effortlessly into the bathwater. Then, he leaned over her and picked up the bar of soap from the chair and lifted it to the young girl's nose, and watched her surprised reaction when she smelled its faint perfume. Smiling, he took the soap and lowered his right hand into the water and began to rub it over her dark body.

Jan Muller was beginning to struggle with the restraint he had forced on himself. In his mind, he could see himself lifting the young girl from the bathwater and bending her dripping body over the bath edge and having his way with her. The soap slipped from his fingers. He forced himself to remain calm and reached between the young girl's legs to retrieve it. Then, slowly, very slowly, he began to wash her. He was in control of his emotions now. He tested his resolve by fondling the young girl's breasts with his soapy hands, feigning thoroughness as he continued his ministrations.

When he had finished washing the Aboriginal girl's body, he cupped his hands and scooped bathwater onto her hair and rubbed the foaming soap into her scalp with his big hands, stopping occasionally to rinse the soapy water from her eyes when she wriggled her head from side to side with discomfort. Finally, when he was satisfied, he lifted her from the bathwater and stood her on the board floor and reached for one of his cotton towels.

In the light of the hissing lamp, the young girl's body shone like coal lifted from a bucket of clear water. Muller wrapped her in the coarse cotton cloth and slowly rubbed her dry, again struggling with his self-imposed restraint as he worked the towel over her naked body.

Jiiarnna had enjoyed the pleasure of the warm water and the tender way the huge white man had used his soapy hands on her body. She had been weary after her long, tiresome march through the bush with her grandfather and her people, and grateful for the pleasure and relief he had given her aching body. She waited patiently on the water-stained floorboards as the big white man patted the coarse cloth around her legs, stumbling occasionally as he rubbed her dry. She looked across at the soapy bathwater. It had been an innocent and wonderful experience for the young girl. However, she was totally unaware of the big man's hidden desires.

Muller dropped the wet towel to the floor and looked down again at the silky nest of hair between the native girl's thighs. 'You certainly are a pretty little black princess, aren't you?' he whispered. 'There's another little game I'd like to play with you, but we'll wait just a while longer for that.' The station manager was now almost overcome with animal lust for the naked native girl, but he knew if he frightened her she would probably disappear into the bush at the first opportunity. He decided he would wait until she had gradually settled into the ways of the station and then he would satisfy his dark desires on that sweet black body.

Jiiarnna could not understand any of words the big white man was whispering to her but she smiled with innocent pleasure as he began helping her into the clothing the old cook had given him.

Muller slipped the loose-fitting, white cotton shirt over the young girl's shoulders and drew it down over her dark breasts, and then he knelt and opened the faded blue shorts Santiago had given him and helped her as she stepped awkwardly into them, enjoying her hands on his head as she struggled for balance. The perfumed smell the soap had left on her dark skin filled his senses, thrilling him with carnal desire. With her body so close, he felt his resolve begin to waver once again and found himself struggling with the almost overpowering urge to push his hand between her legs—to touch her—to feel her moist womanhood with his fingers before he buttoned the shorts that would cover her naked hips.

Jan Muller had rarely shown restraint during his life. Usually, if he wanted something, he simply took it, no matter what. But he reasoned that with this Aboriginal girl if he was careful and patient, she could become his regular plaything. She may even grow to enjoy the games he would eventually play with her. He forced himself to concentrate and pulled the faded shorts up over her hips and began to fasten the buttons. When he was finished, he turned the young girl to one side and patted her thigh gently with one of his big hands as final victory over his dark desires.

Muller stood up and unlocked his wash-house door and led the young Aboriginal girl back to Santiago's rooms at the rear of the kitchen and banged on the old cook's door.

He knew he had to get away from her. But now the thought of just letting her go seemed to inflame him even more. He felt his resolve begin to weaken—and then completely disappear. He would take her back to his cottage and tear the clothes from her young body. Yes, he would have his way with her. He reached for the young girl's hand.

'Coming—coming . . .' he heard Santiago yell from inside his room.

He let go of her hand and left her outside the old cook's door.

'Next time, Princess, you and me will have some real fun,' he whispered, his voice thick with desire. 'So don't you go running away now?'

Muller left her and hurried back toward his cottage. He had almost lost control. After he had gone a short distance, he stopped behind a clump of low, sweet-smelling grevillea bushes. His breathing had become constricted and difficult. He fumbled with his trouser buttons for a few moments, until his erection sprang out from the painful restriction of his dungarees. He grasped it urgently with his right hand and, with hurried strokes, relieved the tension that coursed through his body, sending his seed into the dry leaves at his feet. 'Ag, *my klein swart prinses* . . .' he groaned in thick Afrikaans as his body jerked with spasms of pleasure and relief.

# 3

# The Spirit Man

Goonagulla led his people back through the boab trees and off toward the north at a hurried pace. The old man was happy that they had been given food at the white man's station. But he was also relieved that there had not been any trouble with the big white man with the cruel eyes. He knew he would miss his granddaughter, but he also knew beyond any doubt that he'd had little choice in the matter. However, it did not concern him. Goonagulla knew if his granddaughter became unhappy living with the white men she would soon run away and find her way back to them. The old man swung the sack of bloody kangaroo meat he was carrying up onto his shoulder and increased his pace. Behind, his weary people followed without question.

* * *

Cockatoo Creek's dining room resembled an army mess hall. Wooden trestles, roughly planked with flooring boards, were set in neat order around the big room, with long hardwood benches on each side for seating. Over time, a collection of assorted paraphernalia had been attached to the pressed iron walls of the long room. There were several faded pictures of screen sirens, Greta Garbo, and Myrna Loy. A pair of old spurs an ancient muzzle-loading shotgun with a missing hammer, and a couple of long stockwhips that someone had hung in a looping display around the bleached skull and horns of a wild banteng bull. And, in pride of place above the tea urns, a framed photograph of a magnificent Shorthorn bull, with a nameplate below it that read:

Leopold Maximus, Cockatoo Creek Station. 1929.

The long room with its fly-screened wooden windows was separated from the kitchen by a well-worn wooden servery that, on this particular morning, was covered with a dozen various sized serving platters. One held thick slices of Santiago's home-cooked bread, while another had been heaped with slices of buttered toast. Platters of fried eggs sat alongside blackened trays filled with crisp bacon and homemade beef sausage, while nearby, bowls of sliced melon of at least three different colours had been placed on a side table alongside jugs of cold water and stained urns of steaming tea.

Fifteen people were employed permanently on Cockatoo Creek Station. Several of whom were away droving a herd of more than two thousand head of cattle into Derby for transfer there onto ships bound for Fremantle and the markets in the south. They would be the last of the cattle that would be sent south before the wet season arrived, bringing with it the onset of the seasonal rains. Moving cattle any later was always difficult with the boggy conditions, the swarms of bloodsucking buffalo flies, and the bush tick that seemed to materialize with the early wet season rains.

Of the station workers remaining, not all of them ate in the long dining room. Jan Muller, the station manager, always ate alone in the manager's cottage. Pearl and Rosie, the two older native women who were employed on the station as cleaners and laundry maids, ate together on the tiny verandah at the rear of the kitchen. But always after one of them had delivered the station manager his meal, and that was always done before anyone else had eaten.

The long dining room was a noisy place at mealtimes, and this particular morning was no exception with the main topic of conversation still being what some were now calling the native attack on the station. Several of the men seemed disappointed that it had not developed further, while others disagreed and were glad of the final outcome.

Santiago and his new helper, Anna, were busy with their work in the kitchen, preparing breakfast for the hungry stockmen. It had been a couple of weeks since Anna had first arrived at the station, and each day, as they worked, Santiago continued to teach the tall Aboriginal girl his version of the English language. The old cook was constantly surprised at how quickly Anna seemed to grasp the meanings of the simpler words and found he enjoyed the young girl's company and the responsibility Jan Muller had given him—to teach her the ways of the white man and the workings of the huge cattle station.

Anna had grown very fond of the old cook as well, and enjoyed working alongside him and was quickly beginning to get the hang of things in the kitchen, although her work consisted of little more than scraping plates, washing dishes, and watching the talented cook at work preparing and cooking food.

Earlier that morning they had both eaten a hurried meal of sausages and eggs on their tiny back verandah before the cooking and the rush that always followed had started. The young Aboriginal girl was still having some difficulty coming to terms with the easy access to food after her time with her own people. She knew only too well the struggle they faced just getting enough to eat each day through these difficult times.

Anna missed her grandfather terribly. Most of all, she missed the stories he used to tell them at night as they sat around their campfire under the endless star-lit heavens. In particular, she remembered the story he had told her about her mother and her father and the sadness she always felt when he spoke about her mother. Her mother was Goonagulla's only child. She had been called Yilla, which, her grandfather told her, meant bright star. Her father was called Warrai—the goanna—the dragon lizard of the desert.

Goonagulla told the young girl that her mother, like her grandmother before her, was a very beautiful woman and that both of them had the same strange eyes and features. Because of this, he explained, her mother was considered very special among the Ngarinyin people. He told her that long ago, some of the Ngarinyin had interbred with the Makassar people, the boat people who came each year to fish for the 'trepang' along their remote northern coast. These Makassar, he told her, had travelled to their land each year since ancient times in their strange boats that were blown by the winds. The Ngarinyin had helped these fishermen, and in return, they had been given knives and metal for their spearheads, and many other amazing gifts. The Makassar fishermen taught the Ngarinyin how to carve canoes from a single log with metal axes instead of the traditional, stitched-bark canoes they had always made. They showed them how to tie bamboo outriggers across their canoes, making them more stable in the rolling swells of the estuaries so they could more easily hunt for the dugong out beyond the reefs.

Their people, he told her, learned many valuable things from these strange fishermen, and for many generations, they had worked together. It was not uncommon, he told her, for the Makassar to take Ngarinyin women for their wives, and as time went by, there were many children born from these unions.

Anna's mother, Yilla, was a descendant from these unions and, except for her dark skin colour, bore a striking resemblance to the Makassar people. Goonagulla told his granddaughter that because of her mother's great beauty, all the young men in their tribe desired her. But Yilla only had eyes for Warrai who, her grandfather told her, was a bad-tempered and jealous man who never trusted his beautiful daughter. One day, when Warrai returned from a hunt, he found Yilla talking to another man and became enraged. Yilla had told him they were only talking about a Dreamtime story of a fish that could fly from one billabong to another. But Warrai would not believe her and, in a jealous rage, he struck her on the side of the head with his nulla, the wooden fighting club the men carried. Warrai had not meant to kill Yilla, only to frighten her, but the blow was far too hard, and Yilla had died that night in the arms of her father. Warrai knew he had done a terrible wrong, and that same night, while the rest of his people slept, he disappeared into the bush.

The following day, out of respect, Goonagulla and his people painted their bodies with coloured ochre, tied leaves around their waists, and danced for many hours to wish Yilla's spirit a safe journey to Baralku, the spirit world. As he danced, Goonagulla threw dirt into the air in anger and frustration. The death of his beautiful daughter had broken his heart.

Three days later, Goonagulla decided he would set out and try to track down his daughter's killer and make him pay with his life for what he had done, and it would be many weeks before he would return to his people. Goonagulla had followed Warrai's tracks tirelessly for many days across wide spinifex plains and along desolate stony valleys, sometimes struggling to find them as they became windblown and difficult to follow. Finally, after many days' travel, the old man lost the killer's tracks completely when they had entered a long, rock-filled gorge. Weary and frustrated, the old man decided he would return to his people. However, near the river, they called Pulurrji, "*the snake that bites its own tail.*" Goonagulla came upon a small group of the Worla people. The Worla welcomed the Ngarinyin man, and he sat with the men for many hours, and they listened patiently as he told them of the murder of his beloved daughter and of his failed quest to track down the killer, Warrai.

One of the Worla men who sat listening to Goonagulla's story was the spirit man, Pirramurar. Unlike the others, Pirramurar remained silent as he listened to the sad tale of the murdered Yilla. But the spirit man could sense the terrible grief Goonagulla carried with him.

Pirramurar was held in almost fearful respect among the Worla people. It was said among them that he possessed strange, supernatural powers and that he could travel the land as a great eagle—a spirit bird. It was also whispered among the Worla that the spirit man knew the magic of the ancient ones, the Uru, "*The star watchers.*"

Goonagulla had a deep respect for the spirit men and their role among the tribes. These men were called upon to dispense justice when a serious crime had been committed among the people. To the Ngarinyin, these men were also called, Kurdaitcha and were spoken of in fearful whispers around their campfires.

When Goonagulla had finally finished telling his sad tale to the Worla men, he turned to Pirramurar and gave him the strands of hair that he carried with him. The blood-stained hair he had taken from his daughter's dead body.

The spirit man took the strands of dark hair and silently wound them into a rope circle and placed it in the small string bag he carried at his waist and nodded his understanding to the Ngarinyin man.

The following morning, Pirramurar woke Goonagulla at dawn and told him to return to his people and to watch over his granddaughter, Jiiarnna. 'She carries with her the spirit of her dead mother, and it will walk with her always,' he told him. As Pirramurar spoke, he placed one of his hands on the Ngarinyin man's head and began to chant a strange, mournful song.

Goonagulla felt a mystifying calmness wash over him, and when the spirit man removed his hand, the old man felt the terrible sorrow that had haunted his soul for so long suddenly lift and become more bearable. The old man left the Worla that morning to begin the long trek back to his own people not knowing whether the Kurdaitcha man, Pirramurar, would help him, or if he would set out in pursuit of the killer Warrai. However, he no longer felt the terrible sadness that had haunted him for so long and he suddenly longed to return to his own people.

After the Ngarinyin man had left to travel back to his people, Pirramurar went into the bush that same day and sat beneath a massive boab tree. A tree so old it was said that the Wandjina, once sang their songs beneath it to summon the rains. After several hours sitting alone under the huge, swollen tree, he went into a deep trance, and in the trance, his spirit became that of a huge wedge-tailed eagle, the graceful bird that has the keenest eyes of all living things.

For more than two hours his mind swirled with strange, disjointed images as he sat silently beneath the great tree, while above him, in a clear sapphire sky, the huge eagle extended its massive wings to catch a warm current of air. The graceful bird flew in wide, effortless circles, its keen eyes tirelessly searching the harsh land below.

Bush flies began to settle on Pirramurar's face and crawl into his open eyes. Red ants stung his legs and feet, but the spirit man was unable to move, a deadly mulga snake more than eight feet long slid across his thigh and continued around the trunk of the great tree as it searched for small lizards in the dust and cracks of the hard earth.

Slowly, the swirling images began to clear, and Pirramurar's eyes became the dark omniscient eyes of the great eagle as it circled patiently above him. Just before darkness fell that night, Pirramurar saw the killer, Warrai's faint tracks leading across a powder dry clay-pan far off to the north. The great eagle circled the desolate clay-pan for several minutes before turning back the way it had come. As it banked away, it screeched a long, plaintive warning across the empty landscape.

Pirramurar's body trembled, and his heart raced as the vision faded, and again his mind swirled with strange disjointed images. It was then that he saw a strange yellow-eyed beast watching him from the shadows, a sinister, evil thing that had no place in this, the sacred land of his ancestors. When he finally woke from his trance, his face wet with perspiration and his body weakened as if from some great exertion, Pirramurar had a terrible premonition of some future danger haunting his mind.

Once his strength returned, the spirit man set about the ancient task that only he, a Kurdaitcha, could perform. He began to collect the materials he would need to make the Kurdaitcha shoes. These strange, slipper-like shoes were made by weaving together the soft inner feathers of the emu and the skin of a young kangaroo and were held together with blood and the sticky sap from the spinifex bush. When he had finished his tedious work, Pirramurar turned the feather-and-hide shoes in his hands to study them. Satisfied, he put them in the small string bag at his waist and lay down to rest.

The following morning, Pirramurar set off toward the north. He carried only a single spear, a woomera and a long killer boomerang, the fighting weapon of the Aboriginal warrior. This carefully made weapon over four feet long could be used as a club in hand-to-hand combat or thrown with great skill to cripple or kill an enemy with deadly efficiency. As he walked toward the north, he looked up at the bruised clouds that darkened the morning sky and was reminded that the wet season was soon to arrive.

For twelve sunrises and twelve long days, he headed toward the north. In the cool of the mornings, he would jog through the bush. But in the afternoons the fierce heat would force him to walk, but his eyes never left the ground as he searched for the tracks left by the wily Warrai. Finally, on the morning of the thirteenth day, he cut across Warrai's tracks near the dried-out clay-pan he had seen through the eyes of the great eagle. Pirramurar laid his spear and boomerang on the ground alongside the Ngarinyin man's tracks and went down on his knees to search the faint footprints for sign. Perspiration trickled down his dark face, and his chest heaved with exertion as he studied them. Finally, he scooped up a small amount of dirt from one of the tracks and rubbed it between his fingers, feeling for any moisture that would help him determine how far ahead his quarry could be. He let the dirt fall from his hand, and looked out across the dried-out clay-pan and smiled. The man he was following was now no more than three days ahead of him.

Pirramurar had one more task to perform before he could go on. He lit a small fire of twigs and leaves from carefully chosen pituri bushes and sat cross-legged in front of the spluttering flames of the tiny fire. Using his hands, he drew the fragrant smoke back into his face and began to chant an ancient song. Slowly, he went into a trance, and in the trance, he saw the face of the man he hunted—and in his eyes, he saw his guilt.

With this strange ritual complete Pirramurar slipped the feather shoes he carried in the small bag at his waist onto his feet and fastened them securely with strands of kangaroo hide. Then, he attached strings of blood-soaked feathers and leaves to his chest and legs with spinifex sap and daubed his body with frightening slashes of white ochre he had made by crushing small, soft stones he'd gathered from a creek bed and mixing them with clay and spittle. With his preparations now complete he set off toward the north, following the faint trail left by the woman-killer, Warrai. The only traces of his passing were soft, barely noticeable abrasions on the ground that would soon disappear with the afternoon breeze.

*   *   *

Far ahead, Warrai was walking steadily toward the north, to what he hoped would be his safe haven. He was heading for the coast and the rocky lands along the water's edge, where it would be impossible for anyone to follow him. Once there, he knew he would be able to hide in the many caves and stony valleys that could be found along that difficult shoreline. He would fish for crabs and oysters to keep up his strength. Perhaps he would build a small log raft to hunt for the dugong, whose delicious flesh he had only eaten once in his life. Then, he would work his way along the coast toward the northeast, where he would start a new life far from the lands of his own people, in lands that were unknown to him, the lands of the Gwini people.

However, some strange instinct had begun to make Warrai sense that someone was following him. He imagined that it could be Goonagulla, or perhaps some of the others of his people on a mission of revenge for his murder of the beautiful Yilla. Warrai had had this uneasy feeling for quite some time and cunningly decided he would circle back until he cut across his own tracks. He would then know for certain if someone was following him, and if they were, he would wait until they slept, kill them, and continue on his way.

After two days of travelling in a wide circle, Warrai finally crossed his own tracks near a thicket of bloodwood trees. The young warrior approached the trees carefully, his spear at the ready and his senses keen to the sounds of the bush. Small birds flitted about among the shadows. A wallaby, suddenly startled by his careful approach, bounded through the trees ahead of him. And from somewhere nearby, a crow called out in lazy indifference. Finally, satisfied there was no one hiding in the trees, he stooped to carefully study his tracks. He breathed a sigh of relief. The only tracks he could see were his own. He imagined that the old man, Goonagulla, had probably given up if indeed he had been following him at all. Then he noticed something on the ground nearby. He reached down and picked up the tiny emu feather and lifted it to his nose. He instantly recognized the unmistakable odour of the big bird, but just for a moment, he thought he could smell something else—the odour of spinifex sap. This puzzled the Ngarinyin man, and a tiny alarm seemed to ring in his mind. He sniffed at the feather again, but this time he caught only the odour of the emu. He looked about for the bird's tracks, but strangely, there were none. Frowning with disinterest, he threw the tiny feather aside and swung the long spear he carried over his left shoulder and set off toward the north once again, confident now that he was not being followed.

As the sun set that day, Warrai stopped near a muddy waterhole he had found among a small stand of paperbark trees to rest his weary body. He would move on before the sun rose the following day and try to make it to the coast before nightfall. Using his spear, he dug down in the dry dirt at the base of a mulla mulla bush and found a cluster of fat witchetty grubs buried there among its fibrous roots. He plucked out the tasty morsels, shook the dirt away from their plump bodies, and wolfed them down. When he'd finished his meagre meal, he made his way down to the water's edge to drink from the muddy waterhole.

*   *   *

Several hours earlier, the spirit man, Pirramurar had seen the shimmering, distorted shape of a man approaching from the west. He had slipped back into the trees and waited. An hour later, the man he had been following for so long made his way cautiously in among the trees and circled about, staring at the ground. In an instant, Pirramurar knew that Warrai must have been concerned that he was being followed and had decided to circle back to check his tracks. Pirramurar watched Warrai crouch among the bloodwoods and study his own tracks and then pick up something from the ground and lift it to his nose. He watched the Ngarinyin man hesitate for a few short moments before shouldering his spear and casually moving off toward the north once again.

*   *   *

The leaves of the paperbarks that grew around the muddy waterhole where Warrai stooped to drink began to whisper softly in the faint afternoon breeze, their dappled shade dancing lightly across the brown, tepid water. In the branches above him, dozens of thirsty birds waited, some screeching their impatience as the Aboriginal man leaned forward to drink. It was hot—very hot.

Warrai slurped down the muddy water, ran his wet hands across his face and sat down in the mud of the waterhole. He looked up at the noisy birds—something didn't seem right. Then, as if in reply to his concern, the birds took to the air, swooping low across the water and then away through the trees. Warrai got to his feet and looked back the way he had come. Muddy water ran down his naked body and trickled into the waterhole. It was then that he saw the painted stranger walking slowly toward him . . . !

The stranger's coal-black skin was covered with startling slashes of white ochre, and from his chest and shoulders, hung long bunches of leaves and feathers. His hair was pasted down to his scalp with red ochre, and two frightening circles of white ringed his dark, expressionless eyes . . . ! The painted stranger's sudden, unexpected appearance confused Warrai, and for a moment he found himself unable to move.

'Where had he come from—and why had he suddenly appeared . . . ?'

Dumbfounded, he stared at the painted man. His legs felt weak and leaden. He watched in bewildered confusion, as the strands of feathers and leaves that hung from the tall man's painted body swayed from side to side in mesmerizing rhythm with each of his approaching steps.

Suddenly, Warrai woke from his stupor and realised he was staring at a Kurdaitcha man—a tribal killer! He leaped to his feet and pulled his nulla from the string belt at his waist and hurled it at the grim, terrifying figure walking toward him. His heart began to hammer in his chest—he turned and ran for his life.

Pirramurar lifted the long boomerang in his right hand and effortlessly turned away the hastily thrown club. Then he turned the long weapon in his hand and swung it out in a low arc.

Grunting with exertion Warrai clambered up out of the waterhole and raced off toward a distant stand of trees. In his panic to get away, he tripped and fell headlong into a clump of spiny spinifex bushes. In an instant, he was on his feet and racing toward the trees a short distance ahead. He was young and strong and he could easily outrun most men. If he could just make it to the trees, he knew he would stand a chance. He would use the cover of the trees and his physical stamina to put as much distance as possible between him and the fearsome man behind him. He ran on, not daring to look back.

He'd almost made it to the trees when he felt a sudden, sharp pain. His legs gave out from under him. The Kurdaitcha mans' killer boomerang had broken both of his ankles. He tried to rise on his crippled legs and continue, but with a shriek of pain, he fell back to the ground. Terrified, he scurried forward, dragging his maimed limbs behind him. In a blind panic, he turned to look back . . . The painted stranger had disappeared! Gasping with relief, he turned to continue on his painful way toward the trees—and then he stopped. The stranger was standing directly in his path.

'This could not be—how could he have moved so quickly . . . ?'

Warrai had never known fear such as this in all the days of his life. It had sapped his strength and taken away his will. He dragged himself to his knees to face the man who now stood blocking his path and stared into his cruel, remorseless eyes. He attempted to speak—to plead for mercy. But found he was struck dumb with fear. And then he watched in horror as the painted man began to lift the long spear he carried. He looked past him at the stand of trees. They were so close—he had almost made it!

Then, as if in slow motion, the tall stranger stepped forward and drove the long spear he carried down into his chest with a powerful thrust. Warrai grasped hopelessly at the spear shaft as it cut into him. He felt his rib bones try to resist the thrust. Grunting with pain, he grabbed at the shaft even harder, only to feel it slip through his sweating fingers and cut into his strong young heart. He fell back to the ground, his eyes wide and white with terror and in a sudden paroxysm of agony, his knees shot up to his chest, and a dark stream of faeces sprayed out onto the dirt behind him.

Pirramurar released the spear, and the Ngarinyin man rolled onto his side, his legs kicking at the red dirt beneath him in a desperate, final attempt at escape. Dark heart blood pumped from the dying man's chest in time with his racing heart and ran along the blackened shaft of the Kurdaitcha man's spear.

Warrai felt a frightening darkness begin to wash over him, and for fleeting seconds, strange visions raced through his mind. He saw, Yilla, his woman, the woman he had killed with his nulla. She was standing next to her father and they were smiling at him—and then the darkness overcame him completely.

Pirramurar reached down and tore the spear free from the now-dead body of the killer Warrai, and from the small bag at his waist, he removed the long hollow bone he had taken long ago from the dried wing of a brolga, the dancing bird of the bush. In a low voice, he began to chant an ancient ritual, and as he chanted, he pushed the bone down the side of Warrai's neck and into his chest. Then he removed the feather shoes from his feet and sat back in the blood-soaked sand next to the dead man's body.

Bush flies had already begun to settle around the jagged wound on Warrai's chest and into the corners of his now-lifeless eyes. Pirramurar crossed his blood-spattered legs and began to sway from side to side as he continued his chant, patiently waiting for the long, hollow bone to draw out the Ngarinyin man's very soul as his final punishment for the killing of the beautiful Yilla.

It was almost a year later, on a rainy late afternoon that Goonagulla saw the Kurdaitcha man again. The strange man had suddenly appeared near his bush camp and seemed to be waiting for him in the trees. When Goonagulla approached him and looked into the tall man's dark eyes, he knew at once his daughter's killer was dead. The two men greeted each other respectfully, and Pirramurar asked Goonagulla if his granddaughter was well. Goonagulla replied that she was indeed well and growing faster than the grasses that grow after the first rains of the rainy season.

The spirit man nodded and then warned Goonagulla that the girl must watch out for a strange beast with yellow eyes, for he had seen a sign in one of his dreams.

Goonagulla thanked Pirramurar for all he had done and wished him a safe journey back to the Worla people.

But before Pirramurar left, he handed Goonagulla the small string of human hair that had belonged to the old man's daughter. Goonagulla looked down at the tiny rope of blood-darkened hair, and his mind swam with the memory of his beloved daughter. When he looked up, the Kurdaitcha man had disappeared.

# 4

# A Letter Arrives

A nna felt a wave of sadness wash over her, as it always did when she remembered the sad tale of her mother's death. She would miss her old grandfather and his stories. The old man was so wise in the ways of her people, and yet so loving. To Anna, her grandfather had taken the place of her mother and her father, and she loved him dearly.

For the next few weeks, the Aboriginal girl spent her spare time with Santiago, usually sitting on the small back verandah at the rear of the kitchen, coming to grips with the old man's version of the English language and she was proving to be a good student and a fast learner. In the afternoons, in the few hours they had before it was necessary for them to begin the evening meal preparations they would sometimes walk the homestead grounds. Santiago had begun by showing Anna the station buildings and explaining to her what they all were used for. He showed her, the machinery sheds and the huge workshop, the store and the two small diesel-powered generator buildings with their rows of batteries. One of which, he attempted to explain, was used to supply power and light to the owner's house and the other, for the kitchen, to power the 32-volt refrigerators and the lighting in the long dining room.

As they strolled past the owner's empty homestead set among its own private gardens of tropical trees and arbor's of bougainvillea and mandeville vines, where white painted chairs sat unused beneath the shady trees. Santiago explained with an expansive stretching of his arms that the owner lived a great distance away and only visited the station once a year, and sometimes, not even then. The old man showed Anna the beautiful African tulip trees with their huge red, cup-shaped flowers, the magnificent royal poincianas with their canopies of fiery, orange-red blossom, and frangipani, covered in bunches of white, sweet-smelling flowers that seemed to glow among the deep green of their leaves. Santiago plucked a single flower from one of them and put it to Anna's nose and watched the young girl smile her surprise as she sniffed its heavenly perfume.

They continued on past a huge mango tree laden with ripening fruits, under trellised vines of passion fruit, grapes, and dragon-fruit, past banana palms, paw-paws, and neat rows of vegetables. The old cook led her around luxuriant vines that sprawled across the ground, heavy with sweet melons ripening in the warm tropical sun. He showed her the hen houses filled with happy, cackling birds and the long pens of pigs that were the progeny of a litter of feral pigs that a couple of the stockmen had caught two years earlier.

As they made their way around the station grounds, Santiago tried to explain to Anna why the station buildings had been built on the natural rise that was surrounded by the huge boab trees. The young girl nodded her understanding that it gave some security from the occasional floods that would cover the surrounding plains in the worst of the wet seasons. Down from the low plateau, and some half a mile from the ring of boab trees that circled the homestead grounds, a huge dam had been constructed. It had been built in a natural depression that at one time would have covered two, or perhaps three, acres. Now, this massive dam covered closer to two hundred acres. This natural depression was the confluence of both the Cockatoo and Ambush Creeks, and now, because of the huge dam, only the Cockatoo Creek made its way onward toward the distant sea.

The owner, Mr Michael Montinari, had seen the potential of this natural depression on one of his occasional trips to the station and had sent contractors soon after and had them scrape out and enlarge the area to its current size. During its construction, they had used the scrapings and overburden from the dam to increase the height of the sloping perimeter banks to almost seven feet. At the northern end, they'd installed sluice gates that effectively stopped the creek from flowing out on its natural course, thus conserving all of the flow to increase the dam's huge capacity. In the wet season, when the dam was full, these gates could be opened manually to let the excess flow out into Cockatoo Creek, where it would wind its way toward the north once again to eventually merge with one of the many rivers that would carry its waters to the sea.

They had named the dam Death Adder Dam because some of the deadly adders had been seen among the fallen leaves of the small trees that ringed the dam. A couple of the station dogs had met a painful end running carelessly through the trees on their way to swim in the dam's cooling waters.

Anna and Santiago strolled along the earthen bank and gazed out across the open expanse of water. At this particular time, it was down to less than one-third of its capacity, the result of the particularly long and rainless dry season that they all hoped would soon come to an end. As they made their way along the edge of the dam, a flock of whistling tree duck lifted from the water and passed over their heads, alarmed by the intruders that had suddenly appeared. The sleek birds banked away and headed out across the silver water. The rush of air from their wings seemed to thrill the young Aboriginal girl, and she clapped her hands with excitement as they streaked by.

Santiago pointed to the small, galvanized pump shed built high on the bank with its two diesel engines inside that were used to pump water from the dam. He attempted to explain their purpose by pointing to the station buildings and then back to where they stood, using his finger to trace the steel pipe that carried the water up the low plateau to the concrete catchment tanks near the station buildings. The station's drinking water was taken care of by the galvanized rainwater tanks that were located next to each building.

The larger diameter pipe that ran off in another direction used the other much larger pump to irrigate almost five hundred acres of maize and a specially imported sorghum they called, Giant Grass. These irrigated crops were used for stock feed and grain, and the hay kept in a large open-sided shed, built purposely to let the air circulate through. The grain was stored in metal silos that were set on sturdy timber stands alongside the massive station workshop.

Adjacent to these irrigated fields were a dozen or so fenced paddocks of around fifty acres each. These were used to hold stock and to feed and improve their condition if necessary before they left on their long trip with the station drovers to Derby for shipment to the markets in the south.

These fenced paddocks could hold up to two thousand head of the big Shorthorn cattle, but only for a limited time, as they had to be hand-fed the irrigated fodder, which was always in short supply.

Cockatoo Creek Station usually ran around twenty thousand head of cattle. Mostly the hardy Shorthorn breed, but some of the Indian cattle, the Zebu had been trialled as well in recent years. This particular year, with the dry weather they were experiencing, several thousand head had already been sent off to Derby for shipment south.

The huge station covered an area of more than five thousand square miles, or almost two and a half million acres, and was greater in area than some small European countries. In most years, with the normal seasonal rains, there was plenty of feed for the stock. But this was not always the case, as they had found over the past dry season and the poor wet season that had preceded it.

In very dry times, water for the stock was sometimes a problem as well, but with the addition of the twenty three big Simplex windmills, eighteen of which had been installed in recent years, this had been lessened dramatically. The windmills that pumped the precious artesian water to the surface had been placed above bores in areas where there were few creeks and waterholes.

As the days passed, Anna began to enjoy the station life immensely, and she grew even happier as she became more proficient in the language of the white man and slowly began to understand their ways. The kind and ever-helpful Santiago made learning pleasant for her, and they quickly became the closest of friends. The young Aboriginal girl soon became very popular on the station and made friends with most of the stockmen, Golly in particular. Even though Golly was a full-blood Aboriginal like Anna, their only similarity was their colour. Golly had been raised by the white man and had spent all of his years on cattle stations, so their worlds were vastly different. But the young girl quickly grew to like the friendly and good-natured Aboriginal stockman.

As time went by, Anna got to know all the station hands by their names and gradually became familiar with their duties on the vast station. She liked the ever polite Billy Anders, the stock foreman, a popular man with everyone on the station. The wiry Billy possessed the finest horse skills of anyone on the property and was the man they all turned to when opinions were needed in regard to horses or when any basic veterinary work was required. Then, there was Curly Jim Davis, a stocky, rather short-tempered individual, but a capable stockman. Curly Jim was about as close a friend to Jan Muller as that man would allow. The two of them sometimes played cards together in the manager's cottage and drank the dark rum Muller kept there under lock and key.

Another of the white stockmen Anna had grown to like was the very handsome Fancy Dan Miller. Dan had only been on the station for a little over a year. The stockman was only nineteen years of age, a friendly lad with the not-so-common habit of always trying to look clean and tidy, a trait his dear mother had instilled in him as a small boy on their tiny farm down south. Then, there was bow-legged Bob Nugent, the station mechanic and general handyman, a hard worker, and a loner, but a man capable of repairing or rebuilding almost anything on the station.

There were seven white stockmen on the station in total, the rest of the hands were coloured boys. Of the native stockmen, she had gotten to know them all. There was Beans, the short, rather rotund individual so-named because of his love for canned baked beans, Famous Feet, one of the older Aboriginal stockmen who, at one time, had been a well-known black tracker for the Derby police. Anna soon found she liked them all and enjoyed the fuss each one of them, both black and white, made over her.

The only other women on the station were Pearl and Rosie, the two Aboriginal women who were employed as cleaners and laundry maids. Both women had taken a keen interest in Anna's welfare and helped her wherever they could. The women, both in their forties, had their own separate bedrooms some distance away; at one end of the big building, everyone called the store. Obvious by its name, the store was used for the storage of chemicals and branding equipment. It was also the tack room for saddles, bridles, and other paraphernalia. Slabs of hardwood lined its walls where rows of sturdy shelves had been stacked with coils of rope, rolls of wire and drums of creosote. Heavy steel brackets randomly screwed to the walls, held shovels and spades, pickaxes and fencing equipment. The station manager, on his arrival some years earlier, had forbidden any of the coloured stockmen to visit Pearl and Rosie in their little rooms at the rear of the store for sexual favours. Those favours were reserved for the white men on the station, and all but Fancy Dan and Jan Muller did this on quite a regular basis. Dan had not yet plucked up the courage to visit the two friendly coloured women, and the station manager considered both of them used goods and far too ugly for him to bother with. The favours that Pearl and Rosie gave came at a small cost to the white stockmen. The payment required was two shillings for a fuckie-fuckie, as the two coloured women called their services, and payment was always required in advance.

The first of the rains had finally arrived in the last days of November. They had started with a heavy downpour that had lasted for more than an hour and then had abruptly stopped. But everyone could feel the season was about to change. The air had become humid and thick with the promise of rain, and at night, occasional lightning tore at the heavy sky. At that same time, the drovers who had taken the last herd of cattle into Derby finally arrived back at the station, all pleased to be back to their own beds instead of the hard ground they had slept on for the past six weeks. Sam Belsen, the stockman Jan Muller had put in charge of the drive, had spent the entire trip on the old buckboard they used on their trips away. The heavy buckboard was pulled by a team of two huge draught horses and carried all the food and supplies for the men while they were on the drive, and on the return trip, it was used to bring back the station supplies and any mail that was waiting for collection at the post office.

As soon as they had arrived back, as his first priority, Sam took the all-important canvas mailbag to the manager's cottage and knocked on his door. Jan Muller already knew the stockmen had arrived. He was annoyed. They should have been back at least three days earlier. He opened his door and stepped out onto his small front verandah and took the mailbag from the trail-weary stockman.

'You fellas sure took your bloody time getting back,' he grunted, with his usual unfriendly manner.

'A couple of the men got in a fight in the Spinifex pub while we were there, Boss. One of them wound up in the Derby hospital and needed sewing up. Poor bastard got cut up bad by a bloody pearler.'

'Stupid bastards can't handle the piss, that's the trouble,' Muller grunted again. 'So—did you sort things out?

'In the end, I did, but we had to wait till the Doc let Steve out of the hospital. He was concerned that maybe he'd get an infection from the pearler's knife.'

Steve Gibbs was a close friend of Sam and always seemed to be getting into trouble one way or another. The young stockman had a big mouth and considered himself to be a bit of a hard man and handy with his fists.

'So how much time did you lose waiting there, then? It'll be coming out of their wages you know—and that goes for the lot of you.'

'Two days, that's all, Boss. Anyway, the boys needed a bit of a break after the drive,' Sam replied with noticeable bitterness in his voice.

'If I had been there, I would have banged their fucking heads together and fired Steve on the spot. I still might yet,' Muller grunted. 'Anyway, I'd better check the mail; I'll talk to you later on.'

'Alright, Boss,' Sam replied. Realizing that was the end of the conversation he turned and made his way down the verandah steps and headed for the dining room.

Muller took the mailbag back inside his cottage and sat down at his desk. There was quite a bundle of letters for him to get through. Several were for the white stockmen. These he put aside. Among the rest, were accounts for chemicals used on the station from their stock agent in town, an account for feed and yarding while stock waited for shipment in Derby, and accounts for food supplies from Carters Store in town. In a separate, carefully wrapped parcel were several cattle breeding magazines and a couple of rolls of newspapers addressed to the manager of Cockatoo Creek Station.

Muller sorted through the accounts and checked amounts with his own order book, ticking off entries as he went. When he was finally happy with the figures, he put the accounts aside, unrolled the bundle of the now-several-week-old newspapers, and took a quick look at one of them.

'*The severe financial depression that devastated the Australian economy seems to be finally easing. The Prime Minister, Joseph Lyons, said in parliament today.*'

Muller put the newspaper back down on the desk. He would read it later when he had more time. He noticed a longer envelope among the remainder of the scattered mail. He picked it up and looked at the neat, flowing handwriting. He knew in an instant who it was from. The station owner's writing was easily recognizable to Jan Muller. It was probably the neatest handwriting that he had ever seen penned by a man. He opened the long envelope, carefully unfolded the pages, and began to read the letter from the man who was his employer. A man he secretly envied because of his massive wealth and power. Michael Montinari was a very powerful and influential man, and Jan Muller knew he did not suffer fools gladly.

*The letter began:*

*Montinari Constructions*
*Spencer Street, Melbourne*
*Post Office Box 3740*
*12th October 1932*

*To: Mr Jan Muller*
*Cockatoo Creek Station*
*Private Bag 53*
*Derby. W.A.*

*Dear Jan,*

*I hope this letter finds you well, and that all is progressing profitably on the station. I received your last monthly statement of affairs, and I thank you for its concise attention to detail. I have been concerned with regard to the unseasonably dry weather you have been having in your area, and I am glad that you sold off the several thousand head that you did. This would have made things a little easier for you. Although, the receipts I received for the stock sold were not as good as I would have hoped. However, that was to be expected with the long dry season forcing many other beef producers to sell as well.*

*I hope the addition of the dam and the irrigation equipment and, of course, the installation of the last of the windmills has helped along the way. Please give my regards to all the men and thank them for their hard work during the long dry.*

*I have heard through the radio and the press that some of the stations in the Kimberley have had trouble with the local bush natives and that there have been a few attacks in some areas. This concerns me greatly, and I understand the difficulties that these problems can bring. However, I must also impress upon you the damage that this sort of trouble could do to my reputation, should various sectors of the press decide to take it on themselves to cover a story, if we at Cockatoo Creek were ever to become involved aggressively toward the Aboriginal people. Please treat the native people with respect, and impress upon the hands that we certainly do not want to provoke any situations with them at all. After all, they are the traditional owners of these lands. So let us not see the problems arise with them such as has happened in America in times gone by with their native Indians. Let us hope also, that we do not see any more of the problems that occurred many years ago in some areas of the Kimberley as well, with the unnecessary massacre of these people and the bad feelings this caused between blacks and whites.*

*Now, on a completely different topic, I have some news for you, and I ask you for your cooperation in this matter. My daughter, Isabella, has returned from her travels in Europe and England, having completed her studies there in fine art. I am very proud of her achievements and have seen first-hand the exceptional talent she has acquired. I only wish her mother, Rosa, was alive to see the great progress she has made in her chosen field. Isabella has told me she would like to travel up to the station and spend a month or so there travelling about and painting the beautiful and rugged landscapes that make the Kimberley such a unique place. While I am more than happy to have her visit and spend some time at the station, I am concerned about her safety while she is there. Isabella is a very headstrong woman. She has told me that she is quite confident heading into the bush in search of suitable scenery to paint by herself. But I am not so sure. As you quite obviously have a heavy load with the station work that needs to be done, I certainly would not ask you to act as her chaperone. I have instead contacted my very good friend and hunting guide Jack Ballinger to assist me. Jack has acted as my guide on a couple of my hunting trips into Arnhem Land in the Northern Territory and has agreed to help me out. He will look after Isabella while she is at the station and when they travel into the bush. Jack is an accomplished bushman and more than suited for the task. Jack is also a returned serviceman. He was wounded in France in 1918 and shipped back home with shrapnel wounds to his back and legs. They were quite severe wounds, but thankfully, he has made a full recovery. I should also tell you that Isabella is not happy that I have employed Jack to act as her guide. She feels that it is all very unnecessary and that he is not needed, even though she has never met the man.*

*Of course, while at the station, Isabella will stay in the homestead, as will Jack. Jack should be comfortable in one of the guest rooms. Would you please give them both all the assistance they require? While they are there, I think it would be a good idea to have Golly act as a guide and helper for them during their stay and, of course, during any trips into the bush, as he knows the country well. Golly has acted as a guide for me during some of the very infrequent hunting trips I have made there and is a very capable man. I am sure that they would also enjoy the services of a cook while they are away as well, since they may spend quite a considerable time in the bush. I have no doubt that Isabella will want to visit some of the wild country along the coast while they are there, which, as you know, is a significant distance from the homestead itself.*

*As you may or may not know, Isabella has visited the station with me before, although that was almost five years ago and a little before your time as manager. During that time she did get to know quite a few of the hands while we were there and seemed to get on well with Santiago, Golly, and some of the others.*

*Please arrange for Pearl and Rosie to tidy up the homestead and have everything in order, including the stocking of the refrigerators. They are also to offer their assistance if required while the two of them are there as well. Isabella will fly from Melbourne to Perth and will then board the West Australian Steam Ship Company's ship, the S.S. Minderoo in Fremantle. While en-route, they will pick up Jack Ballinger in Geraldton when the Minderoo calls there. Jack has decided to visit a fisherman friend there—an old army pal from the war—for a few days. They will both arrive in Derby on the nineteenth of December. I would like you to pick them up in the station truck and transport them back to the station.*

*Isabella will probably have a considerable amount of luggage, which, of course, will include all her art supplies. Please assist them in every way possible during their stay, Jan, and I sincerely hope it does not conflict too much with your work on the station. Also, please make sure that there is a good supply of diesel at the station, as they may want to take out the Citroen that I had shipped there last year from France for their trips into the bush.*

*I look forward to seeing you some time in the not so distant future, Jan. However, unfortunately, work commitments here are very heavy and require my constant attention. Now that the depression seems to be easing, the construction industry is beginning to start again. Once again, I thank you for your professional management of the station and look forward to an agreeable future.*

*Yours Sincerely, Michael Montinari*

Muller folded the neatly written letter and put it back in its envelope. He had met Michael Montinari on just two occasions in the four and a half years he had been the manager of Cockatoo Creek Station. Muller had been impressed with the clever, intelligent businessman and with his calm demeanor and his natural ability to master most things, including the workings of a cattle station. He also knew that the main reason for the wealthy man's purchase of the big station was as a tax relief from his more profitable ventures and because the station had some of the best hunting in the country.

Michael Montinari was a keen hunter. Huge razorback pigs were plentiful on the station and, at times, were a nuisance because of the way they broke up the ground around the creeks and waterholes. Wild duck were in their thousands when there was adequate water, and deep among the rocky escarpments toward the coast was an elusive herd of Chital deer. These deer were a native species of the Java islands and how they got into the Kimberley, no one seemed to know. The deer were very difficult to locate and to stalk, and to Michael Montinari, this made the challenge even greater.

In the billabongs and creeks close to the coast, there were plenty of the big, dangerous saltwater crocodiles. These had to be hunted with extreme caution—as they were quick, unpredictable, and aggressive killers. And in the remote country near the Mitchell River, there were still plenty of the wild banteng cattle, descendants of the first cattle that were brought into the Kimberley from the Indonesian islands many years earlier. The big, heavy-bodied bulls were quite reclusive and usually stayed in the thick bush country, and would charge with very little provocation if they were disturbed. Hunting was probably Michael Montinari's only other passion, apart from his work. However, in recent times, it had become more and more difficult for him to get away, and so his visits to the station had become very infrequent.

Jan Muller had never met Michael Montinari's daughter, Isabella, and he knew very little about her except what he had just read in the letter from her father, but he was already of the opinion that she was almost certainly a spoilt brat and probably wanted for nothing. He was glad that his boss had decided to have the babysitting done by this Jack Ballinger; he was more than welcome to the task, whoever he was.

'Spoilt arty bitch—what a bloody waste of time and money,' Muller grumbled as he began to put all the letters in order and tidy his desk. 'So—he doesn't want any trouble with the blackfellas, eh . . . ? Well, I guess he never should have bought himself a bloody cattle station. Maybe better the big man should just stay in the city well away from the dust and flies—and the nigger trouble.'

Muller slammed the desk drawer closed and got up to take the station hands their letters.

'Leave the fucking blackfellas to me, I know how to handle them,' he growled as he headed for the door.

# 5

# A Strange Apparition

Goonagulla had led his pitiful group away from Cockatoo Creek Station toward the north for almost two weeks, and once again, they were having difficulty finding enough to eat. The young ones and the two older women were suffering the most. The kangaroo meat they had been given at the white man's station had only lasted two days before it had putrefied. The potatoes, stale bread, and dried beef that the old cook had packed for them had kept them going for a while longer, but now that was gone as well, and they'd begun to suffer once again.

Goonagulla had managed to spear an old crippled kangaroo as it had come in to water at a tiny soak they found among some trees, but it had only lasted for one meal. On most days they managed to find grubs and small lizards and sometimes gathered the nuts of the boab tree and chewed on their astringent piths. Along the edges of some of the shrinking waterholes, they pulled tiny boab seedlings from the ground and chewed on the roots, but these were eaten sparingly as they could sometimes cause stomach upsets. Goonagulla knew that the young ones and the two older women would soon become weak and not able to travel at all if they were unable to find more sustainable and nourishing food.

The first of the wet season rains had fallen and then stopped again just as quickly as they'd started, but all of them could feel the wet season's impending arrival. Dark clouds passed low over their heads during the day, and at night they watched in awe as jagged lightning tore at the night sky. One night, while they watched, a fearsome bolt of lightning struck an ancient boab tree near where they were camped. It had split the great tree asunder as if it had been smitten in two by some angry spirit from the Dreamtime. The huge tree, many hundreds of years old, perhaps even thousands, had fallen to the ground with a weary sigh. The water trapped in its swollen trunk seemed to boil and fizz as it bubbled out onto the dry ground near the frightened natives. To Goonagulla's weary group, it was as if it was the very life-blood of the ancient tree. The lightning had been so close they could smell the ozone in the air for several minutes after it had struck the ancient tree and its power so intense, it made the hair on their heads stand strangely erect for several hours. Goonagulla saw this as a bad sign, although he never spoke of it to his people. But in his heart, he knew beyond any doubt that something evil lay ahead.

Two days later, after they had walked many more weary miles through the sparse bush, in the shimmering distance, they could see a great shining structure with a huge glittering circle at its top turning lazily in the warm afternoon breeze. They approached this strange apparition cautiously, and while they did not understand its purpose, all of them knew it belonged to the same white men who had filled their land with the hungry red beasts.

As they drew closer, they could smell the water, and when they were closer still, they could see the sparkling liquid sloshing its way into a long shining container at its base. The natives stopped in a grove of trees and watched from the shadows as the giant wheel turned slowly in the faint breeze. To Goonagulla, it seemed to creak out a dire warning: 'White man . . . White man . . . White man . . .'

Cautiously, Goonagulla and his hungry group left the cover of the trees and made their way forward. They could see cattle filling their starving bellies with the sparkling water. Clouds of dust rose from their shuffling, weary hooves as they milled about in the late afternoon heat.

Suddenly, Balun, the only remaining young buck of their group, sprang forward and ran ahead of them. As he ran, he notched a long spear to the woomera he carried, and with a heave of his sinewy right arm, he sent it on its way toward the beasts at the trough. The Aboriginal man's spear hit a young heifer low in the belly. With a plaintive cry, it left the others at the trough and trotted off toward a clump of acacia trees, the spear dangling from its now badly bleeding belly.

Goonagulla berated the young buck, cursing him for what he had done, but the old man knew it was already too late, and they watched in silence as the now-staggering heifer made its way into the trees. The young animal stood swaying from side to side for several minutes, the long spear hanging from its body. Finally, it collapsed in the shade of the spindly acacia trees.

Goonagulla knew that they were not to spear the red beasts, as they belonged to the white man. But the old man had always wondered why they had need of so many of them, for it was their voracious appetite that had decimated the grasses, the very food the kangaroo and the wallaby fed on, which had now made their lives so much of a struggle.

They gathered up as much firewood as they could find and stacked it around the unfortunate beast and lit their fire and waited patiently for it to cook. Later that night, Goonagulla and his people had the greatest feast in all their lives, gorging on the tender meat until they could eat no more. As they sat around their fire resting from their feast and readying themselves for sleep, they could hear hundreds more of the red beasts come in to fill their empty bellies with the strange-tasting water beneath the spinning wheel.

Goonagulla and his people slept a satisfied sleep that night in the little grove of acacia trees. But just before dawn, the old man woke from a strange and frightening dream. In the dream, he saw a fearsome yellow-eyed beast, a strange, evil thing almost as large as the red cattle that drank water from the spinning wheel. Goonagulla watched the strange beast cast its eyes about as if it was searching the land for his tiny group.

Early the next morning, as they readied themselves to continue their weary march toward the north and away from the spinning apparition, Goonagulla instructed the women to drag bushes behind them as they walked to hide their tracks from the white men should they happen to find the remains of the dead beast in the trees. As they left, a faint breeze began to blow through the acacias. The slowly spinning wheel creaked and swung back toward them. To Goonagulla, once again, it seemed to cry out a dire warning. 'White man. . . White man. . . White man . . .'

\*   \*   \*

Many miles to the south-west of Goonagulla's pitiful group, two native stockmen were working their way along the widely scattered line of windmills. They were riding on one of the station buckboards, which was being pulled by an old roan mare. The two Aboriginal stockmen, Henry and Wooloo were jokingly known on the huge cattle station as the windmill boys. Their job was to check the windmills and, if necessary, repair any broken parts. They would see to it that the ballcocks were working properly on the long metal troughs and grease any creaking joints they found in need of lubrication and move on to the next windmill. Because of the unusually dry weather they were experiencing on the station, they were also instructed to cut fodder for the hungry cattle near the troughs. When they arrived at each of the windmills, they would use the buckboard and cut as many low branches from the nearby boab trees as they could and leave them on the ground for the hungry cattle to feed on. They had started their work on the western side of the property and had been away from the station for eight days.

The two men arrived at windmill nine just as the sun was setting and pulled the old buckboard to a stop in the shade of a few small peppermint gums. They climbed down, dusted themselves off, and set about unhitching the old mare and tying her to one of the larger of the trees. One of them made his way across to the windmill to fill their billy, while the other started a small fire. But as Wooloo, the stockman who'd gone for the water, dipped his billy into the trough, he noticed two large wedge-tailed eagles feeding on something in the fading light. He called to his friend and pointed to the feeding birds. Henry the older of the two, walked over to join him. He was not really interested in what the eagles were feeding on. Probably just a kangaroo he'd thought,

51

but the rapidly fading light made it difficult to know for sure. Both men had a long drink from their billy, rolled themselves cigarettes, and, after a short discussion, decided to take a look. As the two men drew closer, the eagles, both of them huge birds with wingspans of more than eight feet, began to unfold their wings and ruffle their dark feathers in warning until finally launching themselves clumsily into the darkening sky, only to land again in the high branches of a nearby tree and wait patiently for the intruders to leave so they could return to their partly eaten meal.

The stockmen could now see that it was a steer and not a kangaroo that the birds had been feeding on, and from its condition, they could tell it had been dead for many weeks. But there was something not quite right with the carcass, and it wasn't until they were close that they saw the hole in its hide and its missing legs. The steer had been speared to death. The jagged hole in its withered hide was plainly visible to both men.

That night the two stockmen ate a frugal meal of dried beef and damper, washed down with mugs of sweet tea. They never spoke of the speared steer until they had eaten their meal. But as they sipped their tin mugs and smoked their cigarettes, they began to discuss what they should do. They knew if they returned to the station with the news of speared stock, there would be hell to pay. They knew their boss only too well. However, both men felt some compassion for the natives that had killed the animal, after all, they were Aboriginal themselves—and they knew it had been a difficult time for the bush natives because of the unusually long spell of dry weather. After they'd finished their mugs of tea, they decided they would do nothing at all. It was only one steer, and it seemed a terrible penalty to have to pay with your life for just two legs of beef, which they both knew would probably be the penalty if Jan Muller were to find out. They put out their cigarettes and crawled into their bedrolls, but both of them slept poorly that night.

The windmills on Cockatoo Creek Station had not been set out in any real order but had been erected above bores that had been drilled over the last few years. The two men knew each of the twenty-three mills that were spread across the huge station, not only by their numbers but also by their singular peculiarities, and, of course, the best way through the bush to each of them.

The following day, after their visit to mill nine, the two coloured stockmen set out across the heavy scrub country to their northeast and headed for mill twelve, and after their maintenance on that mill, they set up camp for the night. The following morning they would head due north toward windmill seventeen.

But what the two stockmen were unaware of was that the young bucks that had broken away from Goonagulla's group and had headed in on the long walk to Derby had killed the steer that had been speared and butchered near nine. They, like the others, had been desperate for food. They had seen a large mob of the red beasts near the strange spinning water wheel and had been unable to resist the temptation. They had speared the beast and followed it across the dusty flat until it had dropped to the ground. They had then clubbed it to death and later that night, they'd cooked the legs and feasted on them until they could eat no more. The following morning they gathered up the few bones that still had meat on them and continued on toward Derby.

Two days after Henry and Wooloo had camped at nine, they arrived at mill seventeen. It was late in the afternoon, and darkness was almost upon them. They set up their camp, ate a hasty meal of dried beef and damper, and rolled out their bedrolls. As they settled under their dusty blankets and smoked their last cigarette of the day, they could hear the cattle at the nearby windmill, bawling hungrily to each other as they shuffled about near the stock trough. The sky above the two men that night seemed like liquid crystal, the glittering stars, boundless and breathtaking, and so clear that neither man could ever remember the heavens so wondrous.

The following morning, they both woke with the dawn and set about relighting their fire with the few sticks they'd kept from the night before, and it wasn't long before a billy of strong tea had been made and poured into their tin mugs and the first of the day's cigarettes lit.

Henry took a sip of his tea and a long drag on his cigarette. As he exhaled he could see what looked like the white ashes of a fire near a clump of spindly acacia trees.

'What's that over there near them trees? Can't be no fire—no fires bin lit here since we was here last and we camped right here,' he mumbled through his cigarette smoke.

Wooloo looked over at the trees and squinted in concentration. 'Maybe we better take a look. Probably just some fire a couple of blackfellas lit to cook up a lizard or somethin.'

'Musta bin a bloody big lizard I reckon,' Henry replied.

Both men got up, patted the dust off their sweat-stained trousers, and headed over toward the grove of trees. As they drew closer to the remains of the fire, what they saw lying near the ashes sent a chill through both of them.

Scattered about were the scant remains of a young heifer. Just a few white rib bones and a broken skull with patches of burnt skin still stuck to it. Some hooves lay near the ashes, but most of the heavier bones had been scattered about by scavenging birds. The stockmen went back to their breakfast fire and sat down. Henry poured mugs of the still-hot tea and they rolled themselves cigarettes and began to wonder what they should do.

# 6

# Death Adder Dam

The fly door slammed behind Santiago as he made his way across the kitchen verandah to the hollow steel pipe that hung there on one of the posts. The old cook picked up the steel rod that hung next to it and whacked on the pipe, clang—clang—clang. 'Breakfast—come and get it!' he yelled across the dusty yard.

Cockatoos began to screech from somewhere nearby in reply to Santiago's vigorous efforts on the hollow pipe, their raucous calls amplified in the stillness of the morning air. Station hands began to spill out of the long bunkhouse and make their way across the few yards that separated the two buildings, some stopping near the dining room door to take their last puff on their first cigarette of the day before tossing the butts in the dirt and heading inside.

Dressed in fresh white aprons, Santiago and Anna were busy placing heaped platters of bacon and fried eggs on the long wooden servery, along with plates of toast and bowls of Santiago's homemade butter. It was Sunday—pancake day. Two huge plates stacked with hot pancakes sat in the centre of the well-worn servery, along with bowls of sweet bush honey and the ever-popular mango jam. On Sundays breakfast was always a little later than usual and a little more casual, usually somewhere between seven and eight. It was a day of rest for most of the station hands,

55

except, of course, for the cooks, and sometimes for the hands who had been assigned to the irrigated pastures for feeding out any cattle that were in the holding paddocks. Sunday lunch was also a casual affair, usually sandwiches, cold meats, and salads. This meant that Santiago and Anna could have most of the day off themselves, just as soon as breakfast was over and the lunch hampers had been prepared for the men and placed in the big refrigerators.

However, later, at around three o'clock in the afternoon, they had to be back in the kitchen in time to prepare the Sunday evening meal, which was usually roast beef, occasionally roast pork, but always with lashings of brown gravy and onions, sweet potatoes, and whatever else Santiago's amazing garden was able to supply.

Rosie had delivered Jan Muller his breakfast of bacon, fried eggs, pancakes, and a big pot of strong tea earlier. But when she returned to the little verandah at the rear of the kitchen to enjoy her own breakfast with Pearl, she had a troubled look on her face. The Aboriginal woman went directly to the back door of the kitchen and called out over the clatter of pots and pans. 'Hey, Santiago, can you come here, please?'

The old cook put down the pot he'd been scrubbing, threw the dishrag into the soapy water, and walked across to the door. 'Rosie, what's wrong? Does the boss want somethin special this morning?'

Rosie had a concerned look on her face. 'No, no—his breakfast is fine. He wants Anna to go over and see him after dinner tonight. You'd better tell her, Santiago.'

The smile on the old cook's face dissolved into a frown. Santiago did not like the big South African.

'Okay then, I'll tell her after breakfast is all done,' the old cook replied in a lowered voice to the concerned Aboriginal woman. He went back to the sink and picked up the dishrag floating among the unwashed pots.

Anna had never mentioned the night Muller had taken her to his cabin for a bath on her first night at the station and he had never spoken of it to her, but it had certainly worried the old cook. He knew his boss was an evil man, and he knew he disliked coloureds, but when Anna returned that night she had seemed happy enough. He remembered how innocent she seemed as she paraded shyly in front of him in her new clothes. Santiago simply thought that perhaps he'd been worrying about nothing, so he'd tried to forget that night altogether. But the old cook had a good memory. On many occasions, he had seen his boss do extremely brutal things to the coloured stockmen. He had watched in fear as the vicious streak in him rose like a volcano and exploded in blind rage far too many times to forget. On one occasion, Santiago had seen him lay into one of the coloured hands with his stockwhip for simply mishandling a steer in a cattle crush. The man had to be dragged away from the flying lash by two of the white stockmen before he was cut to pieces or lost an eye. On another occasion, Beans spat on the ground quite by accident just a little too close to Jan Muller's boot. The station manager had punched him in the face so hard that he knocked the poor man unconscious, and while the stockman lay in the dirt, he'd kicked him in the chest so viciously he had broken two of his ribs. The old cook spent several hours that night pulling Beans' nose back into some sort of alignment and taping it in place and when he'd finished with his face, he'd taped and bandaged the groaning man's chest. The coloured stockman had been confined to the bunkhouse for more than a week while he healed.

Santiago could sense trouble, and he feared for Anna. But there was little he could do about it. He decided he'd wait until the stockmen left the dining room and the breakfast dishes were washed before he spoke to her.

As always, Fancy Dan was the last to leave the dining room. The handsome young stockman had fallen madly in love with Anna. The old cook had seen him talking to her while he was served his dinner, and later he watched Anna give the young stockman a discreet wave when she left the servery to head back to the kitchen. Santiago watched him get up to leave and then linger at his table for a while longer, obviously hoping to catch another glimpse of Anna before he left, but the Aboriginal girl was still busy with her work in the kitchen. The stockman left the table and walked across to the door and Santiago watched him waste more time reading the movie poster and looking back toward the kitchen a few more times.

Sunday night was film night at the station, and the film to be shown was always posted on the dining room wall. The poster Dan was reading was a western, *The Bronco Kid*, with Hoot Gibson and Yvette Mitchell and even though he'd seen it several times, it was one of his favourites. He looked back toward the kitchen one last time, hoping for a final glimpse of Anna and then, disappointed, he left.

The station had quite a library of movies, and even though most of them had been shown several times it didn't seem to concern the men as long as it was a western. The station owner, Michael Montinari, had sent the precious movie projector to the station four years earlier, and every few months several new movies would arrive, causing great excitement. Sunday night was the big night of the week and over time it had become an important social event and most of the hands dressed in their best clothes for the night. The films were usually shown outside in the cool, unless it was raining, then they would be shown in the dining room, which usually meant a hurried reorganization of the trestles and stools.

It was a night looked forward to for another reason as well: it was the only night alcohol was allowed to be consumed on the station. This rule had been set some years ago by Michael Montinari himself to help stop the drunkenness and fighting that usually occurred with regular drinking. It was a condition of employment, and to break this rule meant instant dismissal. However, the owner knew that the men needed an outlet, and it made for a happy workforce to allow them one night of the week to have some fun.

Beer was the only drink allowed, and it was supplied free of charge by the station and kept under lock and key in the store. On Sunday morning's Santiago would take six dozen large bottles of beer out of the lock-up and put them in one of the big kitchen refrigerators. They would then be passed around just prior to the picture show beginning, and when it was gone, there would be no more until the following week.

And for the two good-natured Aboriginal women, Pearl and Rosie, Sunday night was a night when both of them made a little extra from a few well-dressed but usually somewhat inebriated callers to their rooms after the excitement of the evenings' movie.

After Dan left the dining room, Santiago and Anna cleared away the dishes from the tables and wiped them down in readiness for the evening meal, and then began to work their way through the piles of dirty dishes. It was still hot in the kitchen, and they were both wet with perspiration when Santiago finally decided to speak to Anna about the message Rosie had given him.

'Anna, the boss wants to see you over in his cottage after dinner tonight.' The old cook watched the young girl's face for a response.

Anna put down the saucepan she'd been wiping and looked at Santiago. 'Oh—I wonder what he wants?' she replied, with a surprised expression.

Santiago was amazed at how fast Anna had learned to speak quite passable English. The old cook knew his young friend was a highly intelligent woman, but she seemed to constantly surprise him with so many things. He had grown very fond of her, and they'd become the best of friends.

'Just you be careful, Anna. He don't like coloureds you know, so watch what you say.'

'I will—I will. He frightens me, Santiago. I don't like him very much,' Anna said quietly. She thought back to the night when she first arrived at the station—the night Jan Muller had taken her to his wash-house. She remembered being naked and uncomfortable in front of the big man. He had not harmed her, and yet she clearly remembered feeling vulnerable and helpless.

'Just you be careful,' Santiago said again, pointing his finger at Anna as he spoke.

'Don't worry, I will. I wonder what he wants, though.'

After the breakfast dishes were washed and the kitchen wiped down, the two cooks prepared and wrapped the lunchtime hampers of sandwiches and fruit and carried them to the refrigerators. When they were both happy that all was in order, they hung up their aprons and left the kitchen to enjoy the rest of their day.

Anna was excited, during breakfast Dan had asked her if she'd like to join him for a picnic lunch down by the dam. She liked the shy young stockman and was looking forward to their day together. She waved goodbye to the old cook and hurried out to the small wash-house she shared with him for a shower and change of clothes. She had grown very fond of the ever-persistent Dan.

Santiago made his way across to the pig pens carrying the morning scraps. He had decided to spend his day in the gardens, where he could be alone while he tended and weeded his precious plants. It was a time when the old man contemplated his life and all that was happening around him. However, for Santiago, all was not well; the old man had a very deep concern for his innocent friend.

Fancy Dan looked even cleaner and smarter than usual when he knocked on Anna's door. His dark brown hair had been slicked down with pomade and neatly combed into place. The dungarees he wore were a little faded but clean and smart, and his white shirt neatly pressed and complete with a fashionable red neck-tie that almost matched the faded red braces that he wore.

Anna opened her door and gave the young stockman a big smile. The clothes she had on had been fashioned from the many bits and pieces she'd been given by her good friends Pearl and Rosie: a pretty green blouse that had been altered and made to fit her by Rosie and a pair of long cotton shorts made from three different coloured pieces of material that were sewn together by Pearls' skilled fingers.

The young girl's long, dark hair was pulled back in a simple ponytail and tied in place with a faded green ribbon. The Aboriginal girl shone with the beauty of her youth and her innocence.

'Hi, Dan, I won't be a minute,' she said cheerfully. 'I just have to grab something from the kitchen.'

She left Dan and went into the kitchen to get a brightly coloured metal lunchbox with the words Hammond's Cattle

Salve stamped on its lid. She had filled the box with sandwiches and fruit earlier, and placed it, along with a glass bottle of cold water, in one of the big refrigerators, ready for her day with Dan. She picked up the metal box and the bottle of water and went back outside to join the nervous stockman.

Dan had been smitten with Anna from the very first time he had seen her standing in the shadows alongside the old Aboriginal head man when they came to the station to beg for food. At first, he hadn't noticed her, and it was only when the old man had stepped forward and pointed his fingers into his mouth signing they needed food, that he saw her. His first impression was that she was somehow different from the rest of her little group. Like the others, her skin was as black as the coal he used to collect for his mother's stove near the train lines that cut through his parents' dairy farm near Dongara in the south. But it was her features that were different—noticeably different—in particular, her eyes. They were almond-shaped, dark, and strangely oriental. Her hair was long and straight and seemed to shine as it framed her dark face. She was very tall, and to the young stockman, she seemed elegant and graceful, like a beautiful bird. She had reminded him of a photograph he'd once seen in one of his mother's 'Women's Weekly' magazines of a beautiful Balinese woman, except of course, for her coal-black skin.

Dan knew that it all could have gone terribly wrong that afternoon had it not been for Golly stepping forward in an attempt to stop Muller from firing on them. It had been a close run thing and he knew it. But the young stockman had been puzzled why his boss had suddenly had a change of heart and had asked for the girl to be left at the station. It made no sense to him at all. Everyone on the station knew that Jan Muller had no time for coloureds. Even more confusing was the fact that he had given them food.

However, even though Dan had been mystified with his boss's behavior, he was certainly overjoyed when he saw the tall native girl take Santiago's hand and walk with him toward the kitchen. To Dan, there was something very special about Anna, something wonderful, and he had loved her from the very first moment he had seen her. Each day, the young stockman looked forward to his meals in the dining room just so he could catch a glimpse of her. For some time, all he could find the nerve to do was to smile at her as she served him his food. Until, finally, he'd raised the courage to ask if she would like to go for a picnic with him, and he had been beside himself with joy when she had agreed.

The young couple strolled beneath the shady poinciana trees and made their way down the rise toward the shining waters of Death Adder Dam. As they walked, Dan took the metal box and bottle of water from Anna in a rather obvious attempt at good manners and felt a flush of excitement as he touched her hand. Dan could feel his heart racing as they strolled down the narrow path toward the dam, and he was not too sure what he should talk about, but he started by asking Anna about her life with her people before she came to live at the station.

Anna was feeling awkward and shy herself, but she began by telling Dan about her grandfather, Goonagulla, and the others of their little group who had visited the station with her. Anna was pleased Dan had asked her. She was proud of her people and their ancient culture. The Ngarinyin were a peaceful race that had survived in this harsh land since the beginning time. As they strolled, Anna used Ngarinyin words to tell Dan the names of the trees and bushes that were scattered around the station grounds. When they passed one of the many boab trees that ringed the homestead grounds, she explained, that in her tongue they were known as larrkardy, the upside-down tree. She told him that once, long ago, the tree was thought to be too vain and proud and so the ancient ones had pulled it from the ground and turned it upside down.

'This is why the tree now looks as if its roots are growing up into the sky,' she told Dan proudly as they strolled past one of their bulbous trunks.

Anna explained that, like so many things in the bush, the great swollen tree had many uses for the Ngarinyin people. The bark was used to treat fever, the seedpods could be broken open and eaten as food in desperate times, and the hollowed-out seedpods were used to carry water when her people travelled great distances in dry times.

The Aboriginal girl went on to explain to the young stockman why the Dreamtime was such an important part of Aboriginal culture, even though she knew it would be difficult for him to understand. She told him that in the Ngarinyin world, the past, the present, and the future were all woven into one. For them, everything is tied together with the invisible threads that weave all things to the earth.

'We are all simply a part of the earth,' Anna explained. 'The air that we breathe is the same air that the ancestors once breathed, and the eyes with which we see are the same eyes that the ancestors sometimes use when their spirits walk with us.' When Anna finally finished her story, she looked at Dan, wondering if he had become a little bored—after all, she thought, the ways of the white people were so much more interesting than the simple beliefs of her beloved people.

They found a shady tree near the bank of the big dam and sat down. Anna opened the coloured metal box and handed Dan a thick sandwich and the bottle of water. The two of them ate their meal of sandwiches and sliced melon in silence. When they had finished, they sat close to each other, looking out across the silver water watching the birdlife that had made the dam their home.

'It's real nice here, Anna,' Dan said nervously.

'Yes, it is, and it's nice to be away from the homestead for a while,' Anna replied.

Whistling tree duck lifted in front of them and whirred across the water's surface, calling noisily to each other as they flew by. Farther along the muddy bank, they watched a pair of graceful white herons busily feeding in the shallows, and on the far side of the silver water, they could see a magnificent jabiru crane wading quietly along the shoreline, stopping occasionally to dip its head into the water to feed.

The young stockman lifted his right arm and put it around Anna's shoulder as they gazed across the water at the wading bird, and to his surprise, Anna leaned her head against him in casual response. They stayed like that for some time, until the shy Dan plucked up the courage and kissed Anna on the cheek.

Anna turned toward the bashful stockman and they embraced, tenderly at first, and then the embrace became deeply passionate. Dan had never been with a woman, and he was very unsure of what he should do, but the affection he felt for Anna drove him on.

Anna had not expected to feel the sudden flush of excitement that she experienced, but somehow it all seemed right to her. They were like two innocent children, both totally unaware that anyone else existed in their little world by the water's edge.

Dan could feel the rise and fall of Anna's breasts beneath the flimsy blouse that she wore. With his heart racing, he reached down and caressed one of them. Anna sighed with unexpected pleasure. She had never in her young life felt the emotions that now seemed to be flooding her mind. She reached for Dan and held him in her arms. 'Dan, oh Dan,' she whispered. And then, suddenly and to Dan's surprise, she untangled her arms from his neck, pushed him away, and stood up.

'Is there something wrong?' Dan was confused and began to think he had done something to upset her.

'No, Dan, it's just that it's hot, that's all.' Anna replied and began to undress.

Dan watched in disbelief as the beautiful Aboriginal girl slipped her shoulders out of her homemade blouse and dropped it on the ground next to the metal lunchbox, and then unbuttoned the shorts she wore and wriggled her way out of them and let them drop to the ground. When she turned back to him she was naked, and to Dan, beautiful beyond all of his wildest imaginings.

'Come on, let's go and cool off,' she squealed and ran out across the dry bank and into the dam and splashed her way out through the shallows into the deeper water.

Dan took off his shirt, fumbled with his trouser buttons for a moment or two and hurriedly removed his clothing and ran after her.

'What's the water like?' he called out.

'It's cool and wonderful,' Anna called back and then dived beneath the surface.

'I'm coming.' he yelled back and ran out across the dry mud and into the water, feeling very self-conscious of the erection he knew was there in plain sight.

A flock of whistling tree duck that had been sitting peacefully out on the silvery surface suddenly took to the air and passed over their heads with a rush of wings.

Anna pointed up at the birds as they flew by and laughed with excitement as they suddenly banked sharply and disappeared through the trees, whistling their annoyance at being disturbed.

The two young lovers swam together for more than an hour, enjoying the cool water on their naked bodies, the beautiful, dark-skinned Aboriginal girl and the white stockman. Eventually, they made their way, hand in hand, from the now-muddy water back to the shade of their little tree and sat down. They embraced, awkwardly at first, both of them conscious of their nakedness, until a wonderful passion seemed to enfold them both.

'Anna, Anna, I love you,' Dan whispered.

'Oh, Dan,' Anna replied, her voice a whisper as well.

Anna had never felt like this in all her young life. She wanted more than anything to stay beneath the shade of their wonderful little tree forever. She reached for Dan, encircling him with her arms and holding his naked body against hers as tight as she could.

Dan pushed himself clumsily between her legs and began kissing her wet breasts. 'I love you, my darling.'

Anna lifted herself to Dan. 'Oh, Dan, I love you too,' she whispered back.

Dan reached down and guided himself into the woman he loved more than anything in this world.

Anna gasped with sudden pain, and then joy. She reached up, put her arms around Dan and pulled him into her body, pushing back against each of his impatient thrusts. A rapturous urgency suddenly seemed to overcome them, and their bodies began moving together, pushing and driving clumsily at each other.

'My darling, my sweet darling, I love you so much.' Dan whispered when their lovemaking finally came to an end.

'It was so wonderful, Dan—so wonderful. . .'

They lay together, exhausted, in each other's arms, both of them deeply aware that something wonderful had happened, something that neither of them had been able to stop, even if they had wanted to.

They stayed that way for some time, hugging each other and kissing until they both began to feel the day's heat once again. When they looked into each other's eyes, it was almost as if they could read the other's thoughts. Smiling, they stood up and ran naked back into the dam again to enjoy its cool water on their bodies and to luxuriate in the deep pleasure their lovemaking had given them.

It was as if a veil of love surrounded them, cocooning them from the eyes of the world. They had travelled to another place, to another dimension, a place where they were the only ones who existed. Waterbirds flew above them, their cries soft and pleasant, willing them to stay. Time seemed to stand still, and the earth had become a wondrous place. Finally, they walked, hand in hand, from the water and back to their tree to dry themselves in the warmth of the afternoon sun.

'I should be getting back, Dan, Santiago will be waiting for me in the kitchen,' Anna murmured, rubbing her dark fingers along Dan's shoulder.

'It's been so wonderful, Anna. I wish it would never end and we could stay here forever. But I suppose you're right, we'd better get back.'

He sat up and looked down at Anna, lying naked beside him, and felt as if his heart might burst with joy.

The lovers dressed and, still holding hands, made their way back toward the homestead, giggling and laughing at the smallest things as they went.

When they were almost ther, Dan turned and wrapped his arms around Anna. 'Will you sit with me at the pictures tonight?'

'Of course, I will. I want to be with you always,' Anna replied, smiling.

'I love you, Anna,' Dan replied. 'Hell—it's all happened so fast, but I really do.'

'I have to go over to the boss's cottage after dinner. I'm not sure what for, but as soon as I can, I'll be back,' Anna whispered, leaning lovingly against Dan.

'Look for me, my darling; I'll be waiting for you.' Dan kissed her one last time, and they walked through the ring of trees that circled the station grounds and made their way back to the kitchen.

Santiago had two large cuts of beef already roasting in their pans when Anna came through the kitchen door.

'Potatoes—start peeling the potatoes, and get some onions out as well.' The old cook passed Anna her apron.

Anna could see her friend was annoyed at her for being so late. 'Sorry I'm late, Santiago, but time just seemed to fly,' she said happily, taking the apron from his outstretched hand. 'It's been such a wonderful day.' She tied it around her waist and picked up the heavy bucket of potatoes. When she looked back, the old cook was smiling and shaking his head with understanding.

# 7

# Muller's Cottage

As was usual for a Sunday night, the dining room was a hive of activity. It was filled with clean, well-dressed stockmen eager to get through their Sunday meal and to then mill about outside while they waited impatiently for Santiago to bring out the Sunday beer and for the movie to begin. Anna could not help smiling at each of the well-dressed stockmen as they lined up to fill their plates. She had never been so happy. The roast for the night was beef, with baked sweet potatoes, carrots, and onions, all topped with a thick gravy followed by Santiago's ever-popular treacle pudding with custard spooned over each serving.

The station hands were certainly a happy lot, many of them lining up for second servings of both the beef and the pudding. Both the cooks were kept constantly busy, as they usually were on Sunday nights until the noisy dining room was finally empty. Of course, once again, the last to leave was the love-struck Fancy Dan.

After Santiago and Anna had washed all the pots and pans and the benches had been wiped clean, and there was order once again in the kitchen after the chaos that always followed meal-times. Santiago rinsed his dish-rag under the tap and wiped down the big galvanized sink, which was always his final job for the night. The old cook undid the tie around his waist and slipped his soaked apron over his head and turned to speak to Anna.

'Anna, it's time for you to see the boss.' he had a concerned look on his face.

Anna hung her apron next to his and smiled at her friend. 'Yes, I know,' she replied. 'I'm sure it will be alright.'

'Just you be careful,' the old man said sternly. He'd been thinking about Anna's meeting for most of the day.

'I will, Santiago. But he's the boss, so I had better go and find out what he wants,' she replied. 'Anyway—I'll come and see you when I am finished with him and tell you what it was all about before I go to the pictures.'

'Okay, my girl—you had better go, then,' the old cook replied. 'I'm getting old, and I suppose I worry about things far too much these days.'

Anna kissed Santiago on the cheek and gave him a comforting smile. 'Don't worry, I'm sure it's nothing important,' she replied. But Anna could not help but feel a little nervous herself as she left the kitchen and made her way through the now-dark kitchen gardens toward the station manager's cottage.

Jan Muller had drunk close to half a bottle of navy rum when he heard the soft tap on his door. He put both of his hand's palms down on his desk and pushed himself to his feet, shook his head to gather his thoughts, and walked unsteadily across the room and opened the door.

'Ah, the cook's little helper!' Muller greeted the Aboriginal girl with a noticeable slur. 'Come in—come in, my dusky little princess.' He reached for Anna's hand and led her inside the untidy cottage, turned back and locked the door.

Anna looked around the room as Muller guided her toward a chair covered with newspapers. The cloying smell of rum filled her nostrils. She saw the long rifle on the wall above the door and the holstered pistol that hung next to it. She noticed even more newspapers in an untidy pile next to a worn timber desk that had a half-empty bottle of rum and a glass on it. Several shirts and a pair of worn dungarees hung stiff on a piece of cord that had been strung between the head of Muller's iron cot and one of the nearby window pulls.

'So, are you enjoying your work in the kitchen?' Muller asked indifferently. He'd forgotten he'd asked the young girl to his cottage. He tried to shake off the effects of the rum.

'Yes, I am Boss. I really enjoy my work,' Anna replied nervously.

'That's good—that's very good.' Muller shrugged with obvious disinterest.

'Everyone has been so very kind to me. I am learning more and more each day,' Anna said uneasily.

'You smell of meat and gravy and pots and pans, my dusky little princess.' Muller's voice was thick with the effects of the rum. 'I think it's time for another nice bath my pretty one.'

'No. No! I'll have one in Santiago's bathroom when I get back,' Anna replied. 'What did you want to see me about, Boss?'

Muller stared at the girl. He could see she was frightened. 'So—do you like your job here at the station, or would you rather be back out in the bush?' He was starting to lose his patience.

'I like it, Boss. I like it very much. I have made many friends, and Santiago has been so good to me. He has helped me learn the white man's words. Yes—yes, I am happy here—very happy.' Anna was starting to panic.

'Well, that's all right then. I think you better come with me.' He took the Aboriginal girl by the hand and led her out through his back door and along the verandah to his wash-house. 'I reckon you enjoyed yourself the last time we did this, so there's no need to be afraid now.'

He pushed open the door and led Anna inside the small, weatherboard wash-house, turned back and locked the door.

Anna watched him push the bath plug into the drain and turn on the tap. 'Please Boss, don't do this again, it's not right and I don't want to,' she whispered.

Jan Muller's mood suddenly changed, he seemed to grow in size as the anger on his face became plain to see.

'Just take off your clothes—and right now,' he hissed menacingly.

Anna looked away from the big man's eyes and began to fumble nervously with her shirt buttons. 'Please, Boss, don't make me do this,' she whispered.

'Get them all off.' Muller barked.

Anna took off her clothes and put them on the chair next to the bath and once again, the beautiful native girl stood naked in front of the big Afrikaner.

'See, that wasn't so bad, was it?' Muller slurred, trying to relax the young girl with another of his insincere smiles, but this time it did little to calm the Aboriginal girl.

Anna covered herself with her hands and watched the station manager unbutton his shirt and slip it from his shoulders. She felt a tremble of fear course through her body as she saw the beast with the yellow eyes and the blood-tipped spears on the big man's chest again.

'Now, let's get you cleaned up good.' Muller patted Anna on the back in what he imagined to be a comforting gesture, and then placed both of his huge hands around her waist and lifted her effortlessly into the bathwater.

The young girl sat silently in the galvanized metal bath as Muller ran his hands over her body. This time she was repulsed by the big man's touch and by the pungent smell of the rum on his breath as he leaned over her. She closed her eyes and hoped in her heart it would soon be over.

When he had finished washing her, Muller lifted her from the bathwater and wrapped her in one of his coarse cotton towels and patted it against her shoulders. The Aboriginal girl's dark breasts and shoulders glistened like wet coal above the faded towel. He started to rub her young body with the coarse cloth. Muller was now deeply aroused, and a dark, carnal lust was beginning to overtake his reasoning. He shifted the towel down to the young girl's thighs and slowly rubbed each of her long legs dry.

Anna stood on the water-stained floorboards, quietly hoping it would soon end. She wanted more than anything to be back in her little room behind the kitchen, dressing for the picture show and looking forward to seeing her, Dan once again.

When he had finally finished rubbing her body dry, Muller tossed the wet towel over the chair. Still swaying a little from the effects of the rum, he reached down and ran his hand over the silken mound between the young girl's thighs.

'Ah, you are a pretty one, aren't you? I think it's time we had a little bit of fun,' he whispered, his voice now hoarse with desire.

Anna stepped back and covered herself with her hands again. She looked past Muller at the locked door . . . There was no escape. 'Can I please go now, Boss—the pictures are starting soon?' she pleaded, looking into the big man's eyes. The sickly smell of his rum breath had begun to make her feel ill.

Then, Jan Muller did something that he had not done on Anna's last visit to his wash-house, and it sent a shock through the young girl. He reached down and undid his thick leather belt, ripped it from its trouser loops, and threw it against the wall.

'Like I said, it's time we had a bit of fun,' he said and started to remove the rest of his clothing.

Anna stared at the water-stained floorboards. She was starting to panic. When she looked up, the station manager had removed his trousers and underwear. He was completely naked. He stood at the side of the bath with his hands on his hips and a perverse smile on his face, his clothing in an untidy pile at his feet.

Anna gasped when she saw his huge erection. It was almost as thick and as long as the young girl's forearm. She looked desperately around the room and then back at Muller's naked body. She was trapped. She began to sob.

'No Boss—please no—I belong to someone else. It's just not right!'

'Most likely one of them bush blackfellas you come here with eh . . . ? Well, they're long gone now. It'd better not be any of the hands here or there'll be trouble—big trouble,' Muller replied. 'Anyway, my little black princess, this will be much more fun, I promise.'

Anna thought of Dan and realised that if she were to even mention his name, Muller would probably fire the young stockman or perhaps even kill him for having anything to do with her. She understood now the big man considered her his private property—his very own plaything. She looked down at his massive erection. She knew what was coming. She began to shake with desperation.

'Come on now, let's play a little game I like to call hide the African sausage.' Muller reached for Anna's waist, grabbed her with his big hands and pushed her toward the chair that held her clothing and the wet towel.

'Bend over and hold onto that chair, my pretty one, and spread those long black legs of yours,' he ordered.

Anna could feel his erection brush against her back as he pushed her toward the chair. She began to struggle. 'Please don't, Boss!'

'C'mon now, spread those long black legs of yours,' he slurred and pushed her head down until her face touched the seat of the chair.

Anna grabbed the base of the chair before she lost her balance and fell forward. 'No—no—please, Boss, you must stop—you must!'

Anna felt him try to push her legs apart with his feet. She struggled against him, trying to force them closed, but he was far too strong for her. And then she felt a sudden sharp sting, as he smacked her cruelly across the backside.

'Open those legs of yours or I'll beat the shit out of you, you black bitch,' he hissed menacingly. Jan Muller was losing his patience.

Anna knew there was nothing more she could do. She stopped struggling and allowed him to push her legs apart and braced herself for what was to come. For a few seconds, nothing happened, and then she heard him spit into his hand, readying himself for her.

'Please don't, Boss,' she whispered as she felt his big hands reach between her thighs, and his fingers probe her. She tried to struggle against his powerful body. But it was no use.

'Stay still, woman,' Muller groaned.

Anna sobbed and held onto the chair as tight as she could and tried desperately to shut out what was about to happen from her mind.

Muller clamped his big hands around the Aboriginal girl's waist and, using his knees to force her legs apart even farther, forced himself inside her with a steady push of his powerful thighs.

'No, Boss—please don't! Please stop—stop—stop!'

Anna looked down at the floor. She could see his crouched knees between her thighs, and then she felt his hips start to drive into her with urgent, brutal thrusts, hurting her with his savagery. 'No, Boss,' she pleaded. 'No, please stop—stop—stop.'

But, Jan Muller had no intention of stopping instead; he started to groan with satisfaction.

Anna held on to the chair, desperately trying not to lose her balance on the wet floorboards. She felt her feet start to slip as the big white man rammed his hips against her, forcing her to open her legs even wider so she wouldn't fall.

Muller saw this as some form of consent. He reached for the young girl's breasts and squeezed them painfully with his big hands and continued to drive into her again and again.

'Yes—yes move those lovely black hips of yours, my pretty one,' he slurred, his voice thick with pleasure.

Anna could feel his perspiration start to drip onto her back and his rum-smelling breath on her neck. She felt like an animal, crouched and subservient, as the man behind her rode her like some cruel, evil beast. She held onto the chair. There was nothing she could do to stop him now—nothing.

'Stay down, woman—stay down.' Muller's voice was now barely a whisper.

Anna started to sob as her head began to painfully hit the seat of the chair in time with each of his animal thrusts. Then, after what seemed to her to be a nightmarish eternity, she felt him start to quicken his sickening violation of her even more. She felt the chair start to slide along the floorboards, creaking in time with each of his thrusts.

'Yes—yes,' Muller moaned his voice hoarse with pleasure.

Anna felt as if she would soon be sick. She could hear the big white man begin to gasp with increased enjoyment, and then she felt him pull away from her and shudder in a spasm of animalistic rapture. The chair continued across the floorboards. Anna held on tight as it slammed against the wall. Then she felt his warm seed spurt onto her back.

Muller groaned with satisfaction. 'We don't want no little half-breeds running around the place, now, do we?' He whispered as he stepped away from the Aboriginal girl.

'Wasn't that fun, my little black princess? If you behave, I'll let you visit me again sometime soon.' He turned to the bath and washed his now flaccid member in the bathwater and rinsed his hands to wash away the smell of the Aboriginal girl. When he finished he turned back to her.

'You'd better get yourself out of here, and say nothing about this to anyone or I'll cut your throat and skin that pretty black arse of yours,' he said menacingly as he reached for the towel to wipe his hands.

Anna stayed as he had left her, her body bent over the chair and her hands still gripping its wooden base. She began to cry.

Jan Muller reached down and picked up his clothing from the floor. 'You just keep your mouth shut about this and we'll get along just fine,' he said in a low voice as he retrieved the key from his trouser pocket. He unlocked the wash-house door, and walked, naked, out across the back verandah and into his cottage. It was as if the taking of the young girl was of little or no importance to him at all.

Anna let go of the chair and tried to stand. Her eyes were swollen from sobbing. She felt a terrible pain between her thighs, and her hips hurt where his hands had held her. The strength had now completely gone from her body. She swayed unsteadily toward the bath. The room was unnervingly quiet. She looked around the wash-house for some confirmation that the nightmare she had just endured had actually happened. Then, she saw her blood on the floor near the chair. She wanted to be sick. The man was a devil, an evil, sinister devil. Anna hated him now with a passion that made her tremble with its intensity. She felt unclean. She wanted to run, but first, she needed to wash herself and dress. She looked at her clothes still folded on the chair and partly covered by the wet towel. She had to calm down. She stepped into the bathwater, crouched down and splashed water up onto herself. Then she cupped her hands and rubbed the soapy water between her thighs as hard as she could bear; trying to wash away the horror she had just endured. Sobbing, she lay back in the bathwater and rinsed her lower back as best she could of all traces of the man who had raped her.

Sobbing, she stepped out of the bath, dried herself and put on her clothes. When she was dressed, she opened the wash-house door as quietly as her trembling fingers would allow and stepped out onto the narrow verandah and looked at the door that led into Muller's untidy cottage. She felt a rush of fear as she imagined him coming out to have his way with her again. With her heart hammering in her chest, she crept across the verandah and down the steps and ran as fast as she could.

# 8

# The S.S. Minderoo

*Port of Fremantle, Western Australia.*

*14th December 1932, Mid-morning*

Captain James Hedley Bradford, skipper of the Western Australian Steam Navigation Company's ship, the *S.S. Minderoo*, took a puff of his old bent-stemmed, briarwood pipe and watched as the last of the passengers who were to sail with him made their way up the gangway. *The Minderoo* carried around 160 passengers in second-class and forty in first-class. Although, on this trip, the numbers were well down due to the effect the Depression had on most things, including shipping. The well-built ship had a multi-purpose role: apart from passengers, she carried up to 550 head of cattle and more than 1,200 tons of cargo.

Among the passengers, the captain watched boarding, were white station workers returning to the north, school-teachers heading to new postings in remote northern towns, and some, just Depression drifters heading north in search of work on the huge cattle stations there.

Most of those boarding were carrying their own baggage, and the captain watched them struggle up the narrow gangway. That is, all except the last one. Three able-bodied porters were carrying

77

the baggage of the last passenger he was watching board. However, Captain Bradford was prepared for this particular passenger, even though he had never laid eyes on her until now. He had received special instruction in regard to this particular passenger. Isabella Montinari would be travelling first-class and he had personally reserved cabin eleven for her. That particular cabin was probably the best of the first-class cabins on board. It had its own small en-suite bathroom and was set apart from most of the others. The cabin was often used by state politicians on government business for their trips to northern ports. The old captain had entertained many important people at his dinner table as they had travelled north on board the *Minderoo*, to Broome and Darwin and even Singapore. Many of them, bureaucrats or politicians enjoying government-funded holidays, while the rest of the country suffered through the long and difficult Depression times.

At first, he couldn't see her; the last of the boarding passengers were blocking his view. Then, he saw her. Captain Bradford slipped the small photograph he was holding in his right hand back into his jacket pocket. Isabella Montinari was dressed in a fashionable white, tropical suit with loose-fitting slacks covering her long legs and comfortable-looking white canvas shoes on her feet. The captain drew in a breath; she was beautiful, stunningly beautiful. Her long mane of dark hair was tied back in a casual ponytail and protruded out from the back of the wide-brimmed, white hat that she wore. The captain noticed she had tied a sash of pale blue silk around the hat, the tails of which hung down with her dark hair, and moved from side to side with each of her unhurried steps as she made her way gracefully up the timber gangway followed closely by the three struggling porters. The captain had never seen a woman wearing sunglasses before, but he did know they were becoming fashionable, he had seen pictures of women wearing them in a shipping magazine in Fremantle. He was aware, that movie stars and some European women wore them, but he had never seen a woman wearing them in Australia, until now. It was difficult for the old captain to keep up with the fashions of the times, and 1932 had come around all too quickly for him anyway. As he watched from the head of the gangway, the woman looked up at him and smiled. The sun glinted off the blue lenses, and the captain noticed the colour seemed to match perfectly the sash she had tied around her hat. Isabella Montinari was indeed a rare beauty. Captain Bradford guessed her age at possibly thirty or perhaps a little less. He noticed she carried herself with the confidence of a woman who had led a privileged life, which was not surprising, after all, she was the daughter and only child of Michael Montinari, one of the country's richest men, if not the richest.

Captain Bradford had read all the newspaper articles and had followed with great interest, the tales of the enigmatic Michael Montinari's rise to the top of the Australian construction industry. The man's ability to read market conditions and his uncanny capacity to invest wisely had carried him through the recent Depression that had devastated the rest of the Australian economy almost unscathed. It was rumoured that he had invested in several struggling machinery companies just prior to the war breaking out in Europe, and later, as Australia entered the conflict and the country was mobilizing for the terrible months that were to follow, he had won contracts building armaments, aircraft parts, and other equipment for the war effort in his hastily re-tooled factories. Even though Michael Montinari was Italian-born, he was hailed as a great patriot. He had rallied to the war effort with all the capacities at his disposal. At the same time, it had made him a staggeringly wealthy man.

Captain Bradford had been instructed by his employers to offer the Montinari woman every possible assistance and comfort on her voyage from the port of Fremantle to the port of Derby, some 1500 miles and several days' steaming to the north. On her arrival there, she was to be met by the manager of Cockatoo Creek Station. A huge cattle enterprise owned by Pegasus Pastoral Holdings, one of the many Montinari families group of companies. Once there, the woman was to be offered assistance with the transfer of her baggage and any further help she may require.

The captain hurried down to where Isabella Montinari stood waiting for her baggage to be safely boarded, and smiling, he introduced himself.

'Welcome aboard the S.S. *Minderoo*, Miss Montinari; Captain James Hedley Bradford at your service.'

'Good morning, Captain Bradford. Please—call me Isabella,' the beautiful dark-haired woman replied with an educated voice.

'Certainly, Isabella, I will be more than happy to.' The old captain smiled, warming to the Montinari woman immediately. He offered her his hand, which she shook politely.

'Would you like me to show you to your cabin, my dear,' he offered.

'Thank you, Captain,' Isabella replied.

The old captain led the way up a short flight of recently painted steel stairs toward cabin eleven, with the porters carrying Isabella's baggage struggling behind. Captain Bradford smiled to himself as he led the Montinari woman away from the boarding area toward her cabin. He had found himself unexpectedly besotted with her.

Cabin eleven was located on the main deck. It had a small folding table and two canvas chairs near its door and an unimpeded view from the starboard side of the ship out over the ocean. The captain unlocked the door and handed the key to Isabella and they both stepped back to let the struggling porters make their way inside.

'There is iced water in your cabin, my dear. If you would like anything else, just press the buzzer near the bed and a steward will happily attend to you. I do hope you enjoy your voyage with us.' The captain bowed politely. 'Perhaps when you are settled and have taken some rest, you will allow me to welcome you on board as a guest at my table for dinner this evening.'

'I would be glad to, Captain. And just what time is dinner served?'

'At seven, my dear, and I should tell you, we have a very talented cook on board the *Minderoo*. I do believe you will find the meals quite satisfactory. Perhaps after you have eaten, you may enjoy a glass of a very fine Chablis that I keep refrigerated in the galley for my own personal use.'

'Thank you, Captain, that would be most refreshing,' Isabella said politely. 'Captain, I would rather you not offer me any special consideration because of my father, sir. As I am sure you have been told who my father is.'

'Yes, my dear, I do know who your father is,' the captain replied. 'In that case, Isabella, all of the *Minderoo's* first-class passengers shall be treated to a glass of my Chablis this evening.' The old captain smiled at the beautiful woman standing opposite him and chuckled briefly at his little joke.

'Well then, Captain, I am sure that we shall have a happy group of first-class passengers, on our very first night at sea on board your sturdy ship.' Isabella thanked the captain for his help, bid him goodbye until dinner, and went into her cabin.

Captain Bradford returned to the bridge just as the gangway was being hauled on board and secured for sea. He flicked on several switches at the helm.

'Engine room—Mr Butfield, make ready for sea, sir. On the deck—stand by to cast off.' He waited for a few seconds for a signal from the engine room before continuing, 'Stern and mid-ship lines away and slow ahead, Mr Butfield.' The captain watched his first mate spin the ship's wheel expertly to port and a few moments later he felt the stern swing out and away from the wharf.

'Bow lines away—stand clear and slow astern, Mr Butfield,' he said almost mechanically to the engine room below. *The Minderoo* began to slowly move astern from her moorings.

'Come hard to starboard, Mr Anderson,' the captain said unnecessarily to his first mate. 'Slow ahead, Mr Butfield, and all hands make ready for passage north.'

The S. S. *Minderoo* came about steadily and headed away from the wharf. They were underway.

Captain Bradford cleared his pipe with a few taps to the palm of his left hand and began to refill its bowl with the aromatic 'Old Holborn' tobacco he carried in the small leather pouch in the pocket of his crisp, white linen jacket.

'Thank you, Mr Butfield,' he said unnecessarily to the now silent, engine room intercom. He lit his pipe, drew a long inhalation of the sweet-smelling smoke into his lungs, and flicked off several of the switches at the helm. He smiled as he drew on his pipe. He was looking forward to his dinner date with the very beautiful Isabella Montinari.

The deck-hands had followed the captain's commands like second nature and the S.S. *Minderoo* was once again underway

81

to ports north. Most of the passengers had quickly stowed their baggage in their cabins and were back on deck walking about, familiarising themselves with the ship. The morning breeze was refreshing and several of them were leaning over the rails watching Freemantle disappear behind a long peninsula of scrubland.

The S.S. *Minderoo* had been launched in 1910 and had very attractive lines for a ship of her type. She had a total weight of 2,720 ton, a top speed of around thirteen knots fully laden, and a draft of fourteen feet. This made her ideal for plying the coastal waters to the north and making her way into its many ports as she steamed up the Western Australian coast on her regular voyages from Freemantle to Singapore and return. Her facilities and fitments were up to the minute and included a card lounge and a beautifully fitted-out saloon reminiscent of luxury liners of days gone by. The saloon had recently been refurbished, its centre-piece now being the new timber and brass bar. The bow-shaped bar was a beauty to behold. It had been fitted with a magnificent top made from solid Australian blackwood inlaid with an African ebony border and a hand-carved mahogany paneled front. A sturdy brass foot rail in the same bow shape as the bar had been fitted, complimenting the fine workmanship that had gone into its construction. Its latest innovation, an ice-maker, had been recently installed next to the glass-doored refrigerators and was proving popular with patrons as the ship travelled toward the north and into the tropics. A short walk from the saloon was the timber-paneled dining room, which was divided into two separate areas. One was for the second-class passengers and the other, for those in first-class, with a pair of superb mahogany and leadlight doors linking them. Both rooms were appointed with the very best of fitments. The upper sections of the walls were covered in a rich burgundy wallpaper, on which hung framed photographs of the S.S. *Mindaroo* and her sister ships. The teak ceilings were fitted with brass and rattan ceiling fans, each having a gold braided control tassel hanging at the ready. Set along the centre of these two tastefully decorated rooms, were several magnificent Italian chandeliers. The cabin the captain had reserved for Isabella was well appointed as well, and very comfortable and complete with its own, small bathroom. Fresh white towels had been folded and placed on the bed, along with several bars of 'Brent's of London soap' and a white toweling bathrobe with the monogram 'S.S. Minderoo' sewn stylishly onto its pocket with burgundy thread.

Isabella had been quite tired when she came aboard and had slept for several hours. When she finally woke, she could feel the comforting throb of the ship's engines far below. She rolled over and looked around her cabin. She felt adventurous—she was at sea and soon she would be back to her beloved Cockatoo Creek. The steady throb of the ship's engines gave her the feeling that they were well underway. She checked her small travel clock on the bedside cabinet. It was a little after six. Time, she decided, to shower and dress for her dinner date with the very charming, Captain James Hedley Bradford.

# 9

# Santiago

Santiago lay on his bed reading his battered old copy of 'The Complete Home Gardener,' a book he had read from cover to cover many times. He loved the illustrations and the neatly drawn diagrams that showed the novice gardener how to do most of the things that needed to be done in their garden. There were simple pictures that illustrated the best way to trellis beans and passion-fruit vines, simplified instructions on how to build windbreaks using bamboo and brush. How to harvest seeds and easy to follow instructions for drying fruit. That book and his bible were the only books the old cook owned, and he loved them both.

Santiago never watched the picture shows on Sundays. More often than not they were cowboy films, and the shooting and killing always made him feel uncomfortable. To the old man, it seemed to show the world as a violent, aggressive place. Santiago was a peaceful man and he detested violence of any sort. He would rather read his books and dream his dreams.

The old man had just shut off the kerosene lamp next to his bed when he heard the sound of running feet across his back verandah. He could still hear the noise coming from the pictures that were being shown outside the dining room, or at least the occasional loud voices, cheering, and gunshots. He knew that Anna had planned to meet Dan there after her visit to the station manager, but now, something didn't seem right. He felt tiny prickles of fear begin to crawl across his skin as he realised beyond any doubt that the running feet belonged to Anna. Then, he heard her door slam shut.

Anna had run back to the kitchen in total panic. She had no idea what she should do or where she should go. Perhaps, she should take her few belongings and disappear into the bush and try to find her grandfather. She was confused and unsure, but one thing she did know was she must not see Dan. She just couldn't face him, not now, not after what the boss had done to her. She ran across the narrow verandah, went into her room and fell onto her bed and started to cry. Spasms of desperation shook her young body and tears poured down her distraught face. 'I am so sorry, Dan—so very sorry,' she sobbed.

There was a knock at the door. It was Dan; she knew it—it had to be him.

'Go away—I am sick. Please go away,' she cried. She heard the door creak open. She lifted her head and looked through her tears at the smiling brown face of Santiago—her best friend.

'Please leave me alone, Santiago. I am sick,' she whispered.

'What has that evil man done to you, my sweet darling?' the old man asked. As soon as he'd looked at Anna, he knew something was wrong, terribly wrong.

'What has he done to you, Anna? You must tell me,' he asked again, softly but insistently as he walked toward her.

'He has hurt me, Santiago. He pushed himself inside me in his wash-house.' Anna began to sob again. 'He made me feel like one of the station dogs—I hate him, Santiago. I hate him.'

'I'll kill him! I'll kill the bastard! I'll get my old axe and cut his heart out and feed it to the dogs!' Santiago cried out and exploded into a rage, flailing his arms about in frustrated anger. Then, just as quickly, his rage gave way to tears and the old cook put his arms around the young girl, and they cried together. The old cook was devastated. He should have known something like this would happen.

While they cried together, Santiago began to wonder what they should do. It seemed to him that perhaps the safest place for

Anna would be back with her own people. But he did not want to see her go. He knew it would break his heart. He loved the young girl as a father loves a daughter, and he knew she was happy with her new life at the station. But, Santiago was an old man, and with age comes hard-earned wisdom and an ability to see reason when reason seems almost impossible. Slowly, the old man began to realise a plan, a way for Anna to get through the next few days. He slowly undid the tangle of her arms around him and drew his face away from hers and looked into her red, swollen eyes.

'Anna, I will go and see Dan in a few minutes and tell him you are not well and that you will see him as soon as you feel better,' he said softly. The old cook could see the turmoil of emotion in the young girl's eyes, but he continued, 'I don't think that bastard Muller will bother you again for a while, and if he does, you must refuse to go near him.' Santiago had a cold, distant look on his face. 'Curly Jim has told me the owner's daughter, Isabella, is coming to the station soon, so this is what I think we should do.' He tried to smile as he told Anna his plan, but the smile seemed more of a grimace. 'I know Isabella, she is a beautiful person, and she has a peaceful and loving soul. When she arrives, we must go to her and tell her what has happened and she will tell us what must be done.'

He wiped the drying tears from his wrinkled brown face. 'You will like Isabella, and I am sure she will like you, my sweet darling. But until then, we must carry on as if nothing has happened. It is the only way.' The old man's voice was little more than a whisper.

Anna finally stopped crying and wiped the tears from her face with her crumpled bed sheet. 'If you think that's what we should do, then I will wait until Isabella arrives to tell her what that evil man has done to me. But, Santiago, I am not sure if I can face Dan ever again. He must know the truth, and I don't think I can tell him.'

'I will go and find him now and tell him you are not well. Then, let us just see what each day brings as you begin to feel better. You need not tell him what has happened, at least, not yet for a while.' Santiago kissed Anna's cheek and stood to leave.

The Aboriginal girl reached for the old man's hand and looked into his eyes. She tried to smile. 'Thank you, Santiago. What would I do without you?' she whispered.

'Get some rest, my sweet, and if you need me, just tap on my door.' He kissed the young girl's cheek again and smiled back at her as he opened the door. Then, he was gone on his mission to find Dan.

At four thirty the following morning, as Santiago was tying his apron around his skinny waist and wondering if his helper was feeling any better, he heard the kitchen door creak open. He turned to see Anna walking toward him. She gave him her usual, cheerful smile and went across to where her apron hung and took it down.

'Now, what would you like me to do Santiago?' she asked in a timid voice.

Santiago could not believe his eyes. Outwardly, Anna looked as if nothing had happened to her at all. But as she drew closer, the old cook could tell she was barely managing to keep her emotions in check. He smiled back at her. 'I'll start the eggs, while you start slicing the bacon,' he replied. Tears welled in the old cook's eyes as he watched his friend tie her apron around her waist.

Breakfast was, as always, a busy time for Santiago and Anna. As usual, Dan was trying constantly to catch Anna's attention as she rushed in and out with plates of food for the servery. But the young girl managed to keep busy and avoided his attention as best she could. After the cooks had finished their breakfast chores and the cleaning of the dining room, things were quiet once again. Santiago paced around among the heavy tables pushing stools into place. He was still deeply annoyed that his Anna had been assaulted by the station manager. When he'd finished, he stepped behind the wooden servery and headed for the kitchen to hang up his apron. He stopped—he had heard something—the metallic jangle of wagon traces. He looked out in the direction of the sound and saw Henry and Wooloo sitting round-shouldered and weary on the hard timber seat of their old buckboard heading down toward the manager's cottage. Like the two despondent-looking men who sat behind her, the old roan mare looked equally done in and was carrying her head low as she plodded steadily down the station's dusty grounds.

'It's Henry and Wooloo. Something's not right. . .

They're not due back for another week.' Santiago called across to Anna and pointed through the window to the two men making their way toward Jan Muller's cottage.

'Maybe one of 'em's hurt or sick or something,' Anna replied and joined him at the window.

'Maybe, but I'm not so sure. They don't look too happy; if you ask me. I reckon something happened out bush.

# 10

# Henry and Wooloo

Jan Muller was still in his cottage readying himself for his day out with several of the hands. He was almost ready to leave when he heard a soft tapping on his door. He walked across the room and jerked it open. Two very dirty and nervous black faces looked up at him.

'G'day, Boss,' Wooloo greeted him anxiously.

'What the hell are you useless bastards back here for?' he snarled.

The two stockmen were covered in dust. Their shirts were stained white with perspiration and both of them looked extremely worried. Henry decided to take over from his nervous friend. 'We got a bit of trouble out near a couple of the mills,' he mumbled.

'Did the pair of you bugger something up on one of them? C'mon, tell me, what the bloody hell is going on?' the station manager snarled.

'No, Boss, we bin fixing 'em up real good. We found a couple of them ballcocks on three and fifteen bent outa shape by stock, but we fixed 'em up proper like—no leaks now, Boss, everything's just fine.'

'So why the hell are you back here, then?'

Muller was becoming angry and impatient, and it showed.

'Getting scared of a few bush niggers out there, eh? Don't like the idea of a spear in your black arses? I'm telling you right now, you'd better have a good reason for coming all this way back when you still have work to do,' he hissed at the two frightened men.

'No, Boss, we bin doing this too long now to be scared of them black buggers. But like I was sayin, we found something out near nine and seventeen, Boss.'

'Found what? Come on, what the fuck could be so important for you to come all this way back?' Muller grunted impatiently.

'We found some stock speared by bush blackfellas out there, Boss. One of them bin roasted real good over a big fire,' Wooloo blurted out.

The colour drained from the station manager's face. 'And what makes you so sure it was bush niggers?'

Muller seemed to grow in both the stockmen's eyes. They could see the anger rise and swell in him.

'That one out near seventeen, they picked his eyes out with sticks. We could see them scratch marks on the skull; only blackfellas do that, Boss. Anyway, we saw the spear hole in the other one out near nine. Clear as day, I reckon,' Henry said shuffling about near the door.

'Black bastards . . . !' Muller whispered.

'We didn't find no fire with that one, Boss and we looked round real good. We reckon it was killed a while back though. The legs was cut off and taken away. Bush niggers for sure. After we found that second one near seventeen, we came straight back as quick as our old horse could bring us, Boss,' Wooloo explained nervously.

Jan Muller could feel the anger boiling inside him as he listened to the two men. 'Black Bastards, we can't have it. Once it starts, there's no bloody stopping it,' he snarled, staring at Wooloo's nervous face.

'Sorry, Boss,' Wooloo whispered.

'You two get yourselves over and see Santiago, and get him to give you both a good feed. You did the right thing coming back to tell me. Get Santiago to see if he can find Beans, and tell him to come and see me straight-away,' Muller whispered. He was angry—very angry.

The two stockmen hurried down the verandah steps and headed for the kitchen.

Muller went back inside his cottage and sat down at his desk. He picked up the letter opener that lay next to some opened letters and slapped it against the palm of his left-hand several times as he contemplated what to do. Then he drove it down into his desk with such force that it snapped in two. He looked at his left hand. One of the pieces had cut him quite badly; blood was dripping from his palm onto the pile of letters. 'Black bastards . . .!' He threw the broken pieces of letter opener across the room just as there was knock at the door.

Beans had run across to the manager's cottage as soon as he knew he was wanted and tapped on the door. Wooloo had told him there had been some stock speared out near a couple of the windmills. He knew there was going to be trouble. The door opened, and Jan Muller, his left hand wrapped in a dirty handkerchief, looked down at him with obvious disdain.

'You took your bloody time getting here, you tub of lard. I suppose you have heard about the spearing?'

'Yes, Boss, bad business—very bad business you know. Once they start, the buggers won't bloody well stop. They'll reckon its easy pickings, eh, Boss?' Beans stammered, imagining that was what his boss wanted to hear.

'You're right about that.'

'Err—I spose we gotta do somethin about it, Boss,' Beans mumbled. He was feeling uneasy; he'd noticed the blood-spattered paperwork on the station manager's desk.

'I want you to ride out now and get every hand on the place back here as quick as you can,' Muller said calmly. 'I want you to them all that they are to see me just as soon as they're back here.'

'Yes, sir, Boss. I'll get saddled up straight-away. I reckon I should be able to have 'em all back before nightfall.'

'Well, go on—get fucking moving, then,' Muller snapped and turned to go back inside.

'Okay, Boss,' Beans replied and hurried away.

It was almost sundown before the hands were finally back at the station and following Bean's instructions; they were all gathered outside the manager's cottage, waiting for Jan Muller to appear. A thick cloud of cigarette smoke rose above them and wafted away through the boab trees as they milled about whispering their concerns to one another.

Suddenly, the cottage door opened, and a very calm and controlled Jan Muller strode out.

'Good evening, boy's, thanks for getting back here so quickly,' he began in a matter-of-fact manner. 'You have probably heard, we have lost some stock to marauding blackfellas, and as you all know, that is a practice that will not be tolerated by the cattlemen of the Kimberley.'

The stockmen shuffled about in the dirt, puffing nervously on their cigarettes and watching the big man's face.

'Too much time and effort has gone into this station to tolerate cattle spearing. We are duty bound to do something about it—and quickly,' Muller announced with noticeable calm. 'There have been two separate instances of spearing that we know about on the station, one near mill nine the other near seventeen, and according to Henry and Wooloo, the steer that was killed near nine is the older of the two. Now, I want you all to listen very carefully to what I want done.' Muller studied the nervous faces of the stockmen before he went on. 'Beans, you, Fancy Dan, and Steve will take Henry and Wooloo and head on out to nine and work your way along the western boundary of the station, looking for blacks. I want you to carry rifles with you in case you are attacked,' he said calmly. 'Before I go any further I must add that I have been instructed by the station owner, Mr Montinari that we are not to engage in any ruthless attacks on scrub blacks. You are only to use your firearms if you are under attack. If you do come across any blacks, I want you to round them up and, under armed guard, escort them to our boundary. Once you get them there, you are to let them go with a severe warning, and if necessary, by firing a few shots above their heads. Just make sure they get the message and get the hell out of Cockatoo Creek country—do I make myself clear?' Muller said quietly. He watched Beans, Dan, Steve, and the windmill boys nod their agreement.

'Famous Feet and I will head out to seventeen to see what we can find there. If we come across the group that speared the steer there, they will be roped together and escorted to our eastern boundary along the creeks that run into the Drysdale and sent packing. The Durack's can have the pleasure of their bloody company. I want them off this station. They will be warned not to return here again or there will be trouble, big trouble,' Muller said calmly.

'The rest of you will be staying at the station and will carry on with work here.' Muller paused for a moment and looked at everyone's faces again to make sure he was being understood, 'Billy, you will be in charge while I am gone. There is still fencing to be done on the paddocks down near the dam, and there are irrigation channels to be cleared and the last of the cut feed to be carted out to stock.'

The stockmen mumbled that they had understood and began to move off toward the dining room and their evening meal, thinking that was the end of their instructions.

'Hold on. I haven't bloody well finished yet,' Muller snapped, his calm demeanor momentarily disappearing.

'Beans, I want horses saddled and ready to leave at sun-up, and you had better make sure that both groups have a packhorse. Tell Santiago to put together supplies for what could possibly be a two-week trip. I'll see you in the morning.' With that, he spun around and went back inside his cottage.

After he had eaten his evening meal, Dan made his way around the back of the kitchen, in the hope he could see Anna and say goodbye before he left for the western boundary the following morning. Pearl and Rosie were just finishing their meals on the kitchen verandah when he made his way up the steps.

'Good evening, ladies. I hope you're enjoying your meal?' Dan said politely to the two good-natured Aboriginal women.

'Hi there, pretty boy. When are you gonna pay us girls a little visit?' Rosie asked the handsome young stockman.

'Not tonight, ladies—not tonight,' Dan replied with a self-conscious laugh.

'Just for you, we'll drop the two bob for your first visit and you can give us both a ride. What do you say, sweetie?' Pearl giggled.

'I'm sorry, ladies, but I'm here to see Anna,' he replied shyly, and made his way past the two laughing women and rapped on the kitchen door.

A few moments later Santiago opened the door and gave Dan a sympathetic smile. 'Like I told you before, Dan, she's been a bit sick, and she's still not too good. Maybe you should come back and see her when you get back from your trip,' Santiago said convincingly.

'I just wanted to say goodbye to her, Santiago, that's all. There may be trouble out bush, and I could get myself speared or something. Can't I see her for just a couple of minutes?'

Just then the door opened wider, and Anna brushed past Santiago and stepped out onto the verandah.

'It's okay, Santiago. I'm feeling a lot better now, and I want to see Dan before he heads out in the morning anyway.' The Aboriginal girl smiled at the old cook and patted his shoulder as she brushed by him.

'Don't be too long, Anna; we've still got work to do,' Santiago replied with a concerned expression on his face.

'I won't be too long, really.' Anna turned back quickly and kissed the old cook's cheek.

'Come with me, Dan.' Anna took Dan's hand and led him down off the verandah and away from the prying ears of Pearl and Rosie.

'You save yourself for Pearl and me, Dan. We'll teach you some tricks, sweetie,' Rosie teased and blew the young stockman a kiss across her dark palm. Both women burst into raucous laughter.

'I've missed you, Anna. I've really missed you. I know you have been sick, but I just wanted to say goodbye before we left tomorrow, that's all,' Dan blurted.

'I'm sorry, Dan. I've missed you too,' Anna replied. She squeezed Dan's hand and felt tears begin to well and fought them back.

'I love you, Anna.' Dan leaned forward and kissed Anna's cheek.

'I'm sorry but should be getting back, Dan. Santiago needs me to help him. But as soon as you get back, come and see me.' Anna's voice sounded ready to break. She stepped away from Dan and started back toward the kitchen.

'All right then, I'll see you when I get back,' Dan called after her. 'I'll be thinking of you every day while I'm gone—every single day.' The lovesick but very confused young stockman turned and headed off toward the bunkhouse.

The following morning, as the first rays of daylight crept through the boab trees and cast their long, distorted shadows across the dusty grounds, the horsemen who were to take part in the search were gathered outside the manager's cottage. The stockmen were mostly silent as they set about their last-minute preparations. Saddle leather creaked as girth straps were tightened and final adjustments were being made. Rifle scabbards were being buckled into place, saddlebags secured and bedrolls tied with rawhide thongs behind well-worn saddle seats.

The early morning quiet was suddenly broken as Jan Muller stepped out of his cottage, his clay pipe clenched firmly between his teeth. The station manager was carrying his long Rigby rifle and the heavy Schofield revolver was already holstered and buckled around his waist.

'Good morning, boys—are we all set, then?' He greeted the waiting stockmen with a half-hearted smile and hefted a set of leather saddle-bags and a scabbard for the Rigby up onto his shoulder and headed down the verandah steps toward the horse Beans was patiently holding for him.

'Have you got plenty of tucker on those packhorses and enough water like I told you?' he grunted at the portly stockman.

'Yes, Boss—all set to go, Boss,' Beans replied a little too quickly and spat out his cigarette in his eagerness to answer. He looked down at the wasted cigarette on the ground and decided to leave it where it was.

'Right then, you all know what to do, so let's get moving,' the station manager barked. He tied on his saddlebags and waited impatiently while Beans buckled the heavy Rigby rifle under his right-side saddle flap. The riders climbed into their saddles, split into their two groups, and walked their horses out through the boab trees and set off in their different directions.

Santiago and Anna were watching from the dining room windows as they rode out through the trees. Anna was worried about Dan and hoped he came to no harm. However, the native girl was even more worried about her grandfather, Goonagulla, and her tribespeople. She hoped in her heart that it was not his group that had speared any of the cattle. She knew there would be trouble if they had been the guilty ones and Jan Muller managed to catch up with them.

Several hours later, as Dan's group were working their way toward the west on their long ride to windmill nine, warm tropical rain started to spot their shirts and saddles.

Dan pulled his hat down and looked across at Beans.

'I hope this rain don't get no heavier, Beans.'

His friend turned to him and smiled. 'This ain't nothing— just wait till it really pisses down,' he replied and hunkered down in his saddle

'How long do you reckon before we get to nine, Beans?' Dan urged his horse up alongside the Aboriginal stockman's.

'Three days at most, I reckon,' Beans replied. 'Shouldn't be no more.'

Back at the station, Billy Anders and several of the hands were busy with the fencing work the station manager had given them. The rest were cleaning the irrigation channels. All of them could smell the sweet promise of rain in the humid air.

Santiago and Anna were busy working in the gardens. They had picked the last of the cucumbers earlier and were now clearing out old melon vines and tying long bean runners up onto a trellis that Santiago had put together from a simple design he'd found in his old gardening book.

Anna had a worried look on her face. 'I hope there's no shooting or fighting with the bush natives while the men are out bush, Santiago. They're just hungry, that's all,' she said and threaded a runner into place on the sturdy trellis.

'The boss said he don't want no killing, we all heard him,' Santiago replied. 'He said they're just gonna escort them off the station with a warning. That's if they ever find the black buggers . . . Sorry about that, Anna.' But the old cook had a bad feeling about it all. He wasn't too sure what Dan's group would find. After all, they were stockmen, not trackers. But he knew if Famous Feet came across any tracks he would find them easily. He was probably the best tracker in the Kimberley, and everyone knew it. But what really worried the old cook was what Jan Muller would do if Famous Feet did manage to track them down.

'I hope you're right, Santiago. Anyway, it was just two steers, that's all,' Anna said quietly as she tied another curling runner into place.

'The silly buggers shouldn't have speared the cattle, though. There's always big trouble when stock gets speared, one way or another.'

Two days later, Dan's group arrived at windmill nine just as the sun was setting. Henry and Wooloo led them across to the withered, legless carcass of the steer that had been speared. They dismounted and stood around the dusty remains. Steve took off his battered hat and slapped it against his thigh. 'That's a spear hole all right. Stupid buggers, they know they aren't allowed to touch the stock, no matter what.'

'I was sort of hoping it was all a mistake. But you're right, it's a spear hole for sure,' Beans said quietly.

'Let's set up camp near the trough over there, and tomorrow, we can start working our way south of here and see if we can pick up any tracks,' Dan added wearily and lead his horse back toward the trough, hoping in his heart that they came across none.

The following day, they set out early on their search of the area and spent the next two days working their way through the bush along the station's western boundary. But they found no sign of Aboriginals at all, other than the faint windblown tracks they had followed earlier that led from the carcass and on toward the west. They all agreed that that group had disappeared out of the station country soon after the spearing and had headed off in the general direction of Derby. They had now been away from the station for four days, and from where they were, many miles north of windmill nine; they knew it would take them a good four days to get back. Even though there was still plenty of food left on their packhorse, it was beginning to look as if their mission was all a waste of time.

After the few showers that had fallen when they had first set out from the station, there had been no more rain, but the humidity had become almost unbearable. Each day as they travelled, there were heavy clouds above them, and at night, lightning ripped across the sky lighting up their campsites and frightening the horses. In the evenings they hobbled their horses carefully, and as an extra precaution, camped well away from any big trees.

As they set up their camp that night and rolled out their bedrolls, they decided among themselves they would begin their long ride back to the station at first light the following morning. The whole trip had just seemed a waste of time. They were saddle-sore, hungry, and missing Santiago's cooking more and more as each day wore on.

Dan gathered up a few sticks and soon had a good fire going, and it wasn't long before a billy of tea sat in the coals with their cooking pot next to it and the last two cans of beans bubbling in the heat of the coals.

'That's the last of the beans, just damper and dry beef from now until we get back. Do you reckon you'll survive, Beans?' Steve remarked and tossed a generous pinch of salt into the bubbling red mess.

'One day at a time, Steve. We got beans tonight, so I'm a happy blackfella for now,' he replied, patting his ample belly. Four long days in the saddle hadn't seemed to strip away any of his ample proportions.

'Hey, Dan, a few more days and you'll be back in the arms of your sweet little black gin,' Steve continued sarcastically.

'Shut your dirty mouth, Steve, and keep your filthy thoughts to yourself.'

'What seems to be wrong with our love-struck gin jockey tonight, eh?'

'Give it a rest. Anyway, Rosie tells me every time you visit her, it's the fastest two bob she makes on the station,' Dan shot back. The others burst into good-natured laughter.

'Watch it, Fancy Pants, or I'll give you a bloody hiding, right here and now.'

'You can hand it out, but it's not so nice coming back, is it?'

'Just bloody well watch it, or look out.'

Dan had had enough of Steve's dirty mouth and his snide remarks. He could take no more, and he didn't care if he got a hiding. He had had enough.

'Anytime you want to try me, Steve, just let me know. But for now, just keep your filthy mouth shut.' Dan stood up as he spoke and walked toward Steve, expecting the man with the fighting reputation to come straight at him. But Steve stayed where he was.

'Can't take a little joke, eh, Fancy Pants? You're just too sensitive for your own bloody good, I reckon.' Steve stood up, stared hard at Dan for a few seconds and went across to his bedroll. 'As I said, you're too bloody sensitive. Anyway, now ain't the right time Danny boy.' He reached down and patted his bedroll into position against his saddle. When he finished, he leaned over and grabbed his rifle scabbard. He was angry he'd been challenged by the usually timid, Dan. He slid out the Lee Enfield and slammed the bolt back and forth, feeding a round into the chamber.

Dan stood waiting, his hands at his sides, his fists bunched.

'As I said, now ain't the right time, Danny boy.' Steve put his rifle next to his bedroll and walked off to relieve himself.

Dan shrugged and went back to his own bedroll. He sat down, slid off his boots, and started to massage his sore

# 11

# Famous Feet

Jan Muller and Famous Feet had been pushing their mounts hard as they headed out toward the northeast and windmill seventeen when the rain hit. Muller was beginning to worry. He knew if it got any heavier, the tracks of the marauding natives could become very difficult to find, and follow. He looked across at the thin black tracker riding alongside him.

'Famous, can you follow tracks if this rain really starts coming down?' he asked with an impatient grunt.

'Yep, I think so, Boss. Once I find them tracks and I know what they're doing, I reckon I'll just start thinking like them and keep me eyes open.'

'I hope you're bloody well right,' Muller mumbled. 'I just hope you're right.'

Two days after leaving the station, Famous Feet and Jan Muller arrived at windmill seventeen. It was late in the afternoon, and even though darkness would soon be upon them, Muller wanted to see the remains of the fire where the heifer had been cooked before they set up their camp for the night. It only took Famous Feet a few minutes to find the ashes, and the two of them stood there for more than a minute looking down at the cold remains of what would have been a very large fire.

'Bastards are going to be sorry for this,' Muller whispered and kicked one of the dried hooves that lay nearby through the ash. He began looking around for sign left by the Aboriginals, but he could see none. 'Famous, I want you to do a circle around and see if you can pick up their tracks.'

'It's getting pretty dark, Boss, maybe we better wait till morning.'

'Circle around and see what you can find—and right fucking now, you lazy black bastard,' Muller replied with a menacing stare.

Famous Feet tied up the packhorse and began walking around the long-dead fire, looking for any trace that had been left by Goonagulla and his weary group.

Muller went back to the windmill and began to set up camp. By the time he had a small fire burning and a billy of water resting against the coals, Famous Feet had strolled back.

'Well . . . what did you find?' he grunted and threw a handful of sticks onto the fire.

'It's getting a bit too dark to be sure, Boss, but it looks like they tried to brush away their tracks by dragging bushes along behind 'em.'

'You're the famous bloody black tracker, can you find them or not?' Muller snapped. He pushed a long stick into the fire which sent a small explosion of sparks into the now dark sky.

'They went off to the west, Boss, and circled around for a bit, I reckon. Like I said, they was dragging bushes behind 'em trying to fool us. Then the smart buggers tied bushes to their feet and headed off to the north.'

'Can you track the bastards tomorrow or not?' Muller was getting frustrated and angry listening to the tracker's pointless babbling detail.

'Yep, I reckon I can, Boss. I think I found where they took them bushes off their feet and kept heading on to the north. I know what they're thinking now, so we'll be right, I reckon. Anyway, Boss, this is the same blackfellas that was at the station. I know the old buggers' tracks from before,' Famous replied confidently.

'Jesus, you found all that out in half an hour, just wandering around in the dark?' Muller grunted. He threw a heavy log onto the fire and watched yet another explosion of sparks. He was grudgingly impressed by the tracker's skill, but he was still impatient to get on with the job.

'I guess that's why they call me, Famous Feet, Boss,' the thin tracker replied with a nervous laugh.

'One thing I hate is a smart-mouthed blackfella. We'll see how fucking good you are tomorrow,' Muller grumbled. 'Unpack that packhorse and get the animals tied up for the night.'

'Don't you worry, Boss, I'll find 'em easy now,' Famous replied. He led his horse across to the packhorse and tied it to the same tree.

Muller watched him and frowned. 'In the morning, I'll tie the packhorse behind mine. You can follow the tracks on foot ahead of me. I don't want you to lose these bastards, Famous—you hear me?'

'Okay, Boss. But we'll be right, I reckon. Right now I gotta see to the horses like you told me.'

At sun-up the following morning, the two men ate a hurried breakfast and set off toward the north. Famous had his head down, following the tracks left by Goonagulla and his weary group as they'd headed away from the small pile of broken bushes they'd used to cover their tracks. The old tracker was leading his horse and walking at a steady pace, searching for any signs of deviation or trickery by the bush natives.

Jan Muller was following on horseback with the packhorse tethered to his horse's tail. A plan was beginning to form in his ruthless mind. He urged his horse up close to the tracker.

'Can't you move a bit quicker, Famous? We'll never catch up with the bastards at this rate.'

'I don't want to lose 'em, Boss. That old fella up there is a smart bugger; he might try to trick us, I reckon,' Famous replied. He pointed toward the north and made an unconvincing attempt to increase his pace.

'Keep moving then, quick as you can.' Muller grunted. He slumped down in the saddle and stared at the tracker's skinny legs. Muller had begun to worry that he may have to call off the search if they didn't find the natives soon. He had counted the days since they had left the station and realised the date was December the eighth. He had to get to Derby to pick up Isabella Montinari and her minder Jack Ballinger on the nineteenth. It was, at the very least, a three-day ride from where they were, back to Cockatoo Creek. He was fast running out of time.

Late that afternoon, Famous Feet stopped in a small grove of young boab trees and began wandering around among them.

'They camped here, Boss. Right here in these trees. They don't seem to be in a hurry anymore—I reckon they think they're free and clear now.'

'How far ahead are they, Famous, can you tell?' Muller had been feeling more and more frustrated as each hour went by.

'No more than half a day, maybe even less, Boss. They're just a few miles ahead of us now.' Beans pointed in the general direction of the travelling group of natives. 'That way, Boss. Not too far now.'

'How can you tell? How the bloody hell could you know they were here only a few hours ago?' Muller grunted, in obvious disbelief.

'The tracks are still all in one piece, Boss. The sides are still straight—I don't reckon they started to crumble in just yet,' Famous replied, pointing down at the tracks.

Muller looked down at the faint man tracks in front of his horse. 'Sounds like a load of bullshit to me. I don't see any straight sides, just bloody tracks is all I can see. Anyway, that'll do us for today.' He reined in his horse, climbed down and began undoing its girth strap. 'We'll stop here for the rest of the day; the horses could do with a bit of a spell. Get your saddle off and take the load off that packhorse. You get them watered and fed, while I get a fire going.'

'Still, a bit of light left, Boss. We could get a bit closer if we kept on.' Famous Feet knew the Aboriginals were not too far ahead, and he wanted to go on for a while longer to prove his point.

'We'll wait till tomorrow—and no fire tonight just in case they see it, or maybe smell it,' Muller replied. Now that he knew the natives were not too far ahead, he had begun to feel a lot more relaxed. Time was not such a problem for him now. 'No bloody cigarettes either,' he snapped, as he put his saddle on the ground and his bedroll next to it.

Jan Muller had a plan, and, tomorrow, he would set it in motion. He slid the Rigby out of its scabbard, placed it next to his bedroll and went across to his horse. He pushed Famous out of his way, unbuckled one of his saddlebags and slid out a bottle of the dark navy rum he had packed back at the station. He wrapped the remaining bottle carefully, slid it back into the side pocket, and buckled the saddlebag.

'Don't even bother to ask me, Famous, you'll just be wasting your bloody time.' He walked back to his saddle, sat down, opened the bottle and took a swig.

# 12

## The Captain's Table

Captain Bradford had decided not to use his usual table
for dinner and had instead chosen a small table in a quiet
corner of the ship's first class dining room, away from most of
the other guests. The stewards, under careful instruction from the
captain, had placed a freshly laundered and pressed, white linen
tablecloth on its top, along with a crystal vase of pale pink roses,
and had set the table with the very best of the ship's silver cutlery
ready for the captain and his guest.

When Isabella entered the dining room, at first, she couldn't
see the captain at all. She had expected him to be at a traditional
captain's table along with several other personally invited guests,
but this did not seem to be the case. Then, she saw him. Captain
Bradford was sitting at a small, intimate table in a quiet corner
of the dining room, well away from the other passengers. She
smiled and waved and made her way past several passengers
already dining and headed for his table. The captain returned
the wave with an even wider smile and stood up. Isabella was
intrigued by the effort the captain had gone to. He seemed such
a charming man.

'Captain Bradford, you have gone to too much trouble, sir.'
She reached for the captain's hand and shook it lightly.

'Good evening, Isabella. I hope you feel rested and refreshed, my dear, and I do hope you like roses. These, in particular, seem to have a wonderful perfume.' The old captain bowed graciously and pointed to the vase of flowers in the centre of the table. Captain Bradford was dressed in his best, white ships uniform for the dinner, and it seemed to match perfectly his carefully brushed white hair.

'I love roses, Captain. They are one of my favourite flowers,' Isabella said politely.

'Let me help you with your chair, my dear.' The captain made his way around the table and pulled back Isabella's chair. When he returned to his own, he leaned across the table to the beautiful woman opposite him. 'My dear, it is no trouble whatsoever. After all, how often does an old man such as I have the chance to dine with a beautiful, well-travelled woman such as you? Who knows, perhaps I can learn how things are in these troubled times in other parts of the world, for I have been informed that you have travelled widely, my dear?'

'Thank you for your flattering words, Captain,' Isabella replied. She reached across and patted the captain's hand. 'Yes, I have travelled quite extensively, but no more than many, I would think. But if I can help you with any knowledge that I may have, I will be only too glad to do so. However, at this very moment, I am famished.'

'Well then, perhaps we should order.' The old captain was thoroughly enjoying himself.

'Do we have a menu, Captain?' Isabella inquired with a smile.

'There is a menu, my dear, but I didn't think we would need it,' the captain replied. 'Let me explain: tonight is Wednesday night, and the tradition on board is to offer passengers two separate choices for each night while they travel with us. As I mentioned before, the cook we have on board the *Minderoo* is a very capable man and a real talent at his trade.' Captain Bradford then went to great lengths to explain the ship's traditions to his beautiful dining companion. 'This evening's choice will be freshly caught local southern crayfish cooked in seawater, chilled and served with salad greens, cantaloupe, and Lady de Coverly grapes, complimented with the cook's very special chili and mango chutney.'

'Lady de Coverly grapes, Captain? I don't think I have heard of them before.'

'Sultanas, my dear—they are simply sultanas. The cook, Henri, is a Frenchman and he seems to like putting on the airs and graces. But I do believe they are one of the best grapes one can eat, and I feel we must forgive him his little eccentricities.'

'Well, it certainly all sounds rather delicious, Captain,' Isabella replied, smiling. 'And what would the other choice be?'

'The second and equally delicious choice this evening will be an American-style rib-eye steak cooked exactly as you like it and topped with a red wine sauce, along with baked potatoes, minted peas, and tender young carrots, cooked with just a splash of honey. Both are most excellent dishes, my dear.'

'You have given me a difficult task, Captain. Very difficult indeed,' Isabella replied.

'And, my dear, the dessert this evening will be Henri's Wednesday night special.' The captain was enjoying his elaborate presentation of the French cook's dishes.

'What would that be, Captain Bradford, please tell?' Isabella found herself enjoying the old captain's company immensely.

'Small, delightful hot puddings filled with chopped dates and raisins and topped with a tasty chocolate sauce. Henri likes to call his little creations, *'Un Savouries Plaisir,'* but I have absolutely no idea what it means.'

'The cook certainly has flair, Captain. But it simply means, 'A tasty pleasure,' Isabella replied and they both laughed lightly at the simple description of the desert.

'And which dish do you think you will choose this evening, my dear?'

'I think I shall be more than happy with the crayfish and salad, and perhaps just a small serving of the pudding.'

'An excellent choice, my dear, one of the stewards should be along at any moment to take our order.' The old captain pushed back his chair and stood up.

'Now, I shall get us a bottle of that tasty Chablis I told you about.'

'Captain Bradford, please do not forget your earlier promise—a glass for each of the first-class passengers.' Isabella smiled as she reminded him.

'Yes Isabella, I have not forgotten. I shall see to it directly.' The captain gave Isabella a bow and turned for the galley.

The dinner that night was a great success, and as the night wore on, Isabella and the captain became firm friends. Their discussions covered many topics, including Isabella's joy at being able to return to Cockatoo Creek Station, the huge cattle holding the Montinari family owned. As their discussions continued, Isabella found that one of Captain Bradford's great passions was the Aboriginal tribes of the Kimberley and of Arnhem Land.

'Isabella, the native tribes from the areas along the Kimberley coast and farther up and into Arnhem Land, including the many islands, most certainly have a fascinating history. There has been a considerable amount of research done in regard to contact they may have had with traders from other countries and the effects it has had on their culture,' the captain began.

'Yes, Captain, I have heard a little of some of the explorers that are supposed to have arrived in this country well before the British. I know that Captain Willem Janszoon from Holland landed here in 1606. I believe there are records in Holland that confirm this,' Isabella added enthusiastically.

'Ah, yes, that is so . . . However, there are those that believe this country has been regularly visited for many hundreds of years, perhaps even thousands, by travellers from other places even prior to that.' The captain stopped for a moment and reached for his wineglass to take a sip.

'Really, Captain, please go on,' Isabella replied.

Captain Bradford went on, explaining that his interest lay in the early history of the northern tribes and their interaction with the seafaring Makassar people. These people, he explained, had visited the northern areas of Australia long before any Europeans had ever arrived in this land we now call Australia, including the Dutch.

The Makassar, he said, had travelled here each year during the northern wet season, to fish for trepang, or 'Bêche-de-Mer' as they are sometimes called. He explained that this fish was found in the shallow rock pools among the inshore reefs, a delicacy that was traded by the Makassar people with the Chinese when they returned to their home country of Sulawesi, a part of the Indonesian islands once known as the Dutch East Indies. This trade has been documented for many hundreds of years by the Indonesian people and could well have been going on for much longer. These Makassar befriended the Aboriginal people of the north and worked with them to harvest the trepang each year. The natives helped these fishermen to set up permanent camps during their many visits. The remains of buildings made of stone: smokehouses and small homes for the fishermen; have been found at many locations along the northern beaches and islands. At some of these sites, tamarind trees have been found, the seeds having been brought across by the fishermen from their homeland. The Macassar taught the Aboriginal people many things. Among them, how to make dugout canoes with small outriggers, instead of their traditional, but flimsy, sewn, bark canoes. This then allowed the Aboriginal fishermen to venture farther offshore and to more easily hunt for the dugong, a great delicacy for the Aboriginal. In return, the natives helped the Makassar harvest the trepang at low tide and were paid with knives and metal for their spearheads. Even tobacco was used as trade, as was alcohol and, it is rumoured, sometimes the sexual favours of native women as well. There are even stories that some of the Aboriginal women were taken back to Sulawesi as willing wives for a number of the fishermen. However, evidence of this is sketchy, and quite possibly supposition. I have been told Aboriginal cave paintings have been found clearly showing Makassar sailing ships and the sailors that travelled in them to the northern lands each year. He went on, telling Isabella that many of the words that the northern tribes still use in their language today come from the Makassar language, words such as '*Jama*' for work and '*Balang*' for white man.

'I hope this is not too boring for you, my dear, but once I start, I can't seem to stop,' Captain Bradford said apologetically and smiled at Isabella.

'Not at all, Captain, not at all. Please go on, sir,' Isabella replied.

'One of the most interesting things that have come to light,' he explained, 'is that there is a possibility the Makassar people introduced Islam to the northern natives. There is evidence of this in some of their Dreamtime stories. But, of course, as time has passed by, this has been diluted and has faded into their folklore.'

'Tell me, Captain, why was the trepang such a prized item with these Makassar people?' Isabella asked.

'The fish was partly dried on the beaches and smoked in their smokehouses and then taken back to the markets in their home country, where it was regarded as a great delicacy. I believe it was also used for medicinal purposes by the Chinese that traded with the Makassar, and some say it may have been used as some sort of aphrodisiac as well,' the captain explained.

'I suppose when you think about it, the northern waters of Australia are certainly very close to some of the Asian countries, in particular, the Indonesian island of Timor,' Isabella offered.

'There is legend also of an ancient people called the *Beijini* that visited this land long before even the Makassar came here. Some say this may well be as far back as a thousand years, or perhaps even more. This may or may not be so, of course, and could well be just a fanciful legend. However, interestingly, there have been ancient coins found on an island off the coast of Arnhem Land that came from Kilwa an African sultanate; I have been told these coins date back to the fifteen hundreds. This, they say, suggests that the northern parts of Australia could well have been part of some ancient and well-used trading route.'

'It's all very fascinating, Captain, and it seems such a shame that the Aborigine have no written language and that all we really have to go on is cave paintings and beach fossicking. But I am sure that there is much truth in what you say,' Isabella replied.

'Now, Isabella, enough of my stories. Tell me a little about yourself, my dear. Tell me why a beautiful woman such as you, travels alone. Surely there is a man in your life?' the captain inquired. He smiled warmly and waited for Isabella to reply.

'Captain Bradford, normally I would say to anyone inquiring about my private life that it is, indeed, private. But I feel that, in you, I have made a confidante and a friend, and I suppose talking can do me no harm. Perhaps it may well do me some good; after all, I have few people I can talk to in confidence these days. My father, whom I love dearly, always seems to be too busy for anything other than work and simple pleasantries,' Isabella replied with a hint of sadness noticeable in her voice.

'Consider me a true friend, Isabella. What we speak of this evening shall go no further, of that you have my word. Who knows, perhaps I can give you some guidance. After all, I have lived a long life and have gained some small amount of wisdom, I believe,' Captain Bradford said earnestly.

'Now, Captain, you asked me why I have no man with me on this trip and whether there is a man in my life. The simple answer to that is no, there is no man in my life at this time,' Isabella said quietly. 'There have been several men who have meant a great deal to me, but unfortunately, true love seems to hide itself. For me, it is as elusive as the pot of gold at the end of the rainbow.'

'Well, Isabella, I wish that I were younger. I would have treated you well had I known you when I was a young man. I can sense that there is a beautiful person inside that matches perfectly the beautiful woman who is there for the entire world to see.' The captain whispered, reaching across and touching Isabella's hand affectionately.

'Thank you, Captain. Thank you very much.  As you already know, I have spent the last few years of my life in Europe, and while I did travel widely when I was there, I spent most of my time in France, in Paris mostly,' Isabella began. 'In Paris, I met a man who changed my life completely. He was certainly very different from the men I had been with before. Most of the men I had been in relationships with previously were, as time proved, not really my type. They either drank too much or thought more of their friends, or perhaps football or some other sport than they did of me. I had become disillusioned and alone, but comfortably alone, if you know what I mean,' Isabella said with sadness in her eyes.

'And this man you met, my dear?' the captain inquired, sensing the sadness in the beautiful woman opposite. 'What was he like?'

'He was a very tall and handsome man, but that was not the reason that I became attracted to him at all. At that particular time in my life, I was quite content to be alone. After all, I had my studies, and Paris is the art capital of the world. There is just so much to see—the museums, the architecture, the works of the great masters, and, of course, the city itself.'

'Tell me more about this handsome man who caught your eye, my dear,' the captain continued delicately.

'His name was Alain. He owned an art gallery that I visited quite frequently. It was a small, but quite exclusive gallery and not far from where I lived, where I would sometimes wander about on days away from my studies. As time went by, Alain and I got to know each other quite well. We seemed to have so much in common. He was very supportive and even liked some of my early work. He encouraged me to put one of them on display among some of his prized paintings, and we were both pleasantly surprised when it sold quite quickly. But, of course, I do believe he used his influence to help make that sale. We had a lot of fun in those early days. Alain was a native Parisian and knew his city well. We became good friends and confided in each other about all of the things that seemed to be of importance to us both. About the city, about art, and about the great masters themselves. As time went by, he opened many doors for me in the art world. We attended some very private functions together, where I met some of the most important artists still living, Matisse and Duchamp to mention just two of them.

Thinking back, I suppose I was overwhelmed by Paris. It was almost too much for a young woman like me to comprehend.' Isabella stopped for a moment to take a sip of her wine. 'More than anything, I loved the lifestyle. Paris is a truly wonderful city, Captain. Once, while I was sitting alone enjoying an espresso in a small café that I frequented, a tiny place called the *Café de la Rotonde*, I saw Pablo Picasso sipping wine and smoking cigarettes with a beautiful dark-haired woman. Isn't it strange how some things remain in your mind? I clearly remember Picasso wore a faded beret over his white hair, and the woman he was with wore a low-cut green dress and very red lipstick. The two of them seemed to be having a rather animated disagreement about something or other, and soon after, the woman with the green dress departed, leaving her long cigarette holder on their table.'

'It is a wonderful story so far, my dear, but tell me more about this mysterious gallery owner.' The old captain reached across to top up Isabella's glass.

'Well, I suppose what happened is we began to fall in love. It was all very wonderful, and I began to believe my life had changed for the better. The two of us did everything together, the cafés, the galleries, the parties. However, as you would have already guessed, Captain, Paris was not the city it had once been. The Depression had hit Europe hard, and in particular, France. But I am fortunate, my father is a rich man, and I am his only child. Even though the city had lost some of the flamboyance and excitement of the twenties, when Hemingway and Fitzgerald frequented her streets and drank in her bars, it was still most certainly a wonderful place to be.'

Isabella took a sip of her wine and smiled at Captain Bradford. 'I was in love with Paris and in love with Alain. I was content, and I was happier than I had ever been. But after we had been together for more than a year, something quite terrible happened, something that I have had great difficulty coming to grips with as a woman.'

'What did the French swine do to you, my dear?' The old captain was noticeably annoyed that anyone could mistreat such a beautiful and intelligent woman.

'Early one afternoon, I came back from my classes to our little flat above the gallery, on the *Rue Auber*. I had a terrible headache. I needed rest and a quiet place where I could sleep. When I opened the door to our flat, I found Alain in bed with one of our friends.' Isabella was close to tears as she related the story to the old captain.

'Another woman . . . : the swine! You must have been hurt beyond belief, my dear.'

'Not a woman—that would have been bad enough. No, it was a man.' Isabella looked sadly at the captain. 'Of course, I left, and quickly, I never even bothered to collect my belongings,' she whispered.

'Well, my dear, I believe you had no choice in the matter, really.' The captain reached across the table and touched Isabella's hand tenderly.

'Of course, Alain was hurt as well, and he came to see me, and I do believe he loved me deeply. He asked for my forgiveness, but what was done was done. There was no trust left between us. I left Paris two days later for Barcelona and stayed there for the next year, burying myself in my studies.' Isabella reached for her wineglass and took a small sip.

'A very sad tale indeed, and, of course, one that will be kept in confidence, I promise you,' the captain replied. He leaned across and took Isabella's hand in his for a few moments. 'But I am sure much happiness still awaits you, my dear.'

'And that, Captain, is the sad tale of my love life up until now. But please do not concern yourself, time enough has passed by now that I feel I am healed from the pain of my sad affair in Paris. However, I do not regret it, and, as they say, Captain, life goes on, does it not?'

'It does, my dear, it certainly does,' Captain Bradford replied.

Isabella drank down the last of her wine and passed her empty glass to the captain. 'But, I must say, I am still a little fragile when I hear accordion music, or that magical voice of Gaby Montbreuse,' Isabella added and attempted to change the subject. 'Captain, do you think it would be wrong of us to have another bottle of your wonderful Chablis?'

'It certainly would not, and I believe we both could do with a little more anyway.' The old captain pushed back his chair. 'I shall get another, and when I return, we shall plot a path toward future happiness for you, my dear. You most certainly deserve it.'

'Thank you, Captain. You are a sweet man.' Isabella smiled up at the old captain.

Captain Bradford brushed the white hair away from his eyes and stood up. 'I won't be too long, my dear.' He looked down at Isabella and his expression momentarily changed. 'Perhaps this Ballinger chap we are picking up in Geraldton may show some promise, my dear.'

'I think not, Captain. Too much like my father, I fear, and most probably a little too raw and rough around the edges for me. But please don't tell my father—he is the only man I truly love.'

'Keep smiling, Isabella, I shall be back directly.' Captain Bradford straightened his tie and jacket and started for the bar.

# 13

# Cattle-Spearing Bastards

As dawn broke through a dark menacing sky, Jan Muller rolled out of his bedroll and walked off into the trees to do his morning duties. As he walked away from the campsite, he yelled back at Famous Feet, 'On your feet, Famous, and start packing up the gear, I'll be back in a few minutes.'

Famous turned his blanket down, uncovering his thin black frame, yawned and stretched his arms up toward the sky. 'Okay, Boss, I'm up already,' he replied. The old tracker struggled to his feet and let out a loud fart.

'Too many beans, Boss—too many bloody beans. Geez, them blackfellas could smell that one.'

A few minutes later Jan Muller returned to the campsite and tapped the Aboriginal tracker on the back.

'Famous, there's a change of plans for today. I want you to leave me a couple of full water bottles from the bladder on the packhorse, a bit of the dry beef, a bag of flour, and some salt. You pack up the rest, take the packhorse with you, and head on back to the station,' he said and watched the black tracker's face for a response.

'You need me with you, Boss. You need me to show you where them blackfellas are.'

'I'll find them from here on without too much trouble. When I do, I'll tie them all together like I said I would and lead them off the property right quick. So you go on and head back to the station.'

'Will you be able to handle them by yourself, Boss—you know, tying em together and all?'

'You get on back, I'll be fine. It's just a few blackfellas. I'll be back at the station in a few days,' Muller replied a note of finality in his voice.

'Okay, Boss. Okay then . . . Watch it, though—they got spears and boomerangs—black bastards. Just you watch yourself, Boss.'

'Pack up and get moving, Famous. I'll be all right. Go on now, quick as you can.' Muller knelt down and began rolling up his bedroll.

Twenty minutes later, Famous Feet had set off on his long ride back to the station, and Jan Muller was in his saddle moving steadily off toward the north once again. The station manager was smiling. Now he could set his plan in motion. He dug his heels into his horse's flanks and pushed forward at a steady walk, keeping his eyes glued to the tracks that led out of the little grove of boab trees.

Six hours later, he noticed a low ridge of coloured stone off in the distance. When he drew closer, he reined in his horse, dismounted, and led it over to a shady copse of acacia trees and tied it up. He undid the girth strap, slid off his saddle and laid it on the ground well away from the horse's hooves. It was hot—very hot. He took off his hat, wiped the sweat from his forehead, and gulped down a few mouthfuls of water from one of his canteens. His horse whickered softly at the smell of the water and waited while Muller filled his hat with the remains from the canteen and laid it on the ground. The horse, thirsty after six hours of steady travel through the dry savannah country, pushed the big man aside and nuzzled into the hat.

Muller checked the Rigby and the revolver while he waited in the sparse shade next to the horse. A short while later, his horse started to push the empty hat about in the dirt. Muller picked it up, shook out the last drops, put it on and headed up the stony rise, enjoying the coolness of the damp hat on his forehead. Keeping low and hugging the weathered rocks, he made his way to the crest.

There were no trees on the little ridge, just a few ancient boulders scattered along its highest point. When he reached the crest, he sat down near one of the bigger boulders, leaned back on it, and slid out his old binoculars. Before he lifted them to his eyes, he checked the position of the sun in the afternoon sky. Hooding his hand over the lenses so no reflection would give away his position, he began to glass the tree-stunted country below him. After a few minutes, he saw them. He counted them; there were six of them in all. They were walking in an untidy single-line, and leading the way was the old chief he had seen back at the station.

'Cattle-spearing black bastards!' he hissed. 'I've got you at last.' He spat on the ground and lifted the glasses back to his eyes. The bent old chief was leading them, and following close behind was the only other buck. He turned the focus ring slightly and noticed they were the only two carrying weapons. The two women and the children following looked to be struggling to keep up. One of them was limping badly and using a stick to help her walk.

Muller watched the Aboriginals for the next fifteen minutes and smiled when they stopped near a small stand of boab trees that circled a muddy waterhole he could see glinting through the trees. As he watched, they began to settle in the shade. There were still a few hours of daylight left, and he was surprised they had decided to stop, but he guessed the women and children had probably made it necessary. He began to glass the area around their camp, searching for a way to approach them and remain unobserved. He noticed a dry creek to their left that snaked almost all the way back to just below where he sat on his rocky hilltop. It would be a long and indirect approach, but it would be the only way he could get close to them without being seen unless he waited for darkness.

'You cattle-spearing bastards are going to have a visitor before this day is over,' he whispered.

Muller slipped the strap of his binoculars back over his head, got up and worked his way down from the ridge and back to his horse. As he sat down, he looked across to where his rope lay next to his saddle.

'I don't believe you'll be needed after all,' he whispered.

He leaned back on the spindly tree next to his horse and pulled his hat down to shade his eyes. He had the sudden urge to light up his pipe, but he knew the tobacco smell could easily drift across the rocky plain to the natives, so he decided against it.

An hour before sundown, Jan Muller made his way around the stony ridge and down into the creek-bed. He would have to follow it very carefully, and at times he would need to keep low as it snaked across the dry plain toward the natives. Crouching low, he set off, following its many twists and turns. The dry creek was little more than a shallow depression in the surrounding dusty plain. In most places it was around four or five feet deep, enabling Muller to travel fairly quickly along its sandy bottom. Near one of its many tight turns, it dropped into a much deeper hollow, and he had to skirt carefully around a nest of mulga snakes writhing about in a tiny mud pool chasing brightly striped rock frogs.

Just before sundown, he was in position. Before he had left his vantage point on the ridge-top, he had taken careful note of an old, almost skeletal acacia tree on the bank of the dry creek bed not too far from the little ring of trees where the natives were camped. Muller had calculated it to be about a hundred yards from them and in easy range for the Rigby. He looked up at the crooked little tree above him and smiled—he was ready.

It was hot his clothing was saturated with perspiration. He laid the Rigby across a huge spinifex bush that protruded out from the side of the creek bed, removed his hat and sweat saturated shirt and draped them over a sun-bleached log that lay in the loose sand nearby. Then, with the bank burning his bare skin, he worked his way up the side of the creek until he was next to the trunk of the crooked tree and into the small amount of shade it afforded. He lay very still for several minutes before slowly lifting his head and looking out across the hundred yards that separated him from the natives. He was suddenly annoyed. The boab trees obscured his view of the sleeping natives, except for one, the young buck. He noticed the buck had placed himself near the outer edge of the trees, probably to keep watch in case someone approached. But he had not been careful enough.

Muller slid the Rigby off his back and put it to his shoulder. His breathing was coming too fast. He would need to rest and let it settle for a while. He was excited, very excited. He had killed before, but that was back in Africa and long ago. It had been part of the reason he'd left his home country. He'd disappeared before inquiring police decided to visit him on the farm where he'd worked in the Eastern Cape after his father had died. It had been a coloured there as well, and, in a way, it had been unfortunate. But he'd been wild in those days, uncontrollably wild. It was his insatiable lust for women that had been the reason for the murder of the Shona woman. She had fought him and tried to stop him from having his way with her. Perhaps had she not fought he may have let her go, perhaps not. But, she'd fought him, so she had to be silenced. It had been many years ago, but he still remembered every little detail. He had enjoyed himself as he violated her dark body, and later, as he had cut her throat with his skinning knife and watched the life drain from her eyes. It was his little secret, and sometimes at night, when he remembered, it would excite him so much he would masturbate.

He could feel his breathing was now coming more slowly and the excitement he felt coursing through his body was under control. He eased the safety on the Rigby forward to fire and drew a careful sight on the resting Aboriginal. Flies buzzed incessantly around his face. He flicked at them with the fingers of his right hand. It was hot. He concentrated his eye along the iron sight of the Rigby. Sweat began to run down his face in crooked little rivulets and drip onto the dry ground beneath him. He wiped his eyes with the back of his hand and settled his face against the rifle stock. It was quiet, very quiet. He exhaled slowly and squeezed the trigger.

The sudden shock of noise was deafening as it reverberated through the trees and along the dry creek bed. The heavy, soft-nosed .350 calibre bullet smashed into the chest of the young Aboriginal buck, killing him instantly. Muller watched as his body slid down the side of the tree he had been resting against. The bullet had torn straight through the Aboriginal man's chest and into the bloated trunk of the boab tree behind, leaving broken bark and gore staining its trunk.

Muller got to his feet and calmly worked another cartridge into the chamber of the Rigby and readied himself should there be an attack. But there was none, only silence.

Bush flies continued to buzz around his sweating face and crawl into the corners of his eyes as he stared hard at the ring of trees. 'Where are they—where the hell have they gone?' He whispered into the stock of his rifle. Suddenly, two women ran out of the trees, crying and screaming with terror. One of them was carrying the small child he had seen before; the other held the hand of the young teenager, pulling her along as fast as they could run. They were heading away from the trees to what they hoped was safety by distancing themselves as quickly as they could from the direction of the rifle shot. They were running at an angle away from him, but they were still within easy range of the Rigby. Muller grinned, his face a sinister mask of malevolent delight. He looked along the iron sights again and concentrated.

Four shots rang out in quick succession, and three of the natives lay dead in the dust. Only the small child was still alive. She was kneeling next to the body of the limping woman who had been carrying her. Muller cursed his aim. The rifle roared again, and the small child joined the others in death.

Goonagulla had tried to stop the women and children from running, but they could not be stopped. The old man watched as they raced out of the trees and sobbed helplessly as each shot slammed into them, leaving their bodies ruined and lifeless in the dust. A sudden, terrible feeling of loneliness gripped Goonagulla. His people were gone—gone forever. His heart was broken. Tears began to run down his face as he stared at their bodies lying out on the dusty flat. He knew that this would be the day he was to die. But, he was not afraid. He was an old man. His fear of loneliness was now far greater than his fear of death. From the small bag he wore at his waist, he pulled out the woven string of his daughter, Yilla's, hair and touched it to his lips.

'Who will dance for our safe journey to Baralku to live among the ancestors?' he asked as he hung the woven strands of hair on a low branch of the boab tree he had been sheltering near.

The old man looked around the little grove of trees. It was as if he was saying a spiritual goodbye to their bloated trunks. He turned and walked out toward his people who lay dead on the dusty flat and as he walked toward them, he whispered a single word, 'Jiiarnna.'

Muller had emptied the Rigby, and he was about to reload, when he saw the old chief stumble, unarmed, out into the open. His face twisted into an evil grin. He leaned the Rigby against the little acacia tree and walked out to meet the old man. He was enjoying himself. The madness that had always been there had risen to the surface once again, and he found himself consumed by a killing fever, a crazed and totally mad killing fever.

Goonagulla watched the big white man walk toward him. This was the same white man he had seen when he had pleaded for food for his people at the white man's camp—the man with the evil eyes. The old man noticed his body was not covered with the clothing the whites wore to protect their pale skin. Then he saw the terrible beast with the yellow eyes on his chest! This was the beast that Pirramurar had spoken of so many years before. The same beast Goonagulla had seen in his dream as he slept near the spinning wheel that sucked water from the earth.

Jan Muller lifted the big Smith and Wesson revolver from its holster and waited until he was no more than a few paces from the old man before he spoke. 'You were told not to spear the cattle, you stupid black bastard,' he said to the old man.

Goonagulla looked back at the bodies of his people lying in the dust. The terrible loneliness he felt in the trees still clutched at his heart. He turned and stared at the big white man and the terrible beast with the yellow eyes Pirramurar had spoken of so long ago. He could not understand what the white man was saying to him, but he wondered why he should be smiling when they were surrounded by so much death.

Muller pulled back the hammer of the revolver and fired. The heavy .45-calibre bullet hit the old man in the chest and knocked him off his feet as if he had been struck with a giant hammer.

Goonagulla lay in the dust, choking and gasping for a breath that would never come through his ruined lungs. Pink blood gushed from his mouth and from the neat round hole in the centre of his chest. His eyes were wide and white with shock, and his scarred old legs kicked and jerked at the hot sand beneath him. The old man rolled onto his side and looked up into the eyes of the man who stood above him and watched as he lifted his pistol one last time.

The noise of the final shot echoed back as it hit the heavy trunks of the boab trees in a deadly staccato, reverberating out across the lonely landscape. The bullet had taken the top of Goonagulla's skull away and splattered its contents across the sand behind him in a bloody mess. A small, curved piece of hair-covered skull had cartwheeled into the air and embedded itself in the sand next to the old man's body.

Muller slipped the pistol back into its holster and looked about. He counted the bodies lying in the dirt. There were six of them—he had killed them all. He felt elated. Once again, he had taken lives, and once again, it would be his secret. They were blacks and they had speared cattle. They had been warned. They were cattle killers—it had to be done. 'It had to be done,' he said aloud, giving voice to his thoughts and nodding his head.

Jan Muller began to calm down from the killing madness that had taken over every fibre of his being. He knew what he had to do. First, the bodies must be taken care of. He would burn them, he decided. He looked back toward the creek. He would drag their bodies into the dry creek bed. He would lay logs on top of them, and burn them. He would burn them time and time again until all that remained was ash and charred bones. He smiled with satisfaction and patted the holstered Colt. Once the rains came, the creek would wash the ash and the last of the burnt bones away, scattering them along the creek for miles. No one would ever know.

Muller walked across to Goonagulla's fly-covered body. 'It's time to clean up, old man,' he whispered. He reached down and took hold of one of the old chief's legs and began dragging his remains toward the dry creek. He was thinking clearly now. He had a plan, and he knew what had to be done.

# 14

# Pirramurar

A little more than a mile away, a lone Aboriginal man had been making his way down the side of a broken ridge of red and yellow stone when he heard the first rifle shot. The sudden, unexpected sound echoed along the valley floor and through the trees below him. A crow that had been sheltering from the heat in the shade of a tall bloodwood tree took to the air, its call, plaintive and melancholy. The tall Aboriginal man stopped and looked back along the ancient valley toward the direction of the sound. Coloured pebbles, loosened by his sudden halt, rolled down the side of the stony ridge and chased each other to the valley floor. A single shot rang out first, then several more, and a while after that, another two. Strangely, the last two were not as loud as the others, but the Aboriginal man was certain they came from the same direction, and with each of them, he felt pain tear through his body. The Worla spirit man knew beyond any doubt that something evil had just happened, something that would inexorably affect his life.

Pirramurar had learned to trust his instincts and to believe in the strange and unexpected feelings that often racked his body, and he had learned to heed the terrible visions that sometimes flooded his mind. He had known for most of his

124

life that he possessed an inexplicable, even supernatural, ability to see things that others could not.

Sometimes he was able to see into the future, but mostly visions such as those came to him as broken, disjointed images that passed through his mind with no apparent meaning, and almost always left him confused and exhausted. To the Worla man, the strange abilities he possessed made his life a constant struggle. Like him, his mother had had the gift as well, but she had gone quite mad when he was still a young boy and had sacrificed herself to a huge crocodile because of a terrible vision she had seen. Perhaps this was why, as a young man, he had been cast into the role of a Kurdaitcha—a tribal killer—a spirit man.

When he reached the bottom of the coloured ridge of stone, he turned in the direction of the gunshots and set off. The tall Aboriginal spirit man carried a long killer, boomerang, a woomera, and a single spear, around his waist, he wore a small string bag tied together with plaited strands of blackened kangaroo hide. He worked his way over several more ridges of coloured stone, travelling steadily toward the direction of the gunshots until finally in the distance he could see a long plume of smoke working its way up into the darkening sky. Pirramurar stopped and stared at the distant smoke for several minutes before moving on.

A strange vision began to swim into the spirit man's mind, a frightening vision he could not understand. He saw a beast covered in fur with a great golden mane growing from its huge snarling head. Pirramurar knew this strange beast was not from the land of his ancestors but came from another, distant land. Fear clutched at his heart as he watched the beast turn its head toward him as if it sensed an intruder. It was then that he saw its pale yellow eyes, hideous eyes that seemed to glow like the coals of a campfire made with the seeds of the larrkardy tree. He had seen this beast in a vision long ago . . . !

He shook his head to clear his thoughts, and continued toward the smoke, but carefully now, his senses heightened by the danger that he knew lay ahead. Like the fish that is part of the ocean in which it swims, the spirit man was part of the land, bound to it with the invisible strands of his ancient culture.

Several minutes later he stopped in the shade of a small grove of flowering acacias. Tiny bush bees flitted in and about the sweet smelling blossom above him. He could now see the faint glow of the fire itself, and to the right of the fire, he could see a small ring of bloated boab trees. He studied the open ground between himself and the fire.

Pirramurar knew he would need to be cautious, for he had been told the white man's weapon could kill a man as far as the eye could see. Something moved just to the left of the boab trees, he was almost certain it was a white man, but the smoke that swirled back on the faint breeze made it difficult to be certain. Hundreds of the tiny bush bees had settled onto his dark shoulders and into his dusty hair. He shook them away, indifferent to any discomfort and turned back into the trees.

Like a shadowy wraith, he moved through the trees, distancing himself from the open ground until he was certain he could make his way into the ring of boab trees without being seen by the man at the fire. Finally, hidden from view, Pirramurar made his way in among their bloated trunks. He stopped and looked up, concerned that birds should give away his presence. But there were none just a strange, sinister silence. He moved forward from tree to tree, until finally, he stood in the shadows of the outer ring. Concealed by the boab trees and the fading light, he peered out.

Even though the daylight was now almost completely gone, he could now see the man at the fire clearly. He had been right it was a white man, a huge man. The white man was sitting on a small pile of logs looking at the fire as it hissed and crackled sending long yellow flames up into the darkening sky. His face was smudged with soot and shone with the perspiration of his labours. He wore only trousers and on his feet, were the heavy boots the white men wore to protect their soft feet. As Pirramurar watched, the white man dragged several logs to the edge of the fire and tossed them into the flames. An explosion of sparks and yellow flame shot up into the sky, illuminating the creek banks in a blaze of light. The white man returned to the pile of logs, picked up his weapon and started up out of the creek bed.

Pirramurar slipped back among the trees, his spear at the ready and waited.

When he was clear of the sandy bank, the big white man stopped, fumbled with his clothing for a few moments, and began to piss.

Pirramurar felt a sudden fear clutch at his heart. He had seen the painting on the white man's chest. He had seen the fierce head and the savage yellow eyes of the great beast—the very beast he had seen in his strange vision! He could now barely see in the rapidly approaching darkness, but he knew what he must do. He would work his way back out of the trees and wait, and when the first light of dawn came, he would return to the edge of the trees and watch, and perhaps then he would find what evil had been done by the huge white man.

As the final dark cloak of night fell, Pirramurar was safely back among some acacia trees, resting in a little hollow he had found. He lay against the warm bank, in the distance; he could still see the faint glow of the white man's fire flickering through the trees. In the quiet of the long night, well before the dawn came, Pirramurar heard the white man call out strange words into the darkness, and then the deafening thunder sound from his terrible weapon. Birds that had been sleeping quietly in the trees took flight, and tiny animals scurried about in the darkness. Pirramurar sat very still and waited. When dawn finally came, he rose from his little hollow and set off across the open ground and back into the trees.

* * *

Just before dawn, Jan Muller had walked out of trees where he had spent the night and made his way down into the creek bed to the remains of the fire. As he walked along the edge of the still-glowing coals, warming his body from the morning chill, he could see that very little remained of the natives he had burnt. Satisfied, he walked back along the creek to the spindly acacia, where he had left his shirt and hat, and put them on. Then, with the Rigby in his hand, he came up out of the dry creek bed just as the sun began to creep above the horizon and set off toward the ridge where he had left his horse. After he had gone a short distance, he stopped and looked back. He had a sudden, unnerving sensation that someone was watching him. He lifted his hand to shade his eyes from the morning glare and stared hard at the ring of trees, and just for a second, he thought he saw the shadowy outline of an Aboriginal man. He curled his hand closer to his eyes to shade them even more, but now all he could see were the dark shadows that fell among the trees. A crow flew in toward them and turned away, alarmed by something below it. Finally, the bird swung back and landed quietly in the treetops. Muller took his hand away from his eyes. He'd spent the night among those trees; he knew there had been no one else there. He turned and continued toward the distant ridge where he had left his horse.

\* \* \*

Pirramurar had watched the big white man as he went down into the creek to look at the smouldering fire, and he'd slipped back farther into the shadows when he saw him come up out of the creek bed. But when he realised the white man was leaving, he crept out to the edge of the trees to watch which direction he would take across the stony ground that led away from the dry creek. As he watched, he could see that he was heading toward a distant stony ridge.

Suddenly the white man stopped and looked back. Pirramurar slipped back in the shadows and waited. When he peered out again the white man had gone.

As Pirramurar made his way out of the ring of trees and headed toward the dry creek and the now-dying embers of the white man's fire, the earth seemed stilled with sorrow. Tiny petals of ash swirled up on the faint breeze and were scattered away like lifeless butterflies across the silent landscape. A strange vision suddenly began to writhe and swim into the spirit man's mind. He stopped and waited for it to pass. In the vision, he saw a massive boab tree silhouetted against a darkening sky. Rain was falling and dripping from its twisted limbs. Near the base of the bloated tree, he could see a narrow opening. The huge ancient tree was hollow. Crouching inside its belly, he saw the yellow eyes of the beast he had seen in his dreams. The same terrible beast the white man had painted on his body.

Pirramurar continued on toward the creek. The smell of death filled his nostrils. He made his way past a small, skeletal tree and down into the creek bed. When he reached the edge of the still smouldering fire he looked down at the ashes.

# 15

# Call Me Jack

It was mid-afternoon on Monday, the sixteenth of December when the S.S. *Minderoo* eased her 2,720-ton hull slowly alongside the Geraldton wharf. Captain Bradford was attending to his duties from the wheelhouse and watching the practiced routines of his crew as they tossed their heavy lines down to the wharf to be secured by the port's workers to bollards fore and aft. They were to be in Geraldton for four hours. Just enough time to unload a small amount of cargo and to pick up a single passenger. While the deckhands were making their final adjustments to the timber gangway, most of the *Minderoo's* passengers were leaning over the rails admiring the well-maintained port facilities of the bustling coastal town.

Isabella was watching as well. But she was looking out for the passenger who was to join them, and apart from a port official waiting for the gangway to be secured, there seemed to be no-one on the wharf waiting to board at all.

She looked across toward the shipping office just as a man stepped out and headed for the gangway now being set into position. The man was tall and well-proportioned, with a shock of hair the colour of beach sand that spilled down in an unruly tangle over his shirt collar. Isabella noticed he carried only one small, battered leather bag. He was certainly a handsome man in a typically Australian way—lean and athletic, and there was a pleasant casualness about him.

Isabella turned and made her way back to her cabin. She was still annoyed that her father had supplied her with a guide and chaperone. It just was not necessary. She was a grown woman, for heaven's sake. She could easily have used one of the station hands as a guide. But she loved her father dearly for making such a fuss over her.

Jack Ballinger swung his old leather bag up onto his shoulder and headed up the narrow wooden gangway. At the top, he noticed a very correctly dressed captain waiting patiently.

'Would you be Mr Jack Ballinger?' the captain called down to him.

'That would be me, alright,' Jack replied.

'Mr Ballinger, Captain James Hedley Bradford at your service, sir.' The captain announced.

'Call me Jack, Captain. Just call me, Jack. So you've been told I was to board, then?' Jack replied. 'I wasn't too sure about that, mate.'

'We certainly were, Jack that is, if you're sure you don't mind me calling you, Jack?' The captain answered.

'Jack's just fine, Cap,' the sandy-haired man said as he reached for the captain's hand.

'Alright then, Jack it is,' the captain replied. 'We have a very nice first-class cabin waiting for you, sir.'

'Great, just great—but ease up on the sir business, Cap. Like I said, Jack will do me just nicely.'

'Of course, Jack. Sorry about that. If you would like to follow me, I'll show you to your cabin.'

Captain Bradford led Jack up a freshly painted white steel stairway to the upper deck, where folding wooden chairs and brightly striped umbrellas had been set about in inviting order. They had almost reached Jack's cabin when the captain turned back.

'Jack, it would give me great pleasure if you would join me at my table for dinner this evening.'

'Sounds like a good idea, Cap, I'd be glad to,' Jack answered enthusiastically.

'There will be someone joining us whom I shall be pleased to introduce you to,' the captain said as they turned into a long passageway.

'No worries, Cap. I take it you are referring to the Montinari woman,' Jack answered. 'Her father, Michael, is a good friend of mine. But as yet, I've never met the little lady.'

'She is a very charming woman, Jack—very charming indeed. Isabella has done me the honour of dining with me these past two nights, and it has indeed been a great pleasure, sir.'

'There you go with the sir again, Cap. Call me Jack, mate— just plain Jack.'

It was a little after six o'clock when Jack Ballinger walked into the saloon. He was showered and dressed neatly in a pair of light tan slacks and a matching cotton shirt. On the left breast pocket of his shirt were four neatly sewn, but empty cartridge loops. There were no pretenses with Jack Ballinger; he was a hunting guide and proud of it. It had only been fourteen years since the war to end all wars had finally come to a close, and he had been in the thick of it. Jack knew that many men still felt the need to remain familiar with firearms, and he was one of them. Like so many, the horror of war was still fresh in his mind and constant in his thoughts.

'I'll have a scotch and soda, mate, with a bit of ice if you have it,' Jack ordered his drink and gave the barman a friendly smile. 'Bit of a crowd in here, mate, must be a popular spot.'

'Yes, sir, it seems to be tonight. We do have ice, sir. I won't be a moment,' the barman replied. He reached down to take a small metal bucket from behind the bar and turned to head for the ship's new ice machine.

'Jack, mate—just call me Jack. You're as bad as the bloody captain, sir this and sir that.' Jack laughed.

'Excuse me . . . Would you be, Mr Jack Ballinger?' Jack heard an educated woman's voice ask from somewhere behind him.

'That would certainly be me,' Jack replied cheerfully. He turned and looked down at one of the most beautiful women he had ever seen.

'I should introduce myself, Jack. I am Isabella Montinari. You know my father, I believe.'

The tall man with hair the colour of beach sand looked down at Isabella with the most piercing, pale green eyes she had ever seen. The eyes of an adventurer—tough, reliable and trustworthy were the words that came quickly to Isabella's mind. Jack Ballinger was a very handsome man, a man most women would be instantly attracted to. Isabella waited for his reply.

'Err, yes—your father—yes, I know him well. I am very pleased to meet you, Miss Montinari.' Jack was taken off guard by the beautiful woman smiling up at him, and it took him a moment to regain his composure. 'Well now, I knew Michael had a daughter, but I guess I wasn't expecting one as beautiful as you,' he mumbled and was suddenly sorry he had made that comment and felt his face redden.

'You flatter me, Mr Ballinger, and I thank you for your kind compliment. But there is something I should like you to know, sir,' Isabella began. 'I realise you are a close friend of my father, and that you have come on this trip as a favour to him, but I must tell you, I feel it is all totally unnecessary, and I have told my father so.'

'Oh . . . I'm sorry, Isabella. I didn't realise that you weren't in favour of me tagging along. What can I say—Michael is a good friend, and I just wanted to help out, I suppose. But I am deeply sorry if it is inconvenient for you,' Jack replied, with obvious disappointment showing on his tanned face.

'Please don't take offense, Mr Ballinger; I just wanted to make that point at the very outset. I am sure we shall get along just fine.' Isabella had found herself somewhat unnerved by the tall man's rugged good looks and emerald coloured eyes. Her mind drifted to a sandy beach she had once frequented in Barcelona. She found herself remembering its pale green waters lapping lazily against the sand and the warm Mediterranean sun on her body.

'I hope we do, my dear—I certainly hope we do. But let's drop the mister and the sir, for a start. Perhaps we could start over, what do you say?' Jack replied.

'That sounds like a good idea, Jack. Perhaps you could buy me a gin and tonic before we head into dinner with the captain?' Isabella said politely, forcing herself to concentrate.

'I'm certain we will get along just fine, Isabella, and I must say, I have been looking forward to this trip for some time,' Jack replied and turned back to the bar to order the drinks.

# 16

# Steak and Kidney Pie

The rain had started at last, badly needed rain. The wet season seemed to have finally broken as Dan and Steve, Beans and the windmill boys arrived back at the station.

The last day of their journey back had been in constant rain for most of that day, but it had not been uncomfortable. It was hot, and they'd enjoyed the cooling rain on their bodies, and to the weary group of stockmen, even the horses seemed happier.

Golly greeted them as they rode into the station grounds. He took the packhorse from Wooloo and walked alongside as they headed for the yards. He was eager to find out if there had been any trouble with the bush natives and seemed relieved when he was told there had been none.

After Dan and his group were told Jan Muller had not yet returned and that Famous Feet had been sent back alone and had arrived at the station two days earlier, they were as puzzled by that turn of events as everyone on the station. However, they all agreed their boss was a capable bushman and so decided not to concern themselves. With Golly's help, they took care of their horses, hung their saddles and the packhorse gear in the store, and went across to the wash-house to get cleaned up in time for dinner. All of them glad to be back at the station and looking forward to their soft beds and Santiago's cooking once again.

Dan was feeling particularly happy with himself as he stepped into the showers. The stockman picked up a half-worn bar of soap and began singing softly as he rubbed it under his arms, 'Pack up all my cares and woes—here I go singin' low. Blackbird . . .'

'Tonight's the night, eh, Danny boy? You're back with your little black gin at last. Give her a good poke for me, mate,' Steve yelled above the hiss of the showers so that everyone could hear him. 'I might have to call on her meself sometime soon, so don't you go wearin' her out, Danny boy,' he added with a sarcastic laugh.

'Give it a rest, Steve. Anna don't deserve that sorta talk,' Beans yelled from one of the far showers reserved for the coloureds.

'I warned you about your bloody mouth, Steve!' Dan yelled back. He returned the bar of soap he had been using to the soap holder, calmly rinsed his hands, shut off his tap and made his way along the open cubicles to where Steve was showering. 'You've got a nasty mouth, Steve, and it's high time someone shut it for you!' he yelled to the surprised stockman.

Steve threw up his hands to protect himself, but Dan was far too quick and far too angry to be stopped. The punch hit him high on the bridge of his nose and smashed into his left eye socket, the blow so hard that it knocked him back into the shower with tremendous force, splattering the galvanized metal wall with his blood. The startled stockman fell to the floor with his hands to his damaged face.

'Jesus—you broke me nose, you bastard. It was only meant to be a joke,' he sobbed through bloody hands. The shower continued to rain down on him sending his blood and soap suds swirling into the drain in a crimson whirlpool.

'Righto, that's enough, you two. Fighting's not allowed on the station and the pair of you silly buggers know it.' Billy Anders yelled. He pushed Dan aside and reached down to help the bleeding Steve to his feet.

'Jesus, Billy, it was only meant to be a fucking joke, that's all.'

'Shut the fuck up,' Billy snarled. He pulled Steve out of the shower cubicle and shut off the tap.

The three naked men stood facing each other in the narrow shower hallway. Steve with his hands to his face and blood running through his fingers, Dan still smeared with soap suds, his fists clenched by his sides, and the stock foreman with a hand on each of them.

'I warned him not to talk about Anna like that,' Dan yelled! 'I won't have it, Billy. It's just not right.'

'Dan, get the fuck out of here,' Billy yelled and turned to Steve. 'Perhaps now you'll watch your mouth a bit more. The lad had every right to give you a smack for what you said about young Anna. We all like the lass, and you shouldn't be saying the things you said, so that's an end to it. Now, clean yourself up and get over to see Santiago and ask him to have a look at that nose.'

The dining room that night was a hive of activity when Dan stepped through the door and began looking for Anna. He noticed a group of men near the servery being served by someone just out of his sight. Then, he saw her. She was busy placing huge slices of steak and kidney pie and mashed potatoes on a stockman's plate. Dan picked up a plate and took his place in the line behind Famous Feet and waited. It seemed an eternity, but, finally, it was his turn to be served.

'Hi, Anna, it's good to see you again. Have you been busy?' Dan inquired nervously.

'Yes, really busy, I've been helping Santiago in the gardens. But I'm really glad you're back, Dan,' Anna replied with a shy smile.

'I'm glad to be back too, that's for sure. The whole trip seemed a bit of a waste of time if you ask me.'

'What happened between you and Steve, Dan? Someone said there was some sort of trouble.'

'Nothing really, we just had a bit of a misunderstanding, that's all. We sorted it out, though," Dan replied and changed the subject. 'I've missed you, Anna. Can I see you after you've finished tonight?'

'Of course, you can. But it won't be for a couple of hours yet.' Anna placed a generous-sized slice of the pie on Famous Feet's plate and waited for him to move along.

'That's okay. I'll be waiting out the back of the kitchen in a couple of hours then.' Dan grinned as Anna scooped up a massive slice of the pie for his plate.

'Would there be any chance of getting something to eat?' one of the stockmen waiting patiently in line asked.

'I'll see you then, Dan.' Anna turned back to her work.

Dan found an empty table and put his plate of food down and went back to the tea urns to get a mug of tea. When he returned, Beans was sitting across from him.

'Hey, Dan, you did the right thing giving Steve a bloody hiding, mate. He deserved it, silly bugger. You whacked him real good, though. They reckon he's gonna have one hell of a shiner. I just hope the boss don't find out or there'll be trouble. Still—I don't reckon anyone will say too much about it.'

'I shouldn't have done it, Beans. It was the wrong thing to do, I guess. I just lost me temper.'

'Like I said, he deserved it, I reckon,' Beans replied and then changed the subject. 'I wonder why the boss sent Famous back to the station and went on alone to round up those bush blackfellas.'

Dan was busy with a fork full of the pie. 'Geez, this pie tastes bloody good. Next time we go bush we should take Santiago with us.'

'I was talkin' to Famous, and he told me there were six of them. It could get a bit dangerous out there for the boss you know.'

'I reckon he would have fired a couple of shots into the air or something to frighten them first before he roped them all together and took 'em off to the boundary. I don't know really, but I reckon he can look after himself pretty well,' Dan replied and reached for his mug of tea.

'Yeah, I guess you're right.' Beans was having difficulty talking and eating at the same time. 'Anyway, spears and boomerangs ain't much good against guns. This pie's bloody good. I think I better go and get me some more before it's all bloody well gone.'

'Me too I reckon.' Dan picked up his empty plate and the two stockmen stood up just as Anna came out of the kitchen carrying more food and headed for the servery.

'You're a lucky bugger, Dan. That Anna is a real beauty, for sure.'

'She sure is, Beans—she sure is.'

Dan had been waiting at the back of the kitchen to see Anna for what seemed like forever, and he was getting impatient. Finally, the kitchen fly door opened with its familiar creak, and Anna stepped outside. She was still in her work clothes and had even forgotten to take off her wet apron; she had been in such a hurry to see Dan.

'Dan—Dan, I've missed you so much—it's been a long time.' She put her arms out.

'It's been too long for me as well,' Dan replied as he went to her.

'Can we go somewhere, Anna? Maybe go for a walk or something?' He pleaded.

'I've just finished work. I smell of steak and kidney and smelly tinned peas. And look—I forgot to take my apron off.' Anna undid the ties that held her wet apron in place and slipped it over her head. 'Let me have a shower first, and then we can go somewhere.'

'Okay, but hurry, it's been too long.' Dan bent down and kissed Anna on the cheek, and patted her back as a sign of his impatience.

'I won't be long.' Anna hurried off to the wash-house she and Santiago shared. When she returned, she grabbed Dan by the hand. 'Where shall we go?'

'You smell great.' Dan took her hand. 'Let's go down to the machinery shed. There won't be anyone there this time of the night.'

139

It was dark as they headed off through the trees. A few minutes later, a couple of the station dogs caught their scent and began to growl.

'Shut up, mongrels, keep it quiet now,' Dan whispered to the dogs. The dogs recognized his voice and moved back among the trees where they'd been lying, and the two young lovers hurried on to the machinery shed.

Dan pushed open the heavy door. 'There's no one here— it's deserted. Come on,' he whispered.

They stepped into the dark interior of the massive machinery shed and looked about for somewhere they could be comfortable. Dan found a canvas cover thrown over one of the implements. He slid it off and laid it on the ground. It was dark and they could only just see each other in the weak moonlight that shone through a leaf-covered skylight above them. Dan took Anna's hand and pulled her down to the canvas and wrapped his arms around her. 'It's been far too long,' he murmured and buried his face into her neck.

Anna was overjoyed to finally have Dan back in her arms and back in her life. But she was afraid that if they made love again, it would not be the same. She was unsure of herself and nervous that Dan may begin to think that something was wrong. She didn't want to tell him what had happened in Jan Muller's cottage—not yet.

They lay together for several minutes, kissing and hugging each other. It was as if they had been apart for an eternity.

'I love you, Anna, and I want us to be together, forever,' Dan whispered. He started to unbutton Anna's blouse.

Anna reached for Dan's hands to stop him. 'No, please don't, Dan,' she said softly, unsure of herself.

Then, when she looked at Dan's troubled face in the moonlight, she suddenly felt wonderful again. She was in love—it had to be right.

'What's wrong, my darling?' Dan was confused and cursed his impatience.

'Everything is just fine. Let me do it,' Anna whispered. She stood up and undid the remaining buttons of her blouse and slipped it off, and then she reached down and removed her homemade shorts and underwear and let them drop to the canvas as well. She was naked when she sat back down—naked and in love.

But the beautiful Aboriginal girl had a secret locked away in her heart, and it would stay there until she spoke to Isabella Montinari, and that, she hoped would be soon.

'I love you, Dan,' she whispered and reached for the man she loved more than anything in her world.

# 17

# The Hollow Tree

Fifteen miles to the north of the station and in steady rain, a very tired Jan Muller was walking his horse through light scrub, searching for somewhere dry to camp for the night. Eventually, in the fading light, he noticed a solitary boab tree amongst a stand of spindly melaleucas, a bloated, ancient tree very probably more than a thousand years old. Its massive girth was gnarled and broken, and its grotesque twisted limbs were covered with the first of the new season's leaves that signalled the approaching wet season. Near the base of the massive tree, he could see a dark opening. The strange misshapen tree was hollow.

Muller stopped his horse and looked around among the smaller trees, while the rain continued to fall. He was soaking wet and bone tired, and there seemed to be no other dry place. He needed rest desperately. He swung down out of the saddle, tied up his horse and began searching about for dry wood for a fire. The rain continued to fall as he wandered about, but he managed to find some small dry sticks and a couple of the big egg-shaped seed pods near the base of the old tree. As he struggled with the fire, the rain started to ease and then it stopped altogether. He smiled, glad it had stopped. He crouched over his tiny fire and watched the half-dry twigs catch and begin to flame up. When he was satisfied, he wandered off and found a couple of wet logs and put them on the flames, dry side down. The logs hissed for several minutes and then began to catch.

Muller squatted near the flames in an attempt to dry himself, and it wasn't long before steam began to rise from his wet clothing and he had to back away. He started to feel a little better. Suddenly, two small wallabies crashed through the wet scrub only a few feet from where he squatted. He jerked his pistol out of its holster, fell back on his haunches, and fired. The wallabies turned away in alarmed panic and bolted through the trees. The heavy .45-calibre bullet ripped a piece of bark from a small melaleuca, just inches to the left of one of the fleet-footed animals. Then, as suddenly as they had appeared, the wallabies were gone. Muller cursed his aim, knowing only too well how tasty fresh wallaby meat was.

After the fire had burned down to a bed of coals, he mixed a little flour, salt, and water together and made a sticky dough, patted the mixture around a wet stick and pushed it in among the coals. A few minutes later he was breaking off pieces of the tasty damper from the burnt stick and hungrily wolfing it down. He had run out of tea, there was only water from his canteen left for him to drink. He had drunk the last of his rum the night of the killing of the bush natives—almost three-quarters of a bottle of it.

Muller had not slept at all that night. He had been too excited. He'd spent the night in the trees well back from the stench of the big fire he had used to burn the bodies. He'd sipped at the rum bottle at first, trying to calm the excitement that coursed through him from the killing. But eventually, he had been quite drunk, and with his body still charged with adrenaline, sleep had become impossible.

Once, during the long night, he had thought he heard something not far off, and he'd fired several shots into the darkness. But he heard nothing more and thought it was probably just night birds scratching about.

When he'd finished his damper, he took a big swallow of water from his canteen and went off to check that he had tied and hobbled his horse securely. When he was satisfied; he headed across to the old boab tree to take a look inside the hollow. As he hurried over to the bloated tree, he looked up at the now ink-black sky. He knew there was a full moon above him somewhere, but the thick layers of cloud had shrouded it in darkness.

The rain had now almost stopped, and the sky seemed oppressive, dark and menacing. He stopped outside the opening of the huge tree and took out his matches, struck one, and peered inside the hollow. It was empty, and it looked dry and comfortable and there were no troublesome snakes for him to get rid of. He looked up once more at the grim, obsidian sky and was glad he had seen the old tree—very glad. He picked up his bedroll, the Rigby, and his saddlebags and threw them inside the hollow and went across to the now-roaring fire and kicked wet dirt over it. When he was confident it was almost out and that no one would see its glow during the night, he went back to the old tree and crawled inside to roll out his bedroll. With it in place, he laid the Rigby comfortably close by, stretched out his legs, and pulled his blanket up to cover his body. He was desperate for sleep.

An hour later Jan Muller was still awake. Even though his body ached and yearned for sleep, it just would not come. He could feel an incessant throbbing behind his eyes and a terrible bone-aching lethargy in his body. He turned onto his side and reached for the saddlebags that were somewhere behind him. He fumbled with one of the buckles for a moment or two, before pulling out the oilskin pouch that held his clay pipe, his tobacco, and extra matches. A few moments later he had his old pipe lit and burning steadily with each draw. He began to relax. A few more drags and he knew he would be able to get off to sleep easily. Even the pain behind his eyes had started to ease. He took the pipe from his mouth, shook the spit out of the stem, and decided he'd have a last good pull before he dozed off. The clay pipe hissed and crackled as he drew the pungent smoke into his lungs, and just for a second, the light from it lit up the ceiling of the hollow above him with an eerie incandescence.

In that short, fleeting moment, Jan Muller saw something above his head that unnerved him. On the ceiling of the hollow, he saw a primitive, stick-like painting of a stooped man carrying a spear leading a group of five natives in a single file toward a stand of trees. He felt his skin crawl with tiny prickles of fear.

What the fuck . . . ! He took another drag on the pipe and felt the mouthpiece burn his lips. He saw it again—six natives in a single file. The one leading the group was slightly bowed with age and looked to Muller just like the old chief he had killed with his revolver.

'This cannot fucking well be . . . !' he said aloud. He took another nervous pull on his pipe. This time he reached up and touched the painting above him. He pulled his hand back with fright—the painting was still wet.

'This is just not possible!' he shrieked. 'Not fucking possible!'

Jan Muller was suddenly very afraid. His mind began to race. He was trying to reason why the painting was there—and why the paint was still wet, and who had been there before him?

'This is just not possible!' he shrieked again, his voice now bordering on hysterical.

Who could have crawled into the hollow and painted the picture of the natives, and how the hell did they know he would decide to sleep in that damn tree? There could only be one explanation, he thought. He tried to shake that thought from his weary mind. 'Black magic—it had to be black magic!'

He began to panic. His heart hammered in his chest, and now the pain had returned to the back of his eyes. He crawled out of the hollow tree and dragged his gear with him. As soon as he was clear, he got to his feet and stumbled toward the steaming fire, his eyes wide with terror. When he reached the fire, he spun around and stared into the darkness. 'Fuck off, whoever you are—get the fuck away from me, you black bastards!' he screamed, his voice shrill with hysteria. 'You're dead, all of you—dead, and fucking burnt!' He jerked out the Smith and Wesson and opened fire. His first shot almost took his right foot off in his haste. Wet dirt blasted up and stung his face. But he kept firing until the pistol was empty. He started to feel better. The gunshots had calmed him. He was back in control. He reached down and took six shells from his belt and calmly reloaded the pistol. Comforted now by the acrid smell of the gunpowder in the damp night air, he spun the pistol on his finger in an exaggeration of calmness and slid the heavy revolver back into its holster, but his bloodshot eyes betrayed the calmness he thought he was feeling and fear soon crept back to haunt his thoughts.

The rain had now stopped completely. Muller was suddenly aware of the ominous silence that surrounded him. He stared at the ancient boab tree illuminated by the faint light from the hissing fire. It seemed to be glowing and its twisted limbs looked to be moving, clawing at the night sky.

He turned away and hurried across to see if he had shot his horse in his panic. It was still there, and alive. He struck a match. The nervous animal pulled back in fright, its eyes white with terror. He could see it had tried to break its tether, but fortunately, it had held. He went across to the hollow tree and picked up his scattered gear and walked over to the smoking remains of the fire. A light rain had started to fall again. He rolled out his bedroll and crawled inside, the loaded pistol in his hand and the Rigby alongside.

Once again, he tried to sleep, but sleep just would not come.

The rain continued through the rest of that night, and Jan Muller cowered beneath his canvas bedroll, tossing and turning and staring into the darkness until the dawn finally arrived.

In the early morning, once he could see well enough to move about, Muller rolled up his damp bedroll and began to pack his gear. He untied his horse, took off its hobbles, lifted the saddle onto its back and cinched the girth strap. Then, he tied on his saddlebags and bedroll and strapped on the rifle scabbard. He was ready to leave.

Vaporous breath snorted from the horse's nostrils as he climbed into the saddle. The nervous animal spun around in a tight circle, not trusting its rider after the chaos of the night before. Muller jerked savagely on the reins and, with an open hand; he smacked the anxious beast across the head. The horse staggered backward, its front legs splaying out awkwardly, its eyes white with terror.

'Settle down, fuck you, or I'll put a bullet in your stupid brain,' he snarled and wrenched at the reins even harder.

Just as he was about to dig his heels into the frightened animal's flanks, he looked back over his shoulder at the hollow tree. None of what he had seen the night before seemed to make any sense to him.

'It's only a bloody tree,' he whispered. He swung down from his saddle and stood next to his confused horse for a few moments staring at the massive tree. It looked different in the morning light. He decided he would take one last look inside the hollow. He patted the horse's quivering neck in a half-hearted attempt to calm the confused animal, tied the reins to a small bush and walked across to the old tree. The headache he'd suffered from the night before had returned and now seemed even worse. He bent down and looked up at the ceiling inside the hollow tree. *There was nothing there . . . ! Not a thing!* Just a few shrivelled leaves caught up in the cracks of the old tree and the dried remains of a small bat hanging in an untidy mess of cobwebs. Muller could feel its empty eye sockets mocking him as he stared up at the place where the painting had been.

'What the hell!' he whispered. His head was now throbbing painfully in time with his racing heart. In a panic, he ran across to his horse. *'Black magic . . . ! It has to be black magic!'* He leapt up into the saddle and dug his heels savagely into his horse's quivering flanks and rode away.

It was the middle of the morning when he rode back into the station grounds. He had pushed his horse hard. The animal was exhausted, its body stained white with salty sweat and its flanks bleeding from its cruel rider's spurs.

Golly saw him first and ran down to where the big man was undoing the girth strap from his weary mount.

'Boss, you're back—is everything okay? Has someone been chasing you? Your horse looks fucked.' Golly commented nervously.

'Just a long ride, that's all—and what the hell has it got to do with you, anyway, you stupid black bastard?' Muller replied angrily and stumbled backward a few steps with exhaustion.

'Sorry, Boss. Glad to see you're back, though. How did you go with them blackfellas out there?' He asked as he undid the bridle from the exhausted horse and patted its head.

'I rounded them up and took them over to one of the creeks that runs into the Drysdale and sent them packing into Durack country, just like I bloody well said I would. They can have the bastards.' Muller grunted and undid his saddlebags. He turned to Golly. 'Get your black arse over to the kitchen and tell Santiago I want a big feed sent over to my cottage. And since you're so fucking interested in my horse, you can get it cleaned up and fed and put in the yard.'

With that, Muller took his bedroll, saddlebags, and the Rigby and headed off to his cottage. He was bone-tired. He needed a bath, a meal, and sleep. But first, he needed a few stiff shots of rum.

The following morning, when Rosie delivered Jan Muller his breakfast, he sent her to get Billy Anders, the stock foreman. He'd just finished a huge plate of sausages and eggs when there was a knock at the door. He got up and, carrying his mug of tea with him, went across to the door and jerked it open.

'Come on in, Anders.

'Thanks, Boss.' The stock foreman nodded to Muller and entered the room.

So . . . has everything been going okay while I've been gone?'

'No problems here, Boss. I hear you sorted the blackfellas out all right,' Billy replied.

'They're the Durack's problem now, and they can have them. I gave them all a warning about coming back into Cockatoo Creek country, but I'm fairly sure we have seen the last of that lot of cattle-spearing bastards,' Muller said convincingly.

'That's good, Boss—real good. Glad you didn't have too much trouble,' Billy replied.

'What did the boys find out there with that other speared steer?'

'They never found any blackfellas, Boss. But they did find some old sign that led from the dead steer off in the general direction of Derby. They reckon they were long gone though,' Billy explained.

'Now, Billy, I have to go into Derby today for a few days. On the nineteenth, I have to pick up the owner's daughter from a state ship. I'm bringing her and some bloke who will be looking after her back to the station so she can paint pretty pictures of the place.'

'Righto, Boss, I'll keep me eyes on things here while you're gone. No need to concern yourself.'

'Tell Santiago to give me a list of any stuff he wants, and if anyone has any letters to get posted, they'd better get them in the tin box on my verandah real quick,' Muller said and continued. 'Has there been much rain here?'

'A bit, I suppose, Boss. Not a lot, really. I guess it's gonna hit us before too much longer, though.'

'That's good, then. The creeks shouldn't be too high on the way in,' Muller replied. 'Get the truck fuelled up for me; I'll be heading into town within the hour.'

'Will do, Boss, will do.' Billy could see that was the end of the conversation, so he let himself out and hurried over to the kitchen to see Santiago. Then, he would need to find out if anyone had any letters to go to town.

# 18

# The Dancer in the Trees

Lightning flashed across the tropical sky, illuminating the ring of boab trees where the solitary Aboriginal man danced with flashes of eerie brilliance. The small fire he had made sent flickering tongues of orange flame into the night sky. A sudden peal of thunder crashed across the lonely landscape, sending tiny animals that had been sheltering among the leaves and detritus of the small clearing scurrying away from the trees and out across the spinifex stunted flat. The tall Aboriginal man continued his ancient tribal dance. His body was daubed with ghostly splashes of white and from his waist and upper legs hung clusters of leaves and feathers. Dust rose from his shuffling feet in time with the words he was chanting as he continued around his fire. The spirit man had been dancing for more than six hours. Wearily, he continued, and as he danced, he rattled his long killer boomerang against the woomera he held in his left hand.

Pirramurar had wept when he'd found the charred remains of the Ngarinyin people lying among the burnt logs and ash in the dry creek bed. Very little was left of their bodies, just a few blackened bones, and crushed skulls.

He had left the remains where they lay and returned to the ring of trees. His cries of anguish had echoed out across the spinifex stunted plain for more than an hour. For two days he had sat among the bloated trees and wept, and as he wept he could feel the souls of the dead swirling aimlessly around him. Finally, he made his fire and began his dance to ensure the safe passage of the Ngarinyin people to Barulku to live peacefully among their ancestors.

# 19

# The Blue Peacock

Jan Muller was on the outskirts of Derby just before sunset on the 16th December. He'd pushed the big Herrington 4x4 truck hard along the rough tracks and across the still-low creeks and had made it in good time. He had three days left before the *S.S. Minderoo* arrived in port, and he knew exactly where he wanted to go.

It was almost dark when he walked into the front bar of the Spinifex Hotel and ordered himself a double shot of rum. He was glad to be away from the station for a while. He needed to see a few new faces and have a bit of fun, and that is exactly what he intended to do. He took a swallow of his drink and reached into his top pocket for his pipe. He'd lost his old clay pipe chasing the blacks. But fortunately, he'd had another back in his cottage. He filled the bowl with freshly bought tobacco, rammed it tight with his thumb, and struck a match.

'You aren't a local, mate. Where are you from?' the barman asked, trying to be friendly.

'Cockatoo Creek Station, not that it's any of your business anyway. What about you get me another drink and keep your curiosity to yourself,' Muller grunted. He tossed down the last of his rum and pushed the empty glass across the bar.

'I'm just trying to be friendly, mate, that's all,' the barman replied and filled the big man's glass with the dark rum.

'I don't need any more friends,' Muller replied. 'I got too bloody many already.'

Just then, a tall, thin half-caste man walked into the bar. To the big South African, the man looked as if he'd slept in his clothes for several nights. His appearance was unkempt and dirty and his face ugly, scarred, and unshaven. Muller took a sip of his rum and watched the man carefully as he walked along the bar, attempting to get one of the patrons to buy him a drink.

'What the hell are you doing back in here? You won't get no drink from me,' one of the drinkers snapped at the tall half-caste.

'Why don't you just get out of here and leave us all alone?' another drinker yelled.

'Fuck the lot of you! You're just a bunch of miserable bastards,' the half-caste hissed back at the drinkers and continued along the bar.

Muller could see the man had had a little too much to drink and was becoming very angry. He watched him make his way past the last of the drinkers at the long bar, until, finally, he came to where he was standing.

'What about you give me that rum you're drinking there, mate. I reckon I need it more than you.' The half-caste gave him a rotten-toothed grin and started to reach across to take Muller's drink.

The bar went quiet. Everyone watched to see what the outcome would be.

'Do not touch my glass, you piece of shit, and step away, you smell like a mangy dog that just pissed itself,' Muller said in a lowered voice. He wasn't concerned; it was just another drunk, and a coloured drunk at that. He picked up his glass and took a sip of his rum.

'So, where the hell are you from, mate?' the troublemaker asked sarcastically.

Jan Muller said nothing. He took another sip of his rum and puffed on his pipe.

'He's from Cockatoo Creek Station. So why don't you leave him alone and get the hell out of here?' the barman replied for the silent Muller.

'I got rights, mate. I'm allowed in here just like you lot. I'm not some scrub nigger. So to hell with the lot of you,' the half-caste replied and turned back to Muller.

'Cockatoo Creek Station, eh? I cut a man up from out there a few weeks ago. The miserable bastard wouldn't buy me a bloody drink. When I finished with him, they had to take him off to the hospital and get him sewed up.'

Jan Muller put down his drink and looked carefully at the ugly half-caste. 'So you're the piece of shit that cut up one of my boys, eh?' he whispered. He took the pipe out of his mouth. Put it on the bar and stepped out to face the half-caste pearler.

'Watch him, mate. He's a bad bastard that one,' the barman whispered.

'You don't know what bad is. Just pour me another rum, and fill the damn glass up this time,' Muller snarled and bunched his fists.

With that, the troublemaker stepped back and slid an evil-looking knife out of his trousers and began swaying from side to side in readiness. 'Looks to me like I'm gonna get your rum one way or another.' He grinned through rotten teeth.

'Hey, put that knife away and leave him alone, Jimmy! You're a bloody menace. Get the fuck out of here!' the barman yelled.

'Just as soon as I've drunk this bastard's rum,' the pearler whispered back.

Muller held up his hand to stop the barman talking and moved forward. 'You just pulled a knife on the wrong man, you derelict piece of shit. Now you're going to pay the price, my ugly friend.'

There was total silence in the bar now. Everyone was watching the half-caste.

His mouth twisted into an evil sneer. 'Fuck you, cow fucker. You'd better hope the Docs, not outta town.'

The pearler suddenly bent into a knife-fighting stance, stepped forward and made a lightning thrust at Jan Muller's belly.

Muller was surprised by how fast the man could move. He was obviously not as drunk as he'd thought. He sidestepped quickly, and just as the knife thrust passed his belly he hit the back of the pearler's hand with the bunched knuckles of his left fist and sent the knife skating across the floor between the feet of two of the drinkers. One of them, an old man, bent down, picked it up and slid it across the bar to the barman and turned back to watch the two men facing each other.

'You're a brave man when you got a knife in your hand; you piece of shit. But let's see how you go now.' Muller snarled and charged straight at the half-caste.

His first punch was a vicious left hook and it caught the pearler full in the solar plexus and sent him backward with his arms flailing about, searching for support. Muller kept moving forward, following the man across the room as he staggered back gasping for air, and hit him with a tremendous right to the jaw. The punch knocked the pearler instantly unconscious and sent him crashing to the floor.

Several of the drinkers moved away from the bar as stools spun crazily across the floor and into the bar front. It had all happened so fast that no one could believe it. None of the drinkers had ever seen a big man move so fast. A mighty cheer went up around the bar.

'Good on ya, mate. He's a fucking pest, he deserved a bloody hiding,' one of the drinkers yelled loudly.

'Someone, buy that man a drink,' another yelled, holding his glass of beer in the air and slapping the bar.

Muller walked back to the bar, tossed down his rum, and pushed his empty glass across the bar to the barman.

'Fill the fucking thing up this time,' he grunted at the now smiling barman. He looked along the bar at the cheering drinkers. 'What the fucks wrong with you people, letting shit like that in here,'

He waited for the barman to fill his glass, drank it down and walked back to where the unconscious man lay and looked down at him. 'You pull a knife on me and you'd better be sure you know how to use it, you piece of shit.' He lifted his left boot up and crashed it down into the pearler's face, smashing the unconscious man's nose to a pulp and shattering both his cheekbones with a sickening crunch.

The clapping stopped and the bar was suddenly silent. No one moved and no one spoke.

Muller began to lift his boot again. 'You piece of shit,' he roared, his face a mask of contempt for the unconscious man on the floor.

'Jesus, ease up, mate; you'll kill the poor bastard,' the barman yelled.

Muller stopped and looked across at the barman. 'Like I said, you shouldn't be letting shit like this in here then you wouldn't have this sort of trouble,' he snarled.

Two men put down their drinks and ran forward and grabbed Muller before he could bring his heel down into the pearler's face for the second time.

'Take it easy, big fella; I think you proved your point,' one of the men yelled as he struggled with the huge Afrikaner.

Muller shook them off easily and turned to face the barman again. 'No-one pulls a knife on me and gets away with it—no one.' With that, he turned and walked out onto the verandah and headed for the steps.

'Hey, mate, you forgot your pipe,' the barman yelled after him, as Muller strode across the verandah still cursing.

The barman grabbed the pipe and matches from the bar-top and followed the big man outside. 'You're a hard man, mate, and I guess he deserved a thrashing, but Jesus, you could have killed him. Anyway, here's your pipe.' The barman handed Muller his pipe and matches and turned to head back behind the bar.

Two drinkers had walked over and were watching the conversation from the doorway.

'You're too bloody soft, the lot of you. He's just another piece of black shit,' Muller said menacingly. He was angry—very angry.

The two men watching quickly made their way back to the bar. They could see the man standing outside was ready to fight anyone who crossed his path.

Jan Muller spat on the verandah floorboards in a gesture of disgust and stepped down onto the dusty street. 'Your rum tasted like shit anyway,' he yelled back over his shoulder and started down the dark street.

A few minutes later, the cooler night air began to make him feel a little calmer. He filled his pipe, lit it, and went on along Clarendon Street. He hadn't wanted any trouble, but sometimes it just seemed to follow him, no matter what.

He looked along the street. It was dark, but he knew where he was going. At the end of Clarendon Street, he turned into Fairbairn and then into Delawarr Street. A couple of dogs growled in the darkness as he made his way past several run-down old cottages. Muller hissed at the dogs, daring them to come out onto the street. The growling stopped. He walked on past a couple of vacant allotments until he came to number 7 Delawarr Street.

He stopped outside the big old run-down house that was built up on high stumps like so many in the tropics, in an attempt to keep them cooler. In the moonlight, he could see it had been freshly painted since the last time he had visited. Now it looked like a dark shade of cream. The little picket fence that ran along its front had been freshly painted as well but in a different colour. Muller tried to recall the colour the old house used to be, but he couldn't remember. Green, he thought, but he wasn't sure. Two Chinese lanterns hung on freshly painted posts on either side of the path that led to the front door. The brightly coloured lanterns illuminated a sign that had been screwed to the front gable: The Blue Peacock. The words were written beneath a painting of a beautiful peacock, its fantail of a hundred eyes watching all who entered. He flipped the latch, pushed the little gate open, and walked up the path to the front door.

Muller felt a happy anticipation begin to course through him as he opened the door and made his way inside. There were only a few people in the tiny café, and all of them looked up as he entered. He sat down at a small table near a doorway that led to the kitchen and slid the menu out from between the salt and pepper shakers. '*Lu Zhi and the Blue Peacock welcome you.*' The words were written above a magnificent peacock at the top of the red-and-gold cardboard menu. He looked down the list of dishes and thought he would try the deep-fried duck and noodles. He was still tapping the menu with the bowl of his pipe when Lu Zhi came through the kitchen door.

'Ah—Mr Jan, my very good friend, you have come to visit us again,' Lu Zhi said with a wide smile. 'It has been far too long.'

'Yes, Lucy, I have come to visit you again. Are you well?' Muller asked politely.

Lucy Lu was a very attractive woman. She was part Chinese and part Indian, and while Muller never knew for certain, he guessed her age at around forty, possibly a little more. Lucy was dressed in a pink, silk Cheongsam. The tiny turned-up collar of the traditional Chinese dress had two blue dragons entwined, almost as if they were mating, sewn delicately in place with golden thread.

'I am well, Mr Jan. What delights can we offer you, my friend?' she asked politely. As she spoke, she looked around the room at the other diners concerned that they should hear.

'First, Lucy, I would like to start with a large plate of the duck and noodles, and a glass of your tasty rice wine as well, and perhaps later we could talk again.' Muller replied, looking around the room himself.

'I will see the cook now, and for you, it will be very special, my generous friend. If you will excuse me for a moment, I shall bring you a bottle of my wine and a glass.'

Lucy disappeared through the kitchen door, and a few moments later, reappeared with a tall, thin bottle of her homemade rice wine and a delicately made blue glass that had tiny peacocks etched in blue and white around its rim.

'Enjoy your wine, my friend, I'll be back soon.' Lucy bowed and left him and went to attend to another table of diners.

Muller poured himself a glass of the wine and sipped it respectfully, immediately feeling the warmth course through his body. He looked down at the delicate glass and smiled. He had no idea what was in the sweet-tasting wine, but it was certainly refreshing. He made short work of the first bottle and ordered another just as his meal arrived.

He set about eating the wonderful-smelling duck and noodles with anticipated relish, and when he'd finished, he called the waitress back and ordered a second helping. He had almost forgotten how tasty the restaurant's food could be. After he had eaten, he pushed his plate back and lit up his pipe. He was enjoying himself. The café was empty now and the street outside, quiet and dark, and from somewhere nearby, a lone dog howled. Above him, a huge wooden-bladed fan turned slowly, its long cedar blades wobbling slightly as they cut through the hot, humid air with a pleasant hum. He puffed contentedly on his pipe and watched one of the attractive waitresses clearing the tables. A short while later, the kitchen door opened, and when he looked around, the beautiful Lucy Lu was smiling at him.

'Now, my dear and generous friend, is there anything else you desire?'

'Yes, Lucy—yes, there is. Perhaps a little entertainment first, and then later, I would like to chase the dragon once again.'

'Well then, you must come with me, my friend—but first, you must put out your pipe.' Lucy gave the big man a warm smile and pushed the well-used, pearl shell ashtray across the table.

Muller tapped the ash from his pipe, got up and followed Lucy through the kitchen door. They made their way past the kitchen staff, still busy with their work washing pots and pans and up a creaking stairway to the first floor. At the head of the stairs, Lucy led him into a large room with walls that were covered in silk cloth. Small red candles had been placed around the room, giving off a strange, surreal light, and from somewhere nearby, a hidden incense burner filled the room with the pleasant smell of sandalwood. A large bed sat in the centre of the room covered in brightly coloured silk cushions of red and gold, each with embroidered pictures of classically dressed Chinese women sewn delicately onto them with silken thread.

Above the bed, a beautifully made Chinese lantern with long golden tassels hung from the rafters, illuminated by the single red candle in its centre. Its tiny flame seemed to make the blue dragons that were painted around its border lift out in relief from the delicate paper.

Lucy led the big man across the perfumed room to the bed. 'Sit down and make yourself comfortable, my friend. Li Li and Mayli will be with you in a moment,' Lucy whispered. She bowed and left the room through a door hidden behind one of the silk-covered walls.

Muller sat on the cushioned bed and waited. He felt whole again, refreshed and invigorated and ready for the joys of life. But he had not begun to relax until he had arrived back in the town. Ever since the incident in the hollow tree, he had worried about his sanity. Even now, he was unsure what had really happened that night. He knew there was probably a simple explanation for the painting he had seen inside the hollow tree, and then its mysterious disappearance. Perhaps he was simply dreaming, or a little delusional. Not enough sleep can certainly do that, he'd reasoned. But he was still concerned.

'Hello, Mr Jan. How are you?'

Muller heard the two female voices speak, almost in unison. He looked across the room toward the hidden door.

'Hello, girls, it's been quite a while, but I see you are just as beautiful as I remember you both,' he answered graciously and got to his feet to greet the two attractive prostitutes.

The Chinese girls giggled softly, politely covering their mouths as they did so.

'Do you wish to enjoy the pleasures of us both tonight, Mr Jan? Or perhaps you may be happy with just one of us?' Li Li asked, smiling shyly.

Muller noticed the prostitute's long dark hair seemed to glow a deep silken red in the candlelit room.

'Tonight, I need the loving of you both, my sweet darlings. Come here to me,' he whispered.

The two pretty Chinese girls walked gracefully across to where Muller sat and stood next to the bed.

'Ah, you are rare beauties indeed, my sweet darlings,' He said softly. Muller felt his desire for the two women begin to rise within him. He sat back on the bed and watched as they slipped their feet out of their brightly coloured slippers and undid the shiny sashes that held their silken robes in place and let them slip from their shoulders and drop to the floor.

The big South African and the two Chinese prostitutes made love for more than an hour. The women lavished the big Afrikaner with all the lovemaking skills they knew, some of which were very special and were of Indian origin and had been taught to the two attractive women by the fastidious and very professional Lucy Lu. In a final act of carnal pleasure, Muller lifted both of the women off the bed and onto their hands and knees in front of him, and like a rutting dog, he mounted one and then the other, until finally, the three of them collapsed to the floor with exhaustion.

From behind one of the silken wall coverings, Lucy Lu watched with aroused pleasure. The elegant madam was fascinated by the sheer size of the big man's manhood. She had watched the two prostitutes with her special clients before, but she had never been as aroused as she now felt watching these three in their final acts of carnal pleasure. As she watched, she caressed her small breasts through her silken gown and groaned quietly with voyeuristic pleasure.

The two Chinese women finally whispered their goodbyes to Muller and slipped on their robes and, carrying their slippers in their hands, they quietly left the room.

Jan Muller lay back, exhausted, on the embroidered cushions. The big man was close to sleep when he heard a door open. He looked back toward the sound. Lucy Lu was standing near one of the silk covered walls, holding a tray with two glasses and a bottle of her wonderful wine.

'Some refreshment for you, my friend, I feel you may need it.' Lucy said softly.

Jan Muller was still naked, his muscular body spread out across the bed.

'Yes, please, Lucy. Your girls have worn me out. I am very thirsty indeed,' he replied politely and sat up on the edge of the bed as Lucy poured them both a glass of her wine.

'Jan, my wine is made from a secret recipe that I tell to no-one. In my homeland, it is known as 'Huangjiu,' the beautiful madam said mysteriously and gave the big man a secretive smile.

'I always enjoy your wine, Lucy. It seems to refresh me,' Jan Muller replied.

'Tonight, Jan, I am going to add a little extra something just for you.' Lucy retrieved a tiny glass bottle from her robe pocket and removed the delicate glass stopper from its neck and carefully added several drops of a smoky liquid into each of their glasses.

'You are always full of surprises, Lucy, my sweet friend, but you have never visited me like this before,' Muller whispered, pointing at his naked body with an open hand.

'I'm sorry if you feel uncomfortable, my friend. But, as you would already know, I am more than familiar with the beauty of the naked male form. However, if you would rather dress, I could return in a few moments,' Lucy said with a polite smile.

Muller smiled back at the beautiful madam. 'Please stay, Lucy. I'm more than comfortable with your company, and I have no desire to dress at this moment. But tell me, what is that secret potion you are putting in our wine?'

'It is a rare concoction, my friend. It is made from several secret herbs and powders and the dried parts of a small beetle that comes from Spain. In some lands, this tiny insect is called a fly. However, that is not correct. It is indeed a small flying beetle and a rather insignificant one at that. These ingredients I then crush to a fine powder and add a small amount of my boiling wine. This refreshing elixir is something that I save for my very special customers. I am sure you will find it a pleasant and rewarding experience. I have the ingredients sent to me from an herbalist in Durban. In the language of your home country, it is sometimes called, '*Spaanse Vlieg.*' Lucy smiled and handed Muller a glass of the spiced wine and lifted her own to her lips. 'Here's to our very special relationship, Jan.' she drank down her wine and waited patiently for Muller to do the same.

The big South African smiled at the beautiful madam and lifted his glass to his lips. 'Here's to us, Lucy Lu,' he replied and drank down the spiced wine.

The two of them sat talking for a few minutes more and then, quite suddenly, Muller could feel a raw carnal desire begin to course through his naked body once again, charging him with a powerful sexual urgency. He felt his manhood start to rise, and in full view of the beautiful Lucy Lu.

'Ah, the monster lifts his head toward the stars again. Perhaps we should entertain him once more, Jan,' Lucy whispered. The tiny madam stood up and slipped the robe she wore from her shoulders and smiled at the big man. 'I must tell you my little secret, Jan. I have been watching you from behind the curtains. You are highly skilled in the art of lovemaking, my friend. However, there is still more for you to learn.'

'You are a wicked woman, Lucy Lu. You should be punished for watching such things,' Muller whispered back. He was surprised by the potency of the aphrodisiac Lucy had given him. His body seemed suddenly charged with powerful animal lust.

'Yes, yes, I am very bad indeed, and I agree, you should punish me,' Lucy whispered, her eyes fixed on his erection.

'Did you enjoy what you saw, Lucy?' Muller asked softly, admiring the tiny madam's beautiful body standing so close to him.

'Yes, yes, it made me want you for my own pleasure. You are so big.' She sighed and ran her hands down her belly to the neatly shaved mound between her thighs. 'I must be punished for what I have done.'

'You are indeed a wicked woman, Lucy. But how shall I punish you?'

'Jan, you must tie me to this bed, and then you must thrash me, and when you think I have suffered enough, you must make love to me until I can take no more. That is what you must do.'

'But there are no ropes to tie you with, Lucy,' Muller whispered, as he got off the bed.

'I have ropes in my gown, ready for you,' Lucy replied breathlessly.

Muller reached for the naked Lucy Lu and lifted her onto the cushion-covered bed, and from one of the pockets of her robe, he took out the four lengths of red silk rope, which he then secured to the bedposts.

'You must punish me, Jan. I am indeed a bad woman for spying on you. Tie me tight and show me no mercy, my savage master.'

Muller carefully tied Lucy Lu spread-eagled across the bed with the silken ropes around her hands and feet. When he had finished, he looked down at the tiny madam. She was helpless now, and this sent an additional rush of excitement through the big man.

'Please, Jan—now you must punish me.' Lucy moaned with feverish anticipation.

Muller reached across Lucy to check her bonds. The aphrodisiac-infused wine had now inflamed his senses completely. 'And now, Lucy, you will pay for your indiscretion,' he whispered into the beautiful madam's ear. He walked around the bed to where his clothes lay, reached down and slid the thick leather belt out of his trouser loops.

Lucy watched him fold the heavy belt in half and smack it hard across his left hand. She looked up at him and wriggled her body from side to side in eager anticipation of what was to come.

Muller walked slowly around the bed and, using the belt as a whip, he flayed it down onto the tiny woman's body. The blows were not so hard that they would harm Lucy, but hard enough to sting her painfully. He continued around the bed for several minutes, thrashing the leather belt down onto her naked body until her breasts, her stomach, and her thighs were crisscrossed with red and rapidly swelling welts. Satisfied finally with the punishment he had inflicted on her, he tossed aside the belt. 'You are a wicked woman, Lucy, and I hope you have learned your lesson,' he whispered.

Muller climbed onto the bed and knelt between Lucy's legs and began to softly stroke her body, paying careful, almost apologetic attention as he caressed the livid red marks that covered her delicate skin.

Lucy writhed with pleasure as he ran his hands across her body and lifted her hips up in wanton submission as he slid a hand down over her belly and between her thighs. Sighing with relief, she pushed her hips against his hand, groaning as she was shaken by her first orgasm.

'Jan, please untie me now. I need to hold you,' she pleaded, her face a mask of wild pleasure.

Muller reached across her body, and as he untied her bonds, he kissed the tiny madam passionately on the lips. 'I must have you, Lucy,' he moaned, his voice hoarse with wanton pleasure.

'Soon, Jan—soon, but first, I must give you the pleasure you have given me. Lie back and let me look at you.'

Muller lay back on the bed and looked up at the glowing lantern above him. The aphrodisiac in the wine had inflamed his body and his mind with a strange, potent sexual energy that was almost frightening in its intensity. Above him, the blue dragons seemed to suddenly come alive and begin to chase each other, as the Chinese lantern rotated slowly, driven by the heat of the red candle in its centre.

Lucy covered his muscular body with soft, tender kisses and ran her hands all over the Afrikaner's huge frame. Stroking and kneading, she massaged his shoulders, his thighs and his manhood with practiced techniques of Indian origin.

Jan Muller had never felt such pleasure before. He knew it was mostly because of the aphrodisiac. But it was also because of the pleasure he had felt as he inflicted pain on the beautiful madam's body. But now, he could take no more. He lifted the tiny woman up and onto him. Then, with his big hands around her waist, he drew her slowly down.

Lucy gasped with pleasure and began to work her hips urgently against each of his savage upward thrusts. 'Yes, master, yes—yes—yes . . .'

Finally, Muller felt the aphrodisiac consume him completely. 'Lucy—Lucy,' he groaned. You are wicked beyond all belief.'

Lucy grasped his thighs and held on as she felt his climax begin and arched her back with the pleasure of it until another deep and wonderful orgasm overcame her completely.

Finally, the two of them fell back onto the bed, exhausted from their lovemaking. Both profoundly aware of the effect the wine had taken on their bodies. As they lay there spent, they watched the slowly turning lantern above them. The blue, almost translucent dragons now seemed to be moving much more slowly as they followed each other's tails around the flickering red candle.

# 20

# Through The Dragon's Eye

Jan Muller closed his eyes, he needed to rest. Lucy Lu slipped quietly from the bed, kissed the big man tenderly on the forehead and left the room through one of the doors hidden behind the silken curtains.

Two hours later, a refreshed Jan Muller awoke to find a very happy Lucy Lu sitting on his bed with a cup of sweet tea in her hands. 'Drink this, my friend, and you will feel better.' She handed Muller the delicate teacup.

Muller smiled sleepily. 'Thank you, Lucy.'

Lucy Lu had showered and brushed her long dark hair and had changed into a green, beautifully embroidered silk robe that covered the livid marks Muller had inflicted on her body.

She smiled as she watched the big man struggle with the tiny teacup. 'And now, Jan, do you still wish to chase the dragon?' she asked.

'Yes, yes, I do, Lucy,' Muller replied, kissing the madam's tiny hands and smiling in grateful anticipation.

'Then, you must follow me,' she said softly.

Muller drank down his tea and placed the delicate china cup and saucer on the rumpled bed and followed Lucy out of the silken room and along a brightly lit passage. They passed two doors the Afrikaner thought were probably Li Li and Mayli's bedrooms. At the end of the long passage, Lucy stopped in front of a tall linen cupboard and opened its door. Inside, the sturdy shelves were stacked with neatly folded sheets and towels. Lucy removed a hidden pin and pushed against the shelves. The carefully built cupboard swung back on concealed hinges to reveal a small, windowless room. The beautiful madam led Muller across the room and instructed him to lie on one of the padded mats that had been laid out in the centre of the room and set about lighting a few small, coloured candles.

Muller sat down on one of the mats and watched Lucy finish lighting the candles and then hurry across to a beautifully carved, camphor-wood cabinet and take out a long pipe with a carved mouthpiece of ivory on one end and a clay bowl on the other. She filled the discoloured clay bowl with the tar-like opium and went back to where Muller sat waiting expectantly and handed him the pipe. Then she lit a perfumed candle and placed it in a brass candleholder on the floor next to the padded mat.

'Lie down, my sweet, and may you travel in peace to the land of your dreams,' she whispered.

'Thank you, Lucy, you are indeed a friend.'

As he lay back, Lucy slid a small, curved wooden frame under his head and watched as the big man turned the bowl of the long pipe down toward the candle flame and began to inhale the pungent smoke, in short, urgent inhalations.

Jan Muller felt a great peace come over him as he lay there. Every sinew and muscle in his body began to slowly relax in a way that only chasing the dragon can do. Then the dreams began to come. They came slowly at first, strange dreams that he had no control over. Faces flashed through his mind—faces from long ago. The long pipe hissed and bubbled with each of his impatient inhalations, and Muller continued down through the opiate-induced mists of his past.

Languorously, almost without conscious effort, he laid the long pipe on the floor next to the flickering candle and sighed as a wonderful calmness washed over him. As he dreamed, a thin fog seemed to clear in his mind, and he saw a yellow sun shining brightly through the crooked limbs of a flat-topped thorn tree.

He was in Africa, the land of his birth. Jan Muller was a young boy at home on his family's farm near Jansenville playing with the Ndebele boys. They were chasing their dogs in and among the round, wonderfully thatched buildings of the Ndebele village and singing a silly childish song, while his friends' sisters laughed from their doorways. He was happy, so very happy. He looked down at his hand held tight by the dark hand of Abasi his best friend, and they laughed together as they ran through the maze of thatched homes.

Suddenly, he saw a horse flecked with salty sweat, exhausted by its cruel rider. Leather groaned from the rider's great weight as he turned his body in the saddle. His friends were suddenly gone. He looked up at the rider. It was his father, with his long hippo-hide whip coiled in his right hand. He was afraid, very afraid. His father reached down and lifted him effortlessly up onto his saddle and they were gone. Then, he found himself in a different place. He was outside in the sunshine. Something burned his wrists. He was tied to a horse rail with baling twine. He struggled against his bonds, and then he heard his father's familiar voice.

'I told you what would happen to you if I ever caught you with the blacks again, Jannie.' His father spoke to him in Afrikaans. 'They are black—they are below us, boy. Black is black and white is white,' his father snarled.

Jan Muller could not move and it was no longer a dream. He watched his father uncoil the whip. There was no-one to help him. He began to cry. Then the whip cut into him. Again and again, it cut into his young back, until, finally, he passed out and darkness washed over him.

Slowly, through the mists of his almost-forgotten past, the dream continued. He was gone from the rail now. He lay face down on a bed and someone was holding him, comforting him. It was his mother—his beautiful mother.

'What has he done to you, Jannie? What on God's dear earth has he done to you?' his mother whispered.

Muller could feel his long-dead mother's tender hands as she stitched his torn back with her cotton thread and swabbed his wounds with the yellow Iodine she kept in the cabinet in her kitchen. He felt her tears fall warm onto his body. He was there at last—he was back with his wonderful mother. He was home.

His mother had died long ago when Jan was just a boy, and she had left him alone with his father. He hated his father and all his harsh rules. Even though he had been just a boy, he knew his father had killed his mother with the hard work he had expected of her. She had once been so beautiful and so very happy, but slowly, he had killed her with his anger, his cruelty, and his violence. But now he was with her again. He was happy, so very happy.

The dragon continued to carry him through the long-forgotten mists of his past. Now, he was back in the home of his childhood walking quietly from room to room. He stood for a moment in a doorway and watched his mother cooking a meal on the huge open fire in the room that was her kitchen. He saw the smoke-stained walls and the heavy wooden table covered in a thousand cuts and chips. His mother was smiling at him, and he saw then, for the very first time, how sad her eyes were.

He moved on from room to room until he was standing in the doorway of his father's study. On the walls, he saw the horns of Kudu, of Eland, Impala, and the beautiful Sable antelope. He saw his father's great writing desk, the rack of oiled guns, and the polished hardwood floor covered with the skins of zebra and leopard. He continued down the narrow passageway past his mother's holy cross that hung above the faded pictures of his grandparents, until, finally, he found himself in his childhood bedroom. He sat on the narrow cot and looked out through the open window. Yellow grass swayed in the warm breeze. He saw his father on his huge chestnut mare, his battered felt hat in his hand and the Ndebele men around him waiting for their daily work.

And then he found himself in another room, a terrible room. His mother lay on the bed she shared with his father. His mother was dying. He reached for her hand and cried as he looked into her eyes. Then, he heard his own frightened young voice.

'Mama, please don't die and leave me alone. Please don't die.' He continued to sob uncontrollably as he looked into her weary eyes. He was young, but he knew that her time had come. Her once strong heart was frail and broken, and her body could take no more. She was not old, but she had travelled to the end of her road. His mother looked into his young eyes, and then he heard her speak her last words to him. 'Jannie, you be a good boy now and try to live a good life, and always remember that I love you, my darling,' she whispered and closed her eyes for the very last time.

Then, he felt his father's strong hand take him out of the room and away from his mother. Suddenly he was outside in the bright sunshine. He watched his father go back into the house. He began to cry again, and as he cried, a terrible loneliness gripped his young heart.

Lucy Lu came back into the room where Jan Muller lay and looked down at his face. The big man looked sad as he dreamed. She picked up the long opium pipe and took it back to the little camphor-wood cabinet, carefully cleaned it, and placed it back on its shelf and closed the doors. Before she left, she looked down at the big man's sleeping face again and wondered what marvels he had seen as he had travelled with the dragon. But Jan Muller's face was a passive mask. Lucy smiled and brushed her hand through his unruly hair and, just for a moment, she thought he looked like a very young boy.

# 21

# The Port of Derby

Captain Bradford and his two dinner guests had met in the saloon for a drink and a chat before heading into the dining room for what was to be their last dinner on board the *S.S. Minderoo*. The following day, at around midday, they were to arrive in Derby.

'So, Cap here's to you, mate. It's been a great trip on your old tub.' Jack smiled and raised his glass of beer. 'Cheers mate.'

'I agree with Jack. It's been a wonderful trip, Captain, and I feel I have made a real friend. But I'm truly sorry that I bored you with my Parisian tragedy,' Isabella added. She raised her gin and tonic in salute and gave the old captain a conspiratorial smile.

Jack wondered what Isabella had meant by her comment, but when he saw the old captain's impassive expression, he shrugged with confusion and drank his beer.

'Thank you both. It has indeed been a great pleasure. Isabella, you will leave behind a lonely old man who will miss your company dearly,' the captain replied, raising his glass and smiling at his two companions. 'And, Jack, your colourful company was most certainly of great enjoyment to me as well.'

'I sincerely hope, Captain, that there aren't any passengers on board who found themselves disappointed they were not invited to spend time at your table. After all, we seemed to have

171

been privileged with your company at every meal.' Isabella put her arms around the old captain and kissed his reddened cheek.

'My instructions were to give you both whatever assistance you may need, and that, I feel, is what I have done. Now, may I propose a toast?' the captain asked.

Jack and Isabella nodded in agreement.

The captain composed himself, and with an earnest expression, he added, 'To good friends.'

The three of them raised their glasses to the toast. 'To good friends.'

'Okay then, you two, let's go and see what the Froggy cook's got for us tonight,' Jack said and drained the last of his beer.

'It's Sunday, Jack. Beef stew, or casseroled chicken with tomatoes,' the captain replied as they left the saloon and headed for the dining room.

'Sounds good, Cap—sounds good to me,' Jack replied, suddenly feeling quite hungry.

'Surely not, Captain, it just doesn't sound like the words our talented cook would use at all,' Isabella added as she followed the two men through the dining room doors and toward their table.

'All right, then, its *'Boeuf bourguignon'* and *'Chicken Provencale.'* Now—are we all happy?' the old captain replied with a wide smile as he pulled back Isabella's chair.

'That sounds a little better, Captain.' Isabella patted the captain's arm as she sat down.

At eleven thirty the following morning, the S.S. *Minderoo* was making her way steadily along King Sound approaching the port of Derby. Captain Bradford stood next to his first mate on the bridge, watching distant, familiar sight points on the horizon. Derby could be a difficult port to navigate, and great care had to be taken as well as timing. The tides that roared in and out of King Sound were the biggest in the country and at certain times of the year, were as high as thirty-five feet and flowed at speeds of over twelve knots. But the captain had timed it well. They would arrive with the incoming high tide, and as soon as the cargo had been offloaded and Derby-bound passengers had disembarked, the S.S. *Minderoo* would make her way back out of the sound and on toward its next port of call with the outgoing tide.

Jack and Isabella had been invited up on the bridge to watch their arrival in Derby, where Jack was treated to a turn at the wheel and had made a great show of his questionable seamanship. The old captain made a huge fuss over them, showing them the ship's navigation equipment, the map-covered chart table, and her lifeline with the world—her radio communications equipment. From their vantage point on the bridge, they could see a long wooden jetty waiting patiently for them in the distance and the murky, grey-green waters of the port of Derby, the gateway to the Kimberley.

Less than thirty minutes later, the S.S. *Minderoo* was safely docked alongside the jetty, and from the bridge, they watched, as the deckhands lowered the gangway down into position.

Jack reached for the captain's hand. 'Nice work, Cap. You know your stuff, that's for sure. Thanks for a great trip and, of course, for entertaining us so well. It has been a real pleasure, mate.' Jack shook the captain's hand and patted his shoulder. 'I'd better go and grab my old bag and get myself down to the jetty to see if I can find this Muller chap.'

'I do hope we meet again, Jack. Look after yourself, my friend, and be sure to look after Isabella as well,' the captain replied. He shook Jack's hand vigorously and smiled his farewell. Jack made his way down the steel stairway to the main deck and headed for his cabin.

The old captain turned to Isabella. 'Isabella, it has indeed been a great pleasure, you have made an old man very happy with your gracious company, my dear. Sorry about my history lessons and the fishermen's stories. I do hope you were not too bored.'

'I most certainly was not, Captain. The trip has been a lot of fun, and I feel we have become good friends. I look forward to seeing you again. Perhaps in a few weeks, when we leave the Kimberley, we may be fortunate enough to have you as our captain when we travel south. I do certainly hope so.' Isabella hugged the captain fondly and kissed him on the cheek.

'I hope so as well, my dear. You can get a schedule of our ships in the town from the shipping office. It will tell you what ships will call and when. Just look down the list until you find the *Minderoo*.'

The captain gave Isabella a parting smile. 'Till we meet again dear lady, till we meet again.'

'Goodbye, Captain James Hedley Bradford and a fond farewell to the S.S. *Minderoo* and her capable crew as well. Captain, please thank Henri for me. Tell him his meals were as delicious as any I enjoyed while I lived in Paris.'

'That will mean a lot to, Henri,' the captain replied. He straightened his jacket and gave Isabella a courteous bow. 'Farewell, my beautiful friend. I do hope you enjoy your stay at the station.'

Isabella made a fuss over adjusting the old captain's tie, hugged him one last time, and made her way out through the heavy door and down the metal stairway to the main deck to help the porters with her baggage. She knew she was going to miss the old captain.

\* \* \*

Jan Muller stood in the arrivals area of the Derby jetty, waiting patiently for his visitors to arrive. The sea was a dirty grey colour and seemed to swell and roll mysteriously with the last of the incoming tide. A couple of seagulls screeched above him in hungry anticipation as they watched the frenzied happenings below them. The jetty was a hive of activity, as it always was when a ship came in.

A set of rail tracks ran the complete length of the wooden jetty. This, Muller could see, was used to carry goods from arriving ships to the jetty's entranceway. As he watched, more than a hundred forty-four-gallon drums of fuel rattled by followed a while later by large open crates filled with produce from the south. Carriages filled with crates of cauliflower, turnips, bags of potatoes and onions clattered past. He watched as boxes of valuable medicines for the hospital, all carefully labelled and sealed, passed him by.

As he waited in the shade of the small verandah, the seagulls that had been circling above him landed close by and began pecking with obvious disinterest at a couple of cabbage leaves that had fallen from a box of produce as it had passed. Still, more carriages passed him by, some carrying wooden kegs of beer, some filled with crates marked Old Monk Navy Rum and McLean's Finest Scotch Whiskey, all of it bound for the hotel.

Muller had never been down to the jetty when a ship had called, and he could not believe the amount of work that was needed to unload one of these big vessels that regularly plied the coast. He looked back along the jetty at the well-maintained ship. He could see the captain dressed immaculately in white, carefully overseeing the unloading operations while boom cranes swung this way and that above the open holds.

Finally, passengers from the ship began to pass, most of them carrying cases or boxes of belongings and heading toward the town. Muller lit his pipe and continued to wait. He could see there were still more passengers making their way down the gangway. Then, just as another string of rail carriages passed him, he saw a tall, well-built man with sand-coloured hair walking toward him. The man was carrying a well-worn leather bag on his shoulder and walked with a casual step that Muller could see belied a hard man, perhaps even a dangerous man.

'This would be Ballinger,' Muller thought. He was suddenly reminded of a leopard he had once seen long ago, near the Groot River. 'I must be careful with this one—very careful.' He set off toward him. Directly behind the man he thought was Jack Ballinger, Muller could now see a tall, attractive woman, and trailing behind her were three men struggling with what he imagined would be the woman's baggage.

'This must be the Montinari woman,' he reasoned. 'Spoilt bitch has come to paint some pretty pictures, eh?'

As they drew closer, Muller could see that the woman was not only attractive, she was stunningly beautiful. For some reason, he had not expected that. The Montinari woman was dressed in an expensive-looking white cotton blouse and matching slacks with white canvas loafers on her feet. Her long dark hair was partly covered by a wide-brimmed, white sun hat that had a light blue, silk sash wrapped fashionably around it. Muller noticed she wore gold-rimmed sunglasses and walked with the confidence that comes from living a privileged life, a life where money is never of great concern.

Jan Muller had enjoyed his few days in Derby. He had visited The Blue Peacock once more to be entertained by the beautiful Lucy Lu and her pretty Chinese girls, Li Li, and May Li. But he had not smoked the opium again. Even though he could rarely remember the dreams he experienced when he smoked the poppy, he did remember he had seen his mother again, and it had left him feeling empty and sad. But now, he felt refreshed and strong, and he was looking forward to returning to Cockatoo Creek. Back to where he was in complete control. Perhaps in a few days, he would play his little game with the native girl, Anna once again. But he knew he would need to be careful with these two newcomers.

'Would you be Jan Muller, mate?' the sandy-haired man said as he approached him.

'Yes, I am Jan Muller, and I take it you would be Jack Ballinger,' Muller replied. He reached for Jack's hand, and attempted a crushing handshake, only to be met with steely resistance and a pleasant smile.

'Correct, mate. And this lovely lady behind me is Isabella Montinari, as you would already have guessed.' Jack stood aside and waved his free hand back toward Isabella.

'Glad to meet you, Jack, and you, Miss Montinari. I hope you both have had a pleasant trip. We have been looking forward to you arriving,' Muller said, releasing Jack's hand and turning his attention to Isabella.

'Call me Isabella,' the Montinari woman replied pleasantly and removed her sunglasses.

'Very well, Isabella.' Muller suddenly found himself embarrassed by the tall woman's disarmingly friendly manner. Isabella Montinari was obviously very well-educated and certainly not easily intimidated by men.

176

'I am so looking forward to getting out to the station,' Isabella said, smiling at the big South African. 'How are Santiago and Golly, my two good friends from so long ago?'

'All the hands are well. We don't have too much trouble out at the station, just work, and plenty of it. I'm sure it will all be quite boring for someone used to the big city life,' Muller replied with a somewhat condescending tone. He realised this very confident woman had begun to make him feel awkward and self-conscious.

'Perhaps I may be the best judge of that, Jan. Tell me, are we travelling out to the station this afternoon, or would it not be better to travel out in the morning, when it's cooler? What do you have in mind?' Isabella asked politely.

There was something about Jan Muller that Isabella did not like. He seemed arrogant and certainly condescending, and, for some reason, he made her feel quite uncomfortable.

Jack had been listening to the conversation between Isabella and Jan Muller, and he could sense a tension building between the two of them. He studied the big South African. There was something that made him distrust this man, and he couldn't quite work out what it was. He was obviously arrogant, and Jack could sense that he probably had a very bad temper. He had known men like him before, during the war—dangerous men.

'I have made bookings for us all at the Spinifex Hotel for tonight. I thought you both might like a bit of rest. We can head on out to the station in the morning when it's cooler. I hope that's agreeable,' Muller said awkwardly.

'Sounds like a good idea, mate. I hope the beer's cold and the beds are soft,' Jack replied with a laugh in an attempt to ease the tension.

'That will be fine, Jan, absolutely fine. I wonder would you mind helping these gentlemen with my baggage. They seem to be struggling,' Isabella said with a friendly but assertive tone to her voice as she pointed back to the porters.

'Do you have a vehicle somewhere, mate?' Jack asked.

'Yes, I do, Jack, and it's not too far. Now, if you would both like to follow me.' Muller reached down and took one of Isabella's heavy trunks from a struggling porter and hoisted it effortlessly onto his shoulder and headed off toward the parked truck.

Isabella turned back toward the ship in the hope she would see the captain one last time. She looked up toward the bridge, and there he was, looking resplendent in his freshly pressed uniform with his hat in his right hand and, to her surprise, he was waving it at her.

Isabella took off her own hat and waved back. She smiled, she was glad she had seen the old captain one last time. She put her hat back on and turned to follow Jan Muller, a man she had not liked from the moment she had met him.

The front bar of the Spinifex Hotel was full of stockmen from a Kimberley cattle station, rough men who had spent several weeks droving a large herd of cattle into town. They were hungry and thirsty, and the front bar of the Spini had been their first port of call after delivering their cattle to the holding yards out on the edge of the rough-and-ready cattle town. Most of them were quite drunk when Muller parked the big four-wheel drive truck outside the hotel.

Bob Nugent, the station mechanic, had made several major modifications to the big American truck. The cabin had been cut apart and increased in size to enable him to add an extra row of crude but functional seats and the body had been lifted several inches above the springs with hardwood blocks for better ground clearance. Unfortunately, Bob had never completed the project. The capable mechanic had been far too busy with other, more important jobs on the station. The roof of the old truck was now a simple canvas awning attached to a sturdy, welded steel frame and stencilled proudly along the big rig's oversized fuel tank were the words 'Cockatoo Creek Station'. It was a work in progress, typical of many vehicles throughout the Kimberley.

The rowdy drinkers in the bar watched the big cut-down truck pull up outside the hotel in a cloud of dust, and to their total disbelief, they watched a tall, stunningly beautiful woman dressed in white step down from the truck, dust herself off, and set off gracefully toward the entry, the sort of woman rarely seen in the cattle town.

'Hey, beautiful, come and have a drink with us,' one of the drinkers yelled, to a chorus of loud whistling.

'Come and meet some real men, sweetheart, not like those girls out at Cockatoo Creek,' another yelled and joined in the whistling. Two of the drinkers put their glasses on the bar and ran outside. One of them tried to take Isabella's hand and lead her into the bar, just as Jack stepped down from the passenger's side of the truck.

He gave both men a big smile. 'Okay, boys, leave the lady alone. She's just had a big day. She needs a room and a shower and a bit of rest. So be good boys now, and go and have another drink,' he said with a firm but friendly tone.

Just then, Jan Muller had made his way around the front of the truck carrying one of the heavy trunks that he had taken out of the back tray.

'Leave the lady alone, like the man said. I reckon you should go back inside and have another drink if you know what's good for you,' he said and began to lower the trunk.

One of the drinkers stepped forward to face Muller, the larger one of the two. 'If we know what's good for us, eh? Why don't you hop back in your wreck of a truck and piss off and leave the lady to us.'

'You were warned, fellas—don't say you weren't,' Muller replied. He put the heavy trunk on the ground and stepped forward and began to raise his fists, only to feel a vice-like grip grab his right arm and pull him backward.

'No need for any trouble, Jan. The boys have just had a bit too much to drink, that's all. You escort Isabella inside and get her checked in, mate, and I'll take these boys back into the bar and buy them a drink. What do you say, fellas?'

Jack held on to Muller's arm and looked back at Isabella. 'You go on in, Isabella. Jan here will go with you and I'll be along shortly. These boys look like they need another drink.' Jack gave the angry-looking one a friendly smack on the back. 'Come on, mate, let's go.'

Isabella turned back and spoke sharply to Muller. 'There was no need for any of that, Jan. Take me into the office, please.'

Jan Muller felt small. He could not understand this woman. He had been ready to give the two loudmouths a hiding for troubling her, but her knight in shining armour had stepped in, and now the fool was going to buy them a bloody drink.

Jack led the two men back into the front bar and put a five-pound note on the bar. 'Now, fellas, how about we all have a beer with the compliments of Cockatoo Creek Station?' A few of the drinkers booed with discontent, but five pounds buys a lot of beer, and it wasn't long before they were all happily scoffing down their drinks in readiness for another. Jack stayed in the bar until the five pounds ran out, and then he put another pound on the bar and pushed it across to the barman. 'Get them all another round, will you mate. Right now, it's time for me to have a nice cold shower.'

'Come on, Jack, don't go pissing off on us. Have another one on us, mate,' one of the drinkers yelled.

'Maybe I'll see you all a bit later on, fellas,' Jack said happily and headed for the door.

'Make sure you look after that good lookin sheela for us mate,' one of them yelled after Jack.

A short while later, Jack was in his room and about to make his way to the bathrooms, when there was a knock at the door.

'Who is it?' Jack yelled, thinking it was probably one of the hotel staff.

'It's me, Jack. Can I come in?' he heard Isabella ask through the closed door. Jack wrapped the towel he had in his hand around his waist and opened the door.

'Oh—I am sorry, Jack. I've caught you at an inconvenient time. Anyway, I just came to say thank you for defusing what could have been a rather nasty situation earlier. But look, perhaps we could talk a little later.'

'Come on in, Isabella,' Jack said and opened the door wider to let her enter.

'Thanks, Jack. I just wanted to say, if you hadn't stopped Jan, things could have gotten a lot worse out there when we arrived.' Isabella felt a little awkward being so close to Jack now that she could see he was almost naked. She waited for his reply.

'All I did was buy them a drink, that's all—and anyway, that's what I'm here for, I guess. I reckon that's what your father is paying me to do. You know—to make sure no harm comes to you.'

Isabella walked across to the bed and sat down next to Jack's old leather bag. 'I cannot understand why my father would hire a man like Jan Muller. He's a brute, and what's more, I think there is something evil about him.'

'Isabella, I agree with you—up to a point. I've known men like him during the war, men who would use any excuse for a fight. But who knows, perhaps he thought he was looking after you as well. Anyway, your father is no fool, Isabella, and he told me Jan Muller is one of the best station managers up here.'

'That may be so, but I still don't like the man,' Isabella replied sharply.

'Not too fond of him myself, but let's give him a second chance. Maybe we've misjudged him.' Jack was beginning to feel a little uneasy having only a towel covering him with Isabella so close.

'Jack, could I trouble you for a glass of water before I go? I'm still a little unnerved by all that fuss.'

Jack picked up a glass from one of the cabinets near the bed and walked across the room to pour Isabella some water from the jug on his dresser. 'Make yourself comfortable. I won't be a minute.'

Isabella was still shaken by what could easily have been a nasty fight. She watched Jack pour her the water. It was then that she saw his back, or at least what was left of it. Jack's back was covered in reddish-purple lesions from just below his neck to the towel line and probably beyond that, jagged rips that crisscrossed his powerful back, leaving it mutilated and ugly.

'Oh my God, Jack, what happened to your back?' Isabella gasped and was suddenly sorry she had spoken so quickly.

Jack was embarrassed. He had forgotten for a moment that he was almost naked, and he hated people seeing his back. 'That's okay, Isabella. It's nowhere near as bad as it looks. I'm sorry you had to see it, though—it's a bit of a mess, I know,' he said apologetically.

'What happened to you, Jack?'

'A bloody great German artillery shell got a bit close to me at a little place called Hamel in France and knocked me flat. So much for the big adventure and all the free travel, eh? Join the army and see the world, they told us,' Jack replied with a wry grin.

'It must have been terrible.' Isabella realised she should not be asking Jack about the war. She knew that, for many men, it was just too painful for them to talk about.

'Yes, Isabella, it was bad, really bad, and I lost a lot of good mates. But look, I was one of the lucky ones, I'm alive and kicking, and everything is still working all right, you know—two arms and two legs. Better than some of the poor bastards, let me tell you.'

'Sorry I asked, Jack, really I am. You have my respect, all of you men who gave so much. Now I feel terrible, I am truly sorry to have invaded your privacy.' Isabella had begun to feel as if she was intruding. She stood up and headed for the door. 'I had better go. I will see you for dinner a little later.'

'Sorry, you had to see my busted-up old back. Yep, I guess I'll see you at dinner, then,' Jack opened the door for Isabella and waited as she squeezed past him.

The dining room in the Spinifex Hotel was certainly a far cry from the beautifully decorated dining room on board the S.S. *Minderoo*. The walls were lined with simple shiplap boards and battens and painted a dull, rather uninteresting blue colour, and the floor was covered in worn-down and cracked linoleum of an almost indistinguishable grey colour. At one end of the room, there was a set of double doors that led into the dining room from the passageway near the bar area, and at the other, a single, spring-hung door led to the kitchen, and scattered around the room in no particular order, were cheap wooden tables and chairs.

When Jack arrived, the dining room was empty, except for an attractive coloured woman of mixed race busy setting the tables. Jack had seen quite a few women who carried part Asian bloodlines in the hotel, one in the office, and another in the gardens, and a couple of the domestic staff. More than likely, he thought, direct descendants from the pearlers who worked the waters from Broome to Darwin, and on up as far as New Guinea. He knew the pearling masters had brought in cheap labour to work on the boats, Koepangers, Filipinos, Malay men, Japanese, and many others. As a result of this, many of these pearling industry workers had taken wives among the local Aboriginal tribes and among some of the whites as well. The offspring from these unions were scattered throughout the Kimberley and were known locally as Creamies and many of the women who carried the Asian features of their fathers were quite beautiful.

As Jack walked toward the attractive woman setting the tables, he sensed movement near a side wall and turned to see what it could be. A young Aboriginal boy of no more than ten years of age was standing against the side wall pulling a stained rope up and down in a well-timed and regular movement. Jack looked at the boy for a few seconds and then up at the ceiling. The well-worn rope he was steadily pulling on was attached to a series of crude pulleys that were connected to a collection of large grey panels fixed to the ceiling by sturdy hinges. Each of these panels was approximately the size of a door, and there were about twenty of them in neat rows across the ceiling, and all of them were swinging in unison from the boy's steady pulling.

Jack had never seen anything quite like it before, and he watched, fascinated, as the boy sent the huge panels back and forth with seemingly effortless regularity, sending a pleasant breeze down into the room.

'Can I help you, sir?' It was the attractive mixed race woman.

'Hello there. Am I too early for a table?' Jack asked. He was still watching the young boy steadily pulling on his rope.

'No, sir, you can sit anywhere you please. We don't have too many for dinner tonight,' the mixed race girl said politely.

'What's the boy's name over there—and for that matter, what's yours, sweetheart?' Jack asked, pointing to the boy pulling on his rope.

'He's Tommy, and my name is Teresa. Can I get you a drink while you wait, sir?'

'Thanks that would be great. Just a large lager will do me fine, and Teresa, just call me Jack, sweetheart.' Jack smiled and gave the attractive Teresa a two-shilling piece.

'I'll get it for you now, Jack. I won't be too long.' Teresa gave him a smile and headed for the bar.

'Doesn't the lad there get a bit tired?' Jack called out just before she went through the double doors.

'No, Jack, that's his job, he's been doing it since he was little,' the waitress replied and disappeared through the doors.

Jack sat down at a table and waved to the boy pulling on his rope. He was enjoying the cool breeze that blew down from the swinging shutters. The boy smiled back and kept on with his work.

The dinner that night was a rather forgettable experience. The three of them had ordered the mixed grill, which consisted of a small piece of tough, overcooked steak, two sausages, some mashed potatoes, and woody, overcooked carrots. But, they were all hungry and they slowly worked their way through it. Jan Muller finished his meal first and excused himself to go for a walk and a smoke before bed. He was still noticeably annoyed about the incident with the stockmen earlier.

When Jack and Isabella finally finished their meal, Teresa came to take away their plates. 'Did you enjoy your meal?' she asked.

'Yes, it was very nice, thank you, Teresa, and please tell the cook we enjoyed it as well. By the way, Teresa, is there a quiet bar where we could have a drink?' Jack asked.

'Yes, there is the cocktail bar, Jack. It's just out through the doors to your left and across the hallway,'

'Thank you, my dear, and here, take this and share it with young Tommy pulling on his rope over there. I'm sure you both deserve it.' Jack handed the attractive waitress a shiny, new half-crown piece.

'Thank—thank you, Jack,' Teresa stammered with surprise and smiled across at Tommy. The young boy managed a quick smile and kept on with his duties.

'Feel like trying the cocktail bar for a bit, Isabella?'

'I think I would enjoy that?' Isabella smiled and pushed her chair back.

As they left the dining room, she whispered to Jack, 'So, we enjoyed the meal, did we? Compliments to the chef and all that? You're a big fat liar, Jack Ballinger.'

'Little white lies never hurt anyone. Come on, let's go and try this cocktail bar for a bit.' Jack laughed and led the way.

The two of them strolled down the hallway, following Teresa's directions, and turned into the cocktail bar. Jack ordered two drinks, and they sat down in one of the small padded booths that looked out onto the now dark street.

'Well, it's out bush for us tomorrow. Are you looking forward to it?' Jack took a good swallow of his beer and waited for Isabella to reply.

'Yes, I am—I really am. Its rough country out there, but you'll love it. I can't wait. The station is great. They have their own electricity and running water, and the most beautiful gardens you will ever see,' Isabella replied, trying to restrain her enthusiasm.

'I've heard quite a bit about the Kimberley. Good cattle country they say.'

'And, Jack, they have a really great cook out there as well. His name is Santiago, and he is a really sweet man. Then, there's Golly, he's just a lot of fun. I hope we can take him with us when we travel out into the bush.'

'Your father has told me a bit about the place. He says he has spent a fortune out there and hardly ever gets to visit.'

'That's true. But he loves the place as well; he really does, no matter what he says. Anyway, he can afford it. Tell me, Jack, how long have you known my father?'

'Let me see. Pretty well ever since the war ended—what's that? Thirteen or fourteen years, I guess. Your father helped a lot of us messed-up soldiers when we got back from overseas. Some of us were a real bloody mess, both physically and emotionally, let me tell you. I came back just before it ended, and I was bloody glad to be out of it. I needed treatment back in Australia, still had bits and pieces of shrapnel stuck here and there. Your father came and saw a few of us in the hospital to see if he could help. I didn't know who the hell he was. He just came into my room and sat on the bed. I was lying on my side when he came in, my back covered in bandages from my last operation. He asked if he could get me anything. I told him a smoke would be good. But he said he couldn't help me there. Then, he said, 'How about a job when you get yourself out of the hospital?'

'He never told me a thing about any of this—I never realised, Jack.' Isabella was noticeably surprised.

'He helped a lot of us poor buggers, Isabella. Most of them were worse than me though. He found them jobs and helped them to get a start again. Some of them were bad, though, real bad, and when they could take no more and jumped off a bridge or something like that, he made sure they got a decent funeral and sent money to their families,' Jack said quietly. It was obvious to Isabella that Jack was not comfortable talking about the war.

'I just never knew—I was young, and he was always so busy—I just never knew, Jack.' Isabella had tears in her eyes. 'I love him; you know . . . He's always been a wonderful father.'

'Well, that's how it started for me, anyway. I never knew too much about anything before the war. I was just a wild Melbourne street kid. But the war changed us all. Your father could tell I needed some sort of direction, so we talked—we talked a lot, really, about all sorts of things, I guess. About what I wanted to get out of life mostly, I suppose.'

Jack watched Isabella wipe tears from her eyes and continued. 'So, when I finally got out of the hospital, he gave me a job on one of his building sites to get me started. I enjoyed it, I really did. I worked hard, and it wasn't long before I became a leading hand. I went from project to project with Montinari Constructions. It was good for me, and I knew it. But after about eight years, I just got sick of the city life and needed to get away. I guess I really wanted to go and see the country I had gone off to fight for. So, eventually, I gave my notice. I was always appreciative of your father's help, but I was certainly surprised when I was summoned to his office in the city.'

'So what happened then?' Isabella had never realised her father had taken a personal interest in the welfare of any returned soldiers. She had always thought business came first for her father and there was never much time for anything else.

'Then, another talk took place,' Jack replied. 'I explained to him that I needed a change and told him I would like to do a bit of hunting up north. Just bum around for a year or two. I had a few quid saved.'

'Did he try to talk you out of it? He can be convincing, my father, when he wants to be.'

'No, he seemed to understand. He thought maybe it could be the war still messing with me. But I didn't agree with that. Then, he told me he needed to get away himself once in a while. He told me he liked to hunt as well, but just never seemed to get the time.'

'I think that's the real reason he bought the station, you know, Jack,' Isabella said.

'So, eventually, I left Melbourne and headed up to the Territory under instructions from your father that I keep in touch. A few months later, I wound up in Pine Creek. I didn't really know where I was going, I was just having a look around, I guess. Anyway, I met a few locals there and did a bit of pig hunting. I got to know the people who owned the pub there and met a few more locals. I was having a great time, really. Then, one day, a croc hunter came into the pub, an old guy by the name of Dick McGregor. He'd been out in Arnhem Land for a few months shooting crocs for their skins. The old guy offered to take me back out there with him as soon as he had delivered his skins and got himself a few supplies. So, a few days later, we headed out in his old truck through the roughest bush tracks I'd ever seen. It took us a couple of days, but we finally got to a place he called the Jim-Jim River and set up camp.'

Jack smiled and continued, 'It is an amazing place, Isabella. There are huge billabongs, massive un-named waterfalls, valleys, wild creeks, and rivers. I started to feel alive again. It's an untouched paradise. A lot like the wilds of Africa, I would guess. There's wild game everywhere, buffalo in their thousands, amazing birdlife and fish just waiting to jump in your frypan. I had a great time with the old guy, a really great time. We hunted crocs by night in his canoe, just using a torch he had attached to an old army slouch hat. He was a great old fella. He taught me a lot about how to survive out there. We had some great chats around the campfire and I could slowly feel my spirits starting to lift. The bad dreams I had been having about the war never came so often, and I started to sleep like a baby.

Anyway, after a few weeks, we headed back into Pine Creek for supplies and a bit of a break. The old fellow insisted he share the skin money with me and offered me a sort of partnership.' Jack swallowed a mouthful of his beer and kept on, 'I thanked him but turned him down. The life of a croc hunter wasn't really what I was cut out for. But I had an idea. I made a phone call to your father from the pub one night and put my idea to him.'

'So what was this idea you dreamt up?' Isabella was finding herself caught up in Jack's enthusiasm.

'A safari camp out in the wilds of Arnhem Land. My idea was to build a permanent camp for the well-heeled adventurer. A fully-guided experience with showers and comfortable camp bunks to sleep on, the whole bit, all the comforts of home really. A place where hunters and fishermen, even photographers could come to get away from it all. Your father loved the idea and offered to set the whole operation up for me. But that was not really what I was after. However, he insisted, and the sooner the better, he told me. I finally agreed with him, as long as he would allow me to pay him back at some time in the future. He was okay with that and said he would set up a partnership—you know, keep it legal and proper. So that's what happened. That was the beginning of what I now do for a living, the beginning of *Jack Ballinger's East Alligator Safaris, c/- the Pine Creek Hotel.*'

'What is it like up there now, Jack? Is the camp all finished?' Isabella asked.

'Yep, it sure is. I have a hunting and camping permit for a huge area out on the East Alligator plains. I've set up a safari camp near the Jim-Jim Lagoon. It's a wild place, all right. There are plains that go as far as you can see, and game everywhere. Huge herds of buffalo, wild pig by the thousand and the birdlife is just amazing. I'm paying your father back for his investment in me, though I wouldn't have it any other way.'

'It sounds like an amazing place.' Isabella sipped her drink. She wasn't sure if it was the drink or Jack's emerald coloured eyes making her feel light-headed.

'I picked the spot next to the Jim-Jim Lagoon so I could use the water. There's plenty of it, but unfortunately, plenty of crocodiles as well. I've built a shower block and proper long drop toilets, all of the creature comforts, really. I purchased a dozen good quality ex-military tents for the guests and built a comfortable cabin for myself. The cabin has a big verandah at the front with camp chairs and folding tables so we have somewhere to sit around after a day in the bush. I managed to get a couple of "Snow Queen" kerosene refrigerators in Darwin to keep things cool as well—you know important stuff like beer. And while I was up there, I stumbled on a huge old wood-burning stove from a guesthouse that was being demolished and set it up under the verandah to cook on.

It's a great camp, but I can only operate in the dry season. It just gets too wet and difficult to move about for the rest of the year, and the track out from Pine Creek becomes impassable anyway. But as luck would have it, I know the people who own the pub in Pine Creek quite well, and they give me a bit of work to carry me through, you know, bar work, maintenance, and bits and pieces. They're good friends, and it's a big help.' Jack swallowed another mouthful of his beer.

'Are you getting enough guests out there to keep you busy?' Isabella had found herself intrigued by Jack's adventurous tales and his carefree attitude to life.

'Well, yes, thanks to your father. It was a bit of a surprise at first with the damn depression and all. Anyway, he seems to send a non-stop stream of guests up to me. Some of them are people who contract to him and want to get away from it all. Some are politicians he knows. All sorts, really. I have even had a group of people from Cinesound News spend a month with me, filming a newsreel on the wilds of Arnhem Land.

Your father has been up for a bit as well. He wanted to have a look around and to do a bit of hunting for a few days. But he's a busy man, and he had to get back early.

A lot of my guests just come for a break and are happy to do a bit of photography, while others want to hunt and some are happy just catching a few fish. There's some of the biggest barramundi and saratoga you can imagine in the creeks and billabongs quite close to the camp.'

'It sounds amazing, Jack.' Isabella smiled and finished the last of her gin and tonic.

Jack looked across. 'Would you like another drink? I've been going on a bit.'

'That would be nice. Another gin and tonic with a little ice would be great.'

'Right, okay then, a gin and tonic with ice and one large beer coming up.' Jack slid out of their booth and went to the bar, a few minutes later he returned with the drinks.

'Are your parents still living, Jack, if you don't mind me asking?' Isabella asked as she took her drink.

'Never knew who my father was—just never knew. Someone told me he did a runner when he found out Mum was in the family way. I guess it seems a bit odd, but Mum never spoke about him at all. She died a few months before I got back from the war. Some sort of cancer I was told. It was all very sudden. She had a hard life, Mum, she really did. I tried to help when I could. I used to send her most of my pay during the war. She had it tough, though, poor thing.'

'I guess I must look like a spoilt brat to you, Jack,' Isabella said, looking down at her drink.

'No, no, you don't at all. You're just a little luckier than most, that's all, but you've taken the advantages you were given to better yourself. Fortunate is the word I would use, certainly not spoilt,' Jack replied with an understanding smile.

'Thanks, Jack that means a lot. You know, I have always tried to keep my feet on the ground. I know I have been lucky to have the father I have. But I am also aware that my father started with nothing and worked very hard to get to where he is today. It was my father who insisted I get myself a good education and that I use that education wisely.

However, I must tell you, Jack, when I was young and living at home, I wanted nothing more than to work in my father's offices and to help out in any way I could. He was always so busy, and I thought that was one way we could get to know each other better. But he would have none of it and insisted that I get myself a good education and that one day I would understand.'

'I guess parents are usually right. Anyway, you've turned out half-reasonable, I suppose,' Jack replied and gave Isabella a cheeky smile. 'What about your mother, is she still living?'

'My mother died when I was only a baby. It was leukemia, and she was still so very young. I was told it almost killed my father and that he did not want to go on without her. They were just so much in love. They had grown up together back in Italy. Their families knew each other. They were childhood sweethearts, I suppose. It took my father a long time to heal. I was told he just buried himself in his work. He visits her grave on the anniversary of their wedding day every year, you know. He took me with him once when I was very young, and that is the only time I have ever seen my father cry. He placed white roses in a vase at the foot of her grave and sat on the ground next to her headstone with his hand on her name and just wept. He never took me with him again. That was the only time,' Isabella said sadly.

'He's a great man, your father, and I can't tell you how grateful I am to have met him,' Jack replied respectfully.

'I suppose we should get ourselves off to bed. We have a big day tomorrow.' Isabella said. She finished her gin and tonic and smiled at her companion.

'And will that be your room or mine, beautiful?' Jack answered with a cheeky grin.

'Not a chance, Jack Ballinger. Not a chance.'

Isabella slid out of the booth and stood up. 'Goodnight, Jack. Sleep tight, don't let the bed bugs bite and I will see you at breakfast.'

'Goodnight, Isabella Montinari,' Jack replied.

# 22

# A Few Creeks to Cross

The following morning it was raining—real tropical rain. It was pouring down. Water cascaded off the hotel's roof in great translucent sheets, digging deep runnels in the red dirt as it fell. It was hot and humid, and the noise from the rain on the hotel's iron roof was deafening as they sat down for their early breakfast in the dining room. Jack looked about for the young Aboriginal boy, Tommy the rope puller. But he was nowhere to be seen. Then he saw Teresa come through the kitchen's spring-hung door. When she saw Jack, she gave him a huge smile and hurried over to take their orders.

After she had gone, Isabella looked across the table at Jack. 'I think you have won a heart there, Jack,' she teased.

'More than likely it was the half-crown I gave her to split with young Tommy. I wonder where he is, by the way, it's damn humid, and we could do with a bit of breeze in here this morning.'

It was a little after seven when they were finally ready to leave, and the rain was still coming down, although not as heavy as it had been during breakfast. The truck had proven difficult to start, and the battery had finally gone dead. Jan Muller had handed Jack the crank handle to use while he worked the throttle, and it finally started with a healthy roar.

The two men had packed all their bags, Isabella's trunks, and the goods for the station in the rear tray and carefully covered it all with heavy canvas sheets and roped it down between showers. But as they climbed on board, it began pouring down again.

Jack and Jan Muller were in the front of the big Marmon-Herrington and both men were soaked to the skin, and they hadn't even left the remote outback town. Isabella sat in the centre of the rear seat, dressed in a pair of loose-fitting, fashionably faded American denim jeans and a tight-fitting white T-shirt with the words 'La Vie Parisienne' printed proudly on its front. Her protection from the rain that would occasionally blow in through the open sides of the truck was a small canvas sheet wrapped around her shoulders.

'How will the roads be, Jan?' Jack yelled above the din of the rain crashing down on the canvas roof of the old truck as they headed off.

'We should have skipped breakfast and got going at sun-up,' Muller grunted. 'We'll be okay, though. There are a few creeks to cross on the way out. If we can get over them before they get too high, we'll be fine. We should make it out to the station before dark if we get a good run.'

'What's the truck like in the mud?' Jack asked, trying to be friendly.

'Like I said, we'll make it okay, so don't you worry yourself too much,' Muller replied impatiently. He leaned forward, tapped the fuel gauge a couple of times and shifted into a higher gear.

The first creek they came to was about an hour out of town. It was wide but shallow, and they crossed it easily. It was a little over an hour later when they reached the next one.

'Christ, look at that!' Jack yelled above the noise of the rain on the canvas.

The creek crossing was a mess. Torrents of muddy water raced through the spindly acacia trees on either side of the bank. While they sat watching from the safety of the old truck, the rushing water tore several of the weaker, smaller trees loose and sent them away on rolling red swells.

'Perhaps we had better turn back while we still can,' Isabella called from the back seat above the din of the rain.

'It's not as bad as it looks, and this old truck is like a tank,' Muller yelled back. He jerked up the hand brake and jumped out and made his way down to the water's edge to take a closer look. A few moments later he was back and pulling an old hessian bag out from under Isabella's feet, along with a couple of pieces of wire he found down there as well. 'Won't be too long,' he yelled above the rain and made his way back to the front of the truck.

'What do you think we should do, Jack, head back or what?' Isabella asked as she watched Jan Muller busy at the front of the idling truck.

'He seems to know what he's doing, and I suppose he knows what the truck is capable of, so let's leave it to him for the moment. Can you swim, Isabella?' Jack yelled.

'Of course, I can—college champ, don't you know. What about you Jack? I hope I don't have to jump in and save you,' Isabella teased.

Jack suddenly realised that this was a very capable woman, who could probably handle most of the difficult situations that confronted her. 'Sorry I asked, champ. Sorry, I bloody well asked,' Jack yelled back. They both laughed and watched Muller secure the hessian bag over the grill area of the truck with a couple of the short pieces of wire.

'What does he think the bag is going to do, Jack.'

'It will help create a bow wave when we head into the water, and as long as we keep moving forward, it should stop the water from getting into the engine. It's an old army trick,' Jack explained just as Muller climbed back behind the wheel. The station manager was soaked. His hair was flat against his scalp, and his clothes hung limp like rags on his huge frame. But if the big man was feeling any discomfort, it certainly never showed.

Muller never said a word or bothered to look at either of his passengers. He released the hand brake, gave the old truck a quick rev to make sure it was still running smoothly, and as soon as he was satisfied, he locked in the four-wheel drive, and drove forward into the water.

They all felt the big truck's gearbox crunch as he changed from first into second gear a little too quickly. Muller mumbled his annoyance, increased the revs, and pushed forward into the swirling torrent.

Reddish-brown water began to wash over the bonnet of the truck and rush in through the cabin's open sides where they sat. Muller pushed the throttle down a little farther to keep up the forward momentum and gripped the steering wheel tight to keep the truck from slewing out of control. They made it to the centre of the creek without any real trouble, the revving engine almost drowning out the sound of the pouring rain, and white tendrils of steam leaking from the truck's bonnet. Then, without any warning, they felt the truck begin to slide off the gravel crossing and start to lean dangerously downstream with the push of the water. Suddenly a huge rolling red swell smashed into the back where Isabella sat and almost swept her out into the maelstrom of rushing water. She grabbed at the crudely welded steel framework in front of her and held on, while the old truck fought against the torrent of rolling red water.

Muller hit the throttle down hard and wrenched the steering wheel back to counteract the pull of the water. Below them, they could feel the old truck's tyres spin and slip in the gravel of the creek bed. Finally, they gripped, and slowly began to pull the heavy vehicle back toward the crossing under the extra revs. They lurched forward for a few yards and then bounced up over a submerged log or rock, and quite suddenly, they were back in shallow water again. Muller snapped the gear lever into third, and, with a rush, they tore up the opposite bank and into the trees beyond. Once they were well clear of the crossing and back in full control, he stopped the truck and with a relieved expression on his face, he got out, rolled up the hessian bag and climbed back behind the wheel.

'Nice work, Jan—well done, mate,' Jack commented just as the rain began to lighten and they could hear each other without yelling.

'Thank you, Jan. Very well done. I think we were all a little nervous for a moment or two there,' Isabella said pleasantly, almost apologetically.

'All in a day's work in the bush. I guess it's a bit different than the cobbled streets of Paris or London. Like as I said, she's a good old truck. But we'd better keep moving, though,' he replied and let out the clutch.

They pulled away with a shudder and headed off along the muddy track toward the distant station. Heavy rain clouds raced over them as they moved away, and quite suddenly, it began to pour again. Muller gave his passengers a confident smile. He was happy, and he was back in control. He began to push the old truck as fast as he could along the muddy road, hoping there were not too many more high creeks to ford. But the rain continued to pour down and made him nervous about what lay ahead. They all understood that to turn around and head back to town now was out of the question. They had to push on through the rain and mud and hope for the best. There was simply no other choice.

An hour later, they came to another swollen creek. However, this one was much worse than the one they had had trouble with earlier. The water had flooded this creek so badly that it had come up over its banks and was now several hundred yards wide. Muller stopped the truck and got out to roll down the wet bag that he'd hitched up onto the bonnet.

Isabella and Jack used the opportunity to step down from the mud-covered truck and stretch their legs for a few minutes. As they looked out across the swirling red water wondering if perhaps they should have turned back earlier, a chorus of cicadas chirped monotonously from somewhere nearby.

'Perhaps we should have turned back, Jack. It looks rather bad.' Isabella gave voice to their concerns.

'It's a bit late now I reckon. If it's not too deep we should be okay.' Jack replied.

'Okay, we had better keep moving, then,' Muller yelled with obvious impatience as he climbed on board again.

'Won't be a moment, Jan.' Jack was helping Isabella brush away the last of the mud and wet leaves from her clothing. He pulled a small ant-covered branch from the back of her T-shirt and brushed away the few ants that were still stuck to the fabric.

'There you are—ready for another go, I reckon.'

The red water had stained Isabella's white T-shirt a muddy brown colour and made the wet material cling to her ample breasts and emphasize their perfect shape.

Jack turned away while she brushed off the last of the leaves that still clung to the front and they climbed back into the mud-covered truck.

Muller pushed the gear lever forward, gave the engine a quick rev, and they headed into the maelstrom of rushing water. It was difficult for him to know exactly where the track was beneath the swirling surface, but he simply lined up the break in the trees several hundred yards ahead, thinking that was where the creek crossing should be and kept moving toward it. His calculations proved correct, and it wasn't long before they slid down into the rutted creek bed itself.

Once again red water rushed into the cab and around their feet. They braced themselves for what lay ahead and pushed on. The creek was close to five feet deep, and they prayed it would not get any deeper. They forged on with steam now pouring from the engine bay in hissing clouds. Several times they jerked forward in their seats as the engine faltered and then fired again but Muller pushed the throttle down further, trying to create an even bigger bow wave.

It began to look as if it had become a battle between the old truck's dogged ability and the rushing water, and that perhaps the water may soon win that battle, but they kept moving forward, their hopes high. And then suddenly, the rain began to crash down on the old truck again. They continued forward at a steady rate, a muddy red wave lapping over the truck's bonnet, the water's surface now a misty fog of swirling red waves and broken tree branches racing past. Just as they began to feel with uneasy certainty that they would soon be washed away along the roaring creek bed at any moment, they began to creep back into shallower water. Muller wrenched the wheel this way and that, searching for traction, and with a rush, they came up out of the muddy mess and back onto the barely visible track, which was now fast becoming a creek itself.

It was the middle of the afternoon before the rain finally stopped, and as they continued, they began to notice the track becoming a lot drier and much easier to travel on.

For the next three hours, Jan Muller pushed the old truck along at more than forty miles an hour, in the hope he could make up for the time they had lost at the creek crossings.

'How much farther do we have to go, Jan?' Isabella asked, watching the speedometer and bouncing about on the hard seat in the back.

'Do you see those big trees up ahead in the distance there?' Muller replied happily.

'Sure do, Jan, sure do, mate,' Jack replied. He was becoming just as sick of being wet and uncomfortable and bounced around as Isabella was.

'Well, just beyond them and about three or four miles on is Cockatoo Creek.'

'Thank goodness for that,' Isabella replied with a sigh of relief.

Fifteen minutes later, the old mud-covered truck pulled through the ring of boab trees and up onto the plateau where the station's buildings were built.

'Well, here we are, Cockatoo Creek Station,' Jan Muller announced, trying to hide his own relief. He turned the truck to the left and followed the track down toward the machinery shed, just as a welcoming party of more than thirty dogs rushed out to greet them. In their excitement, some of the unruly mob tried to leap onto the truck, while others ran around in wild disarray, barking and snapping at the tyres and each other in their confusion. They had arrived.

## 23

# Cockatoo Creek Station

It was dinnertime, and most of the hands were in the dining room when the truck pulled through the boab trees. Santiago and Anna were still busy serving the evening meal when they heard the low drone of the truck's engine.

'That's the truck. The boss is back from town,' someone yelled, 'and it looks like we got visitors as well.'

Most of the diners got up from their tables and went across to the windows to watch the mud-covered truck pull through the trees surrounded by its welcoming party of yapping station dogs.

'Come on, Santiago, let's go and see them. I think its Isabella. She's here at last,' Golly yelled. He put down his mug of tea and headed for the door.

'You look after things here, Anna. I'll be back soon.' Santiago rushed out after Golly with a wide smile on his brown face.

The waterlogged travellers were a mess. Like the truck, they were covered in partly dried mud, their clothing water-stained and their appearance disheveled and weary. They were certainly not ready for a welcoming committee, but they got one anyway.

Golly and Santiago ran across to them and, totally ignoring both Jan Muller and Jack, surrounded Isabella.

'Miss Izzy, Miss Izzy, you're back. It's been so long. Are you well?' Golly gabbled excitedly.

'Hello, Miss Izzy, it is so good to see you again,' Santiago said quietly, wiping his hands on his apron, a huge smile on his brown wrinkled face.

Isabella put her mud-stained arms around the two men and hugged them to her affectionately.

'Yes, I am well, and it's so good to see the two of you after so long. You both look just the same as I remember. I'm sorry about the muddy clothes—I bet I look terrible.'

'No, Miss Izzy, you look beautiful, just like always,' Santiago said sincerely.

'You must thank Jan for getting us here, though. It was a rough trip, and he did a first-class job of driving to get us here safely,' Isabella replied.

Neither man looked at the station manager or said a word of thanks to him. They both waited for Isabella to continue.

'Now, we have a first-time visitor with us as well. This rather muddy-looking gentleman standing next to me is Jack Ballinger.'

'G'day there, fellas. What were your names again?' Jack asked with a friendly smile.

'Sorry, Jack. This gentleman here is my very good friend Santiago, just the best cook I know, and this curly-haired, smiling fellow is the inimitable Golly, short, of course, for Gollywog, and my very good friend as well,' Isabella said affectionately. She placed a hand on each of their shoulders and gave them a friendly shake.

'Glad to know you fellas.' Jack left them and went to help Muller untie the ropes that held their canvas covered luggage.

An hour later Isabella and Jack were showered, dressed in clean clothes, and enjoying a delicious roast chicken and vegetable dinner that Santiago had personally delivered to the homestead, along with a pot of steaming tea.

Both of them were ravenously hungry and glad to finally be at the station after such a long and difficult drive. They had thanked Muller again for getting them to the station safely, and he had gone off to his cottage to bathe and wait for his dinner.

They heard a knock at the door just as they had almost finished their meals.

'It sounds like we've got visitors.' Jack announced with a smile and got up to answer it.

'That will be our fruit and homemade ice-cream. Santiago makes the best homemade ice-cream I've ever eaten,' Isabella declared, picking at her remaining chicken wing.

Jack opened the door and was greeted by Santiago's smiling face, and tagging along behind him, dressed in a clean white apron, was a very tall and attractive Aboriginal girl carrying two bowls of paw-paw and ice-cream.

'Come on in, Santiago. By the way, the chicken was delicious mate, very nice indeed. I see you have a helper, and a pretty one at that.'

'Yes, this is, Anna. She is my new helper and my very good friend,' Santiago replied proudly. The old cook and the tall Aboriginal girl stepped inside and made their way quietly across to the table. Santiago began clearing away some of the dinner dishes, while Anna placed the bowls of fruit and ice-cream on the big table.

'Miss Izzy, I would like you to meet Anna, my new assistant cook,' Santiago said respectfully. He turned to the young girl, who stood next to him. 'Anna, this is Isabella—but we all call her, Miss Izzy.'

Isabella had not expected Santiago to have an assistant, and certainly not one as pretty as the girl who stood smiling at her. She put down the remains of the wing she'd just finished and wiped her hands on her napkin.

'Anna, I am very pleased to meet you,' she said politely. She got up and made her way around the table to the attractive Aboriginal girl and greeted her warmly. 'I am very glad Santiago finally has a helper in the kitchen. He has always worked far too hard.'

Anna was nervous. She had heard so much about Isabella and desperately wanted to make a good first impression. 'Hello,

Isabella. I hope you enjoyed your meal,' she began shyly. 'I am very pleased to meet you too. I have heard so many nice things about you.' Anna felt flustered and embarrassed as she took Isabella's hand. The young girl had never seen a white woman before, and she simply could not believe her eyes.

'Are you happy here, my dear?' Isabella asked pleasantly.

Anna didn't know what she should say. The sudden memory of her frightening night in Jan Muller's washhouse flooded into her mind. But she knew her discussion with Isabella about that terrible night would have to wait. For some strange reason, she suddenly felt so much safer now that Isabella and her handsome friend had arrived at the station.

'Yes, thank you. I am very happy here. Santiago has helped me to learn so much, and it is hard for me to thank him enough for all he has done,' Anna replied, still struggling with some of her words.

'I am very glad to hear it, Anna. I am sure you and I will be great friends as well and thank you for this wonderful dessert, it looks delicious.'

'You are very beautiful, Isabella. It is true what Santiago has said about you. I hope that we become good friends as well,' Anna replied happily.

'Thank you, my dear, thank you very much.'

Isabella went back to her chair and sat down. 'Now, Anna, this rather rough-looking individual dining with me is Jack Ballinger, my very own personal minder.'

'What is a minder, Miss Izzy? Does he help with the cattle?' Anna asked innocently.

'No, Anna. He is going to protect me from all the wild things in the bush when we travel out there in a few days.' Isabella smiled at Jack.

Anna was a little confused by Isabella's description of Jack. However, she knew there were many dangerous things in the bush, and she thought perhaps it was a good idea anyway. The young girl said no more. She and Santiago gathered up the empty dishes, and both of them politely said their goodbyes and left to go back to the kitchen.

'What a pretty girl. Did you notice her eyes? Very Asian I thought, and her features as well, which reminds me of something Captain Bradford was telling me at dinner one night,' Isabella commented as she finished the last of her ice-cream. 'Now, I think I should show you around this wonderful home my father built.'

'Guide on, oh, woman-I-am-to-protect-from-all-bad-things-in-the-bush—guide on.' Jack put down his teacup and stood up.

'Well, I know you have seen some of it already—the bathroom, and one of the bedrooms, of course. But let me take you for a tour. I just love the place, even if it is rather masculine, but that's my father's influence, I suppose.' She stood up and pushed her chair neatly into place against the huge hardwood table.

Isabella was very proud of the home her father had built at Cockatoo Creek. She'd been at the station with him while it was being built, not quite seven years earlier. Her father had designed the house himself and then had the construction plans drawn up in Melbourne. When he was finally happy with its layout, he'd sent a team of his carpenters, stonemasons, and other tradesmen up to the station on board a state ship loaded with materials to begin its construction. Isabella and her father had travelled up to the station to oversee the setting out of the site in the very beginning and Isabella had had a wonderful time and had taken quite an interest in the home. She had worked alongside her father, pegging out the site and pulling string lines along its perimeters and walking with him from room to room when they were no more than scratched lines in the dirt. She'd listened carefully, as he explained the importance of taking into consideration so many things when siting a home. Critical things, he had told her, such as the sun's path in both the wet and the dry season, the importance of the prevailing breezes and the likely directions of tropical storms.

Her father had designed the home to suit the harsh tropical climate of the Kimberley. It was built about five feet above the ground on sturdy hardwood stumps to allow the night breezes to circulate beneath it to help keep it cool. The walls of the home were constructed with a multi-coloured, local stone, quarried from a ridge several miles from the homestead and carried to the worksite by the station truck and horse-drawn wagon, where it was cut to size by the stonemasons.

The outside walls were more than two feet thick, with a wide verandah that carried all the way around the home, which shaded the windows from the harsh tropical sun. The windows and doors on the outside of the home were fitted with louvered storm shutters, hinged in readiness of severe weather. Most of the rooms throughout the home had beautifully made French doors that opened out onto the wide veranda's to catch the evening breezes, creating a home reminiscent of those built by the British on the coffee plantations of Africa and the tea plantations of India.

The sturdy hardwood flooring throughout the home was made from beautifully figured jarrah, a hardwood that was shipped up from mills in the south and expertly laid on-site by the carpenters, to be later polished to a stunning gloss. The ceilings were high and the exposed rafters throughout were jarrah as well. The doors, door frames, and cabinetry including the magnificent kitchen, were built from karri, another native timber shipped up from forests in the south. The outside walls of the home were left in the natural red and ochre stone of the hills, while the inside walls were bag washed by the stonemasons with a lime and sand plaster and left the natural ivory of the plaster.

Isabella began her tour of the home by leading Jack into the tastefully fitted out great room with its karri bookshelves and magnificent gun cabinets. The huge room's polished jarrah floorboards were strewn with red and white cattle skins, while the walls were adorned with several sets of bull's horns and a framed collection of black-and-white photographs taken during the construction of the magnificent home. Isabella led him across the room, past comfortable armchairs and a massive leather couch that had glass and chrome smokers' stands placed thoughtfully at each end. Near one of the walls and next to a collection of native spears and paraphernalia, Jack noticed a beautifully made American, Steinway Pianola, complete with a glass-fronted cabinet next to it full of neatly boxed music rolls.

'I told you it was masculine, but it's very practical as well, you know, and cool most of the time with its high ceilings and wide verandas.'

Jack was impressed. For some reason, he had expected something far more spartan and certainly much smaller. Perhaps more like a hunting lodge, he had thought. But Michael Montinari had style, there was no question of that, he conceded. For Jack, the home was certainly full of surprises, not the least of them the magnificent gun cabinets and the more than twenty expensive German and English firearms neatly racked and secured behind the locked glass doors.

'I'll get you the keys after I have shown you the rest of the house, Jack, so you will just have to be patient,' Isabella remarked, noticing his interest in the expensive display of her father's firearms.

There were five large bedrooms in the home, each with mosquito nets tied at the ready above the beds, and each with French doors that opened out onto the wide verandas. Next to the master bedroom, a set of double doors opened into a superb study. This magnificent room was fitted with floor-to-ceiling bookshelves and was complete with a comprehensive collection of volumes covering subjects as diverse as cattle breeding and meat production, to poetry and the classics.

Jack noticed volumes on birdlife, local fauna, and two rather rare first edition leather-bound books on African hunting by the great Frederick Selous, both written before the turn of the century. He went across and sat on the edge of the huge timber desk in the centre of the room.

'It's certainly an amazing home, Isabella, and with all the creature comforts you could ever need, that's for sure. It must have cost your father a small fortune to build it out here in the bush.' Jack was having some difficulty taking his eyes off the expensive gun collection in the adjacent great room.

'I would imagine it must have cost a considerable amount, certainly. But he loves it, and so do I. It's an amazing place, and I don't just mean the home. Just wait till we go bush. There is so much to see Jack. There are ancient weatherworn hills of unbelievable colour. Valleys filled with rare plants that exist nowhere else on earth and as you get nearer the coast, great flat-topped plateaus that rise up out of the savannah lands just begging to be explored. It really is a truly magical place, even though much of it I have still to see, and, of course, that is part of the reason for my coming.'

'It sounds fantastic. Remote like Arnhem Land, I guess. But it certainly sounds different as you get toward the coast. Let's hope it doesn't get too difficult with the wet season about to start,' Jack replied, with some concern, as he remembered the difficulty they had on their trip out from Derby.

'I'm not sure if my father told you about another of his projects, Jack. It is something that I know very little about, except to say he imported some sort of an all-terrain vehicle from France about a year ago. A half-track I think it's called. He has had Bob, the station mechanic, working on it, doing modifications of some sort, I believe. That is all I really know, but I guess we could have a look at it tomorrow if you like.'

'That sounds very interesting.' Jack replied.

'So, I think that's enough of the guided tour for now. I'm going to have a gin and tonic and see if I can find some Django Reinhardt to listen to on the phonograph. Would you like to join me?'

'Reinhardt—he's that gypsy guitarist guy. Yep, I've heard some of his work before. Sure, I'd like that. But what else do we have to drink, Isabella? All this walking around has got me a little thirsty.'

'There are two refrigerators in the pantry, Jack and one of them is there strictly for drinks. Let me see if I remember—there is wine and cider, vodka, gin, and, of course, beer, and I am fairly certain there is scotch and bourbon in a cabinet in the great room somewhere. Just name your poison.'

'A cold beer would do me nicely, Isabella. So, where is this record player, then?' Jack asked politely. He was still struggling to come to grips with the grandeur of the magnificent home and with the logistics of building such a home in the wilds of the Kimberley.

'Follow me.' Isabella led Jack back into the great room. 'Take a seat. I'll go and get us a couple of drinks, and then I'll see what I can find.' She pointed Jack to one of the comfortable leather chairs and left the room to get the drinks. A short while later she returned with her gin and tonic and a large, ice-cold bottle of beer and glass for Jack.

'This is certainly nice and cozy. What would you say if I suggested we both move to the couch and maybe get a little bit closer?' Jack suggested as he watched his beautiful companion open a cupboard filled with paper-sleeved records.

Isabella turned back to face Jack with a serious look on her face. 'Please don't get the wrong idea, Jack. Friends are what we are, and friends, I hope, is what we will stay. I am sorry if I gave you any false hopes, but I have no time for men in my life at the moment, and I am certainly not interested in anything casual. I am just not that sort of woman. I suppose I have a few too many memories still haunting me from my days in Paris.'

'Well, you can't blame a guy for trying, you know. If you need to talk about things, I'm a good listener.'

'Thanks, but no thanks. It's all in the past now. Tell me; is there anyone special in Jack Ballinger's life?' Isabella started shuffling through the records again.

'I can't say there is, really. But there was for a while there when I first got out of the hospital. One of the nurses, she was nice, but it just never worked out, and for a short time one of the barmaids at the Pine Creek Hotel, but she went back to Darwin, and that was that. I suppose I've been fairly busy with the camp and buried myself with work since then.'

'I can't seem to find any Reinhart. I know there are a couple here somewhere. My father just loves him. What about Gene Austin?'

'Gene Austin is fine with me,' Jack replied.

He took a long swallow of his beer and watched his beautiful companion continue to shuffle through the piles of records.

# 24

# The Hippo

The following morning, as dawn broke, Jack was up, washed and dressed and walking around the station yard getting to know the place when Golly spotted him and came over to greet him. 'Mr Jack, how are you this morning?'

'Call me Jack, Golly—just plain Jack, mate, and yes I'm fine. You certainly have a great place here, from what I have seen of it so far.'

Just then, Santiago's old metal pipe clanged three times, and stockmen started spilling out of the bunkhouse and heading for the dining room.

'Come and join us for breakfast, Jack. Old Santiago's a great cook. There'll be eggs and bacon, sausages, whatever you want,' Golly said happily. 'I'll introduce you to some of the fellas.'

'Sounds like a good idea to me,' Jack replied.

The two men made their way across to the dining room. Once they were inside, Golly turned to Jack. 'Follow me,' the Aboriginal stockman instructed. He grinned and headed for the servery.

'Right behind you, mate—right behind you,' Jack replied.

The dining room was a hive of activity. Surly stockmen were crowded around the tea urns; others were taking their places in line at the servery, while some were seated and already enjoying their breakfast. Jack noticed the Aboriginal girl, Anna, rush in and place a tray of sausages on the wooden servery.

Jack followed Golly's example and filled his plate with sausages and bacon, eggs and buttered toast. Then, both men filled their mugs with hot tea and went back to one of the long tables. Golly pointed to an empty spot for Jack and sat down on the opposite side of the crowded table.

'Jack, these here fellas are Steve and Fancy Dan, and the fat blackfella there is Beans. That quiet bloke down there a bit further is the station mechanic, Bob. This here fella is Jack Ballinger,' Golly announced and pointed to each of the men as he introduced them.

'Glad to know you all, fellas.' Jack put his plate and mug on the table, tipped an imaginary hat to each of them and sat down.

'A city boy, eh—so what do you reckon you're gonna be doing while you're out here in the wilds?' Steve asked with a condescending tone.

'Well, firstly, I'll be having a little breakfast, and after that, who knows? Why do you ask, sonny?' Jack replied sharply and then set about attacking his breakfast.

'I ain't your bloody son,' Steve snarled, trying to show off in front of the other stockmen at the crowded table.

'Yep, you're right there, sonny. If you were, I'd be taking you outside and giving you a good spanking for being so bloody rude,' Jack replied and casually continued with his meal, not bothering to look at Steve.

'Why don't you shut up, Steve? You're a bloody fool. I reckon this guy could take you out the back and whip your stupid arse just to settle his breakfast,' Dan remarked, glaring across the table at Steve.

There was a murmuring of agreement around the table, and then someone said, 'We thought that pearler in Derby and the hiding Dan gave you would have turned you off scrapping for a while, Steve.'

Steve looked across the table and gave Dan a menacing stare, still trying to impress the station-hands at the table.

Jack shrugged with disinterest. 'Yep, I reckon you should watch what you say from now on, sonny,' he added reaching for his mug of tea and taking a sip.

'Don't take too much notice of Steve, mate. I think his mum dropped him on his head when he was a baby. I'm Dan, mate—pleased to know you.' Dan reached across the table and shook Jack's hand. 'So, I hear you're taking the owner's daughter out bush for a look around the place.'

'Yep, that's about the strength of it, I suppose, and I'm looking forward to it as well.' Jack stood up and reached across the table to Bob Nugent. 'You're the station mechanic, eh, Bob? I'll be coming to see you a bit later on today to have a look at this half-track contraption you've been working on.'

'She's no contraption, mate. She's a bloody beauty, and all ready to roll as well,' the mechanic replied and reached for Jack's hand.

'How's your breakfast, Jack?'

Jack turned and saw Santiago standing behind him with a welcoming smile on his face.

'It's just great, Santiago—just great. Look, if you wouldn't mind, could you get me another breakfast on a tray, along with a pot of tea and a couple of pieces of fruit that I could take back to Isabella? I think she may have slept in.'

'I'll get Anna to do it for you straight away. It shouldn't be too long.' Santiago hurried off to the kitchen.

A short while later, Jack was back at the homestead and tapping on Isabella's bedroom door. 'Wake up, sleepyhead, your devoted minder has your breakfast ready for you,' he announced through the closed door.

'Come in, Jack. I've just this minute woken up.

What time is it?' Isabella called out sleepily.

Jack opened the door and looked across at Isabella. He could see that she had just woken. Her long dark hair was in an unruly tangle across her pillow, she was holding a sheet up over her breasts, and her legs protruded out from under the rumpled sheets. Jack could tell she had slept naked, and he was having trouble tearing his eyes away from her. Isabella Montinari was

210

beautiful and seemed to light up the room with her presence. Jack was suddenly painfully aware that he had very strong feelings for this woman. He felt a rush of confusion.

'Breakfast in bed, my lovely, but don't count on it again real soon.'

'You're sweet, Jack, but there was no need, really. I could have gotten my own a bit later.'

'You asked what time it is, my lady. It's just after eight. You enjoy your breakfast, and I will see you when you're decent,' Jack said, smiling awkwardly.

'Thank you anyway, Jack.' Isabella started to lift herself up onto her pillows.

Jack closed the door and made his way outside. He was painfully aware that he had strong feelings for the woman inside, but it was obvious she did not feel the same way. Just friends, she had said. He had to shake it off and concentrate on the job her father had asked him to do, to look after his daughter, and that is just what he intended to do. He shook his head in an effort to clear his thoughts and headed for the workshop building to see Bob Nugent.

'Morning, Jack. I hope you slept well.'

Jack turned and saw Jan Muller walking toward him with a smile on his face.

'If you or Isabella need anything, you only have to ask.' The station manager reached for Jack's hand.

'We're fine at the moment, Jan, just getting used to the place. It's a great setup you have here, mate.'

'Glad you like it, Jack. Well, I have work to do, so I'll see you a bit later on,' Muller replied pleasantly and headed off toward the irrigation paddocks.

Jack continued toward the workshop. When he was almost there, he could hear the crackle and fizz of a welder from somewhere inside the big building. He pushed open the heavy metal door just as Bob Nugent lifted his welding helmet.

'G'day there, Jack. Come on in, mate. This is where all the real bloody work takes place on this station.'

'So you say mate—so you say. She's a bit warm today, Bob.'

'Yep, it sure is, but we still haven't had too much rain, though.' Bob said as he tossed his helmet onto a cluttered workbench and reached for Jack's hand.

'It was pissing down on the way out here Bob. We were bloody lucky to get through some of the creek crossings. Then it just stopped as we got closer to the station.'

'Yeah, I could tell you had a bit of strife by the state of the bloody truck,' Bob said with a laugh. 'But you won't need to worry too much about that sort of thing when you take 'The Hippo' out, mate, let me tell you.'

'The Hippo?' So you've given it a name, then.' Jack looked around the huge workshop.

The station mechanic noticed Jack's curious expression. 'You'd better come and have a look, I reckon,'

Jack followed Bob to the rear of the workshop, where a large tarpaulin covered something quite high and long in the corner of the building. The mechanic pulled back the faded tarp.

'Here she is, Jack—'The Hippo,' he announced with a proud flourish.

Jack could now see why it had appeared so long. It was not just one vehicle, but two, and one of them was a trailer. A custom-built trailer with racks for equipment and holders for fuel and water cans neatly attached to the outside of its enclosed body. Jack could see by its rugged construction, it had been built specifically to go with the strange vehicle in front. Both of which had been painted a matching military green colour.

'Michael sent me the plans for the trailer and the car about six months ago, with detailed drawings to show me what he wanted, and this is it, Jack. Firstly, the trailer I built from the ground up. It's a fully waterproof set-up, complete with fuel and water drums on the outside, and on the inside, there are containers for most of the things you would need when you go bush.'

Bob opened one of the trailer doors and watched Jack's amazed expression. 'There's a slide-out cooker, a small stainless sink, and rolled up inside, is a collection of top-quality military tents and tarps that Michael sent up as well.' Bob continued walking around the trailer, opening doors and sliding out cleverly made compartments. 'The vehicle at the front here is a Citroen P17 half-track. It arrived here brand new in a bloody great wooden crate, shipped all the way from Paris, France. It was built a couple of years ago and is basically the same as one a team of Frenchmen drove halfway around the world a while back. I believe it made quite a splash in the news back then. My instructions were to cut off the roof and add enough seating for six people, along with a removable canvas top and roll-up side curtains. As far as major mechanical changes, there are very few. I have made and installed an extra fuel tank with tapware on the dashboard to change over from one to the other. On the outside, as you can see, I've attached special brackets to hold more water and fuel cans than you will ever need, and inside you will find a compartment that contains a full kit of tools, along with jacks, ropes, and recovery gear.'

'Wow, she's a beauty, Bob. You have done some really great work, and I like the name tag across the bonnet, 'The Hippo,' Jack replied.

'Well, it's an ugly-looking bloody thing if you ask me, and I reckon she could just about travel underwater, so the name seemed to fit.'

Jack was amazed at the work that had gone into the sturdy vehicle and its trailer. 'When did you get her finished?' he asked patting his open hand on the bonnet of the half-track.

'About two weeks ago. The boss here reckoned I was spending too much time on it, so I had to do a lot of it in my spare time. But she's finally bloody well finished.'

'What's he like, this Muller bloke?' Jack watched the station mechanic's face for a response.

'He's a bloody hard man, too bloody hard if you ask me. He hates the coloureds you know. He gives some of the boys here a hard time, let me tell you. I don't like the man at all. But he's the boss, and I guess I shouldn't be saying too much about him anyhow, Jack—if you know what I mean.'

'I'll keep it under my hat, mate. He looks a bad-tempered bugger.' Jack was fishing for information about Muller. He felt the same as the station mechanic; he did not like the man. There was something about Jan Muller he could not quite put his finger on, and it had begun to concern him.

'Watch him, mate—you watch him. There are a few things going on around here that worry some of us. I won't say no more, Jack. But just be careful while you're here, mate, he's a dangerous bastard, that one.'

Jack could see Bob was sorry he'd said some of the things he had, and that he wanted to say nothing more about the big South African, so he changed the subject.

'How about you and I take 'The Hippo' out for a bit of a trial run tomorrow morning?' Jack decided to get the subject back to the Citroen and all of the mechanic's obvious hard work.

'Love to, Jack. But the boss might not like it, mate, me out cruising around the station enjoying meself.'

'You leave that little detail to me. Is straight after breakfast all right with you?'

'All right then, sounds bloody good to me. I'll see you after breakfast in the morning then. And, Jack, don't go taking any notice of that idiot Steve.'

'He's all right, Bob. Just doing a bit of showing off in front of his mates, I reckon.' Jack reached for the mechanic's hand, shook it, and left the workshop to head back to the homestead.

After Jack had spoken to Jan Muller and had received his grudging approval, he and the station mechanic spent the next few days putting the half-track through its paces, getting to know its strengths and its weaknesses, and it seemed, after fairly rigorous testing in some of the wet areas south of Death Adder Dam, to have very few. The sturdy vehicle seemed tough and reliable, and the half-track drive at the rear of the vehicle was simply amazing over most surfaces. Its only weakness seemed to be that it was quite slow. A comfortable speed of around fifteen miles an hour was possible in open scrub country, and perhaps ten miles an hour through heavy going conditions. But it certainly seemed unstoppable, and both of them were extremely pleased with its performance, in particular, its ability to climb steep terrain.

On their final trial, they hitched up the trailer and took it for a run through the bush to test it as well, and after a few hours of travel through some fairly rough country, they stopped about ten miles out from the station and set up a temporary camp so that Jack could become familiar with all of the equipment. They found a comfortable campsite could be set up in no more than one hour, complete with a canvas shower, a canvas toilet, and a fully equipped kitchen set up on the side of the trailer under its very own canvas awning.

The two men erected a couple of the military sleeping tents and the large central tarp that was to cover the area between the sleeping tents in case of bad weather and were pleased with the outcome and the ease with which it could all be set in place. Jack retrieved the four bottles of beer he had wrapped in a blanket back at the station, and they sat in the comfortable camp chairs and christened 'The Hippo' as a great success with the warm beer.

Jack had enjoyed his few days working alongside the station mechanic checking the equipment and putting the half-track through its paces, and the two men quickly became good friends.

In the evenings, Jack dined with Isabella in the homestead. Most nights, after their meal, they would listen to music and talk for hours about each other's lives. Isabella relived her days in Paris with tales of the museums, the art galleries, and the sidewalk cafés. However, she carefully skirted around her time in the little flat above Alain's gallery on the *Rue Auber*. Jack relived his days with the old crocodile hunter, Dick McGregor, in Arnhem Land and some of the wild times he'd had on leave during the war, in places like Cairo, Port Said, and London. Much like Isabella, he skirted around the difficult memories, in particular, the hell that had been the Western Front.

While Jack and Bob were working on and testing the Citroen half-track, Isabella had spent her days painting some of the unique scenery around the station grounds. She had painted a wonderful scene of the home her father had built set among the bloated boab trees. The painting seemed to capture perfectly the feel and remoteness of the huge station. Her skillful use of colour and shadow had brought the home and the hot tropical atmosphere to life almost perfectly. On another morning, she had carried her easel and paints down to the dam and painted a wonderful scene of several resident whistling tree ducks landing out on the silvery surface just as the golden rays of the morning sun splashed across the cracked mud and out over the water. Her wonderful rendition of that early morning scene captured several of the sleek birds with their webbed feet flared down toward the waiting water and their wings pulling back at the air, while others had already settled and broken the mirror-like surface of the dam in an eruption of silvery ripples that radiated back to where the artist sat with her paints.

On another day, she'd painted a small simple work of the two Aboriginal women, Rosie and Pearl, sitting on their tiny verandah at the back of the kitchen. The two women were casually sipping on mugs of steaming tea, while their hand-rolled cigarettes sat smoking in a chipped ashtray between them.

This small but beautiful work was Jack's favourite. He was simply amazed by it when he first saw it. Isabella had portrayed the two women perfectly, the cheeky smiles on their shiny black faces, their dark unruly hair, and the faded colours of their homemade clothing as they sat sipping their tea and joking with her.

Jack had quickly come to realise that Isabella was an exceptional artist, and as each painting was completed, it was placed by the two of them on a long, open shelf in the homestead's great room to be admired daily by Jack and criticized constantly by Isabella.

After they had been at the station for several days, Isabella invited Santiago, Anna, and Golly to join them for a meal she'd decided to cook in the homestead kitchen. She told them all she had an announcement to make. Santiago and Anna were uncomfortable about the coming evening. They both knew they would feel out of place in the magnificent homestead. Isabella had seen this in their faces and had told them both she needed their help to prepare the meal, and this seemed to make all the difference.

The meal was a great success, a joint effort that the three cooks were very proud of, even if only one of them could understand the dish's name. *Boeuf en Croute*, Isabella had explained, was simply succulent fillet steak wrapped in a casing of pastry and served with a red wine sauce, along with Santiago's runner beans and sweet, honeyed carrots.

'Well, that was just as nice as any meal I have eaten in the restaurants of Paris, even if I do say so myself,' Isabella proclaimed proudly. 'Thank you, Santiago and Anna, for all your help. I believe it made all the difference.'

'Yep, the tastiest meat pie I've ever eaten. Sure beats the Melbourne pie-carts,' Jack commented as he cleaned up the remaining crumbs on his plate and gulped down a mouthful of his beer.

'Now, I'd like to make an announcement while you are all here this evening,' Isabella said.

The diners put down their knives and forks and watched Isabella's face, wondering what was coming.

'In two days' time, it will be Christmas, and I see no reason why we here at Cockatoo Creek Station can't have some sort of celebration like the rest of the world enjoys at this time of the year,' Isabella announced with a smile and watched their faces for a response.

'A party—sounds like a great idea,' Jack said encouragingly. The others at the table remained silent.

'I've brought quite a few things with me—ribbons, tinsel, and all sorts of little things. They are in one of the trunks in my room. Also, my father has given me some gifts he would like me to give out in appreciation for the work that is done on the station. Now, I believe we should start the day off with Christmas breakfast in the station dining room. Santiago could cook up his famous pancakes and whatever else he can think of. Now, tell me, what does everyone think about the idea?' Isabella watched everyone's faces, and except for Jack, the others looked very surprised and a little embarrassed.

Santiago looked at Anna and Golly and then back to Isabella, and said quietly, 'Miss Izzy, are you sure you should be giving us gifts? We love you very much, but we are just workers on your father's station and no more than that. In any case, the boss won't like it—you giving gifts to the coloureds.'

Isabella's face flushed with annoyance. 'Santiago, you are a sweet man, but when I tell you that you are my friend, that is exactly what I mean. You are all more to me than employees, and you are to my father as well. If my father would like to show a little appreciation to you all, then that is what shall be done, and that is an end to it. Mr Jan Muller has absolutely no say in the matter. Also, Santiago, coloureds is not a word I am comfortable with at all, my friend,' she replied with a firm tone.

'All right then, Miss Izzy, if you are sure it will be all right. But can we help you with things?' A smile was beginning to form on the old cook's wrinkled face.

'I'm counting on it. Now, here is what I have in mind. . .'

They all listened attentively as Isabella went on, telling them some of her ideas for Christmas Day.

Two days later when Santiago's old metal pipe clanged to announce breakfast. The dining room was already full of station employees. Even Jan Muller, who had been more than a little reluctant when invited, was seated at one of the tables. He had grudgingly agreed to attend only when Isabella had insisted he come. After all, she had suggested to him, he was the station manager and it was only proper that he be there.

The dining room was ablaze with decorations. There were carefully twisted paper ribbons in a rainbow of colours attached to the iron walls. Balloons tied in clusters to the rafters and glittering silver and gold ropes of tinsel paper hung above the tables. Christmas cards, lovingly designed by Rosie and Pearl with paints supplied by Isabella, were attached to the walls with drawing pins, and at the far end of the long room, Isabella had hurriedly painted a striking picture of snow-clad mountains, below which, neatly painted words proclaimed, 'Merry Christmas to all at Cockatoo Creek Station for 1932.'

Jack and Isabella stood together and watched the station workers filling their plates with the hot pancakes, honey, and canned strawberries that Santiago had opened as a special treat. The long room was a riot of celebration. Plates clattered onto tables and stools were being dragged across the worn timber floor, and everyone seemed to be talking at once, when suddenly, there was the sharp crack from a shotgun blast from somewhere close by. The rowdy diners stopped what they'd been doing and the room was suddenly quiet. Several men went over to the big window that looked out onto the homestead grounds. Santiago and Anna put down their serving utensils and came out from behind the counter and stood next to Isabella and Jack with knowing smiles on their faces.

Down between the boab trees on the well-worn track that led into the homestead grounds, Henry and Wooloo were seated on their creaking old buckboard making their way toward the dining room. In the back, wearing a hurriedly made red suit and a not-so-real-looking white beard was Beans seated on an empty beer crate with a bulging feed sack draped over his shoulder. The buckboard was still quite a way off but they could all hear him clearly.

'Ho, ho, ho! A Merry Christmas to you all!' he bellowed, a wide grin on his black face.

The dining room erupted in instantaneous applause. Only Jan Muller seemed to take offence, and his distaste was plainly evident to anyone who looked at him.

'A black Santa—shit—that's just not right!' he whispered sarcastically. Fortunately, the cheering drowned him out, and even though no one noticed, when he lifted his mug of tea to his mouth, his hand was shaking with anger.

A few moments later, the old buckboard came to a halt outside the dining room, and Beans climbed down. The portly stockman adjusted his beard, hefted the bulging feed sack up onto his shoulder and made his way inside, followed closely by the smiling windmill boys.

'Ho, ho, ho! A very Merry Christmas to you all!' he cackled as he headed for Isabella's table. 'Now then—have you all been good girls and boys?' When he finally made it through the cheering crowd, he put the heavy feed sack on the table in front of Isabella and gave her a courteous bow. Then he took off his beard and hat to more good-natured applause and made his way back to where Henry and Wooloo were waiting next to one of the long tables.

Isabella slid the bag across the table to have it comfortably in front of her, and when the laughter and clapping finally subsided, she began to speak.

'Good morning and a very Merry Christmas to you all. I do hope you have all enjoyed your breakfast and Santa's surprise visit. Sorry about the gunshot, that was Jack's idea. But it seemed the only way to get everyone's attention.' She smiled and waited for more cheering and clapping to stop and then continued, 'I speak to you all on behalf of my father, and myself when I say that both he and I wish you all a Merry Christmas and a Happy New Year. My father has asked me to thank you all for your hard work during the past year, and to tell you that it is certainly appreciated. Now, I have a few gifts for you all to celebrate the day. They are only small gifts, as I certainly did not have a great deal of room in my luggage when I travelled up here.' Once again, everyone burst into good-natured applause.

Isabella put her hands inside the feed sack and began by pulling out a large cardboard box. 'Firstly, my father has given me this box, which contains two new western movies to give to you all. One of them, I believe is, 'Under a Texas Moon.' with Myrna Loy. I have been told it is very good. Anyway, I hope you enjoy them both.' Isabella pushed the box containing the movies to one side amid more clapping and cheering and began removing small gift-wrapped parcels from the bag. 'Now, ladies first, of course—would Anna, Rosie, and Pearl like to come up to receive their gifts?'

The three coloured women made their way through the crowd toward Isabella with shy, embarrassed expressions on their faces, all of them glancing nervously at Jan Muller as they made their way forward. They took their gifts, thanked Isabella quietly, and went back to where they had been standing.

'Now, I have a small gift for Jan, our station manager, to thank him for all his hard work during the year.' Isabella took out a gift-wrapped box and held it in her hand while an embarrassed and annoyed Jan Muller made his way forward.

A couple of the stockmen started clapping to break the silence, a moment or two later, some of the others joined in.

Eventually, all of the gifts were given out to the station employees. Each had been carefully wrapped, and each had a name tag attached to it. The male workers on the station, both black and white, were given a beautifully made leather belt with an oval buckle that had been made in Melbourne by a highly skilled leather craftsman under careful instruction and a design brief from Michael Montinari. The oval buckle was engraved with a set of bull's horns across its centre and the words *Cockatoo Creek*

*Station* at its top and the year *1932* at the bottom. With each of these gifts, there was a simple Christmas card and a crisp new, one-pound note folded neatly inside. Both Rosie and Pearl were given a box that contained a bottle of reasonable quality perfume and a ream of coloured cotton material, along with a card and a crisp one-pound note. Because Isabella had not known Anna had been employed at the station, she had hurriedly put one of her own bottles of *'Vol de Nuit'* perfume in a box along with a card, a folded pound note, and a ream of brightly coloured cotton cloth.

Jan Muller received a beautifully bound book on Africa with a card that contained a crisp, new ten-pound note. Santiago was given a belt, the same as the others, but because Isabella knew that the old man did such a wonderful job in the kitchen and worked such long hours, she had added a beautiful, leather-bound bible and a small book on gardening called *A Chef's Garden.*

The day was a great success. Isabella had earlier instructed Santiago to bring out six crates of beer and to get them chilled for the day's celebrations and later in the day, the movie projector was set up outside the dining room for everyone to enjoy the first of the new movies.

Jack and Isabella stayed to watch the movie and managed to sit all the way through it, even though they could never hear much of what was being said because of the cheering and good-natured fun going on around them.

While everyone was watching the flickering movie through the clouds of cigarette smoke, Isabella noticed Anna and Dan curled up on a blanket at the back of the crowd with their eyes glued to the screen. She nudged Jack and pointed to the two young lovers. Jack smiled knowingly and turned back to the ensuing gun battle on the screen.

When the movie finally ended, Jack and Isabella waved goodnight to the crowd of revellers, took their chairs and empty glasses back into the dining room and made their way across the grounds toward the homestead.

'Isabella, I have to tell you, I feel bad,' Jack admitted with a concerned tone as they strolled through the well-maintained gardens.

'Why is that, Jack?' Isabella rubbed Jack's arm affectionately as they walked.

'I don't have a Christmas gift for you. I'm sorry, but if I had known about your little surprise party, I could have gotten you something nice in Geraldton.'

'Please don't concern yourself, Jack; I don't have anything for you either. The gifts were for our employees here at the station, just to show them they are appreciated, that is all. However, there is something for you from my father in the house. But you will just have to wait until we get inside,' She smiled mischievously at Jack and slapped his shoulder.

'What gift . . . ? Look, your father has helped me out so much already. I certainly didn't expect anything from him for Christmas,'

Once they were back in the homestead, Isabella took Jack by the hand and led him into the great room to the locked gun cabinet. 'My father has asked me to give you this card and to wish you a very Merry Christmas.' She handed Jack a sealed envelope that was addressed simply, To Jack Ballinger.

Jack opened the envelope and read the neatly written words on the inside of the card:

'To my very good friend, Jack Ballinger, I sincerely hope you are having a wonderful time at the station. I must say, I wish I was there with you both. Jack, I would like you to choose one of the firearms from the gun cabinet as a gift from me to you as an appreciation of our friendship. But, I do have one serious request for you Jack. Please look after my Isabella and see that no harm comes to her, my friend.

Merry Christmas to you both, and my best regards,

Michael M.'

Jack was speechless; each one of the firearms inside the glass cabinet was worth a small fortune. They were all hand-made and custom-built by some of the best gunsmiths in England and Germany. He looked at Isabella in disbelief. 'I don't know what to say, I really don't, Isabella.' Jack was suddenly struck short for words and quite embarrassed by the extraordinary act of generosity by Isabella's father.

'Can I read the card, Jack? That is if you don't mind?' Isabella asked her voice hushed, and a little mysterious.

'Of course, you can.' Jack handed her the card.

'My father is a very generous man to those who mean a lot to him, Jack, and it seems that you certainly are one of them. But I do see there are instructions on the card as well.'

'What do you mean?' Jack suddenly thought he must have missed something, something important.

'You have to look after me, Jack.' Isabella stood very close to Jack as she read aloud the neatly written words on the card. *Please look after my Isabella. . . '*

'And that's what I intend to do. No harm will come to you, I assure you.'

'Come with me, Jack Ballinger.' Isabella took Jack by the hand and led him along the dark hallway to her bedroom and pushed open the door.

'B-but . . . I thought!' Jack stammered, finally understanding what this had all been about.

Isabella put her arms around Jack's neck and pulled him down so she could kiss him. 'I have grown very fond of you, Jack Ballinger, my brave protector, and tonight, I need looking after.'

'And I have certainly grown very fond of you, Isabella Montinari. Now, just what sort of looking after did you have in mind?' Jack said with a playful laugh.

'Shut up and make love to me, Jack. I think I've wanted this since I first saw you on the Geraldton docks. I'm sorry about all the mixed signals.'

'I guess you just needed a bit of time to find out what a great guy I am.'

'Please shut up, Jack.'

Jack put his arms around Isabella, picked her up and carried her across to the bed. 'I've wanted you from the very first as well my love.' He reached down and tried to undo the tiny buttons on Isabella's blouse.

'Let me, Jack, you'll break something.' Isabella took Jack's big hands away from the flimsy material and pushed them to his sides. Jack watched breathlessly as Isabella undressed, and when she'd finished she turned to face him. Moonlight filtered into the room through the French doors and washed over her naked body.

'You are beautiful, Isabella, truly beautiful.' Jack had begun to think he had died and gone to heaven as the woman bathed in the moonlight, reached for him and drew him into her body.

Isabella took both of Jack's big hands in hers, lifted them to her mouth, kissed his fingers lovingly and lowered them to her breasts and began undoing his shirt. '

Jack bent forward and kissed her perfect breasts. 'I want you my darling, so much it hurts.'

Jack felt Isabella reach for his belt buckle. He lifted her face to his and kissed each of her cheeks. 'Let me,' he whispered. He quickly removed the last of his clothing and tossed them toward a nearby chair, the belt missing its target by a wide mark and the buckle clattering noisily against the wall.

'This is a Christmas I'll never forget my darling,' He whispered, he reached for Isabella and they fell back onto the bed, locked in a passionate embrace.

'Oh, Jack—Jack—I love you.' Isabella guided Jack between her open legs and locked her arms around his mutilated back.

Jack felt no pain from the embrace, only joy. He was holding the woman he had loved from the very first time he had seen her. 'Isabella—my Isabella, I love you.' he murmured.

They made love—urgent, passionate love. When it was finally over, they were like two spent athletes, both of them exhausted and overwhelmed by the intensity of their lovemaking. They fell back onto the pillows, both silent for some time, wondering what the future held for them, the only sound in the room the steady hum of the slowly spinning ceiling fan.

Isabella reached for one of Jack's hands. 'My God, Jack, I almost fainted. I do love you, my darling.'

'And I love you,' Jack whispered and pushed his arm under Isabella's naked body and pulled her to him once again.

The following morning, Isabella was woken by the screeching of cockatoos from somewhere outside. She turned on her side and pulled the sheet up over her naked body to cover herself from the cool breeze of the slowly turning fan. She smiled as she remembered the night before and their lovemaking. She turned to curl up against Jack, only to discover he was not there. She reached out and felt the bed, still warm from his body. She lay there for a while, reliving the night before, remembering how wonderful it had been. 'Where was he? Where could he have gone?' she wondered, and then she heard the creaking of a cabinet door being opened. She threw the sheet back and got up. She knew exactly where he was.

Jack had tried to open the glass door to the gun cabinet as quietly as possible, cursing softly when he heard the creak of the brass hinges. From the display of firearms in front of him, there was only one weapon he wanted to lift out and heft for balance. He swung the door open and reached for it, lifted it out, and went back to sit on one of the leather chairs in the centre of the room. The firearm he held in his hands was a thing of rare beauty, a Westley Richards .375 Nitro Express, double rifle. To Jack, it was the perfect weapon for dangerous game and a testament to the gun maker's craft. He stood up and began to lift it to his shoulder and at that very moment, he heard the sound of a woman's voice from somewhere behind him.

'What's it going to be, Jack Ballinger—the firearm or me?'

Jack turned to see Isabella, naked, with a smile on her face and her hands on her hips, waiting for an answer. He hurriedly put the rifle back in the cabinet, closed the glass doors, and walked across the room to the woman he loved, the very beautiful, but somewhat impatient Isabella Montinari.

'You were sleeping—I just thought I'd take a quick look. I was coming straight back, I swear.' Jack smiled lovingly at Isabella and took her in his arms.

They made love on one of the huge cattle skins that were strewn across the polished floorboards just as the sun's early morning rays began to filter through the windows, lighting the room with a soft golden haze. This time they made love quietly, affectionately. Kissing and touching each other as if in some form of religious wonderment, until finally, exhausted, both of them fell asleep in each other's arms on the skin-covered floor.

They spent most of that day in the homestead, either making love or laying together and talking about their coming trip into the wild bush country.

In the afternoon, when Isabella went to the kitchen to get them both something to eat, Jack went back to the gun cabinet to pull out the double rifle and marvel at it again. This time he sat on the huge leather couch in the centre of the great room with it across his legs and looked almost reverently at its classic shape and the beautifully figured French walnut stock. His fingers traced the superb engraving on the action, of a cape buffalo and a snarling lion, each surrounded by delicate flowing scrolls and tiny teardrops of pure gold that enhanced the exquisite example of the master engraver's art. He stood up and hefted the rifle to his shoulder. His eye cast perfectly along the centre of the two barrels to the white ivory foresight. He smiled and carried it back to the gun cabinet. He was still, simply overwhelmed by his good friend's generosity.

# 25

# A Meeting

That afternoon, Jack and Isabella decided they would have their evening meal with the stockmen in the dining room. Isabella had asked Jan Muller to join them, as she needed him to be present in regard to some important matters she wished to bring to his attention. They had decided now that Jack was familiar with 'The Hippo' and all the testing had been done, they would head off on their safari into the bush sometime after breakfast the following day.

Jack had spoken to Santiago and Anna at breakfast and asked the two of them if they would join them in the dining room that evening after they had finished their work. Isabella had spoken to Golly and asked him to join them as well. When Jan Muller was invited, he'd grudgingly agreed, but he was not happy about eating in the same room as the coloureds. He had been thinking of asking Santiago to send Anna over to his cottage for another visit. But now that would have to wait. He knew he was getting careless, but the native girl had been a tasty diversion that he had enjoyed. She hadn't run away after he had had his way with her in his wash-house, and he was fairly certain she had kept her mouth shut. Perhaps she had enjoyed their bit of fun just as much as he had. But he couldn't be sure. He reasoned that, once the spoilt Montinari woman and her chaperone were away on their little excursion into the bush, he would instruct Santiago to send her to him again.

The dining room was fairly quiet when Isabella and Jack arrived, even though almost all of the station hands were present. Jack imagined that most of them were probably still suffering the effects of hangovers from the celebrations of the day before. As they looked around the room, they noticed Jan Muller sitting alone at a long table near the back of the room. They went across to join him.

'Good evening, Jan, glad you could join us,' Isabella said warmly.

'My pleasure, Isabella, I'm glad to be able to help,' Muller replied politely, his pleasant smile masking his annoyance.

'Good to see you again, Jan,' Jack said. He greeted Muller with a handshake and turned to Isabella. 'Would you like me to get us both a meal, Isabella? It looks like beef casserole if I'm not mistaken.'

'That would be nice, Jack, and a mug of tea, if you don't mind.' Isabella sat down across the table from the station manager.

The three of them ate their meals quietly, broken only occasionally with small talk about the day-to-day running of the station and Jack explaining to Muller how well the half-track had performed during their tests and thanking him for allowing Bob to spend some time with him. Later, when they had finished their meal and were enjoying their mugs of tea, Santiago, Anna, and Golly joined them. Muller was both surprised and annoyed that the coloureds were joining them, and even though he said nothing, it showed on his face.

'Well, I'm glad you could all make it for our little meeting. Please sit down, and I will try to be as brief as I can,' Isabella smiled warmly as she greeted them all.

'If we can help with anything, Miss Izzy, you only have to ask,' Golly replied earnestly as he sat down.

Anna and Santiago sat together, taking silent comfort from each other, both of them feeling very uneasy being so close to Jan Muller.

Anna hated the big white man and felt a terrible fear being so close to him again. The memory of her night in his wash-house had rushed back to her when she first looked at him. She'd tried desperately to force it from her mind. But now, like a nightmare, she was there again, bent naked, over his wash-house chair, the stench of his rum breath on her body, his knees between her legs, riding her, hurting her with his savagery. She shivered and closed her eyes and tried to force the horror of that night from her mind and concentrate. When she opened them again, Muller was staring at her, and to her horror, he was smiling!

'How can we help, Isabella?' Muller asked politely, turning his attention back to Isabella.

Isabella put down her tea mug. 'Well, Jack and I have decided that tomorrow, before lunch, we are going to head off on our camping trip for a few weeks. Jan, I believe that you were told by my father we may want to take some help with us, so I wanted to let you know what we have decided.' Isabella looked around the table to see that she had everyone's attention. 'Firstly, because Golly knows the country quite well, we'd like him to act as our guide and be an important part of our team.'

Everyone turned to Golly. 'Thank you, Miss Izzy. Yes, I know some of the country quite well, but not all of it, But if that is what you've decided then I will be glad to be your guide, and I will do my best for you,' Golly replied, smiling gratefully at Isabella and glancing nervously at Jan Muller.

'And, because I would like to have a female companion along with us. Anna, I would like you to come as well. You can help me with the cooking and act as my assistant and companion on the trip.' Isabella smiled at Anna.

'No, that will not be possible. Anna is needed here to help in the kitchen.' Muller said suddenly, surprising Jack and Isabella with his interjection.

'I can manage here easily, Boss. I really don't mind at all,' Santiago said nervously. He looked at Isabella and then back to the station manager.

'She is staying here to help you, Santiago, and that is final. I am the manager of this station, and what I say goes. I'm sorry

Isabella, but the station workers are my concern. Anna is needed here, and she will stay.'

'I don't think you should interrupt, Jan. Please let Isabella finish what she has to say,' Jack said quietly, looking directly at Jan Muller.

'Thank you, Jack. Now, there is one more person I would like to have come with us as well. Someone who can help us with the tents and camp gear and that is young Dan Miller. Dan is a learner here on the station, and I am sure you can do without him for a few weeks, Jan,' Isabella said pleasantly.

'You can take Dan—that's fine with me—but not Anna. I'm sorry, but she is needed here,' Muller replied sharply. He was beginning to feel annoyed that the spoilt bitch seemed to have taken no notice of him at all.

'Please do not interrupt again, Jan. I'm sure Isabella will address your concerns in a moment,' Jack said again, this time a little louder and nodded for Isabella to continue.

Santiago and Anna were beginning to panic. They both knew what was likely to happen once Isabella and her party left the station. But it seemed as if there was little hope of her going with them if the station manager were to have his way.

'It's all right, Jack. Now, Jan, with respect to your refusal in regard to Anna coming with us. . . '

'I'm sorry, Isabella, but the station employees are my concern,' Muller interrupted again, smiling briefly at Anna.

'Jan, perhaps I should clear up a few things for you. You certainly are the manager of this station, and I believe you do a very competent job. But there is something you should be made aware of. Firstly, you may or may not know, the lease on this station is held and owned by Pegasus Pastoral Holdings, a subsidiary of the Montinari group of companies. Pegasus is jointly owned, in equal parts, by my father and me. This has always been the case since the lease was first purchased by my father some years ago. It was not my intention to have to bring this up, but I suppose it now needs to be said. I must add, Jan, that my father and I are more than happy with your work here at the station and we realise you have worked very hard at being the manager.

However, I feel I need to bring some finality to this discussion, and so I will say again. Anna will be coming with us—and that, Jan, is final. If you do not agree and feel you have been treated poorly, I will accept your resignation immediately. That is, should you feel the need to take such action? Of course, I'll contact my father as soon as I am able in regard to that unfortunate outcome, should it become necessary,' Isabella replied. She took a sip of her tea, put her mug down, folded her arms, and waited for Muller to reply.

'Well, I—I don't suppose it's really that important. I guess Santiago will be all right. I was just thinking of him and all the work he has to do. I don't know if you are aware, but I was the one who hired Anna because I felt he needed help. But yes—she can go, that's fine,' Muller replied.

Jan Muller was beginning to have trouble with his words. He had no idea the rich bitch had anything to do with the station at all, and he certainly was not aware she was a part owner. There seemed to be little he could say or do about it now. But he was seething with anger inside.

'Well, that's all settled then.' Isabella nodded her confirmation to Muller. 'I wonder if someone could tell Dan we would like him to come along with us as well.' Isabella looked across at Anna's now visibly relieved face.

'I can let him know in a few minutes if that's all right,' Anna replied. She gave Isabella a happy smile. She had seen Isabella looking across at her and Dan the night before at the picture show.

'Thanks, Anna that would be great. Just one more thing: each person coming with us is to pack a small bag of clothing and toiletries, the rest we will have on board, and I sincerely hope that everyone who comes with us will enjoy our trip into the bush.' Isabella stood up and turned to Jack. 'I think we can go now.'

The first to get up were Santiago and Anna. Both of them were smiling as they left the table and headed back into the kitchen. Golly rushed off to the bunk-house in a big hurry to pack his bag. He had never been so happy.

Jan Muller never said another word. But he was angry, and he was beginning to have trouble hiding it. He hurried out of the dining room and headed back to his cottage. He needed a shot of rum, desperately.

'Santiago, what are toiletries?' Anna asked as she and Santiago put on their aprons to start the dishes.

'Just some soap, a toothbrush, and bits and pieces. You will need a small bag as well, but don't worry, after we have finished with the dishes, I'll get my old kitbag from my room for you to take. You had better talk to Rosie and Pearl about what women's things you may need as well,' the old cook replied. 'I told you that Isabella would like you. Now you will be safe, my sweet, and when you are ready, you can tell her what the boss did to you that night in his washhouse.'

'I will speak to her when the time is right. Perhaps some time when we are alone together. But, Santiago, I don't want to ruin her trip for her just yet so I will wait for a little while.'

'She is wise, Anna. She will tell you what must be done.' Santiago picked up a huge pot and pushed it under the soapy water.

'Santiago, I could not understand a lot of what Isabella spoke about. There is still much I have to learn about the white man's words.' She began scraping the plates.

'I am not much better, my dear. However, it seems the boss must take very serious notice of what Isabella tells him from now on, and I don't think he is very happy about it at all,' Santiago replied. The old man was overjoyed with the outcome of the meeting. Now he knew that for a time, his Anna would be safe.

# 26

# Going Bush

The following morning, at a little after ten, all of the excited travellers were on board the half-track, trying to make themselves comfortable in the rudimentary confines of the sturdy vehicle. Anna sat smiling in the centre of the rear seat with Dan on one side of her and Golly on the other, while Jack and Isabella were in the front, with Jack at the wheel listening to last-minute instructions from Bob Nugent.

'Look after her, Jack. I put a hell of a lot of work into this machine, one way or another,' Bob instructed and patted the driver's door as a parting gesture.

'Bob, thanks for everything you have done, mate. We'll have a beer together when we get back.' Jack gave the Citroen a tickle on the accelerator and smiled across at Isabella.

'Goodbye, Bob, and thank you for making such an effort with the vehicle and the trailer, it is certainly appreciated,' Isabella added and waved her goodbye above the revving of the Citroen's engine.

Jan Muller had given all the hands their daily work much earlier that morning and had taken his horse down to the irrigated paddocks with some of the stockmen so he would not have to watch them leave and wish them well. He was still very annoyed that they were taking Anna with them. For now, he had lost his nubile princess. But, he reasoned, when she returned and that annoying spoilt bitch finally decided to leave the station, things would return to normal.

There was no-one else to see them off, so Jack pushed the gear lever into first, checked the gauges one last time, and let out the clutch. He turned the half-track away from the big workshop. They were on their way.

'Hold on, Jack—that's Santiago back there, running down to say goodbye, I reckon!' Golly yelled from the back seat.

Jack stopped the 'The Hippo', pulled up the hand brake, and they sat there while the old cook ran down to them.

'Sorry you had to stop,' Santiago said breathlessly, 'I just wanted to say goodbye to you all and wish you a safe trip. I hope you all have a really wonderful time. Thank you for taking Anna with you, Isabella. She will be safe now that she is with you. Goodbye, and please be careful out there.' The old man reached across Golly and put his skinny arms around Anna and hugged her awkwardly. 'Goodbye, my sweet Anna. Perhaps if you are a lucky girl, you might see your old grandfather out bush somewhere.' He kissed her on the cheek and stood back to let them leave and waved as they pulled away.

There were tears in both Anna's and Santiago's eyes as they drove off and everyone had seen them. Isabella had a sudden feeling there was some hidden secret between the old cook and the young native girl, and she began to wish she knew what it was. Something was not right, and she wondered if it had anything to do with Jan Muller. She was still puzzled by his behavior the night before when she had insisted Anna was to join them on their trip.

Jack turned 'The Hippo' down the slope that led away from the homestead and headed out through the stunted scrubland that surrounded it. For the first hour, they followed a well-worn horse track that led away from the station, and then he turned the slow-moving vehicle toward the northeast. They planned to travel up the eastern side of the station toward the rocky hill country, where the tributaries of the Drysdale and Berkley Rivers begin to work their way down out of the hills. Once there, they would look for suitable passage toward the Prince Regent River. Jack hoped that when they reached that river, they'd be able to follow it as it wound its way toward the sea.

Golly had travelled through a lot of the station country during the years he had been at Cockatoo Creek, but when he and Jack had first studied the map Jack had found in the homestead library, he had explained that once they reached the Drysdale River, that was as far as he had travelled. While the two of them sat pondering over the map, Jack noticed huge areas seemed incomplete, and as his fingers traced the spidery course of one of the many rivers that headed toward the coast, he noticed the word *unknown* written across large areas of the map. Golly had explained that he knew very little about the wild lands farther to the north and told Jack that once the savannah country ended and the steeper hill country began, that was as far as the station ran cattle. The country from there on, he explained, was far too wild to successfully run and muster cattle.

They travelled for about five hours on their first day away from the homestead, passing through a lot of open country visibly suffering the effects of the long dry spell. The little grass that had grown from the occasional rainstorms, had withered and died, and most of the small creeks they passed were powder dry. But the air was thick and humid with the promise of rain, and the sky was dark with low, slow-moving rain clouds rolling above them.

Late in the afternoon, they reached a long, dry billabong. Boab trees of varying shapes and sizes lined its desiccated, red earth banks. Isabella seemed suddenly excited when she looked along the now dry waterhole with its bulbous trees standing silent sentinel on each of its dusty banks. Some of the strangely shaped trees were young, with thin vase-like trunks while others were huge and bloated, looking almost as if they had been the villains that had sucked the dusty billabong dry. Jack slowed and turned toward the dry watercourse just as a huge wedge-tailed eagle lifted clumsily up out of the sandy bottom, leaving behind the dried remains of a small kangaroo. A pair of crows that had been waiting patiently in a nearby tree took to the air, startled by the huge bird as it flapped noisily past, their melancholy calls echoing across the lonely landscape.

'What a wild and beautiful scene, Jack. Can we camp here for the night?' Isabella pointed excitedly along the dry billabong.

'Okay then, but we'll set up camp away from the trees a bit. By the look of that sky, there might be a bit of lightning later on.' Jack swung the half-track away from the line of boab trees and headed for a small dusty clearing he had noticed among some spindly acacia trees.

On their first night away, it took them a little over an hour to set up their camp, and when they'd finished, they were all very pleased with the outcome. Isabella could not believe how comfortable it all was, and she was simply amazed at how much equipment was packed into the camp trailer. The two small tents that were to serve as the camp toilet and shower really intrigued her. When she saw the shower tent erected complete with its folding table, hand basin, and shower enclosure, she unzipped the canvas door and peered inside.

'This is amazing, Jack, it looks like Bob has thought of everything,' she said excitedly and reached up to pat the five-gallon drum that Jack had just set on its stand above the shower rose.

The big tarpaulin was strung up on ropes with its centre raised to take away any rain should it fall, and a folding metal table was placed in the centre, along with camp chairs for each of them. A small canvas annexe was quickly attached to the trailer with thin metal posts and rope strainers and the slide-out kitchen was set in place, along with a small metal table for food preparation.

Jack retrieved a purpose-built three-piece metal stand from the trailer so they would have a place to hang their canvas water bags. These were then filled and hung in place to cool. In a separate, carefully packed wooden box, there were cans of fruit and packs of salt, sugar, and flour. Santiago had packed them a good supply of bacon and dried beef that could be cut up and mixed with the vegetables for a tasty stew. But as time went by, they would need to shoot kangaroo or wild pig if they were to continue to enjoy fresh meat on a regular basis.

Their first meal away from the station was a great success. The two women cooked up a casserole from the small supply of fresh beef Santiago had given them. This was the only fresh meat they had with them, and they knew it had to be used, as it would soon spoil in the heat. Anna and Isabella cut it into small pieces, added onions, and potatoes, and seared it in one of the camp ovens. When it was almost cooked, they added water and seasoning and pushed it back into the coals to wait for it to finish. The men congratulated them on their casseroled beef. It was both tender and tasty, and they mopped at their plates with pieces of damper to soak up the last of it.

'Best stew I think I've ever eaten.' Jack raised his mug of tea to the cooks in salute.

'Thank you, Jack. It was a joint effort, wasn't it, Anna? But that will be the last fresh meat we'll be having until someone bags a kangaroo, or maybe a nice young wild pig,' Isabella replied, smiling at Anna.

'Yes, it tasted nice, but it was just a stew, really, and not as nice as Santiago's.' Anna was feeling a little embarrassed by the attention.

'Jack, I'd like to spend a few hours in the morning with my paints and work on that wonderful scene of the boab trees along that dry billabong over there. Anna could stay with me, and you men could do a little hunting if you wanted to.' Isabella sipped her tea and watched Jack's face to see what he thought.

'Yep, that sounds like a good idea. We'll head off in the morning for a scout around and see what's about the place,' he replied and added. 'In that case, I guess we should stay here tomorrow night as well. That way we won't be packing up camp in the middle of the day when it's hot.'

'That should be fine, Jack. I don't think we are in any hurry. Let's just take our time and enjoy ourselves,' Isabella agreed and wrapped her hands around her mug of tea and stared into the coals of their fire.

They sat around their campfire until quite late that first night and talked excitedly about the wild country that lay ahead. Golly explained that as they got closer to the coast, the country was mostly unexplored by white men. He told them most of the rivers and billabongs were home to saltwater crocodiles and that some of them could grow to over twenty feet in length and were extremely dangerous.

He warned that they had been known to take the occasional unwary stockman and that even horses had been attacked and dragged into the water by these monsters. In the heavy bush areas along the waterways, he told them they would need to be wary of the old boars that lived in the tunnels they made among the dense bush.

Finally, when their discussions came to an end and they were to go off to their tents, there seemed to be some confusion among them. Isabella went off to her tent alone after saying goodnight to everyone, including Jack. Golly and Dan sauntered off to their appointed tents, and Anna went to hers, feeling very confused about the sleeping arrangements. However, less than fifteen minutes later, Jack sneaked across the big central awning and slipped quietly into Isabella's tent, and a few minutes after that, Anna made her way past Golly's to join Dan.

'That took you long enough. Come here, you,' Isabella purred as Jack undressed and slipped into the bedroll next to her naked body.

'Sorry, my sweet, but I wasn't sure if you wanted everyone to know about us just yet.'

'I don't really care what they think. I love you, Jack, and they might just as well know it.'

'I'll bet Anna is in with Dan by now as well,' Jack murmured as he kissed Isabella's neck and put his arms around her.

The following morning, Golly was the first to leave his tent. The stockman set about getting their campfire going with a few sticks that he quickly rounded up. A short while later, Anna came out of Dan's tent to join him at the fire. As soon as the fire burned down a little, she set about cooking up a huge breakfast of bacon, eggs, and tomatoes for them all. She retrieved a loaf of bread from the tuckerbox in the trailer, cut it into thick slices and filled the wire rack they were to use for toasting and put it aside to be ready for the coals as soon as Jack, Isabella, and Dan joined them.

Jack and Isabella woke to whisperings and the smell of bacon in the morning air and both of them were suddenly hungry. A short while later, Isabella emerged wearing a blue silk robe with a towel over her shoulder and headed for the shower, closely followed by a yawning Jack Ballinger, looking just a little sheepish. This was the first any of the others realised Jack and Isabella were lovers. But they all smiled approvingly as they made their way toward the bathroom tents.

Isabella stopped halfway, turned back to Jack, and kissed him on the cheek and smiled at the somewhat bewildered onlookers. 'Anna, I hope Dan doesn't snore as bad as this one does, my dear.'

Anna and Dan both blushed with embarrassment and they all laughed at the obvious comedy of it all.

'Hey, breakfast smells great, Anna. I hope there's plenty—I could eat a horse and chase the rider. I don't know about the rest of you,' Jack announced and followed Isabella into the shower cubicle.

'Same here, Jack,' Dan replied, still feeling a little embarrassed, but happy and somewhat relieved.

Before they had left the station, Jack had taken charge of loading the trailer and trying to fit their gear into the drawers and shelves inside. He had left one complete shelf empty and had gone back to the gun cabinet in the great room and taken out the Westley Richards, his gift from Isabella's father. He'd then selected a nice English Holloway twelve bore, double-barrelled shotgun from the rack and a custom-built .22 Hornet bolt-action rifle. The Hornet had been built by Gibbs of London using a shortened Mauser 98 action and was topped with a quality German, Heinsolt telescopic sight. For good measure, he had taken a holstered .44-calibre, Colt, long-barrelled revolver, and after searching through the cabinets for a while, found leather scabbards that fitted each of the firearms. In another cabinet, he found boxes of ammunition for every weapon that was on display in the gun cabinet. He took out several boxes for each of the weapons he had decided to take and a small metal box containing cleaning gear and gun oil. He'd then carried all of the weapons to the trailer and placed them on the shelf he'd set aside for the purpose and packed them carefully in blankets before closing the steel door to the compartment and pulling down the latches. Jack reasoned he would use the big double rifle for any dangerous game, while the twelve bore would be handy for wild duck and birds for the pot. The Hornet would be his general game rifle for meat hunting any small pigs and kangaroos. This smaller calibre would cause only minor damage to the meat, and because of its accuracy, would enable him to get clean kills at reasonable distances.

When they had finished their breakfast, Isabella and Anna set off for the dry billabong loaded with paints and boxes of brushes, a folding wooden easel, and two camp chairs. The sun was still low in the sky, and the weather was quite cool as they set off, both of them struggling with their loads. After they had said their goodbyes the three men went to the trailer. Jack unlatched the gun compartment and, satisfied that the tightly packed weapons had travelled well he slid the big double out of its scabbard and leaned it against the trailer, then the twelve bore, and finally, the Hornet and for each of these, he took ten cartridges from the ammunition boxes.

'Now, have either of you gentlemen fired a rifle before?' Jack asked his two hunting companions.

'No, Boss, not me, I'm too bloody scared of 'em,' Golly replied with a nervous grin.

'That's okay, Golly. In that case, you can be my gun bearer for the day, and carry the shotgun—and please, do not drop it.' Jack showed Golly how to carry the shotgun safely and gave him the ten shells to put in his pockets.

'Now, Dan, what about you?' Jack looked the lanky stockman up and down as he asked.

'Yep, I've done a bit on my dad's little farm down south. Just rabbits mainly, and that's about it. I used my dad's little old single shot .22,' Dan replied proudly.

'Well, that's better than nothing, my friend. You can carry the Hornet. But please look after it.' Jack slipped three shells into the Hornet's magazine and passed the remaining seven to Dan. He then slid two of the long .375 Nitro Express cartridges into the double, closed it, and pulled back the safety. The remaining cartridges went into the loops on his shirt and into his right-side trouser pocket. The three men then filled their canteens from one of the containers on the side of '*The Hippo*' slung them over their shoulders and headed off.

Jack had noticed a shaded band of trees near what he thought was probably a watercourse some distance away toward the west and they trudged off in that direction.

Less than an hour later, they reached the band of trees. A slight wind was blowing into their faces as they slipped into the heavy shade. They stood there for several minutes, while Jack decided which direction they should head. To their right, they could see a worn game trail that led through the dry bush, and to their left, a muddy waterhole about fifty yards across, where they noticed a good-sized flock of whistling tree duck. To the right of the waterhole, they could see a heavy thicket of dark green melaleuca and spinifex scrub running right up to the edge of the water. Tall bloodwoods grew along the edges of the waterhole and scattered among them were several magnificent livingstonia palms.

Jack spoke quietly to his companions. 'Golly, I'm going to swap the double rifle for the shotgun.' He turned to Dan. 'If we can get up close to the water by keeping to the cover of these trees and then those bushes near the water, I think we can get us a few ducks for dinner. What I'd like you to do, Dan is keep a lookout for any pigs or scrub bulls that may break out of that thick scrub and decide to have a go at us.' Jack pointed to the heavy cover just to the right of the water.

'Right-o, Jack, I'll keep a lookout. But it looks pretty quiet to me,' Dan remarked and unslung the Hornet.

Jack nodded to his companions, and they moved off toward the waterhole.

Golly was starting to feel nervous. The mention of wild pigs had sent a shiver through him. Many years earlier, he had seen a huge cornered boar charge into a pack of station dogs, disemboweling three of them before it finally disappeared back into its bush tunnel. So fast and furious was the attack on the dogs that it had left Golly terribly shaken. It was an experience he had never forgotten.

The three men moved through the scrub carefully, sticking to the heavy shade and watching the trees ahead in case there were any noisy birds to give away their approach. But all they could see were a few flying foxes sleeping silently in the trees above them. Slowly and cautiously, they drew nearer to the waterhole, until, finally, they were within easy range for the shotgun. Jack motioned for his two friends to stay in the cover of the trees, and keeping low, he made his way forward into the clump of melaleuca bush close to the water's edge. Out on the water, the whistling ducks were still happily bobbing about and cackling to one another, totally unaware of the hunter's approach.

When he was comfortable with the range, Jack lifted the twelve bore to his shoulder and pushed the safety forward to fire, but the faint metallic click alarmed the birds, and they took to the air in a whirring of wings. Jack cursed softly, swung the double after them and fired two quick shots, and they watched four plump birds career to the ground near the water's edge, leaving tiny clouds of pale green feathers floating in the morning air.

'Nice shot, Jack,' Golly whispered from behind.

Jack flipped open the shotgun and the spent shells sprang out on their ejectors. He reloaded, and they watched the remaining birds disappear through the trees.

Suddenly, Jack heard a crashing sound from somewhere to his left, the sound of something large tearing through the scrub. It was close—very close. Then, he heard something else, a grunting sound. He swung to his left. Less than fifty feet away, the melaleuca scrub was flying apart from the passage of something very large crashing through it. Something he couldn't yet see. Then he heard it again; the guttural grunting sound of an alarmed animal—a sound he knew only too well.

Jack also knew the danger that usually came with that sound. He raced back to Golly and snatched up the double rifle and thrust the shotgun at the surprised stockman. Golly looked confused but Jack lifted his hand to signal him to stay where he was and stepped out into the open just as a shot rang out. In an instant, Jack could see what was happening. Two huge wild boars had been sleeping in the bush only fifty feet from where they had been standing. The noise from the shotgun blasts reverberating through the trees had woken and confused them. They'd leaped to their feet and charged out from their tunnels in the bush and were heading for the safety of the distant trees. Fifty feet away and standing directly in their path was Dan, feverishly trying to work another cartridge into the Hornet.

Jack started to move sideways, searching for a clear shot just as both boars crashed out into the open and checked their stride. In that instant, both pigs saw the young stockman blocking their path, and with no hesitation, threw down their heads and charged straight at him. Jack kept moving sideways, as Dan fired at the lead boar for the second time, but the tiny bullet from the Hornet did little more than enrage it. It came on, moving even faster now and ripping its head up and down in savage anticipation as it raced toward the young stockman. Jack took another step to his left, searching for a clear shot, and threw up the double rifle. His eye settled down the centre of the two barrels and he swung toward the dark blur crashing through the bush toward his young friend. The lead boar was moving very fast now and grunting with annoyance from the small wound on the top of its head as it closed the last few feet to where Dan stood, still desperately trying to work another cartridge into the Hornet.

Jack swung the double past the nose of the old boar, led him by a few inches to compensate for the speed of the charge, and squeezed the trigger. The roar of the express rifle was deafening through the trees. The huge boar nose-dived into the dirt less than five feet from Dan's feet. The sudden noise of the shot slowed the second, equally large boar down for what was only a split second—and then he came on.

Jack swung the double back and fired the left barrel. The heavy bullet hit the second beast in the heart, the sheer shock of the impact killing it instantly. He ejected the spent shells, reloaded, and swung back toward the bush in case there were any more unwelcome visitors. But there were none. Satisfied, he threw the rifle across his right shoulder and headed for Dan.

'Thanks, Jack that was close. I thought I might have got him there for a minute, but he just kept coming, and I couldn't get another shell in the damn chamber. I guess I'm not too good with these repeating rifles. Dad's old thing was a single shot.' Dan leaned the little Hornet against a tree and reached out to shake Jack's hand in thanks.

'You held your ground, mate, and that takes guts. You just need some practice, that's all. I reckon I'll spend some time with you and see if we can get things right. Meanwhile, it looks like we're having wild duck for dinner tonight, so let's go and pick them up.'

'I guess these two old boars wouldn't be too damn tasty?' Dan remarked.

'You got that right. Now where the hell is Golly?'

The two men walked back to where Jack had left Golly behind some trees and found him sitting on the ground with the shotgun across his lap. The Aboriginal stockman was swaying from side to side and mumbling something neither of them could understand.

'Are you okay, Golly?' Jack reached down and patted the Aboriginal stockman on the shoulder.

'Geez, Boss that was too bloody close for comfort. That big old pig woulda buggered up Dan good and proper. And, Boss, I ain't ever seen shooting like that—not ever.'

'Just a good rifle, that's all—and Golly, you can call me Jack, mate. Jack will do me just fine.'

That night, they feasted on wild duck with the last of the bacon strapped across the breast of each bird and roasted in the camp ovens along with baked potatoes and carrots topped with gravy made in the bottom of one of the camp ovens. After they'd finished their meal, they sat around in their camp chairs, talking about their day. Golly could not contain himself and went into great detail about the day's hunt. While both Jack and Dan tried to play the whole episode down as much as they could. Jack could see that Anna was worried that something could easily have gone wrong, so he promised her he would show Dan how to use the firearms properly.

Isabella and Anna had spent most of their day in the shade of a huge boab tree with their paints, trying to capture the remote and lonely scene of the dry billabong lined with its sentinel trees that they had seen earlier. Isabella had given a small canvas to Anna and encouraged her to try her hand as well, and she had thoroughly enjoyed her first attempt at landscape painting and proudly passed her work around to nods of approval and words of encouragement while they sat sipping their mugs of tea. Isabella put her completed work of the dry creek scene in a wooden storage box, promising to show them all when she had finished several more. She explained that each of her works would hopefully compliment the other as a series. No one really understood what she meant, but they all smiled and nodded knowingly just the same.

The following morning they ate an early breakfast and set about dismantling their camp and were soon on their way. Jack had decided to take bearings on his compass before they left the camp. They were still heading northeast toward the Drysdale River and from there, they hoped to find a way through the ranges to the Prince Regent River and follow it as it made its way through the mostly unknown country on its way to the Timor Sea. All that day, they weaved their way through dry savannah country, passing thousands of Cockatoo Creek cattle, most of them in very poor condition and would probably die if decent rains did not come soon. As they continued across the dusty plains stunted with spiny spinifex and weeping paperbark, they passed two of the huge Simplex windmills, sloshing precious artesian water into their long metal troughs. The slowly spinning mills were surrounded by hundreds of the starving red cattle, while above; the sky was dark with rain clouds. But no rain would fall.

In the late afternoon, they came to a long, shaded billabong surrounded by trees of all shapes and sizes. Huge bloated boab trees grew alongside small acacias and lanky paperbarks, all fighting for position along its moist banks.

The billabong looked to be close to a mile long, and at the very least, two hundred yards wide along most of its length.

Strangely, they noticed there were no cattle to be seen near its dark shaded waters. Perhaps, they thought, because of the proximity of the two windmills they had passed earlier.

Most of the billabong was hidden from their view, but its size could be easily judged by the trees that crowded its muddy banks. Jack changed down a gear, and they wandered in among the trees, the half-track making easy work of the broken ground. It was strangely quiet, and the dark, almost black surface of the shaded water was still in the afternoon's heat. The edge of the billabong was lined with weeping pandanus palms and clumps of rice grass, making its surface indistinct, vague, and mysterious. The leaves of the pandanus and other weeping plants that grew along the water's muddy edge hung down in wild disarray, covering much of its dark, obscure interior. When the rains came, this massive billabong would probably grow to more than twice its size. But even now, it was still a considerable stretch of water.

As the slow-moving half-track weaved among the trees, they noticed thousands of flying foxes hanging silently above them, their skeletal bodies' deathly still in the afternoon's oppressive heat. In places, the flat, shallower banks were badly torn up by wild pigs. But as they travelled farther, the banks became steeper and were not so corrupted by the watering hogs.

Jack swung the half-track in among a clump of beautiful livingstonia palms a good hundred yards back from the water's edge. He'd noticed a small clearing among them suitable for them to spend the night. An hour later they had their camp set up, complete with all of its outbuildings and amenities.

Jack drove in the last of the tent pegs and turned to Golly. 'Can you scout around for some firewood, my friend, and, get a decent fire going?'

'Will do, Boss—er, Jack'.

'And, Golly, if you have time, get a couple of buckets of water from the billabong for the showers,' Jack added as he unfolded the last of the camp chairs.

'What would you like me to do?' Dan asked, his arm draped around Anna's dark shoulders.

'Well now if you can let go of Anna for a while, you and I might head off for a look around. That is if Isabella and Anna don't mind.'

'I don't mind, Jack. We're short of meat, so see what you can find. But please be careful,' Isabella replied, and Anna nodded in agreement.

'Okay then, we'll get out the rifles and head off.' Jack turned back to Golly. 'You will have to look after the ladies, my friend, and be careful where you go, mate; I don't much like the look of this place.'

'Don't you worry about me, Jack. You forget, I'm a blackfella, and anyway, this place don't look so bad to me. I'm pretty sure I was here a year or so ago,' Golly replied with a dismissive grin.

'All right then, but look after the ladies for us, mate,' Jack replied.

'Bit strange we ain't seen any cattle, though,' Golly mumbled as he wandered off among the palms on his quest for firewood.

Twenty minutes later, Jack and Dan were making their way through the trees along the edge of the billabong, stopping each time they saw small clearings ahead. Jack had given the double rifle to Dan to carry, while he carried the little Hornet. They'd been moving from clearing to clearing for about thirty minutes when, up ahead through a dense stand of trees, they noticed a much larger clearing. They moved on through the scrub until, finally, they peered out from the shadows. There was no game to be seen on the clearing at all and it seemed strangely quiet. Then, without warning, a flock of magpie geese streaked in through the trees from their left and settled out on the surface of the dark water and began honking noisily to one another. Jack and Dan smiled to each other, glad of the birds' noisy company, but annoyed they hadn't brought the shotgun with them.

'I don't much like the look of this place. Too bloody quiet for my liking,' Jack whispered. He gave a nod to Dan, and they started to move out of the trees.

'Hang on—what was that?' Dan whispered. He pointed to his left just as two heavy-bodied sows walked out from behind some bushes and began to make their way across the clearing toward the water, followed closely by two separate lines of mischievous piglets. Both men crouched low and watched the approaching animals. The leading sow began to stop every few feet and grunt at her progeny in a vain attempt to discipline them as they made their way toward the water. She was followed closely by the other sow and her own rather erratic line of piglets. Jack counted six of the young pigs in one line and eight in the other and guessed their age at about two months, perfect for the coals of their campfire. He smiled at Dan and pointed to himself to indicate he would try for one of the young pigs with the Hornet and quietly worked a cartridge into the chamber of the little rifle.

The two lines of pigs were angling a little toward the two men as they made their way cautiously for the water. When they were only a few feet from the edge of the billabong, the lead sow stopped and lifted her snout to taste the air, all of them unaware of the two men watching from the shadows. The sows stood stock-still for some time and looked out across the black, mirror-like surface, their ears flicking at troublesome flies and their young milling impatiently at their feet. It was eerily quiet. Even the magpie geese sat motionless out on the dark water. Jack lifted the Hornet to his shoulder and thumbed the safety forward to fire.

The old sow nearest the water finally seemed satisfied and began to lead both groups in to fill their thirsty bellies. Jack chose a plump young animal from the milling piglets and placed the crosshairs on the animal's neck and lifted his finger to the trigger, while Dan stood silently off to his right, holding the big double rifle across his shoulder, waiting patiently for Jack to take his shot.

Suddenly, the whole peaceful scene in front of them exploded, as a massive saltwater crocodile burst up out of the black water. For a split second, the sows stood stiff-legged in fright and then, everything seemed to happen at once. Dark waves lifted up and rolled across the inky surface of the billabong from the sudden shock of movement below. In that same instant, the magpie geese took flight, honking their displeasure at being disturbed. Pandanus fronds that had previously hung becalmed down into the dark water suddenly began to dance crazily along the muddy edge of the billabong as the huge crocodile rushed forward, its hideous jaws wide open. In an instant, it fastened onto the lead sow and began to twist its long body in a deadly dance of death. Black mud flew into the air, as it rolled, its massive tail, carving ugly shapes near the water's edge.

The sow, now screeching pitifully, began to flail its front legs about, searching for the earth below and a chance of escape. Then, as the surprised hunters watched, the crocodile momentarily stopped its rolling, lifted its head high, and tossed the old sow into the air, only to snap its jaws mercilessly around it again. The progeny of the trapped sow milled about in panic, squealing with fearful indecision as they watched the massive beast begin to back into the deeper water, its jaws locked firmly on their unfortunate mother.

In the confusion, Jack fired the Hornet at one of the milling piglets and brought it to the ground, just as the other sow and the remaining piglets bolted for the trees. Satisfied with his shot, he turned back to Dan.

At that very moment, Dan fired the big express rifle at the disappearing crocodile. The blast was deafening as it reverberated out across the billabong's rolling surface, and a geyser of water shot into the air ten feet above the crocodile's head. The recoil from the double rifle hit Dan so savagely he was forced backward several steps and almost fell. When he regained his balance, both men turned back toward the water. The crocodile and the squealing sow it had taken were gone. Dark waves rolled through the pandanus palms and lapped noisily against the muddy bank. Above them, hundreds of flying foxes fell away from their roosts in the trees, their ungainly wings clawing drunkenly at the humid air as they flapped across the dark surface and away through the scrub.

'Are you okay, Dan?' Jack looked at his shaken companion and smiled.

'I'm fine, but this thing kicks like a bad-tempered stock horse.' Dan handed Jack the double and started to massage his bony shoulder.

'Let's go and pick up our dinner, and I'll give you a couple of pointers with both of these rifles.'

The two men walked out of the trees and across the clearing toward the young piglet that lay in the mud near the water's edge. Jack thumbed open the double rifle and reloaded.

'We'll go forward together, mate. I'll keep my eyes on the water, while you grab hold of that pig—but be quick about it.' Jack lifted the rifle to his shoulder, while Dan moved forward and cautiously retrieved the dead animal.

As they backed away from the water's edge, the surface of the billabong continued moving in dark sinister swells, distorting the reflection of the sky above like an oily mirror. Finally, when they were well back from the water's edge, they leaned their rifles against a small tree and began cleaning the young piglet.

'Well, it's roast pork for dinner tonight, mate,'

'It's a pity we couldn't have got another one this size, Jack, we'd have had cold pork for a few days as well.'

'That bloody croc took care of that—sent the little buggers off in all directions,' Jack said as he splashed water on his hands from his canteen. 'Now let's see if we can get you a bit more familiar with these rifles.'

The two men spent the next fifteen minutes with Jack familiarising Dan with both of their weapons, firing them at an old boab tree until Jack was satisfied that he was more confident and capable as a rifleman. At first, Dan was reluctant to fire the double rifle again, but Jack showed him how to shoulder it correctly and had him balance his stance by leaning slightly forward as he fired. The slightly built stockman's first shot hit the old tree dead centre, and he only went backward one small step with the recoil.

After the rifle practice was over, they set off for the camp just as the sun began to set through the trees.

'That croc would have been at least twenty-five feet long, Jack. It looked like something out of my worst bloody nightmare.' Dan was still coming to terms with the size of the crocodile and the speed of its ambush of the unfortunate sow.

'It was big, all right, and I reckon there are probably more of them in there as well. I just hope if anyone goes near the water back at the camp they are bloody careful. We all agreed it looked a dangerous place when we arrived.'

Jack was beginning to feel quite concerned for the safety of those back at the camp.

'Let's get a move on then, just in case someone does something foolish,' Dan said and the two of them began to jog through the trees.

A few minutes later, they could see the livingstonia palms and the tops of the tents and tarpaulins rising above the light scrub of their campsite. When they arrived back at the edge of their little clearing, they were relieved to see Anna and Isabella sitting on their camp chairs, chatting.

'We heard the shots, Jack. It sounded as if you were quite close,' Isabella greeted them and smiled when she saw the plump young pig in Jack's hand.

'Where's Golly?' Jack asked. He watched as Isabella's eyes turned toward the water. 'Bloody hell!' he cursed.

Golly was standing on a low bank a few feet back from the water's edge and as Jack watched, the stockman threw a bucket attached to a short length of rope down into the dark water. Jack dropped the pig at Isabella's feet and ran toward the billabong, loading the double as he went.

'Golly, get back from the bloody water! Get back!' he yelled. Then Jack saw it, a low, pointed wake slowly making its way toward the unsuspecting stockman. He kept running. 'Get away from the bloody water! Move damn you!'

Jack stopped for a brief moment and waved his left arm in an attempt to get the Aboriginal stockman's attention and then he moved on. 'Get away from there, Golly—move damn you!' Jack was starting to lose his voice.

Golly could hear yelling coming from somewhere behind him. He turned away from the water's edge and saw Jack running toward him. 'Something must have happened at the camp,' he began to think as he watched Jack wave. He continued coiling his rope. The bucket of water was now by his side. Behind him, the V-shaped wake rolled silently closer—and then something dark broke through the surface!

Golly kept watching Jack. 'He must need my help,' he thought. 'Something has happened!' Everything seemed to be happening in slow motion to Golly. Jack's mouth was moving. He was yelling—but what was he saying?

Then, he heard the words, 'Get away from the bloody water. Get away!'

Jack kept watching the surface of the billabong behind the Aboriginal stockman. He slowed to a walk and stopped just as a long snout and a pair of evil eyes broke the surface less than fifteen feet from the low bank and directly behind the stockman.

The confused Golly remained motionless—and then the words began to register in his mind. 'Get away from the bloody water!'

The huge crocodile rushed up out of the water, its powerful legs tearing at the muddy bank, its sinister ambush almost complete. Long strands of vegetation hung from its hideous maw as it came up over the low bank and raced toward the legs of the bewildered stockman.

Jack threw up the double, sucked in a breath of air, exhaled, and squeezed the trigger. The double rifle recoiled back into his shoulder. He moved forward again.

Golly heard a violent rush of air as something tore past him, and then he heard the blast. The shock of noise made him drop the bucket he'd just picked up and water splashed over his bare feet. For a split second, he crouched in terror, and then he ran. 'Jack is trying to shoot me!' He raced for the safety of the nearby trees.

The heavy bullet from the double rifle had hit the crocodile halfway along its snout and angled back into its brain, killing it instantly. Jack kept moving forward. He opened the double and slid in another cartridge from a loop on his shirt. The big crocodile's now-lifeless body began to slide back down the shallow bank, its tail flicking from side to side like a headless snake.

Suddenly, the whole scene erupted into a mass of twisting, snapping bodies as several smaller crocodiles rushed up out of the dark water and tore at the dead reptile, thrashing and rolling in the mud in a wild feeding frenzy.

Water boiled around their writhing bodies, and thick black mud splashed up over the low bank.

Jack swung the rifle across his shoulder, staggered back a couple of steps with exhaustion and watched the mayhem unfold in front of him. Above him, a flock of white cockatoos began to screech their belated alarm from the treetops. Suddenly he realised Dan was standing alongside him.

'Jesus, Jack, what a bloody shot.'

'That, my friend, was the luckiest bloody shot ever. Pure luck, that's all it was. I couldn't bloody well breathe.' Jack passed the heavy rifle to Dan and sat down.

'You all right, Jack? You don't look so good.'

'Give me a couple of seconds, mate,' he replied breathlessly.

Dan looked back at the now-silent billabong and waited for Jack to catch his breath, just as another flock of cockatoos took to the air, alarmed by the mayhem beneath them.

Isabella ran across to where the bewildered Golly stood and put her arms around him. 'Golly, are you all right?' She could feel the Aboriginal stockman shaking uncontrollably as she held him.

'I–I thought Jack was trying to kill me,' he croaked, still shaking with fright. Then, he saw Jack walking toward him, smiling.

'What the bloody hell were you thinking, Golly? We spoke about this before, crocodile's, man, bloody crocodiles. You, of all people, should have known better.'

'Sorry, Boss. I was using a rope—I was trying to be careful. I just never saw it coming, and then you fired that big bloody cannon and I didn't know what was goin' on,' Golly blurted, still shaking with fright, but enjoying being held by Isabella.

That night they roasted the young pig over a bed of coals for more than two hours. While they waited for it to cook, Jack retrieved a bottle of twelve-year-old scotch from a secret stash in the trailer and poured a shot of it into everyone's tea, and they all raised their mugs in relief that Golly had not been taken.

'Glad you're still with us, mate.' Jack announced with a smile and lifted his mug into the air.

'Thanks, Boss. Hell, I could be out there stuck under a log somewhere instead of sittin' here sippin' tea.'

He took another sip. 'Geez, Boss, that's the best tea I reckon I ever tasted.'

'Jack, mate—call me Jack, Oh hell, what's the bloody use? Here, have a little more, my friend.'

They were all a little drunk by the time the pig was finally roasted. Even the usually quiet Anna was talking far more than usual as the tender meat was being carved and served. After they had eaten, Jack and Dan heaped more logs on the fire to keep away any visiting wildlife. When they'd finished, Anna came over and took Dan by the hand and led him off to their tent, wishing everyone goodnight.

Golly took his refilled tea mug with him and wobbled off to his tent, singing some song he remembered from a cowboy film he had once seen. 'Drifting along with the tumbling tumbleweeds . . .'

'Well, my big hero, are you coming to bed to receive your reward for bravery above and beyond the call of duty?' Isabella whispered, taking Jack by the hand.

'If you insist,' Jack replied. 'But only if you insist.'

# 27

# The Crystal Pool

The following morning, after they had eaten breakfast and packed up their camp, they refuelled the half-track and were on their way, all of them secretly relieved to be leaving the place they had named The Black Billabong. Toward midday, they reached the Drysdale River, or at least where that river began its winding journey down toward the Timor Sea. The country had now become much more difficult to find passage through, and quite often, they would find their way impeded by sheer walls of craggy limestone. They followed the river as best they could through the rocky terrain, sometimes being forced to backtrack for several hours. Their plan was to follow the Drysdale on its northerly course for some time and then change course to a more north-westerly direction until they eventually came to the Prince Regent River. Then, they hoped to follow that river as best they could as it made its way toward the sea.

As they travelled, they passed hidden valleys of lush rainforest, where rare palms and tall ferns shaded grottos of crystal-clear water. Fairy-wrens and pardalotes; rosellas and red-winged parrots flew in and about among the trees. At one of these grottos, Jack stopped the half-track and they watched dozens of colourful birds splashing into a partly hidden pool to bathe, their feathers ruffled, incandescent blazes of colour. They continued on past great, flat-topped ramparts of multi-coloured stone that rose around them like the walls of some ancient citadel, sometimes forcing them well away from the river itself through chasms of ancient ironstone, eroded and smooth from the passing of countless seasons.

In the middle of the afternoon, they parked 'The Hippo' in a shaded valley of multi-coloured stone. From there, they set off on foot across low plateaus of eroded limestone to watch the mighty Drysdale River as it tore down through an area of descending rapids, linked here and there by long pools of gin-clear water. Each of these pools was somewhat lower than the previous and each connected, in spectacular fashion, with its very own waterfall. The breathtaking scene eventually disappeared below them, as the final waterfall raced over a distant ledge and the river continued its gradual descent toward the Timor Sea.

'Can we camp somewhere close by, Jack? I must try to capture this scene somehow. It's just breathtaking,' Isabella yelled above the roar of one of the waterfalls below them.

'It's amazing all right. Just look at all that water rushing down through that valley. It sure must have been raining somewhere back in them thar hills,' Jack yelled back.

'Let's get back to 'The Hippo' and grab some gear and see if we can find somewhere to camp for the night,' Dan gabbled excitedly. He grabbed Anna's hand and they made their way back to the half-track. They decided between them they would take only what they needed from the trailer for an overnight camp. Jack and Dan carried the bedrolls and water, Golly carried the cooking pot and a billy, while the women carried Isabella's paints and food for their evening meal. By the time they had unloaded what they needed and turned for the river, it was late afternoon and still quite hot.

Jack led them single file back toward the falls. Several hundred yards upstream from where the river broke into the rapids and crashed noisily down through the valley, they stumbled upon a deep pool of crystal-clear water, hidden from view on two sides by rounded hummocks of smooth stone. They found it completely by accident as they were working their way down toward the falls. A tranquil, almost secretive place that seemed to be a part of a small tributary that flowed away from the main river and then back into it somewhere below them. On one side of the pool, huge, flat, weatherworn rocks led down to the water like a welcoming stairway. On the other, a wall of multi-coloured stone, worn smooth from the passage of time rose more than a hundred feet above the surface. High above the crystal-clear water, they could see shady nooks and tiny crevices filled with strange and exotic plants. Tiny palms and luxuriant ferns hung out from these craggy overhangs, while delicate flowering vines cascaded down toward the water in a riot of colour. Rainbow bee-eaters and tiny fairy-wrens darted in among the palms and vines searching for insects sheltering in the cool shade of these lofty grottos.

They decided they would set up a simple overnight camp on one of the huge flat rocks high above the water. It was still hot, and they were all weary from their long day's travel through the rugged hills and valleys. Dan began rolling out their canvas mats on the smooth stone, while Jack and Isabella poured cool water from one of the canteens.

'Golly, can you fossick around and find a few sticks for a fire, my friend?' Jack called across to the Aboriginal stockman.

'Will do, Jack,' Golly replied.

Quite suddenly, their work was disturbed by a high-pitched scream from somewhere below them, the sound distorted, amplified by the walls of stone around them. They dropped their camping gear and went across to the edge of their campsite and looked down. Anna had made her way down the ancient slabs of worn stone and had dived into the crystal-clear water. The beautiful Aboriginal girl was completely naked and swimming on her back, laughing up at them.

'Please tell me there are no crocodiles in that water, Jack?' Isabella asked with a concerned expression on her face.

'There couldn't be, Isabella. This country is far too difficult and steep for them. They stay in the billabongs and creeks down lower. But I imagine when we get down to sea level again we'll be seeing them in the creeks and estuaries there,' Jack replied with a smile on his face as he watched the beautiful Anna swimming naked below him in the gin-clear water.

Isabella turned back to Golly. 'Golly, will you be a dear and go back to 'The Hippo' and get us some towels, please?'

'Okay, Miss Izzy, I won't be too long.' Golly turned and hurried up the rocky path toward the half-track.

'Come on, you two, it's hot.' Isabella kicked her boots off and ran down the flat rocks to the water's edge with Jack and Dan in close pursuit, laughing like schoolboys.

'What's the water like, Anna?' she yelled across to Anna, shamelessly enjoying herself.

'It's so cool and wonderful—you must come in, Isabella,' Anna spluttered back.

Isabella walked out to the edge of the flat rock where Anna had left her clothing and dived in. She went down at a steep angle with powerful strokes for more than a minute before finally turning back for the surface. When she broke through, she lifted her face to the sky and sucked in a deep breath. 'It's wonderful and so cool and deep,' she called back to the two men and then made her way out to the centre of the pool, where Anna was floating on her back, watching birds darting about in the lofty grottos high above her.

'Well, what are you waiting for?' she yelled, her voice echoing across the surface.

Jack and Dan looked at each other and then out across the water at the two women enjoying themselves. Without further encouragement, they both stripped and raced each other to the edge of the flat rock and dived into the cool, inviting water. Anna lifted her hands above the surface and clapped her applause as the two naked white men broke through the surface and raced toward them.

Isabella laughed as well and then swam back to the edge of the impossibly clear water and climbed out. Her long dark hair hung down over her shirt in an untidy tangle and water streamed from her clothing. She stood there for a while, watching the others splashing about like children, and then she called out, 'Well, at least I bothered to wash my clothes first.' She strode across to the untidy heap of clothing that lay scattered across the rock ledge and began to undress. The swimmers watched Isabella struggle out of her clinging clothes, strip naked, and then lay her wet clothing on the warm rock to dry. Then, with a shriek of delight, she raced across the water-stained stone and dived back in.

The four of them splashed about in the crystal pool, enjoying the exhilarating feeling of the cool water on their naked bodies, and for a while, time seemed to stand still until, finally, Golly returned, carrying their towels. They watched the shy stockman put the towels discreetly near the water's edge and turn to go back the way he came.

'Golly, come and join us mate. It's hot, and the water's nice and cool,' Jack yelled up to the Aboriginal stockman.

'No, Boss, not me—you all enjoy yourselves, and I'll come back a bit later on. Maybe I'll just go and have a smoke somewhere quiet for a while.' Golly turned and disappeared out of sight.

The two couples swam about for a while longer, enjoying themselves, until; finally, the men swam back to the edge and climbed out. They dried themselves, dressed quickly, and then, as if they had made some unspoken agreement, turned their backs toward the two naked women making their way toward them.

'Okay, you can come out now,' Jack yelled, holding a towel out behind him.

'Why so prim and proper all of a sudden, Jack? We're all grown-ups, aren't we?' Isabella called back as she breast-stroked to the water's edge, followed by the giggling Anna.

'I don't know—it just seems proper, that's all. Just tell us when you're decent, all right?' Jack said rather prudishly.

'All right, then. Come on, Anna, let's get out. It's not as if they haven't seen every bit of us anyway,' she replied.

The two women climbed out of the water and dried themselves with the sun-warmed towels, enjoying the feel of the rough cloth on their cool bodies. The tall native girl with skin almost as black as coal with a body so perfect she could be mistaken for an Ethiopian princess and the white woman with the classical Roman features of her ancestors, equally tall and stunningly beautiful.

They lit a small fire that night and ate a simple meal of cold sliced pork and damper, washed down with mugs of hot tea, and later, the five of them lay back in their bedrolls on the wide flat rock high above the now-silent pool and gazed up at an endless starry sky.

A sudden, confusing feeling of dread washed over Anna and made her shiver with superstitious concern as she saw several shooting stars streak across the night sky. The boundless eternal heavens above her made her realise that her time spent with the white people and her love for Dan had made her forget if only for a short while, the undying love she felt for her own people. She felt a sudden pang of guilt as if she had deserted them, and it made her realise that she missed them terribly. She wondered if they were looking up at the same wondrous sky at that very moment. Perhaps they were listening to her beloved grandfather tell the same story he had told them all so many times before. She could see him sitting cross-legged near their fire and pointing up at the glittering stars. Strangely, each time he told them the story of the shooting stars, she had listened and enjoyed it as if it were the very first. She kissed Dan softly on the cheek and looked up again at the panorama high above her. It was quiet, and they were all deep in thought when she spoke.

'Would you like to hear a story my grandfather told me on nights like this?' she asked in a dreamy tone.

'Please, Anna, I'm sure we would all be fascinated, my dear,' Isabella replied sincerely.

Jack and Dan murmured their agreement. Only Golly remained silent.

'Among my people, when someone dies, a sacred canoe we call Larrpan leaves Baralku, the place you call the Milky Way. Larrpan the canoe then journeys down to our country to carry that person's spirit back up to Baralku, where it will stay forever among the ancestors. Baralku is a truly wondrous place where no evil can exist,' Anna said quietly as they gazed up at the vast glittering sky above them.

'If you look along the edges of Baralku, you can see the campfires of our ancestors flickering in the darkness and the faint white smoke that moves between them.' Anna was silent for a moment, and then she continued. 'Of course, it is a very long journey for the spirit to travel to Baralku, and once it has arrived safely, Larrpan the canoe farewells the spirit and returns to the earth as a shooting star. The grieving family watches and waits for Larrpan to streak across the sky, for then they will know that the spirit of their loved one has travelled safely to live among the ancestors.' Anna whispered the last few words. She was beginning to fall asleep. Dan put his arm around her, and the two of them closed their eyes.

'What a beautiful story, Jack. Perhaps it is true, who really knows, my darling?' Isabella whispered to Jack and began to fall asleep herself.

Golly lay in his bedroll a few yards away from the two couples. He'd listened to Anna's story carefully as he lay there looking up at the heavens. He wondered if his mother and his father sat by one of those distant fires. He had never known his parents; he had been taken from them as a baby to be raised by white people to work on a station. But he did remember the white station owner's wife. The Boss-Missus was always very kind to him, and he had loved her dearly. But she had died long ago. He had been a boy then, and he had cried for many nights, and now, as he gazed along the glittering edges of the Milky Way, he felt tears well in his eyes once again.

# 28

# The Whispering Cave

The next day, Isabella spent the morning with her paints. Anna sat with her as she worked and watched the roaring white water and the crashing waterfalls spring to life on the talented artist's canvas sheet. While they sat in the shade of an overhang of rock, the men carried their bedrolls and camp gear back up to 'The Hippo' and began readying it for the afternoon's journey toward the coast. Just before midday, the two women came up the path carrying Isabella's paint box and easel and packed them away in the trailer, and a short while later they were on their way.

They stopped late in the afternoon to rest and to eat some of the cold pork and damper washed down with mugs of cool water, and then they pushed on, hoping to find a good campsite before nightfall. Later that day, at the bottom of a rocky valley, they came to an area shaded from the fierce afternoon sun by a long red cliff. Jack idled the half-track along enjoying the cool shade cast by the wall of stone. In the distance, they noticed a copse of wispy acacia growing around a tiny waterhole at the base of the red cliff. As they drew closer, the drone of 'The Hippo' startled two kangaroos drinking from the waterhole. The old buck and its companion, a doe heavy with joey, bounded out of the trees and into the sun, only to disappear down an unseen valley to their left. Jack pulled the half-track to a halt near the trees and shut off the engine. He climbed out, his back wet with perspiration. 'I reckon it's time for a bit of a break, and this doesn't look too bad a spot for us to camp for the night,' he announced, rubbing his lower back.

After stretching their weary legs and wandering about among the trees for a while, they set up their camp on the sandy ground nearby. The women, hot from their exertions, decided to shower before preparing the evening meal. While they showered, the men set off to find firewood, and, they hoped, a wallaby or a young kangaroo for the pot. Jack decided he would carry the Hornet. He passed the shotgun to Dan, and they headed off along the valley floor, keeping to the cool shade of the long red cliff.

A short while later they came to another thicket of acacia trees growing near the base of a low wall of stone that jutted out at right angles from the massive red wall to their right. As they approached the trees, Golly stepped on an ancient piece of bleached seashell, and it broke with a sharp crack. The Aboriginal stockman looked down and cursed his carelessness, just as several black and gold spinifex pigeons burst into the air. Dan threw the shotgun to his shoulder and fired both barrels almost in unison, and five of the beautifully coloured birds cartwheeled into the sand, leaving tiny striped feathers floating in the warm air of the valley floor.

'Nice shot, Dan, well-done, my friend,' Jack remarked and patted his friend on the back.

Golly scurried off to gather up the birds. 'Good tucker these, Boss,' he said happily.

The three of them sat in the shade of the trees and plucked and cleaned the plump little birds. When they had finished, Golly and Dan gathered as much wood from the thicket of trees as they could carry and they headed back to their camp.

That night they made a casserole with the pigeons, the last of the potatoes, and the cold pork in two of the camp ovens. After they had eaten their meal and filled their mugs with tea, they sat around the campfire listening to more of Anna's wonderful Dreamtime stories, until finally, they all drifted off to their tents to get some sleep.

Isabella leaned lovingly against Jack as he untied their tent flap, and the two of them crouched through the narrow opening. They undressed quietly and climbed into their bedroll.

Isabella kissed Jack's shoulder and whispered, 'Jack Ballinger, all that naked swimming yesterday got me a little excited. Would it be too much trouble for you to make wild and passionate love to me?'

'Only too happy to oblige, you shameless, naked hussy, only too happy to oblige,' Jack tossed their blanket back, got up, tied their tent flap, and hurried back to their bedroll.

The following morning, they changed their course to a more north-westerly direction and headed away from the Drysdale toward the Prince Regent River. Later that afternoon they began descending through a long valley of multi-coloured stone. Veins of pink and vermillion sandstone glittered in the sunlight, a spider web of colours against the dark basalt walls that lined the valley. Some of the ancient metamorphic rock had broken away in schist from the cliff sides and lay in untidy heaps on the valley floor, forcing Jack to weave the half-track around them, and occasional, massive, dislocated boulders as they made their way along the valley.

At the end of the valley, they came to a narrow pass that veered to their left under another high cliff. Jack turned 'The Hippo' through the tight corner and up over a stony ridge, and a few moments later they passed out into open country, all of them relieved to be finally out of the confines of the narrow valley. In the distance, they could now see the bright blue of the Timor Sea, or at least the wild, unexplored estuary that formed a part of it. Jack stopped the half-track in a bed of pure white sand covered in places with mounds of bleached and broken seashell.

'These mounds of shell look ancient. Probably old eating spots used by coastal Aboriginals, by the look of them.' Jack suggested as he worked his way around one of the ancient middens and then stopped the half-track.

'They sure look old alright.' Dan Replied.

'This looks like a pretty good spot to set up camp for a few days, while we have a bit of a look around. I'm fairly sure we are pretty close to the mouth of the Prince Regent River now,' Jack announced as he climbed down.

'This looks perfect,' Isabella agreed. 'What a wonderful view.'

Dan filled one of their canteens with cool water from the canvas bags that hung on the heavy bull bar at the front of the half-track and passed it around. They all agreed on Jack's choice of campsite, and an hour later, they had their elaborate camp set up just as the sun began to set through the ramparts of stone off to the west. Their meal that night was a rather uninteresting stew made with the dried beef and onions and washed down with mugs of hot sweet tea.

'We have two handlines in the trailer. I reckon we might try for a few fish tomorrow. That's if we can find something for bait.' Jack slid his fork into the stringy stew and pushed it around his plate.

'I've never caught a fish in my life,' Dan replied, looking equally disinterested with his meal.

'Well, I reckon tomorrow will be your lucky day, mate,' Jack said optimistically to his young friend. 'A few nice snapper or a couple flathead would be good.'

Dawn the following morning found them making their way on foot over a rocky plateau toward the Prince Regent River. Jack had checked his charts before they left and taken a careful bearing with his compass, but with the weaving and backtracking they had done over the last few days, he was not too sure of their exact location.

Anna was the first to hear it, a soft, steady humming sound off to their right as they trekked past a couple of massive flat-topped cliffs. They turned toward the sound and kept walking. Slowly, the noise became louder, until finally, they made their way around a weatherworn cliff of dark stone and looked down at the magnificent Prince Regent River. The scene in front of them was unexpected and amazed them. The river had become a series of clear pools linked together by magnificent waterfalls crashing down from one to the other as it made its way below them. Some of these waterfalls were quite narrow, falling only short distances, while others were massive and thundered down through glistening rocks and crevices to crash into the pools below. At the end of this line of pools, the river widened into a swirling torrent and spilled out over the final cliff into the sea below.

They worked their way down past the pools and waterfalls, marvelling at the sheer beauty of the place as they went. It took them more than two hours, but finally, they stood near the edge of a dizzying cliff and looked down at the final, much wider waterfall, that was in fact, two separate falls that broke through crevices in the water-worn cliffs and plummeted down into the Timor Sea.

The noise was deafening. Blasts of cool spray swirled back on the breeze and wet their faces and clothing. They were dumbfounded by the wild scene below them. The broken falls crashed down into the estuary in a maelstrom of white water and yellow sea foam, while swirling clouds of spray shot up the cliffs to fall again like constant rain onto the glistening rocks below. As they watched, the sun broke free from a dark patch of cloud above and sent translucent shafts of light through the falling water. A rainbow suddenly appeared in the mist of the falls, a blaze of colour against the bright blue of the Timor Sea.

Finally, reluctantly, they turned away from the cliff top and began to look for a way down the steep sides of the falls. For some time they had difficulty finding a safe route, but again, it was Anna who discovered the narrow path that led around a wall of dark stone. They followed the path past steep bluffs and across primitive rock bridges as it made its way down toward the sea. Near the end of a high wall of stone, they noticed the small smoke-stained entrance to a cave that had previously been hidden from their view. The opening was slightly above them, and a series of flat rocks rose up to it through two narrow walls of ochre-stained limestone.

Jack was the first to speak. 'Look at that—a cave entrance. Let's go up and take a look.' He led the way up through the walls of stone, and a few minutes later, they reached the place where the opening should have been, but it had disappeared.

'It must be here somewhere—it has to be,' Jack said, frustrated. He began walking around among the scattered pillars of stone until finally, he found the narrow opening hidden behind a column of rust-coloured sandstone.

'What an amazing place,' Isabella gasped, trying to catch her breath from the steep climb.

'The pathway we have been on for the last half an hour or so has almost certainly been used by others, but not for a very long time I would guess.' Jack declared, breathing heavily himself. 'Some of it is man-made by the look of it. You can see quite a lot of the rocks have been placed into position in some of the more dangerous places near the cliff edges.'

Anna was strangely silent as they stood talking, and Golly had begun to look quite uncomfortable.

'I don't think we should be going in there, Jack. Something don't seem right,' he mumbled as he stared at the dark opening.

'Come on, Golly, it's only a bloody cave,' Jack replied, trying to reassure the Aboriginal stockman.

Cautiously, one at a time, they stepped through the narrow opening into the cave's cool interior and waited for their eyes to become accustomed to the darkness, to be met by a scene that astounded them. The cave was an ancient art gallery, very probably thousands of years old. The massive cavern was at least three hundred feet in length, and approximately fifty feet in width along most of its length, although in several places much narrower. The ceiling was stained black from the smoke of countless fires and soared more than forty feet above them, to where they could see a faint slanting light coming from a hidden opening. Inside, the cave was many degrees cooler than the scorching heat outside and would certainly have been a comfortable refuge for the many travelling Aboriginals that must have used it over the centuries.

The walls of the great cave were covered from end to end with thousands of very detailed works of art. There were paintings of hunters stalking kangaroos across tree stunted plains, women with pendulous breasts surrounded by what appeared to be children playing. Strangely striped lizards and huge fish covered in rows of white spots, stood out in stark relief, surrounded by literally thousands of handprints of varying sizes. The artwork was a riot of primitive colour, reds and ochres, stark whites and burnt umber.

In a small grotto separated from the main cavern by a low wall of soot-covered stone, they stopped to study a strange collection of faded paintings of tall, elongated men with elaborate concentric rings of white circling their heads and smaller rings circling their eyes. Strangely, none of them had mouths. These figures were almost certainly extremely ancient and had deteriorated with the passing of time, although there was evidence that some had been carefully repainted. But even those repairs were very old.

'Wandjina—these are the Wandjina. The rain people,' Anna whispered reverently, gazing up at the primitive paintings of the Dreamtime beings. 'They summon the rains each year—they are the ancient ones.'

As they walked past these faded works of art, none of them spoke. It was as if they had stumbled through some strange portal in time, and, even though they were alone, all of them could sense the presence of the bygone artists and hear the faint whisperings of their voices.

Finally, at the far end of the huge cavern, they saw a scene that puzzled them all. This section of the cave was covered with primitive pictures of sailing ships, small ships, each with a single mast and a square-rigged sail straining against the wind. On each of these craft, they could see men sitting below the sails. Some were holding ropes, others were looking up at the taut canvas above, while below were what appeared to be rocks representing the coastline, interspersed with stick figures waving their arms in welcome.

Anna had never been to this place, but she knew beyond any doubt it was a very special place for her people. She remembered the stories her grandfather had told her about the Makassar people that came to their land each wet season in their strange ships blown by the wind, to fish for the trepang, men who had become friends of the Aboriginal people.

As she continued along the cool stone walls of the ancient gallery, she began to feel an uneasy sensation come over her. The painted walls seemed to be closing around her, separating her from the others. She began to struggle with her balance. She stopped and leaned against one of the painted walls. She looked up and noticed a painting of an old man, bent with age carrying a long spear. She stared at the painting for more than a minute, and then, quite unexpectedly, a vision began to appear in her mind. At first, the vision seemed formless as strange shapes and indistinct colours swam into her mind. She saw a long plume of smoke, but no fire. She heard noises, terrible noises, gunfire, or perhaps thunder. A fearful premonition began to clutch at her heart. She began to sway unsteadily as the paintings swirled around her. Someone called her name. It was a voice she knew. 'Jiiarnna,' the familiar voice called.

She was suddenly confused and afraid. Then, as if in response to her panic, the vision cleared, and she saw her beloved grandfather. At first, he was a great distance from her, but he slowly drew nearer until, finally, she felt she could reach out and touch him. There were tears in the old man's eyes. He seemed to be watching something, something terrible. Anna stared into the mists of his tears, but she saw only her own distorted reflection. Then he called to her again. 'Jiiarnna,' he sobbed. There was a terrible loneliness in the old man's voice.

'Anna—Anna, are you all right? You fell, my dear.' Isabella was sitting next to her patting her hand. Dan had a canteen to her lips.

'It must be the heat or something,' Dan whispered.

'It can't be—it's so cool in here. Perhaps she has just fainted. After all, it is certainly an overwhelming place,' Isabella whispered.

Anna opened her eyes. 'I'm so sorry. I don't know what happened, I really don't. I felt quite strange for a moment, and then I must have fainted.' She looked up at the concerned faces of her friends, and her reasoning started to return.

'Come on now let's get you on your feet and out of here. It's just possible the paintings were a little too much for you, my dear.' Isabella helped her to her feet.

'Sorry about that, really I am.' Anna struggled to her feet and wiped the cave dust from her legs.

They made their way out of the huge cave and back into the bright sunshine of the late afternoon.  Anna leaned wearily against Dan, and the five of them stood staring up at the hissing waterfalls above them, marvelling once more at the sheer beauty of the place.

'Okay, let's get down to the estuary and see if we can catch us some fish.' Jack yelled above the sounds of the falls and started along the narrow path that led down toward the sea.

'Isabella, can you walk with me for a while? I need to speak with you about something that is troubling me,' Anna asked quietly.

'You certainly can, my dear.' Isabella turned to Jack. 'You men go on. Anna and I will follow you in a few minutes.'

The three men left Anna and Isabella sitting on a polished rock that overlooked the last thirty feet of the falls and headed down toward the distant shoreline. Just before they disappeared out of sight, Dan looked back with a concerned look on his face.

'Now, my sweet dear, what is troubling you? Is it the cave? I suppose those paintings must have been done by some of your ancestors long ago.'

'No, it's not the cave, although, for a moment, I thought I could hear my grandfather calling for me. It was quite strange, really. I hope we see him as we travel back toward the station, just so that I know that he is safe.'

'Well then, what would you like to talk about? I will certainly help if I can.' Isabella leaned forward and put her hands on Anna's shoulders and looked into her troubled eyes.

'It's something that happened back at the station, something that I should have told you when I first met you. But you and Jack were so busy planning this trip, and I suppose I didn't want to spoil it. But now I feel I must tell you.' Anna had a distraught expression on her face.

Isabella put her arms around the young girl and hugged her fondly, trying to comfort her. 'My dear you're upset. Tell me what it is?' she whispered. 'I had a feeling something wasn't quite right when we left the station.'

Anna looked very uncomfortable as she began to speak. 'A few days before you arrived at the station, the boss asked me to go to his cottage to see him. He frightens me, Isabella. Everyone there is afraid of him. When I got there, he took me into his wash-house and made me get undressed.'

'He did what?' Isabella was shocked and suddenly very concerned.

'I told him I didn't want to and that I wanted to go, but he'd locked the door and had the key in his pocket. I was frightened Isabella, but I had no choice. He lifted me into the water and started to wash me. He did this to me once before, on the very first night I was at the station. I didn't know what to think then, but I know now that it was wrong. But he only bathed me, gave me clothing to wear, and led me back to the kitchen. This time, after he bathed me, he took off his own clothes.'

'Oh my God, Anna, why would he do such a thing?' Isabella was visibly shaken.

'I was confused and afraid. I tried to stop him, but he just laughed. Then, he made me bend over his bathroom chair and he forced himself inside me.'

'Oh no—my poor, Anna . . . !' Isabella lifted her hands to her face in shock.

'He made me feel like one of the station dogs. I begged him to stop, Isabella, but he wouldn't. After he had finished with me, he told me to keep my mouth shut. I was to say nothing or he would cut my throat.'

'Cut your throat . . . ! My God—the man is a monster!' Isabella replied. There were tears in her eyes. She reached for Anna and hugged her.

Anna broke down and began to cry. 'I know I should have told you before. I am so ashamed Isabella. Now I have ruined everything,' she sobbed.

'That swine—that evil swine, how dare he do such a thing?' Isabella's voice was now barely a whisper. 'You must not blame yourself, my dear, you simply mustn't. And you have ruined nothing, my dear, nothing at all.'

'It was terrible—he hurt me, Isabella. I have lived in fear that he would make me go to him again, and I am sure that he will when we go back to the station. I was so glad when you insisted I come with you on this trip.'

'Tell me, my dear, have you told Dan about this?' Isabella asked, staring into her eyes.

'No, he knows nothing about this at all. I am afraid that I will lose him if I tell him. I wanted to speak to you first. Only Santiago knows what happened, Isabella.'

'Well, my dear, you must tell Dan, of course, but not for a while yet. It is obvious that he loves you dearly, and I am sure he will understand that it was not your fault, and while he may be hurt, he will get over it. But if you tell him now, he will want to confront that monster, and then there will be trouble,' Isabella said firmly. 'Now, my dear, this is what we will do: I will tell Jack, of course, and we will return to the station as soon as we can. When we get back, Jan Muller will no longer be working on Cockatoo Creek Station. I will see to that as soon as we arrive. He will be instantly dismissed and told to leave the station immediately. I will then contact the Derby police on that somewhat unreliable pedal radio we have in the homestead, that is if I can get through, and I will see that charges are brought against him.'

Isabella was extremely angry. She felt partly responsible herself; after all, she and her father were Jan Muller's employers. Perhaps they should have carried out more extensive background checks on the man. Isabella knew her father would be angry when he found out what had happened, very angry, and she knew that she must contact him as soon as possible.

'I'm sorry to have told you, Isabella. Now I have ruined your trip.' Anna began to sob again.

'No, no, don't concern yourself, my dear. You needed to tell me, and I am glad you did, never doubt that. But for the moment, we must try to act as if there is nothing wrong. I will tell Dan and Golly I have decided to head back a little earlier for some private reason. You must try to compose yourself, my dear. I think we should go down to the beach and join them now.'

'Thank you, Isabella. I will do as you ask,' Anna said quietly.

'It will be a good excuse to get back to Santiago's cooking, and I'm sure everyone will agree. But let me ask you one more thing, my dear.'

'What do you want to know?' Anna looked into Isabella's eyes.

Are you with child?' As Isabella asked, she took Anna's hands in hers.

'No, Isabella, I am not, and I am certain of it,' Anna replied and bowed her head in shame.

Isabella put her fingers under the young girl's chin and lifted her face. 'None of this was any fault of yours, Anna, as I'm sure you already know. You must place your trust in me now, that evil man will not harm you again,' she said sincerely.

'Thank you, Isabella. Santiago told me you would take care of things for me. He is very wise,' Anna replied.

'Santiago is a good man. Now, we had better join the others and see if they can catch us some fish for our dinner.'

Both of them stood up and began to make their way down the path that led to the estuary's rocky shoreline.

Dawn the following morning found Isabella and Anna grilling some of the fish fillets they'd smoked the night before. The arduous trip down to the estuary had proved to be worth the effort. They had caught two large flathead and a couple of smaller, golden whiting, and had eaten their fill of the abundant oysters they found among the rocks along the rugged shoreline. The fish had been filleted and cleaned in the seawater and taken back to their campsite to be grilled over the coals. Those that were not eaten were smoked in the small metal smoker they found in the camp trailer.

While they breakfasted on the tasty fish and sipped from their tea mugs, they could hear the distant hiss of the waterfalls in the still morning air. Anna and Isabella sat together while they ate and listened again to the two white men congratulating each other on their success with the handlines the afternoon before.

# 29

# The Stranger

An hour after they had eaten they had their campsite dismantled and packed into the trailer and were on their way back toward the south. For the first few hours, they were mostly silent as they crisscrossed in and around the rocky valleys, working their way back the way they had come. In the middle of the day, they passed the pathway that let down to the crystal pool where they had swum. A short while later the country opened out, and Jack began pushing the half-track faster, and later that day they arrived back at The Black Billabong. Even though no words were spoken as they drove among the silent trees and along the edge of the massive billabong, it was obvious that none of them wanted to camp near that ominous dark water again. Jack kept the half-track moving through the trees and across the occasional muddy clearing. At the far end of the billabong, they watched thousands of flying foxes take to the air and circle above them before flying off on their evening mission to search for food. After the sun had gone down, they pushed on for another hour, until it became too dangerous to travel in the dark through such rough country.

'I reckon this will do us for tonight,' Jack remarked wearily as he swung 'The Hippo' in near a dry creek bed to camp for the night and shut down the motor.

Golly scouted about and found some firewood near a few stunted acacia trees while the rest of them set up their camp, and it wasn't too long before they had a good fire burning and a billy nestled in among the coals.

'I think if we get moving at sun-up and keep going all day, we should only be a couple of days' travel from the station before we have to camp again,' Jack reasoned to the others. Jack had found himself looking forward to a confrontation with Jan Muller. He had grown very fond of Anna, and he had no time at all for men who abused women.

'Look, I must apologize to you all again for my hurry to get back. But as I told Jack, I need to radio a message through to Derby so that a telegram can be sent to my father. I have just remembered his birthday is in a few days, and I had completely forgotten. I know it must sound trivial, but I always contact him for his birthday, no matter where I am.' Isabella looked across at Dan and Golly, hoping they believed the lie she had dreamt up. When she looked at Jack, she felt a twinge of embarrassment as he smiled back at her.

Two days later it began to rain, and it continued to rain for many hours. Before they'd left their camp that morning, Jack had taken a careful compass bearing and decided to change their direction to a more direct course toward the station now that they were out of the rugged hill country. As they travelled steadily toward the south, they saw hundreds of the station cattle in the heavy scrub country. Most of them in very poor condition and stood with their heads down as the rain fell as if they were waiting for the first of the wet season's grasses to appear. Jack and Dan had erected the canvas roof on 'The Hippo' and rolled down the side curtains earlier and they travelled in comparative comfort as the half-track easily managed the slippery ground.

In the middle of the afternoon, as they were making their way through a thicket of tall bloodwoods, in the distance, they noticed a small, almost circular ring of boab trees. The rain was still hammering down as they drew alongside the trees, and for no apparent reason, Jack stopped the half-track. The noise of the rain on the canvas roof drowned out the sound of the idling engine, and for more than a minute, they sat staring into the misty interior. The rainwater that ran down the Perspex side curtains made it difficult to see much more than a hazy, indistinct clearing stunted with spinifex and fallen limbs. Jack pushed the gear lever into first and eased out the clutch. The half-track slipped sideways for a few feet, straightened, and they began to move forward once again.

'Stop, Jack, I think there is someone in there. I can see him,' Anna called out. She had undone her side curtain and lifted it for a better view.

They all turned in the direction she was looking and saw him. A tall Aboriginal man was standing under the cover of one of the huge boab trees, sheltering as best he could from the steady rain.

Jack stopped '*The Hippo*' and looked back at Golly. 'Do you know this man, Golly?' he yelled above the drumming of the rain.

'No, Boss—he's a bush native that one. He's carrying a spear and one of them killer boomerangs. I reckon he might be dangerous. Maybe we better just leave him alone and keep on going. There may be more of them in there somewhere.' Golly was looking very nervous as he yelled his reply. Then, as they watched, the tall Aboriginal laid his boomerang and spear on the ground and held his arms to his sides, as if he was signalling that he meant them no harm.

'I think he wants to talk to us,' Anna yelled as the rain continued to pelt down on the canvas roof. 'Let me go across and speak to him. I should be able to understand him better than anyone.'

'Are you sure, my dear?' Isabella yelled.

'Yes, I am sure—I have a feeling he wants to talk to me. But I have no idea why. Don't worry, I'll be careful.'

Anna patted Dan's leg and reached for the door handle.

'Well, don't get too close to him, just in case, and if something happens, get behind one of those trees and we will come for you.' Jack slid the Colt out of its holster and put it on his lap and nodded to Anna.

'Look, I should come with you,' Dan reasoned as he got out to let Anna out of the vehicle.

'No, Dan, I must do this alone,' Anna said firmly.

'Well, please be careful, then,' Dan said, just as another heavy squall hit the idling half-track, rocking it slightly.

Anna gave them all a nervous smile and headed off.

Jack laid the long-barrelled Colt revolver on the seat and reached for the ignition switch, and killed the engine. 'We shouldn't have let her go alone,' he said nervously, just as the rain started to ease.

'It was what she wanted . . . but I agree,' Dan replied.

'He might be one of them black buggers who did the spearin' of the cattle,' Golly mumbled just as the rain stopped altogether.

Anna made her way across the slippery ground into the ring of trees and cautiously approached the waiting Aboriginal man. As she drew closer, she wiped the rainwater from her eyes and studied him carefully. The stranger was very tall, and certainly not a young man, but neither was he old. His skin was as black as the darkest night and shone like a dull mirror from the water that ran down his muscular frame. He was naked, except for a thin strand of blackened kangaroo skin tied around his waist and attached to a small string bag that hung down over one of his buttocks.

Anna began to sense a terrible danger. She looked back at the half-track and wondered if she had made a mistake approaching this man alone.

'I have waited for you for many days,' the stranger said quietly. He spoke in a tongue Anna could easily understand, but it was not the tongue of her people.

'I do not know you. Why do you say you have waited for me?' she was beginning to feel uncomfortable. There was something very intimidating about this dark stranger. She glanced back at the half-track again.

'You are Jiiarnna, daughter of Yilla, who no longer lives. You are granddaughter to Goonagulla, an elder among your people,' the stranger began, his dark eyes never leaving Anna's.

'Yes, I am Jiiarnna,' Anna replied in her own tongue. She began to shiver with premonition.

'I am Pirramurar of the Worla people,' the tall Aboriginal man said.

The rain had started to fall again, and Anna watched it run down the stranger's dark body. The glistening liquid trickled over the tribal markings etched onto his chest and down his lean belly, into the dark curls of his manhood.

'My grandfather has spoken of you in stories he once told me when I was very young. You are a spirit man, a Kurdaitcha.'

Anna remembered the stories her grandfather had told her about this man when she was a child, and she wondered why he did not appear much older.

'Yes, Jiiarnna, I am Kurdaitcha. I was chosen long ago to carry out the laws of the people. But now you must listen to me. I have waited here for you because there is something you must be told,' Pirramurar's eyes softened as he spoke to the young girl.

'What is it that I must be told, Pirramurar of the Worla?' Anna looked into the tall man's dark, slightly bloodshot eyes and waited.

'I must speak to you about your grandfather, Goonagulla, and your people.'

'What has happened to my people?' Anna felt a terrible feeling of dread begin to wash over her.

'Your grandfather lies dead not far from here, and his people lie with him. I have sung my songs and danced for them for many days here among the trees until I felt their spirits leave this terrible place. At night I have seen their campfire burn new and bright on Baralku.' Pirramurar spoke his words with great respect and reverence to the young girl.

Anna staggered backward a few steps. She had begun to feel faint. 'How—how did my people die? You must tell me!' She felt a great fear clutch at her heart as she waited for the stranger's reply, and for a fleeting moment, she remembered the vision she'd had in the whispering cave two days earlier. She began to feel unwell. Her arms fell to her sides, and she stepped back unsteadily.

'Many days ago, I heard the noise from the weapon of the white man. Each time I heard the thunder sound, I felt a terrible pain in my body. I tried to see through the mists that sometimes swirl in my mind, but I could see nothing. I followed the sound to this place and hid among the trees. I saw a great fire burning and a white man standing at the fire. As I watched this white man, I saw the terrible beast he had painted on his body, a beast with yellow eyes that search the land. I have seen this beast many times in my dreams. This white man is an evil devil, and he carries with him a sickness. But I could not see what evil had happened here, and so I waited through the night until the dawn came. Then, as I watched, I saw the big white man leave. I hid among these trees until he had gone, and then I went to the fire and found what he had done. Your people were killed by the white man's terrible weapon and burnt in his fire until all that remains are bones among the ashes. Soon the waters that renew the land will wash away all that is left.'

Anna fell to her knees in the mud and began to cry. As she cried, she wrapped her arms around herself and began to sway from side to side with grief.

Jack and Dan leaped out of the half-track and raced through the outer ring of trees toward the kneeling Anna. Jack drew the pistol out of his belt as they drew closer, waiting for the tall stranger to make any sudden move toward Anna.

But the Aboriginal man made no attempt toward the weapons that lay at his feet, nor did he look at the approaching men. Instead, he stood with his arms at his sides, silently looking down at the distraught Anna.

'Anna, are you all right? What has happened here?'

Jack held the big Colt at his side, its barrel pointing to the ground while he waited for her to reply.

'This man is Pirramurar of the Worla people. He has waited here for many days to see me. My grandfather knew this man long ago. In the language of the white man, he is a spirit man, a gifted one. Among our people and to the Worla, he is all of these things and more. He is also a Kurdaitcha, a tribal killer. But do not be afraid, he will not harm us.' Anna got to her feet and walked toward them. They could sense something was wrong—terribly wrong. Her voice sounded distraught. She looked upset and seemed to be trembling uncontrollably.

'Are you sure you are all right, Anna?' Dan asked his face pale with concern.

'Something terrible has happened here.' Anna sighed and took a deep breath to settle her thoughts.

'W—what has happened?' Dan started toward her in an attempt to comfort her. But Anna put up her hand to stop him.

'My grandfather and all of my people have been murdered here. They were shot to death, and their bodies burnt by a white man. By the station manager—by Jan Muller! Pirramurar has seen the beast with the yellow eyes painted on his chest, and I have seen this thing you call a tattoo on his body myself. Pirramurar has told me Muller burned the bodies in a fire for many hours, and when the morning came, he watched him leave this place and travel back toward the south—back toward Cockatoo Creek.'

Anna turned back to Pirramurar and looked into his eyes. 'Pirramurar, where are the bodies?' Tears had begun to run down Anna's cheeks.

'The white man burnt them many times, trying to hide the evil he had done. What is left of them lies in a small creek just beyond the trees. Soon, the little that remains will be gone now that the Wandjina has summoned the rains.' The spirit man's expression never changed as he spoke, but his dark eyes sparkled with hatred for the white man who had committed this terrible crime. He walked across to Anna and held out his hand to offer her something he had removed from the bag at his waist. The fierce look in his eyes softened as he spoke. 'This belongs to you, Jiiarnna, daughter of Yilla.'

Anna recognized the tiny rope of hair instantly as the hair of her mother. She knew her grandfather carried it with him always. She nodded to Pirramurar to thank him and looked down at her mother's hair, and for a moment, she was lost in thought.

Pirramurar took another step forward and placed his hand on Anna's head and began to chant a strange, mournful song.

Jack knew now that the tall stranger meant Anna no harm, but he continued to watch carefully, the long Colt pistol at the ready. The rain had now stopped altogether, it was suddenly very quiet and from somewhere nearby, a chorus of cicadas started their monotonous chirping. He heard footsteps behind him, and when he turned, he saw Isabella and Golly standing a few steps back with concerned looks on their faces. None of them spoke; it was almost as if they were unable to. As they watched, the tall stranger lowered his voice almost to a whisper and continued his chant, and all of them began to feel a mystifying calmness wash over them.

Anna had felt the soft touch of Pirramurar's hand on her head while she was looking down at her mother's hair. She began to feel light-headed and strangely euphoric. The earth seemed quiet and peaceful and Pirramurar's strange song a whisper, a soft, relaxing murmur of sound.

A sudden strange vision entered Anna's mind. At first, all she could see was a campfire burning in the night, and then, as she drew closer, she could see herself sitting near the fire. For a moment she thought it was just a memory from days gone by. Then, she saw the faces of the people she had travelled with for so long—her people. They were sitting with her at the fire. She saw Balun the young warrior, the two older women, Jannali and Toora, and the young ones, Alinga and Ekala. Their bodies were gaunt and hollow from hunger, and the young ones wept piteously.

She called out their names, and they turned toward her. Then, across the coals of the fire, she saw her beloved grandfather. Slowly, they started to draw away from her, and their images began to fade. Anna watched them raise their hands in farewell. She tried to call out, but it was too late. They were gone.

Anna felt a mystifying calmness wash over her as Pirramurar drew away his hand. When she looked up, she saw him smile his understanding to her. She knew then that something deep and spiritual had just happened between her and the Kurdaitcha man. The terrible grief she felt seemed suddenly much easier to bear, and when she spoke, her voice was no longer racked with emotion. 'Pirramurar, I would be honoured if you would eat with us tonight.' Anna felt great respect for this man and for the strange powers he possessed. She hoped that he would stay.

'If that is what you wish,' Pirramurar replied in the language of the Worla.

It was then for the very first time that the spirit man looked around at the others and stared into their eyes. As his gaze passed from one to the next, each of them felt as if their very soul was laid bare and their secrets there for the strange black man to see.

They set up their camp that night near the ring of boab trees just as the rain stopped. A little over an hour later they were sitting around their campfire cooking the not-so-tasty dried beef and onion stew. Pirramurar had disappeared while they were setting up their camp, and as they started cooking their meal, he'd returned. The tall Aboriginal was dragging what they all thought was a log for the fire. It was dark, and it wasn't until it landed in among the coals in a shower of sparks that they recognized it as a huge goanna, almost five feet long. The flickering light from the fire and the continuing explosions of sparks lit up the Kurdaitcha man's dark face and the thick tribal markings on his chest as he squatted and rolled the huge monitor lizard in among the coals.

After they had finished their meal, Anna and Pirramurar sat apart from the others, talking for more than an hour in the language of their own people. For some reason, the mysterious man's company seemed to make Anna's grief much easier for her to bear.

The next morning they rose just as the sun's early rays glinted through the trees and began to pull down their tents and tarpaulins. Pirramurar had disappeared long before the dawn. Very little was said as they prepared their breakfast. The terrible news Anna had received had left her devastated, and now that Pirramurar had gone, she began to feel a numbing loneliness again.

After they had eaten their meal and the men were packing their gear into the trailer, she walked across to the creek bed where Pirramurar had told her the bodies of her people had been burnt. She stood there for some time, watching the muddy water rush along the creek. When she returned to the campsite she was strangely calm. She had a plan, and she knew what she must do. But she would tell no one.

# 30

# Back to the Station

Pirramurar stood at the top of the ridge of coloured stone, where he had found the tracks left by the white man and his horse, and watched the strange crawling thing slowly disappear into the distance. During the night, as everyone had slept, he'd had a dream. In the dream, he saw the white man who had murdered Goonagulla and his people. But just before the dream passed from his mind, he saw something he could not understand. The dream had begun to swirl and distort in his mind. He saw the sun chasing away the early morning shadows across a silver billabong, and near the edge of the water, he could see two bodies lying dead on the hard ground. Pirramurar felt a great pain in his heart for Goonagulla's grand-daughter. He had seen too much death in his life. But the Kurdaitcha man knew that Jiiarnna had set herself on a path that would leave her, the beautiful daughter of Yilla and the beloved granddaughter of Goonagulla, dead, and there was nothing he could do about it.

\* \* \*

Just before midday, the rains came down again. Thunder crashed above their heads like gunshots, and great jagged bolts of lightning lit up the dark sky above them with intermittent flashes of brilliance. They continued on toward the south, but the going became far more difficult. Red water had started to fill

283

the hollows and gullies and run along the dry creek beds. They skirted as many as they could, unsure how deep they were, and pressed on. Their experiences had given them great confidence in 'The Hippo' and it churned on through the red mud. The steel tracks at the rear of the sturdy vehicle seemed unstoppable, although, at times, the narrow, front steering wheels had little grip in the mud and they would surge forward, often moving in the wrong direction.

For most of the morning as they travelled, very little was said between them. Jack and Isabella stared out through the windscreen and were silent. Anna sat quietly in the back, while Dan, lost in thought, stared ahead and watched the single windscreen wiper fight its losing battle with the rain. Golly sat next to Anna, he was taking no notice of the country they were passing through at all. The Aboriginal stockman was sorry the trip was finally coming to an end. He'd had a wonderful time. But now he was afraid of what was going to happen when they arrived back at the station and Jack and Isabella confronted Jan Muller. He knew his boss was a violent, dangerous man, and he wondered if the others really understood just how violent and dangerous he could be. He was almost certain their plans could go horribly wrong when the big South African was confronted with what he had done. He knew there was going to be hell to pay when they arrived.

Later that day the rain began to ease, and eventually, it stopped altogether, and as they continued, the country became a lot drier. They kept moving through the scrub as fast as the half-track could travel until just after dark. When it finally became too difficult to see, Jack started to look for somewhere to camp for the night. A short while later, the weak beam of the headlights illuminated a clearing among some scattered trees not too far ahead. Jack swung the half-track into the clearing. It was then that they noticed an ancient boab tree of immense proportions standing on its own among some weeping acacias and ghostly paperbarks and it was only when they came to a halt that they could see its great bulbous trunk was hollow.

Jack reached forward and switched off the ignition. He had roughly calculated they had about fifteen miles to travel in the morning to get to the station. If they left at dawn, they should get there in two or three hours, at worst.

It had been a hard day's travel through the now wet country, and they were all weary from the constant bouncing and lurching of the half-track. They unloaded their sleeping tents and set up a temporary camp for the night.

It had become an almost military routine. Jack and Dan put up the tents as Anna and Isabella got out the pots and pans from the trailer and began preparing their meal, while Golly searched about for firewood and got a campfire going. Less than half an hour later, their tents were neatly pegged down, and a good fire was burning with a cooking pot nestled among the coals. They laid a canvas sheet on the ground and sat down for their evening meal of the not-so-popular stew and damper and hot sweet tea.

'Now, we had better start to plan what we are going to do when we get to the station in the morning,' Jack began seriously, smiling at his weary companions.

'Well, that evil bastard must be brought to justice for what he has done, that is for certain,' Dan replied with a firm edge to his young voice.

'Jack, I suppose you will have to use a firearm when we confront him, and I think we should place him under some sort of arrest and secure him somehow. Then, I think we should take him through to Derby,' Isabella said with a concerned tone. 'After all, murder is a capital offence, punishable by hanging in this country. I also think we should take Anna with us to make a statement about what she was told by Pirramurar. I will insist that criminal charges be laid, and then I will have to call my father to tell him what has happened.'

'I suppose we will have to keep him under lock and key in one of the sheds until we are ready to leave for Derby,' Jack added, he was beginning to look forward to the task ahead.

'My father will be devastated when he finds out about this. He will probably fly across to be here as soon as he can. This is bad, really bad. I feel so sorry for you, Anna. How could anyone be so cruel?' Isabella was deeply concerned about what lay ahead and the course of action they should follow. But for all that, she was even more concerned about how her father would take the terrible news.

Anna sat quietly and said very little as they ate their food and discussed what they should do. After she'd finished her meal, she picked up her mug of tea and wandered across to the old boab tree to be alone for a while.

The flames from their campfire lit up the old tree in a ghostly light. Its strange, twisted limbs seemed to reach above its swollen trunk like so many ancient arthritic arms. Out of curiosity, she knelt at the opening and looked inside, and for a moment, she could see nothing more than the dark hollow itself. But as her eyes became accustomed to the flickering light from the campfire, she saw something. Lying in the middle of the hollow she could see a clay pipe and a small leather pouch. She shivered with fright. She knew in an instant they had belonged to the station manager. She stared at the two items for more than a minute and then finally, she reached in and picked up the clay pipe. Concealing it from the others behind her tea mug, she walked around to the side of the boab tree and dropped it to the ground, and using only her bare feet, she crushed it into tiny pieces.

Jack brought out the last of the whiskey that night, and all but Anna added a good amount to their tea mugs as they sat around the fire and continued their planning. Anna was silent and didn't join in the conversation at all, and when the whiskey bottle was finally empty, she whispered goodnight to them all and carried her empty mug across to the trailer. They were all aware she was suffering terribly, and they were becoming very concerned about her withdrawn behavior. Dan knew she needed rest, so he decided he'd stay at the fire with the others for a while longer before joining her. But the young stockman had a worried look on his face as he sipped his whiskey-spiked tea. Eventually, when their planning finally came to an end, they all went off to their tents knowing that the following day was going to be an eventful one.

Three hours before the dawn arrived, Anna slid Dan's arm from her belly and quietly slipped out of their bedroll, dressed quickly, and crept outside. She looked up at the full moon. There was more than enough light for her to do what she intended. She went across to the trailer, where she and Isabella had prepared their meal the night before and picked up the butcher's knife and its sheath and made her way past the ancient boab tree and out of their camp.

When she was well clear of the campsite, she began to jog toward the station. She knew the way well, even in the moonlight. It was the direction she, her grandfather and her people had used to approach the station in the hope of getting food not so very long ago.

A little over an hour before sunrise, Anna arrived on the outskirts of the homestead. She knew that very soon, most of the hands would be getting up to begin their day. She also knew that Santiago was probably already hard at work in the kitchen at that very moment. A terrible hatred for the man in the manager's cottage raged inside her. He had raped her, and now he had murdered her people. She reached down and ran her hand across the knife in her shorts. She would soon make him pay for what he had done. She slipped through the boab trees that ringed the station grounds and made her way toward the manager's cottage. She had only gone a few steps when she heard a soft growl to her left. It was one of the station dogs. 'It's me, Anna—quiet now.' The dog gave a soft whine of recognition and trotted away.

Anna's bare feet made no noise at all as she made her way up the steps and across the narrow verandah of Jan Muller's cottage. She stopped at the doorway and reached down and slid the long knife out of the sheath inside the waistband of her shorts, and using the metal handle, she knocked on the door. *Tap . . . tap . . . tap.*

\* \* \*

Dan woke with a start from the dream he had been having and shook his head to clear his thoughts. He lay there for a few minutes, trying to remember the dream. It had something to do with a crocodile bursting up out of black water. He was glad he had woken. Moonlight lit up the inside of the tent with a faint yellow glow. It was hot. He could feel beads of perspiration on his forehead, he was not sure if it was from the heat or the dream he had just woken from. A faint breeze blew in through the open tent flap onto his shoulder, cooling him. He rolled over and reached for Anna. But she was not there. He lay there for a few seconds more, not really concerned until he realised the canvas sheet where she had slept was cool. Then, he remembered the night before and how withdrawn she had been. Something was not right. He threw the bedroll back, got to his feet and poked his head through the flap. It was strangely quiet—too quiet. He looked across at the smoldering campfire. Tiny coals glowed like knowing eyes in the cool white ash and pencil-thin tendrils of pale smoke curled lazily up out of a partly burnt log into the pre-dawn sky. It was far too quiet.

'Where could she be?' he wondered as he crouched through the tent flap. 'Where the hell was she?' He looked across at the old boab tree, grotesque and swollen in the pre-dawn light. Just for a second, it reminded him of a picture he had once seen of a laughing Buddha in one of his father's National Geographic magazines. He tried to shake the sleep from his mind and concentrate. Perhaps she had just gone to relieve herself. But as quickly as that thought crossed his mind he cast it aside. The bed was cold—she was gone and he knew it!

He raced across to Jack and Isabella's tent. 'Jack—Isabella, wake up! Anna's gone; somethings not right!'

Jack burst out of his tent, naked, with the Colt in his hand. 'What—where is she, mate? What's happened?'

'I don't know, but she's not here, Jack. I'm sure of it,'

'Let's have a look around and see if we can find her tracks, mate.'

The two of them started to walk around the campsite. But it was an almost impossible task in the faint pre-dawn light.

Isabella had hurriedly dressed and joined them, just as a sleepy Golly stepped out of his tent wearing only his dusty dungarees. He had heard the commotion.

'Light up one of the lamps. We should be able to see her tracks easily in this soft sand, I reckon,' he mumbled and padded across to join them.

Dan quickly lit one of the kerosene lanterns and, holding it low to the ground, they started searching the outer perimeter of the campsite.

'There—there, they are over there!' Golly yelled. 'She's heading for the station, I reckon.'

'The damn knife's gone from the trailer table as well!' Isabella yelled and lifted her hands to her face in despair. 'We'd better get after her. She's gone to confront that monster, Muller!'

Jack put his arm around Isabella to calm her and looked back at Golly. 'Un-hitch the trailer, quick as you can, my friend. We had better get moving.'

Dan ran across to help Golly unhitch the trailer and yelled back. 'It will be daylight in an hour or so. I just hope she's not too far ahead of us.'

Less than five minutes later they were dressed and underway, with Jack pushing 'The Hippo' toward the station at full speed. Thin red mud splashed up over the bonnet of the half-track as he forced it headlong through swollen creeks and washaways. Dan sat next to him in the front seat with the big double rifle at the ready, his eyes glued on the moonlit scrub in front of the bouncing vehicle.

Isabella and Golly were in the back, both leaning forward and straining their eyes through the mud-spattered windscreen, hoping they would soon see Anna's familiar shape in the headlights.

# 31

# The Pump Shed

Jan Muller had been dreaming. He had been having the same dream for the past few nights. In the dream, he lay in his bedroll near a huge, hollow boab tree, watching a line of natives coming out of its dark opening and walking slowly toward him. The natives had no eyes, just maggot-filled sockets that stared at him. He'd raised the Colt to fire, but the hammer fell on an empty chamber. He'd tried again, but the pistol was empty and the natives had continued toward him. But then, something completely different happened. The bent old chief leading them stopped and lifted his spear and brought it down onto the hard ground. *Tap . . . tap . . . tap.*

Muller woke with a start, his body bathed in sweat. He lay there for a few seconds, trying to shake off the remnants of the dream. Then he heard it again: Tap . . . tap . . . tap! It was the door.

He looked at the luminous hands on his bedside clock. It was four in the morning. Who the hell would want him at this hour? He reached for the crumpled bed-sheet that clung to his chest and wiped the perspiration from his face.

*Tap . . . tap . . . tap!*

'Who's there? Who the hell is it?' he yelled. But he heard no reply, only silence.

He got up and went to the door. He was half-asleep and unsteady on his feet and beginning to feel very angry. He reached for the doorknob and jerked the door open. He could see an outline in the doorway. Then he saw an arm raised as if to strike him. He swayed back in instant response. The moonlight came from behind his attacker, showing only an outline. And then he saw the glint of steel rushing down at him.

Jan Muller moved like a panther, down and to his right to dodge the blade, the sleep gone from him in an instant. He came up just as the blade passed, and then he struck. With his left hand, he swung down and grabbed the hand that held the blade and with his right, he hit his attacker hard across the face with his massive open hand to throw them off balance. Then, as his attacker was momentarily dazed from the savage blow to the face, he reached down, wrenched away the knife, and stepped back into the room, dragging his assailant with him. He had the knife now, and he was ready to end it.

Suddenly, he could see who it was as the early light lit up his attacker's face. 'You—what the hell is going on? You tried to kill me, you black bitch!' he snarled, pulling Anna farther into the cottage.

Anna tried desperately to break free from his grip, kicking out with her bare feet. But the big man was far too strong for her.

Muller dragged her across to his bed with his left arm locked around her throat and reached for his matches to light his bedside lamp. 'What the bloody hell is going on here? Where are the others?' he hissed, pointing the thin blade at Anna's face.

'They are coming for you!' she yelled defiantly. 'I left them to come on alone and kill you for what you have done. You murdered my people, you monster. They all know what you have done—you're finished.'

'When will they be here, you black bitch. When—fuck you ..?' Muller took hold of Anna's arms and shook her violently.

'Two hours, no longer—it's over for you!'

Anna started to feel the anger inside her subside and cold fear of the huge man who held her began to take its place.

'Well then, I've got just enough time to do what I must before I get the hell out of this place. But first things first, my little black princess, I think we'd better get out of here.' Muller dragged Anna across to a cupboard on the far side of the room and pulled out a length of cord and began tying her wrists together. When he'd finished, he took the knife and cut off a few feet of the cord and let it hang to the floor.

Anna began to shake uncontrollably. She knew what was coming, she was going to die. She tried to scream, but Muller smashed her across the face with his huge right hand.

'Shut up, you black bitch, or I will kill you here and now,' he hissed and dragged her back to his bed. Holding her with one hand, he pulled on his shorts, picked up the thin-bladed knife, and dragged the frightened girl outside.

Jan Muller knew what he had to do. First, he would take the black bitch down to the pump shed, cut her stupid throat, and hide the body. Then, he would take the station truck and get as far away as he could. He would dump the truck later and simply disappear into the bush for a while and when things quietened down, he would make his way down south. But first, he had to take care of the black bitch. He felt elated—he was beginning to enjoy himself.

Anna stumbled along behind Muller as he made his way toward the dam, her wrists already raw and bleeding from his savage pulling on the cord. When they got to the pump shed, Muller stopped and walked back to Anna and held the knife up to her face.

'You tried to kill me with this, you bitch, now you're going to pay with your worthless life.' He slid the knife up the back of Anna's shirt and ripped the material away from the young girl's body. Grinning, he took one of her breasts in his left hand and squeezed it painfully. 'Pity I didn't have a bit more time before I cut your stupid throat, but unfortunately, it seems I don't. This has got to be done fast, and when it's over, I'm sure no one will find you in there for a while.' He nodded toward the pump shed. 'And while they're looking for you, I'll be long gone and miles away.'

Anna's eyes were fixed on the knife Muller held in his hand. She felt terribly weak. She tried to scream for help, but only a sobbing sound came from her lips. She was going to die, and there was nothing she could do about it.

Muller grabbed a handful of her hair, pulled her head back and lifted the knife to her throat. 'Looks to me like you shouldn't have come on alone, Princess,' he whispered.

'Hey there, Boss is that Anna. What the hell is going on here?' It was Beans, yelling as he walked toward them in the half-light. He'd been up early; his stomach had been playing up. 'Too many bloody baked beans,' Famous had told him.

'Why is she tied up, Boss? You'd better let her go!' the portly stockman called out, trying to sound assertive.

Beans had gone across to the outhouse, and when he came out, he'd seen two people heading down through the trees toward the dam. It was still dark, and he couldn't make out who they were, but it seemed peculiar that two people should be heading down to the dam before breakfast. Something wasn't right, and he knew it.

Muller took the knife away from Anna's throat and put it behind his back. He bent down and lashed the cord around one of the irrigation pipes and walked back to Beans. 'What the hell do you want? This is none of your fucking concern, you fat bastard.'

'What do you think you are doing, Boss—just untie her and leave her alone?' Beans was confused. He had no idea Anna was back at the station. But he did know something was wrong—very wrong.

'Run, Beans run! He's got a knife! Run, now—just go!' Anna finally managed to get some words out and screamed her warning at the bewildered Beans.

But it was far too late. Muller had made the few steps across to the confused stockman. Muller grabbed him by his shirt front and lifted the knife up from behind his back and slashed the razor-sharp blade across his throat. Blood sprayed onto Bean's chest and ran down his ample belly almost instantly. Muller wiped his blood-spattered left hand on the stockman's shirt and stepped back.

Beans put both of his hands up to his throat in surprised fright. Blood gushed out from between his fingers. He looked at Anna and tried to say something, but only a faint hissing sound came from between his fingers. He dropped to his knees, his eyes wide with terror. Blood continued to gush from the ugly gash on his throat and run down his naked chest onto his dungarees. He continued to stare at Anna for a few seconds more, and then his blood-soaked hands fell lifelessly to his sides and he collapsed to the ground.

'That's him fucked. I'll drag the fat bastard in there with you in a minute. Now it's your turn, you stupid black bitch,' Muller hissed. 'Just think if you had stayed with your friends you'd have caught me by surprise. But then, I've always been a bit lucky when it comes to killing.'

\* \* \*

The half-track crashed through the scrub at full speed with Jack at the wheel, desperately maneuvering it around clumps of spinifex and stands of weeping acacias. Dan sat next to him with his right hand tight around the big double rifle, while Isabella and Golly were in the back, holding on for dear life, both staring through the windscreen at the small trees and bushes that were being crushed under the half-track's bull bar. Dawn was beginning to creep through the scrub as they tore along at full revs.

'Can't we go any faster?' Dan yelled above the screaming engine.

'She's flat, mate, flat as a bloody tack,' Jack yelled back his reply.

\* \* \*

Muller wiped the bloody knife on his shorts and walked across to where Anna was tied next to the pump shed. He smiled. 'It's a great pity I didn't have a little more time. We could have had one last bit of fun,' he whispered into Anna's terrified face. Then, using his left hand, he reached behind the Aboriginal girl's back and grabbed a handful of her dark hair. 'But it seems, my dusky little princess, that, unfortunately, I don't.'

Anna closed her eyes as Muller held her head back.

'Dan, I'm so sorry,' she whispered and waited for the knife slash that would end her young life. But nothing happened. She opened her eyes, and to her horror, Muller was still smiling. He was enjoying himself!

'Looks to me like you should have stayed out in the bush and not come wandering into the station looking for food. But now that I think about it, I suppose I would have shot you anyway, along with the rest of those cattle-spearing black bastards.' Muller finished his sadistic farewell to the young girl, smiled one last time, and lifted the knife to her throat.

Anna looked up into the pale, early morning sky. She could see a huge wedge-tailed eagle circling high above her. She closed her eyes and waited—then she heard a dull thud.

When she opened her eyes, Muller had a puzzled expression on his face. In the centre of his chest, almost exactly between the yellow eyes of the fearsome lion tattoo, a barbed spearhead protruded out toward her.

Muller let go of the Aboriginal girl's hair and looked down at his chest in total disbelief. Heart blood, thick and crimson, began to trickle out of the jagged wound and run down his naked chest. He groaned with pain and dropped to his knees. The thin-bladed knife fell away from his right hand and bumped harmlessly into Anna's body as it dropped to the ground between them. He continued to fall back until the long spear shaft caught in a crack in the dam bank, and for a moment, his body lurched at a crazy angle until finally he fell to the ground still facing the terrified Aboriginal girl.

Anna sat back on her haunches and vomited. Her body convulsed and shook as she retched again and again. Finally, she fell back against the irrigation pipe with her head between her legs. She was afraid she would pass out at any moment. Then, she heard a rustling sound, and when she looked up, Pirramurar was suddenly there. The Kurdaitcha man was covered in dried mud and scratches, and his chest heaved with exhaustion. Long strands of feathers and leaves were attached to his naked body, and slashes of white ochre had been painted across his dark face and down his arms and legs. For a moment Anna wasn't sure it was really him.

Blood trickled out of the worst of the cuts Pirramurar had received as he'd travelled through a day and a night, tracking first the strange crawling thing and then the young girl's tracks as she had left her camp and made her way back toward the station. He was worn out, but he still carried himself with an exhausted dignity as he walked silently toward the young Aboriginal girl.

Anna watched as he picked up the knife lying next to Jan Muller and cut away the cord that held her. Then he walked back to the dying man and wrenched out his spear.

Anna heard a hiss of air and a faint groan as the station manager rolled onto his back. Pirramurar crouched beside the dying man and reached into the small bag tied around his waist and pulled out the long, hollow wing bone of the brolga, the dancing bird of his people. Anna began to feel ill again. She had no idea what was about to happen, but she continued to watch with sickening fascination.

Jan Muller looked up into the face of his killer for the very first time. He had never seen this man before, but his mind drifted back to the ring of boab trees, where he had shot the bush natives and the man he thought he had seen standing in the shadows.

The Kurdaitcha man lifted the hollow bone in front of the dying man's eyes, held it there for a few seconds, and then slid it slowly down the side of the white man's neck and into his chest. Then he sat back in the dirt and began to chant while he waited for the hollow bone to draw out the white man's very soul for the murder of Goonagulla and his people. As he chanted, his eyes never left the white man's until they glazed over in death.

\* \* \*

Jack wrenched the steering wheel of the half-track to his left and then to his right as he weaved his way through a dense thicket of melaleuca. Suddenly, in the distance, they could see the station buildings glinting white through the boab trees.

'Can you see her yet?' Dan yelled above the screaming engine.

'Not yet, mate, just hold on till we get through these trees,' Jack yelled back.

'It looks deserted. I hope we're not too late!' Isabella cried out from the back seat.

Jack hit the throttle down hard and they raced up the slope and through the boab trees. Strangely, there was no one in sight. It seemed odd; usually, there would be stockmen wandering in and out of the dining room and a lot of activity at this time of the morning. He swung the half-track in alongside the big machinery shed and cut the engine, and the four of them climbed down and began looking around the seemingly deserted grounds.

'What's that going on down near the dam? Looks like a lot of people standing around near the pump shed,' Jack yelled and grabbed Isabella's hand. 'Come on, then, let's get down there and see what the hell is going on.'

They took off at a run, with Dan and Golly close behind. They raced through the boab trees and down the slope that led to the dam and headed for the pump shed.

It was difficult for them to work out what was happening. Then, they saw Anna. She was being held by Santiago. The old cook was bare-chested, and it looked as if his white work shirt was wrapped around the young girl's shoulders. And then, they saw the bodies—two of them laying a few yards apart. Steve was kneeling next to one of them.

Dan ran forward and wrapped his arms around Anna and hugged her with relief. 'Anna—Anna—are you hurt? Is she all right, Santiago?' he asked breathlessly.

'She is alight now, Dan,' Santiago replied. The old cook was crying.

'What the hell has happened here?' Jack yelled, looking around at the onlookers.

'Beans is dead, Jack. That bastard Muller cut his throat,' Steve cried out. The young stockman was sitting on the dry mud-bank next to Beans' body. He was holding the dead man's hand, and tears were streaming down his face.

Famous Feet and Bob Nugent were kneeling next to the other body. They stood up as Jack and Isabella approached. 'Some blackfella speared the boss—got him good too—he's had it,' Bob Nugent said quietly to the both of them. 'I think Muller was going to kill Anna as well as Beans. But it looks like some blackfella saved her life.'

'So, where's the blackfella now?' Jack looked back along the dam bank.

'He was gone when we got here, Jack. We all heard Anna screaming and came straight on down,' Bob replied and shrugged his shoulders. He was still trying to come to grips with what had happened. 'Famous here followed the blackfella's tracks for a bit. But he says they just stopped and then vanished completely. He wasn't too happy about tracking him anyway. He reckons he was some sort of spirit man or something like that. It has something to do with that hole in the side of the boss's neck.'

Jack looked at Muller's blood-soaked body and then at the old tracker's anxious expression. 'I reckon I have a fair idea who it was, Bob, and it's a good thing Famous here never caught up with him.'

'Well, it looks like the show is over for now, and I'm sure Anna would like a little privacy and support. So if you would all like to go over to the dining room and wait, I'll come over and speak to you in a few minutes,' Isabella said with firm authority to the milling station hands.

'Can I stay, Miss Izzy? Anna is very upset. She was nearly killed by that monster,' Santiago pleaded. The old man had tears in his eyes, and Isabella could see he did not want to leave her side.

'Of course, you can, Santiago.' Isabella turned to Anna. 'What happened here, my dear?' Isabella began to sob herself when she looked closely at Anna's distraught face. She crouched down and took the young girl's hands and waited for her reply.

Slowly, and between bouts of sobbing, Anna told them what had happened. She told them how she had run through the night and about her attempt to murder Muller and her failure to do so, and then all the horrific events that followed.

'And where is Pirramurar now?' Jack asked quietly.

'He just disappeared into the trees some time ago. No one else saw him but me. But it was him alright. He was covered in cuts and scratches from following me through the night. He saved my life. If it wasn't for him, both Beans and I would be lying dead in the pump shed and Muller would be gone. It was terrible. Poor Beans; he was just trying to help me. I should have stayed with you, and none of this would have happened.' Anna broke down again, and Dan put his arm back around her and pulled her gently to him.

'Come on now, let's get you up to the homestead,' Jack said softly.

Dan and Jack helped the distraught girl to her feet, and then Dan and Santiago took her hands and led her toward the homestead. Jack walked back across the dam bank to where Bean's body lay, he unbuttoned his shirt and took it off and placed it over the dead stockman's face in case the crows came.

# 32

# Willie McMullen

Two days later, just after dawn, everyone on Cockatoo Creek Station was gathered at a quiet little place they had chosen among the boab trees that ringed the station grounds. The afternoon before, several of the hands had raked and cleaned the area that was to become Bean's last resting place. Bob Nugent had made the coffin by hand, from timber he'd stripped from pallets in his workshop. He'd welded together a sturdy steel cross and painted it white, and in the centre of the cross, he'd riveted on a piece of brass that he removed from a worn-out machine and hammered flat. Then, using homemade tools, he'd painstakingly engraved the words:

Willie McMullen
'Beans'
Age: unknown
Died: 1933
Sadly missed by all

At first light, Famous Feet and Dan had rounded up the station dogs and chained the confused animals to stop them from running about while the sombre proceedings were underway.

The sky was a dull grey, a light rain had been falling most of the previous night and had continued into the morning. The station hands that were gathered at the gravesite were all dressed in their best clothes, were clean-shaven, and out of respect had refrained from smoking while they attended their friend's funeral.

Isabella had decided to say a few words of comfort to the station hands. She held one of her father's bibles in her hands as she spoke. 'We are gathered here today to pay our deepest respects to our dearly departed friend, Willie McMullen, or Beans as he was known to us all. I would guess that most of you never knew Bean's full name, and I have only just found out myself, by going through the station records. Beans, or Willie, as he was known to his mother and father was born some time ago on Anna Plains Station near Broome, where he grew up. Both of Willie's parents were station workers, and so that became the life that the young Willie would lead as well. The tradition in those times was for native station workers to take the name of the owners of the station as their own and the owners of Anna Plains Station at that time were the McMullen family, so young Willie became Willie McMullen. When Willie was a young man, both of his parents died in a tragic cottage fire on that station, but thankfully, the young Willie was spared. Some years later, he moved to Argyle Downs Station, where he worked for many years until, eventually, he was employed by my father to work here at Cockatoo Creek.

'Willie belonged to the Kardjari tribe of Aboriginal people. I only know these details because my father has kept a detailed file on each of the station employees he takes on here at Cockatoo Creek, and, according to the file, this is the story that Willie told my father when he stated his previous experience. Willie McMullen has worked here at Cockatoo Creek for more than five years. He has always been a hard-working and trusted employee and a dear friend to us all. He will be sadly missed.' Isabella placed her right hand on her Bible and looked around at the sad faces gathered at the gravesite and continued. 'May the Lord watch over you, Willie McMullen, and keep your spirit safe, and may you rest in peace.'

Isabella stepped back and watched as Bean's coffin, complete with his new Christmas belt and a can of beans balancing precariously on top, was lowered into the ground.

Then, as the ropes were pulled away, she stepped forward with a single frangipani flower in her left hand, raised it to her lips in a parting kiss and dropped it into the grave.

Everyone on the station walked by the gravesite, and each of them cast a handful of red dirt down onto the coffin. Some of the stockmen stopped awkwardly for a few seconds to whisper words of farewell, while others removed their dusty hats and held them to their chests before tossing down their handful of dirt. Each and every one of them had tears in their eyes.

Steve had asked Isabella if he could fill the grave, and as the quiet group of mourners made their way back to the dining room for the wake, he stood next to the hastily made cross at the head of the grave, looking down at the coffin of his good friend, a worn shovel in his hand and tears in his eyes.

Jan Muller was wrapped in an old blanket and tied with twine and was buried in an unmarked grave many miles from the station. Jack and Golly had loaded the man's body into the camp trailer and taken it away with the half-track. They had not been sure where to bury him, so they followed the track they'd made through the trees on their return to the station. Three hours later, they found themselves back in the little clearing where the ancient hollow boab tree stood.

Both men decided it would be as good a place as any, so they set about digging his grave. When they had finished, they placed his body in the grave with his head facing the opening in the hollow tree. There was no apparent reason for this that was just the way it happened. Once they had finished filling in the grave, they flattened the earth and tamped it down so there would be no sign that a grave was there at all. Then, they tossed their shovels in the back of 'The Hippo' and headed back to the station. As they made their way back, they made a pact never to tell a soul where Jan Muller was buried—no matter what.

The following day, Isabella called a meeting for all of the employees on the station. The first and most important priority was to select a capable new station manager. Isabella had decided to ask Billy Anders if he would be prepared to act as temporary manager until she contacted her father about everything that had happened.

The meeting was held in the dining room, and all employees were asked if there was any opposition to Billy being made the temporary manager, but there was only cheerful agreement among them. Billy was a popular choice, and everyone on the station knew he was a capable man. The hard-working stockman happily agreed to take on the role until Isabella spoke to her father and secretly hoped it would become his permanent position. For the time being, Isabella decided to have the station manager's cottage remain vacant until after she had contacted her father.

Anna slowly began to heal from the terrible tragedies that had befallen her in recent days. The support and love she received from Dan, and, of course, Santiago and the rest of the hands, helped her immensely, and it wasn't too long before Santiago had her back in his kitchen working alongside him. The old cook loved the young Aboriginal girl dearly, and even though he was deeply worried about her state of mind, he knew it would help take her mind off things.

Isabella had decided not to contact the Derby police on the somewhat unreliable pedal radio. Instead, she and Jack would travel into Derby, taking the station truck. They would then give a full account to the Derby police of all that had happened. They would give particular emphasis to the fact that had it not been for Pirramurar, Anna, as well as Beans, would be dead and that, should any actions be taken against him, it be done after she had spoken to her father in Melbourne by phone.

Five days later, Isabella and Jack made their way into Derby. Most of the creeks were still in flood, but the levels were well down from their last trip. They had left very early in the morning, and by late afternoon, they arrived in Derby. Their first stop was the police station, where the two of them explained in detail what had happened to the sergeant in charge.

Sergeant Pat Collins was an experienced officer with many years in residence in the Kimberley. To Isabella and Jack he seemed an agreeable man, and certainly helpful. However, his response to the tale of the murdered bush natives seemed a little too casual. They sat with the sergeant for more than two hours while he painstakingly typed a full and detailed report, and when he finally finished his work, it was dark outside.

'Well, firstly, thank you, Isabella, for bringing in the deceased station manager's papers. As you have explained, he seems to have no living next of kin for us to notify. Now, in regard to this Aboriginal, Pirramurar, you say his name is. Ordinarily, we would need to get him back here and take a statement from him and then lock him up and let the court decide what happens to him. However, with the language difficulty and the very real possibility that we may never be able to find him at all, I really do not think that would be possible. Also, I feel certain that any tracker we employ will not want to set out after a Kurdaitcha man,' the sergeant said in a matter-of-fact tone and continued. 'I think the statement I shall make to the local press here in Derby will be along the lines of a murder-suicide at the homestead. That will hopefully take away any pressure I get to round up some wild bush native. As far as the other Aboriginals who were murdered out in the bush go, it may be better we keep a lid on that. That's the way we usually deal with these sorts of things up here. Anyway, I reckon the bastard who murdered those poor buggers has certainly paid the price anyway.'

The sergeant pushed back his chair and got to his feet. He put out his hand to Jack. 'It's a pity we had to meet under such difficult circumstances, Jack. But I'm sure we can tidy things up without too much fuss.' He turned to Isabella. 'It's been a great pleasure to meet you, Miss Montinari. Your father is well-known to us here in Derby, even though his trips up this way are sadly infrequent. I wonder if you would mind passing on my regards.'

'Thank you for your help, Sergeant, and please, call me Isabella. I will be speaking to my father as soon as I am able about this whole unfortunate affair, and I will convey your regards to him then.' Isabella smiled and reached for the sergeant's hand.

'Isabella it is then,' Sergeant Collins replied and shook Isabella's hand respectfully.

'Thank you, Sergeant, for all your help and understanding. If there's anything further, you know where to find us both,' Jack added.

'You two had better get around to the Spini and see if you can get yourselves some rooms for the night, I reckon.' The sergeant escorted them to the front door of the police station.

Less than an hour later, Isabella and Jack had showered and dressed and made their way from their room to the Spinifex Hotel's dining room. As they entered the rather drab room, they were greeted with a big smile from the pretty Teresa.

'Hello, Jack, nice to see you again,' the attractive waitress said happily.

'And it's nice to see you again, Teresa. I see young Tommy's back and doing a good job on his rope again,' Jack replied and nodded across at the young Aboriginal boy pulling steadily on his rope.

'Yes, Tommy does a good job alright. Now, would you like a table for two, Jack?' Teresa asked looking just a little annoyed that he was not alone.

'Yes, Teresa, if you can manage it. And by the way, my dear, this is Isabella.'

'Hello, Isabella. I remember you from your last trip; it's nice to see you again. Now, if you would both like to follow me.' Teresa led them across the room to a table that had a neat white card on it that read table six.

Twenty minutes later, they were enjoying a meal of roast pork with apple sauce and fresh vegetables under the cooling breeze of the steadily swinging shutters.

'This is certainly a vast improvement on our last dinner here,' Jack commented, smiling at Isabella.

'Perhaps they have a new cook, Jack, who knows? That boy over there must get tired, poor thing.' They both looked across at Tommy steadily pulling on his rope.

'I'll leave a few shillings for him and Teresa before we go. He does a good job, the young lad.' Jack smiled across at Tommy and gave him a wave.

'Well now, Jack, I think the sergeant was very helpful. However, he did seem a bit casual about the whole terrible business, I must say, but let's just hope that's an end to it.' Isabella had a concerned look on her face. She was still coming to grips with all that had happened and was not looking forward to speaking to her father, but she knew it had to be done, and soon.

'I think it's all pretty well settled now, although he didn't seem too concerned about those poor buggers who were shot out bush. But as he said, that's the way they do things up here. I'm not sure I like it, but I guess he's right when he says their murderer has already paid the price,' Jack replied. 'Now, when are you going to contact your father?'

'I am going to ring him as soon as we have finished our meal. I know he will be absolutely devastated by this. I think he believed Jan Muller was a very competent manager. I know he came with very good references from farms he had been on back in Africa.'

An hour later, they were both sitting in a quiet corner of the cocktail bar discussing Isabella's long phone call to her father. Isabella had had a very serious look on her face when she came out of the manager's office and sat back down. She'd asked Jack to order two strong drinks. She was certain Jack would not like what her father had said about the trouble at the station.

'Well, what did he say, Isabella? You look concerned,' Jack asked, shifting about in his chair. Michael Montinari was his friend, but he was also a man, Jack knew, who had seen the hard side of life in his earlier years. A man whose wisdom and direction Jack eagerly awaited. He leaned forward and watched Isabella's face.

'Firstly, I said he would be devastated, and he was. But after he got over the initial shock of it all, he started to get very annoyed,' Isabella replied quietly, looking across the table at Jack's concerned expression.

'Well, let's face it; it's been a terrible shock for us all,' Jack replied.

'No, Jack, it's not that. He said he would not be part of any cover-up of the murder of the six natives in the bush by Jan Muller. He said it is just not right to treat people as if they do not exist, and he will have no part of it. He is going to contact his lawyers tomorrow morning and set in motion an action that will force the Derby police to carry out a full investigation of the whole ghastly episode. I explained to him that Pirramurar was our biggest concern. However, he told me not to worry and said he would take care of things. After all, as he said, the man saved Anna's life. He is going to try to get up to the station sometime soon, but he said that could take a month or more to arrange. Evidently, he is about to start construction of a large new city hospital and says he will have to stay until all the paperwork is finalized and the contracts signed before he can leave it to his supervisors. He is eager to get up here as soon as he can so that he can meet Anna and make sure she is coping with the tragedy that's happened to her, and, of course, to speak to Billy in regard to his managing of the property.' Isabella stopped for a moment and reached for her drink. 'My father is thinking of making some sort of donation in a trust of some sort for the betterment of conditions for the bush Aboriginals, perhaps along the line of some sort of refuge for them in hard times. He is going to speak to representatives of the Catholic Church's north-west Diocese to see if he can finance some sort of mission for them here in Derby.'

Isabella took another sip of her drink and continued, 'He is very worried what this terrible tragedy may do to his reputation if it gets out, but he says he will have no part at all in sweeping any of it under the carpet.' Isabella's serious composure softened, she smiled at the man she had fallen in love with. 'And, Jack, he sends his regards by the way. He thanks you for all your help in looking after me.'

'It has indeed been a great pleasure,' Jack replied with a wide smile.

'Sometimes, I'm sure he thinks I'm still an innocent young girl in need of constant care and protection every step of the way. But he is really sweet and I love him dearly,' Isabella said and smiled back.

'You are all he's got, my darling,' Jack replied.

'Jack, he says he wants to speak to us both in Melbourne as soon as we can arrange transport,' Isabella finally finished talking and sat back in her chair.

'Well, I think he has made the right decision. It's not right to cover things up and to be honest, I was certainly surprised by the casual way the sergeant handled it.'

'Yes, I tend to agree. I suppose now we have been summoned to my father's office, we will have to find when the next ship heading south arrives so that we can get ourselves to Perth and then we can fly directly across to Melbourne.' Isabella had stated to think of their travel plans.

'I wonder when the *Minderoo* is due back. We should visit the shipping office in the morning and make inquiries, Jack.'

'There is one other little detail we should talk about as well, Isabella.' Jack said with a serious look on his face.

'And what's that, Jack?'

'Will you marry me, Isabella Montinari?'

'W—what . . . ?'

'Will you marry me, Isabella?'

'Of course, I will, my darling,' Isabella replied. She reached across and took both of Jack's hands in hers. 'That caught me by surprise, Jack. Well now, that will be another shock for my darling father to deal with. You do realise my father is a traditional Roman Catholic, and you will have to speak to him first to get his blessing.'

'Yes, I sort of figured that and I'm not really sure he will approve, after all, I am certainly not a rich man,' Jack replied as they held hands across the table.

'Jack, it seems my father sees you as the son he was never lucky enough to have, and I'm sure it will all be fine. I love you, my darling. Now, can we please go back to our room and make love?'

'My Isabella, I love you more than you will ever know.' Jack stood up and pulled back Isabella's chair.

Isabella smiled and took Jack's right hand in hers and lifted it to her lips. 'Shall we go, then?' she whispered and kissed his fingers and the two of them made their way out of the cocktail bar.

# 33

# The Spirit Bird

Anna had woken early. It was Sunday and she wasn't needed in the kitchen until seven to help Santiago with breakfast for the stockmen. Dawn's early light was creeping through the station buildings casting silent shadows across the muddy grounds as she left them and made her way through the bulbous boab trees and down toward the dam. In the distance, she could see the pump shed. She turned away from the main track and took the narrow path that led off to the right away from the long water pipe that snaked up toward the station buildings. She had no wish to visit that terrible place again.

Anna had slept poorly. The dreams had returned again, as they had most nights. Terrible dreams of her grandfather and her people burning in their funeral pyre.

Dan and Santiago had tried to ease her suffering as best they could during the daylight hours, and it had helped immensely. But at night, when she was alone, was always the worst time for her. Her love for Dan had been her one reason to continue, without it she knew she would have suffered even more through the dark days after she had been told by Pirramurar that her people had been murdered.

She had woken from the dream just before dawn. It had left her breathless with grief. She decided she needed to get away from the white man's buildings for a while. She needed to feel the morning breeze on her face and the earth beneath her bare feet. She'd dressed quickly, leaving the treasured leather sandals Santiago had given her beneath her cot, and made her way outside, tip-toed past the old cook's room, and headed for the dam.

She made her way through the trees and down the earthen slope. The dam's cracked banks were ringed in a light fog and its waters still, reflecting the sky above with a strange metallic sheen that seemed almost magical to the young girl. She took a deep breath and sighed as she noticed the small tree where Dan and she had made love that wonderful afternoon. It now seemed so long ago.

The young girl made her way along the bank until she stood beneath the branches of the half-grown bloodwood tree and looked out across the shining water. She smiled as she remembered swimming naked in the dam's cooling waters. It had been wonderful. She looked back the way she had come. She was alone. She hurriedly removed her clothing and made her way down to the water's edge. She wanted more than anything to feel that same happiness again.

She waded out through the shallows until she stood waist-deep in the cool water. Slowly rolling waves moved ahead of her, glinting in the morning light. She took a deep breath and dived beneath the silver water. When she surfaced, she used both of her hands to push back her long dark hair and looked up. High above her, in a cloudless morning sky, she could see a huge wedge-tailed eagle lazily circling the dam. It seemed to Anna that the great bird was watching her. She smiled, and for a moment, the sadness was gone from her eyes. Perhaps it was a spirit bird sent by her grandfather to watch over her. She dived below the surface again and swam until she felt her lungs would burst.

# 34

# Sister Murphy

*Derby District Hospital Clarendon Street, Derby*
*Western Australia 15 August 2008*

Sister Murphy stopped her writing. She suddenly realised that the old Aboriginal woman was no longer talking. She looked down at her face. The poor dear had fallen asleep. The young Irish Sister had listened to the old woman's story with utter astonishment. It had seemed almost unbelievable, like the pages from some brutal history book. She had not been prepared for what she had heard. Some of it had frightened her, and some of it had made her gasp with horror. But the Sister had found herself captivated by the old woman's story, her tales of spirit men and black trackers, racial hatred and murder, and then final and bloody retribution. But most importantly, with Anna's love for the young stockman, Dan, and the conflicting emotions the young Aboriginal girl had felt between the ancient ways of her people and adjusting to the strange ways of the white man. She crossed herself, whispered a prayer for the old Aboriginal woman and stood up.

Sister Murphy realised she had never heard of the Montinari family and began to feel that she should have. She promised

311

herself a trip to the town library as soon as she could manage it. She had run out of pages in her exercise book after a very short while and had asked Anna to wait for a few minutes while she went to the nurse's station and asked if she could borrow some printer paper. The old woman had agreed and waited patiently in her quiet room. When the Sister returned, they'd continued. But now the old woman had fallen asleep.

Sister Murphy looked down at Anna's face and noticed she was smiling as she slept. Perhaps the memories that had been stirred by the telling had returned as pleasant dreams as she slept. She smiled and hoped that was the case. She began to pick up the scattered pages that lay about the side of the bed. Some of them had fallen to the floor, while others were in an untidy pile on the old woman's bedside cabinet. As she gathered them up and put them in some sort of order, she noticed an old, worn book beneath several of the sheets of paper. She picked it up. 'A Chef's Garden,' the title read. She carefully opened its worn and tattered cover and read the faded inscription inside: 'To my good friend, Santiago, wishing you all the very best for Christmas, and a big thank you for all your hard work.

*Love Isabella. 1932.'*

She closed the book and put it back on the old woman's bedside cabinet. She felt a sudden surge of emotion swell within her, and tears formed in her eyes. There was still so much more she wanted to know about the old woman's life out at Cockatoo Creek station. But now, that would have to wait for another day. She gathered up the paperwork and her ballpoint pens and whispered her goodbye to the sleeping woman. 'Good-bye, my dear Anna, and may God bless, and watch over you.'

As she stood to leave, a nurse pushed open the spring hung door that led out to the passageway and wheeled in a small stainless trolley.

'Oh—sorry to disturb you, Sister, but Anna should have had her meds by now. Anyway, I see she has fallen asleep, the poor old thing. I suppose she's been telling you some of her wonderful stories? I should tell you, Sister we all wonder how true some of them are. But she certainly is a treasure, and we love her dearly.'

Sister Murphy smiled at the nurse, excused herself, and made her way out of the old woman's room and down the long corridor. As she passed the nurse's station, she nodded her thanks to the young nurse that had given her the sheets of printer paper. At the end of the corridor, she pushed open one of the heavy double doors at the hospital's entrance and stepped outside. She looked up at the sky. There was not a cloud to be seen, just a vast ocean of blue above her. She made her way through the car park and out through the hospital gates to begin her long walk back to the Holy Rosary School where she both worked and lived.

Just then, a young Aboriginal boy raced past her, his skateboard wheels grating noisily as he slalomed from side to side along the chipped concrete footpath. The sudden noise startled the young Sister. When she recovered she watched the boy turn into Neville Street and continue on his noisy way. One of the earbuds that were connected to the boy's mobile phone by a thin strand of white plastic wire, swung wildly from side to side across the back of the boy's faded yellow t-shirt in time with his skillful maneuvers as he made his way down the untidy street.

The Sister smiled, adjusted the package of paperwork she was carrying and continued on her way.

B. J. Scholefield

314

# COCKATOO CREEK
# PART TWO

B. J. Scholefield

# 35

# Some Old Photos

*Derby District Hospital Clarendon Street, Derby*

*Western Australia 12 September 2008*

It had been the best part of a month since the Sister's last visit to the hospital. The Holy Rosary School had had a visit from the Bishop of the North-West, and as is usual with such visits, there is always so much to do. The Sister nodded her thanks to the young receptionist and made her way down the long passageway toward Anna's room.

On her last visit, the Aboriginal woman had fallen asleep during their conversations about her days living out at Cockatoo Creek Station. The Sister had said a prayer for the old woman and left. But she had made herself a promise that she would visit her again.

During discussions with her students some months earlier, Sister Murphy had decided they would start a project on the early days in the Kimberley. One of the students, a young Aboriginal girl, suggested to the Sister that she should speak to the old Aboriginal woman, Anna Cook who was being cared for at the hospital. The girl explained to the Sister that Anna had spent most of her life out at Cockatoo Creek Station and that she was sure to know what it was like in those early days. The young girl also told her that there was a rumour of some terrible things having occurred out there, many years ago. She mentioned that her parents were told that some wandering Aboriginals had been murdered while Anna lived out at the station. That was all that the young girl had been told, but she was quite sure the story was true. Sister Murphy had told her students that she would visit the old lady in the hospital, and what eventuated was a visit she would never forget

Since her last time with the old woman, the Sister had decided to visit the local library and had begun to collect snippets of information and stories about life on the remote Kimberley cattle stations during those early times. Some of these stations were quite famous for their early pioneering into the cattle industry, stations such as Yeeda, Drysdale River Station, Home Valley Station, and, of course, Cockatoo Creek Station.

During her research at the library, Sister Murphy had, quite by accident, come across some old newspaper clippings that were of great interest, and with them, a couple of rather yellowed photographs. The article she came across had been in the Derby News, dated 18th March 1926 and was titled 'Grand homestead to be constructed at Cockatoo Creek Station'. The article went on to explain that, while specialist stonemasons, carpenters, and cabinetmakers from Melbourne would be brought in to help with the building work. The owner, a Mr Michael Montinari, also from Melbourne, said that he hoped he would be able to use many local tradespeople and suppliers as well during the construction. Mr Montinari suggested that, while it was not a large project, never the less, it would be of some benefit to local tradespeople, suppliers, and the community in general. The article went on to state that, as well as the building of the station home, a dam was to be constructed to help with an irrigation project that was being planned and a while later, the erection of a number of large 'Simplex' windmills.

One of the photographs included with the article had a caption below it that read: 'Michael Montinari and his daughter, Isabella stand proudly next to the completed foundations of the new homestead now under construction at Cockatoo Creek.' While the other photo showed a rather grand, artist's impression of what was to be the completed homestead.

To the young Sister, the pictures were fascinating as they showed the Montinari family that Anna had spoken of so fondly during her last visit to the hospital. While the photographs were black and white, and somewhat yellowed with age, one did show both Michael Montinari and his daughter, Isabella in quite good detail.

Mr Montinari was a tall, well-proportioned man, who looked to be in his early fifties at that particular time, a handsome imposing figure of a man, with dark hair and the noticeably Mediterranean looks of his Italian ancestors. Of even more interest to the young Sister was the woman that Anna had spoken of so fondly. In the photograph, Isabella Montinari stood close to her father with her arm around his waist, and a loving, adoring smile on her face. Even allowing for the photographs somewhat yellowed state, and the obviously dated fashions of the times, Isabella Montinari was certainly a very beautiful woman. She was almost as tall as her handsome father and had the same dark Italian features as well. To the Sister, the Montinari woman looked as if she had just completed some sort of arduous manual work. Her long dark, somewhat unruly hair had been tied back in a sensible ponytail, but several strands of it had still managed to find a way down to frame her smiling face. Isabella was wearing a pair of rather dusty, somewhat baggy shorts and a collarless shirt of an equally voluminous size that looked like it very probably belonged to her father. The photograph showed a series of concrete foundations and footings laid out in a large rectangular design with several heaps of sand and gravel in the background. While directly behind Michael and his daughter, were a couple of large water drums, an assortment of building paraphernalia, and what looked to be a concrete mixer. The Sister had been very excited when she found the old newspaper clippings and had asked the library staff if they could be copied for her so that she could take them to the hospital and show the old Aboriginal woman, Anna, as a special surprise for her.

When she reached the end of the long passage she stopped outside the door to Anna's room, tapped on it and pushed it slowly open. The old woman was awake and beckoned for her to come and sit with her.

'Good morning, Anna. Thank you for seeing me once again,' Sister Murphy greeted the old woman with a warm smile.

'Good morning, Sister. I hope you are well,' Anna replied and continued to pat the bed for the young Sister to sit with her. 'Come and sit close to me my dear. I hope you weren't too bored when you were last here by my stories about the old days out at the station.'

'Not at all, Anna, I found them fascinating. You seem to have had a wonderfully rich life,' the sister replied. She had decided not to bring up some of the sadder parts of the old woman's stories unless she felt it was wise for her to do so.

'It brought back so many wonderful memories for me, Sister. But there is still so much more for me to tell you.'

Sister Murphy gave the old woman a cheerful smile and held up the small case in her right hand. 'Before we begin, I have something to show you.' She laid the case at the end of the old woman's bed, opened it, set her exercise books and several ballpoint pens on the bedcover beside it and lifted the large brown envelope and held it up so the old woman could see it. 'I found this in the town library quite by accident while I was doing some research, my dear. It's a rather old article about some work that was being done out at Cockatoo Creek many years ago. I think you will be quite surprised by what I am about to show you.' She opened the envelope and removed the copies of the newspaper clippings and handed them to Anna.

The old woman took them and reached for her glasses on the cabinet beside her bed. 'Well now—I wonder what you have here!' She lifted the clippings, adjusted her glasses and studied them carefully.

'Well my goodness . . . ! It's Isabella, my dear friend from so long ago, and her wonderful father.'

Sister Murphy could see the sudden shock of emotion on the old woman's face. 'I hope this is not too much for you, my dear,' she said apologetically.

The old woman never answered but continued to stare at the yellowed photographs for some time. She seemed to be lost in thought and the Sister began to think that perhaps she shouldn't have shown them to her.

Finally, Anna put down the pictures and turned to face the Sister. When she spoke her voice was hushed and emotional, her hands were shaking, and there were tears in her weary eyes. 'Thank you, my dear. What a wonderful surprise. It was all so long ago—so very long ago.'

'I'm terribly sorry, Anna, I seem to have upset you.'

'What is your name, Sister?' the old woman asked in a soft voice.

'Kathleen—my name is Kathleen. I'm sorry, I should have told you that some time ago.'

Perhaps you did already. But I'm an old woman and my memory plays games with me sometimes. Well, Kathleen, I believe I am ready to tell you more of my story, that is, if you are still interested, my dear.'

Sister Murphy nodded to the old woman and reached for her exercise book and one of her ballpoint pens.

'Thank you, Anna—and yes, I am ready,' she replied.

The old woman looked down at the photograph of Isabella and her father and smiled. 'I miss them all so much, Kathleen'. There were still tears in the old woman's eyes as she began. 'I suppose the next part of my story should begin with the farewell celebration we had at the station.'

# 36

# A Farewell Celebration

After their visit to the Derby police station and the subsequent reporting of the tragic killing of Anna's people at the hands of Jan Muller, the station manager, and the later murder of the stockman Beans, Isabella had decided she and Jack would travel to Derby and would ring her father to tell him what had happened. Michael Montinari had been both shocked and upset when Isabella told him all the details of what had happened at the station, the killing of Anna's people, her being raped, and the murder of the stockman Beans. This was the first time Michael had been aware that Anna had been hired to work in the kitchen by Jan Muller and he wondered what reason there could have been for Muller not letting him know, as was his responsibility as station manager. The whole tragic episode was of great concern to Michael, and he quickly determined that it should be dealt with properly.

As their conversation continued, Isabella told her father that, apart from the terrible assault on the Aboriginal girl by Jan Muller, Anna had fitted into station life very well, and was a great help to Santiago in the kitchen. She told her father that she and Anna had become close friends during their trip into the bush. She also explained that it was during the trip that Anna told her that she had been raped by Muller. Isabella explained to her father that Anna had been reluctant to tell her of the incident with Muller at first because she was so ashamed to speak of it. She went on to tell her father of their eventual return to the station and about the events that followed.

At the end of their discussion Michael had told his daughter that she and Jack should book passage as soon as possible for their return to Melbourne where he would have further discussion with them in regard to the shocking happenings that had taken place at the station and he would decide then what actions should be taken in regard to further police inquiries. Isabella assured her father they would do so, and told him she would see him soon, and that she loved him dearly.

The following morning Isabella and Jack made inquiries at the Derby shipping office to book passage on the S.S. *Mindaroo* for their trip south. Unfortunately, they had missed a recent southbound trip by Captain Bradford by just a few days and were told if they wished to travel with him they would have a three-week wait until his ship called again on its southbound passage from ports to the north. After some discussion, they decided they would book passage and wait for the Mindaroo as it would be a great opportunity for them to catch up with their good friend, Captain Bradford once again. Isabella sent a telegram to her father telling him of their travel plans, and they had then returned to the station.

In the weeks that followed, Isabella took the opportunity to help Anna with her studies. In the afternoons, in the hours before she was needed in the kitchen, Anna came to the homestead and Isabella took the Aboriginal girl into her father's study and did her best to give her a better education than the basic teachings the old cook, Santiago had given her, and to her delight, she was more than happy with the young girls progress. Isabella soon realised that Anna was a highly intelligent young woman and an eager student, and it became a great pleasure for her to help, and something she looked forward to each day. But as the days wore on it became noticeable to Isabella that Anna was still having trouble accepting what had happened to her people at the hands of Jan Muller. Even though her studies rarely suffered, at times she became quiet and disconsolate, and on occasion, Isabella found herself repeating questions to the young girl.

For Anna, while she enjoyed her studies with Isabella, and her work on the huge cattle property, at times she felt the almost overwhelming urge to leave the station and her new friends and just wander off into the bush. For some strange reason, she felt that she may find peace back in the wild lands of her people. She dreamed of once more sleeping beneath the stars and listening to the comforting sounds of the bush. Anna understood that, while her grandfather and her people were gone from her world forever, she imagined that she may feel some comfort from their spirits as she lay beneath the endless heavens and gazed up at the stars. She was a Ngarinyin and she was alone, and it frightened her.

Most evenings Anna would take wildflowers to Beans' grave and spread them out across the well-tended earth. The young girl still felt responsible for her dear friend's death. Dan had found her weeping at the gravesite several times and each time he would sit with her and wait patiently, and when she grew silent he would help her to her feet and lead her back to her room behind the kitchen. Once, when he helped her onto her narrow cot, she held on to him so tightly that he stayed with her and they had made love. Their lovemaking that night had an intensity that frightened the young stockman. Anna had seemed possessed, frantic, and far too passionate. She had held him so tightly she left marks on his body that took several days to disappear. And later, as the lay together, she had burst into tears. Dan's love for Anna was a gentle thing, a tender wonderful love that would never change as long as he drew breath. But now, it seemed she had changed, she'd become withdrawn, distant, and it worried him greatly.

Santiago had noticed the subtle changes in Anna's behavior as well, and he had tried his very best to help her. But the old man knew that something deep and spiritual was troubling her, and he prayed that she would soon find her way.

Several days before Isabella and Jack were to leave for Derby for their trip south, Isabella decided that they would host a farewell celebration in the homestead gardens. In the afternoon a huge fire was lit so that when it settled into a bed of coals later it would be ready for the two young pigs that were to be roasted on the rotating spit Bob Nugent had hurriedly built in his workshop. Santiago and Anna had spent most of their day preparing and stuffing the young pigs, making salads, and cooking loaves of bread for the eagerly awaited event. Jack and several of the station hands set long trestle tables and chairs into position beneath the shady trees, while others raked away leaves and small fallen limbs from the recently cut lawns in preparation for the farewell celebration.

Pearl and Rosie had spent their leisure time sewing the material that Isabella had gifted them at the Christmas party into pretty new dresses for themselves and a brightly coloured pair of shorts and a pretty new blouse for Anna to wear. Jack and Isabella had earlier strung a large bedsheet onto two posts ready for the movie that was to be shown after the eating and drinking was finished. And, following careful instruction from Santiago, large bowls of salad and sliced melon were set about in careful order on the long trestle tables. Tubs of ice from the kitchen freezer were filled with bottles of Swan Brewery Ale, taken from the store under instruction from Isabella. Isabella, knowing that Anna was having difficulty coming to terms with the murder of her people, had asked her to help with the final preparations for the farewell celebrations.

The two women were busy hanging coloured ribbons among the lower branches of a huge frangipani tree when Isabella spoke. 'Anna, you're very quiet my dear. Is there is anything you would like to talk to me about? She asked sincerely.

'No, I don't think so.' Anna replied softly.

'I am here for you, my dear. If there is anything I can do to help, you only need to ask.'

'Thank you, Isabella. But you have much to do with your planning for your return to see your father. So please don't worry too much about me. Santiago is looking after me, and my work in the kitchen keeps me busy,' Anna replied with a timid voice. The young girl loved Isabella, but she was not comfortable with the fuss that was being made over her by everyone. She was an employee of the station, an Aboriginal, and no more important than her good friends, Pearl and Rosie.

Isabella stopped tying ribbons to the branches above her and climbed down from her stepladder. 'Anna, do you know what I wish I could do?'

'No—what do you wish for Isabella,' Anna asked shyly.

'I wish I could take you with me and take care of you when we leave the station. We could have so much fun travelling down on the *Mindaroo* to Fremantle. You would get to meet Captain Bradford, and I am sure you would like him as much as I do. Then the train trip across the Nullarbor to Adelaide and on to Melbourne. It would be such a great experience for you. You would love my father, and I should tell you, he is very concerned about you.'

Tears began to mist in Anna's eyes. 'Isabella, can I tell you something that I do not want anyone else to know. Not Dan or even Santiago.'

'Of course, you can my dear. It will be our secret if you want it to be.' Isabella could sense the distress in Anna's voice.

'You have been so good to me Isabella, and you will probably not understand. But something inside me is telling me that, to find peace, I must go back to the bush from where I came. Perhaps there, I may find something that will help me to understand the terrible loneliness I feel. Sometimes when I dream, my grandfather comes to visit me and we sit under the night sky and he tells me his stories again, but when I wake he is gone and the loneliness returns. The bush was our home and it is where I was born. Perhaps if I return, I will feel his spirit once again. I hope you can understand, Isabella.'

'Of course, I can, my dear. You feel lost and alone. But you have Dan, and I'm sure he is trying to help, and Santiago, who loves you like his own daughter.'

'Santiago is a wonderful man, and I do love Dan. It makes me feel terrible to even think of leaving him. But I'm sure that when I am well I will return.' Anna had tears in her eyes.

'Have you told him what you are thinking?'

'No I haven't, Isabella. I know he will not understand.'

'You may be surprised.'

'I will talk to him soon, and try to explain how I feel.'

'Where will you go, my dear?' Isabella asked

'I'm not sure. Perhaps back to the hills where we travelled on our trip.'

Isabella reached for Anna and hugged her. 'What would you say if I asked you to come with Jack and me when we leave?' The question came out so quickly that Isabella was surprised by it herself; such was her concern for the young girl.

'You are so kind to me, Isabella. But would that be wise? I am Aboriginal, and I do not know the ways of the white people in their cities,' Anna replied timidly.

'Do you trust me, Anna?' Isabella asked.

'Yes, of course.'

'Well, I think it may be very good for you to leave here for a while,' Isabella replied. 'And we could have so much fun.'

'Do you really think so?' Anna mood seemed to lighten a little.

'Yes, I do.' Isabella had tears of sympathy in her eyes. She reached for the young girl again and put her arms around her.

'But what would, Jack say?' Anna whispered.

'I'm sure he would be more than pleased. He understands much more than you think, and he knows only too well what happened to you, and what you have been through, my dear'.

'What would Dan think if I was to go with you?'

'I'm sure he will understand as well. And perhaps it may be good for both of you.'

'Thank you for your kindness, Isabella. Can I talk to Dan and Santiago first before I decide?'

'And I will speak to Jack as well, my dear,' Isabella put her hand on Anna's shoulder as she replied.

Anna bowed her head in thanks and picked up several of the coloured ribbons that lay on the trestle table and turned back to her task.

The farewell celebration was a great success. Even though the station hands were well used to the great food that Santiago served, the spit-roasted pigs were a real treat. Most of those present ate far too much, and some certainly drank too much of the chilled beer that was set about the garden in cut down fuel drums filled with chunks of ice.

Isabella brought out a portable phonograph from the homestead with a selection of country music records for the station hands enjoyment, and, as the night wore on, Pearl and Rosie found themselves partnered by most of the men on the station to a rough interpretation of the Square dance. Even Anna and Dan got to their feet and attempted a dance that could only be described as a cross between some sort of cowboy jig and an Aboriginal bird dance. Later in the evening, the movie projector was set up and the last of the western movies that Isabella had brought with her was shown to a rowdy crowd of revellers.

When the movie was underway and all of the station hands were glued to the screen Anna and Dan stole away to the machinery shed. Dan spread a canvas tarp, sat down and reached up for Anna. 'Come down here and sit with me,' he whispered'

'Dan, can I ask you something very important first?'

'I know things are getting you down, my love. But I'm here for you. If there is anything I can do, please, just ask.'

'I spent the afternoon with Isabella and she asked me if I would like to travel down to Melbourne with her and Jack when they leave tomorrow. She thinks it will do me good to get away from the station for a while. I don't know what to think, Dan.' Anna had a troubled expression on her face. She was worried about what Dan would say.

This came as quite a surprise to Dan and was certainly unexpected. But he knew it would probably be a good idea for Anna to get away from the station for a while. He would miss her terribly. But he had grown very concerned with her state of mind.

'Do you think you will be able to cope with it all? It will be such a change for you. I have been told Melbourne is a really big place,' he replied.

'I am not sure.' Anna started to cry.

'What's wrong my angel.'

'I have felt so terribly lost for the past few weeks. I miss my people so much!'

'It's been an awful time for you.' Dan reached for her and pulled her to him.

'I was thinking of leaving the station anyway and going out into the bush on my own for a while,' Anna said in a timid voice. She felt embarrassed by her confession.

'I think it would be much better for you to travel with Jack and Isabella. It will be safer, and they will care for you,' Dan replied.

'Yes, I think that it would be best as well. Are you sure you won't mind me going?'

'I will miss you my darling.' Dan knew he would miss Anna terribly. But he knew Isabella would do her best to look after her, and he was certain the change would do her good.

Anna's mood seemed to suddenly change. She felt relieved that some of the confusion that had worried her for such a long time now seemed to lift from her mind. She loved Isabella so much and she was so glad she had asked her to travel with her and Jack. She knew it would be an adventure she would never forget. She got up from the canvas sheet and reached for Dan's hand.

'Do you think we could go down to the dam for a while?'

'But it's dark outside Anna.' Dan was confused.

'No. There is a full moon, and I would like to go for a swim.' Anna smiled. 'Can we please?'

'Okay then.' Dan got up and put the tarp back over the piece of machinery that it had covered, and they made their way outside.

'I will talk to Isabella tomorrow and tell her I will be happy to travel with her and Jack. I hope I am not too much trouble for them.' Anna took Dan's hand and they headed for the dam.

# 37

# Captain Bradford

The S.S *Mindaroo* was somewhere north of the Kingfisher Islands when Captain James Hedley Bradford put down the telegraph message he had just received. Isabella Montinari and two travelling companions, Jack Ballinger, and a Miss Anna Cook were to board the S.S *Mindaroo* tomorrow, mid-morning at the port of Derby. The old captain turned to his radio operator. 'Mr Darcy, please send a reply directly to the shipping office in Derby and advise that Captain Bradford awaits a reunion with Miss Isabella Montinari and her companions with pleasant anticipation. Please include that cabins will be made available, and will be prepared and readied for their boarding'

'I'll get right on it Captain,' the radio operator replied, and waited should there be anything further.

'Thank you, Mr Darcy, that will be all,' the captain said in a matter-of-fact tone and turned back to his chair and sat down. He reached into his linen jacket and took out his old bent-stemmed briarwood pipe and began to pack it with tobacco.

Archibald Darcy turned smartly and left the bridge. The tall radio operator had sailed with the captain for more than eight years, and not once had he ever been addressed by him, as anything other than, Mr Darcy, even though the rest of the crew addressed the affable radio operator as Archie. Still, he thought, that was the captain's way, proper and correct, regardless. But it still irked the Mindaroo's popular shipmate.

Captain Bradford looked out over the bridge at the impossibly blue, tropical ocean spread out before him. It was early morning and the weather was agreeable. He took a draw on his pipe and exhaled the sweet-smelling smoke slowly. He was delighted to hear that his good friends Isabella and Jack were to board his ship in Derby. His long discussions with the very beautiful Isabella Montinari had been a source of great enjoyment to the old captain. He'd listened intently to her retelling of her experiences in Europe. In particular, her days in Paris where she had studied fine art for several years. The captain had also enjoyed the company of the rough and ready, Jack Ballinger after he had joined them in Geraldton as Isabella's travelling companion and minder. The handsome returned serviceman had been hired by Isabella's father, the wealthy Melbourne industrialist, Mr Michael Montinari, to look after his daughter.

Captain Bradford had found himself besotted with the Montinari woman. Isabella was a stunning beauty. But she was also a highly intelligent woman, and their discussions proved a great stimulus for the old captain. They covered subjects as diverse as the art of the great masters, Botticelli, Michelangelo, and Picasso, to name but a few, and then moved on to the mysteries of the northern coast of Australia. Isabella had shown genuine interest in the captain's studies and knowledge of the Aboriginal tribes of the Kimberley, and they had talked for many hours.

The old captain puffed contentedly on his pipe, he knew for certain that the trip from Derby down the coast to Freemantle would now be anything but boring. He looked down at the telegraph message, and read it again. There would be a third passenger, a Miss Anna Cook. He wondered who she was, and hoped he would like her.

## 38

# Tommy the Rope Puller

Isabella pushed the rumpled bedsheet away from her face and looked at her travel clock. It was seven in the morning. It was hot, and she hadn't slept well. Twice during the night she had got up and made her way down the passage to the guest bathroom and showered in an attempt to cool herself, but it had not been worth the effort, as the tap water was warm as well. Isabella was still haunted by the recent events out at Cockatoo Creek and found herself looking forward to getting away from the station. She rolled over and shook Jack awake. 'It's time to get up sleepy-head. We have to pack and get ourselves ready. The Mindaroo arrives in a couple of hours. I think I had better go and check on Anna.'

Jack slid his arm under Isabella and pulled her to him. 'We still have plenty of time, beautiful, and I'm sure Anna is fine in her room for a bit longer.'

'You are incorrigible, Jack,' Isabella replied, struggling with Jack's embrace.

'Alright I give in—anyway I do feel the urgent need for bacon and eggs, and a pot of strong coffee,' Jack announced. He swung his legs out from under the sheet and sat up.

After Jack and Isabella had showered and dressed, Isabella went to the room next to theirs and tapped on the door. 'Good morning Anna, are you up and about?'

332

'Yes, I am. Please, come in Isabella.'

Isabella opened the door. 'Good morning, my dear. Are you ready for breakfast?'

'Yes, I am Isabella.' Anna had been dressed and ready for some time.

A short while later, Jack, Isabella, and Anna made their way into the rather drab Spinifex Hotel's dining room.

'Good morning, Teresa. Could we have a table for three for breakfast, my dear?' Jack gave the attractive mixed race waitress a warm smile.

'I was told you were staying with us again Jack. I hope you and Isabella are both well,' Teresa replied cheerfully. She turned and studied the tall Aboriginal girl who was accompanying them.

'This is Anna, Teresa. She is travelling with us this trip,' Jack added.

'Good morning, Anna.' Teresa was intrigued by the Aboriginal girl's unusual features, her coal black skin, and her slanted, Asian eyes.

'Hello,' Anna replied timidly.

Teresa kept her eyes on the beautiful Aboriginal girl as she spoke. 'I've heard on the grapevine that there's been some trouble out at the station recently, Jack. Some bush natives speared a couple of steers and got themselves shot, so I was told.' She saw the sudden shock of emotion on the young girl's face.

'Yes, that's quite true. There has been a bit of trouble out our way, but it has all been dealt with now,' Jack replied hesitantly. 'Now Teresa—do you have a table for us, my dear?'

'Follow me please.' The waitress led them across the dining room to a table well away from the rest of the morning's diners. 'Will this be okay for you?'

'It will be just fine. Thank you, Teresa.'

Jack pulled out a chair for Isabella and then made his way around the table to do the same for Anna, but Teresa had beaten him to it.

'My dear were you one of those natives that were involved in the attack out there by that bastard, Jan Muller. I know him from some of his trips into town. He was a bad bugger that one. He almost killed a man in the front bar here, a while back.'

Jack and Isabella were taken by surprise by the sudden outburst from Teresa and were caught off guard. They both watched Anna's face and waited nervously for her reply.

'Yes—I was the only one that was not killed among my people,' Anna had tears forming in her eyes when she replied. It was obvious that the question had surprised and upset her. But she had the good sense not to mention, Pirramurar, the man who had killed the station manager.

Teresa put her arms around Anna and hugged her affectionately. 'Some of these white buggers are real bastards, Anna. But you be strong, girl, I'm sure Jack and Isabella will look after you just fine.' Teresa had tears in her own eyes when she spoke.

Jack looked up. The swinging shutters that usually struggled to keep the dining room cool had come to a standstill. He looked back at Teresa and noticed young Tommy was standing next to her.

Teresa looked down at the boy. 'Is this the woman you saw, Tommy?'

The young Aboriginal boy did not reply, instead, he reached up and placed his hand on Anna's arm.

'Anna is it true that you see things—things that sometimes seem to make no sense to you!'

'Yes I do—but not often,' Anna's reply was hesitant and little more than a whisper. It was obvious she was taken by surprise by the question from the waitress.

'Tommy here sees things also, and he has told me about a dream he had, a dream that made him come to me and tell me about it. But please don't be concerned, I'm sure it's just a silly dream that's come about by his overactive imagination. Anyway, he has asked me to tell you about it, and I promised him I would. So I hope you don't mind, my dear.'

Jack and Isabella watched in silence as the strange conversation continued.

'A dream—what dream . . . ?' Anna looked down into Tommy's face. But the boy made no attempt to reply.

Teresa continued, 'He knows who you are, my dear. He saw you yesterday when you first arrived. It was then that he told me he had seen you in his dream. He said that in his dream he saw you crying in a great cave somewhere out in the bush. He said it was a sacred place, could this be possible, Anna?'

Teresa looked into Anna's eyes, and then down at Tommy hoping for reassurance. Tommy nodded.

'Yes that is so,' Anna replied.

The young boy took his hand away from Anna's arm, and went back to his rope and began slowly pulling it up and down. Once again the heavy shutters began to swing back and forth in unison, sending a cooling breeze down into the dining room.

'Anna, he told me you will live a long and happy life, and that your grandfather will visit you many times while you sleep.' Teresa had tears in her eyes when she finished talking. She turned to Jack and Isabella and attempted an apologetic smile. Then she made her way out through the spring-hung doors to the kitchen.

'Are you alright, Anna? Isabella had a concerned expression on her face.

Anna looked across at Tommy, now busy with his work and gave him a knowing smile. She turned back to Isabella and Jack. 'Yes, Isabella, I feel fine. But I am very hungry though.'

'Well, let's see if we can get Teresa to come back and maybe we can get something to eat before we get the manager of the pub to take us down to the wharf to meet the Mindaroo.' Jack stood up and went out through the spring-hung doors to see if he could find Teresa.

# 39

# Avellino

The driver turned the big Packard 845 past the polished brass sign that read, '*Avellino*' and headed down the driveway that ran along the side of the magnificent red brick federation home.

'Damn traffic made the trip from the city a bit slower than usual today, Michael.' Willard Burgess said to the man in the rear of the Packard.

'What was that, Will . . . ?' Michael Montinari took off his glasses put down the papers he had been studying, and looked at the man behind the wheel of the big American car.

Willard Burgess had been Michael Montinari's chauffeur and personal assistant for a little over seven years. The solidly built Englishman had at one time been a contender for the British amateur, heavyweight title. But a brush with the law had unfortunately seen him spend a year in Wormwood Scrubs, which had curtailed his promising boxing career. On release from prison, Willard decided to try and sort his life out, and quite by accident passed a sign extolling the benefits of a life in Australia. In an instant, he had made up his mind, and after a long and arduous sea voyage, he'd arrived in Melbourne. The big Englishman had six pounds and four shillings in his pocket, his few belongings crammed tightly into an old Gladstone bag and absolutely no idea what he should do next. Less than a week later he found himself applying for employment with a building company he had never heard of. A company named Montinari Constructions Pty Ltd.

The quiet Englishman had come to the notice of his employer, Michael Montinari quite by accident. He'd been stacking scaffold parts into a heap ready for later pick up when a well-dressed man accompanied by two site supervisors walked by him. At that very moment, Willard heard an ominous metallic groan directly above him. He looked up, just as a panel of heavy scaffolding swung away from the main structure and hung down the side of the six-story building in a writhing mass of tube-work and wooden planks. Strangely, none of it fell, and at that particular moment, no-one else seemed to hear it. And then the unthinkable happened. The tangled mass of scaffolding began to screech and break free and start to tumble haphazardly down the side of the building, heading straight toward the three men that had just passed him. Willard dropped the long tube he was holding and raced toward the unsuspecting men and crash-tacked them all into an untidy heap beneath a lower concrete awning just as several tons of scaffolding and planks smashed into the earth right next to them.

'Jesus, what the hell just happened,' Mick Smythe, one of the site supervisors gasped, finding himself short of breath from the unexpected, bone-crunching tackle.

'Are you alright, Mr Montinari?' the other supervisor yelled, as the smartly dressed man struggled to his feet.

'I'm fine—I'm fine! But what the hell just happened!' Michael Montinari stood up and began to dust himself off. He looked down at his feet and noticed one of his shoes had come off from the impact of the heavy unknown tackler. 'What the bloody hell just happened?'

'Looks like a section of the scaffold has come away from above us, sir,' Mick, the senior site foreman remarked looking at the pile of twisted metal and timber on the ground near them, concern obvious on his face. 'Heads will bloody well roll for this. I just can't believe it.'

Michael Montinari looked out across the worksite and noticed there were still men working, and most of them seemed oblivious to what had just happened.

'Get someone to shut down those bloody compressors, Mick. Those men in the footing trenches can't hear a damn thing because of the bloody jackhammers, and get across to the site office and sound the alarm—quick as you can.'

Mick Smythe took off at a run toward the site office, yelling to his men as he went. 'Get back away from the main building, you blokes. The scaffolds broke away, and it looks like more of it is gonna come down.'

'I want to know where the man is that just saved us from certain bloody death, that's what I want to know,' Michael Montinari snapped, as he took off his jacket and shook the dust from it. He noticed his missing shoe lying in the dirt at the edge of the concrete overhang. He reached his stockinged left foot out for it. At the same time, he looked up at the tangled mass of steel above him. It was then that he saw a man working his way up the weakened scaffolding.

'Jesus—who the hell is that crazy bastard—and what the hell is he doing up there?' Michael yelled to the other supervisor.

Gerry Knight came across to the overhang and looked up. 'I reckon he's that big pommy bloke we put on a while back. I think he's gone up to try to tie back some of the loose stuff!' he said breathlessly and tried to brush more of the dust away from Michael's clothes.

'Leave my clothes, Gerry. I'm fine. Look at that crazy bastard up there; he'll get himself killed for certain. You'd better get someone up there to give him a hand!'

'Sorry, sir, but I don't think anyone on this site would be that crazy. It'd be suicide going up there right now. This whole bloody side will be on the ground shortly, and that crazy Pommy bastard with it, I reckon.'

Just then another section of scaffold swung away from the main building, sending several, heavy timber planks crashing, end first, into the ground four stories below.

'Get me across to the site office—right now, Gerry.'

Michael could see the obvious sense in his supervisor's words, sending others up the weakened scaffold would most probably be a death sentence. But he was angry and frustrated. There must be something he could do to help the man scrambling up the steel above them. The man had just saved his life!

As the two men raced out from the shelter of the concrete overhang and headed for the site office, a screech of swinging scaffold filled their ears. Without bothering to look up they tore across the open ground, hoping they'd get to the site office before any more steelwork broke free and came crashing down the side of the building.

Most of the construction workers were now well out of harm's way now. Thanks to the high pitched wailing of the safety siren. Only the foundation workers, who had been some eight feet below ground level, were still in danger, but the last of them were now clambering out and heading toward the site office. All eyes were now on the man high above them working his way steadily across the loose scaffold.

Willard Burgess had reacted the only way he knew how when he was faced with danger—fast and straight at it. It was the same philosophy he'd used in the ring—go in and get it done. The big Englishman knew that if any more of the steelwork came loose someone down below could be killed. Something had to be done and done quickly. As he worked his way across a loosened section of the scaffold, high up and to the right of the breakaway, he could see that the structure was securely anchored at each level by a series of heavy clamps fastened to each floor's concrete overhang. But when he reached the area of the breakaway the clamps that were supposed to be connected to the fourth-floor awning were swinging out at least a foot from the main building and not connected at all. Instantly, he knew what had happened. Plasterers he'd noticed earlier working their way down the building floor by floor had removed several of the clamps so they could complete their plasterwork down to that particular floor level. This was a dangerous mistake made by unskilled men who obviously did not understand the rigid principles of scaffold construction. Willard knew that if he could get his hands on the loose and swinging clamp moving about on his side of the breakaway he may be able to clamp it into position on the concrete overhang and anchor that particular section of slowly moving scaffold. To do it he would need to wait until the clamp moved back against the overhang. The Englishman locked his legs tightly around a vertical stanchion and reached out into the void and took hold of the slowly moving clamp and waited for it to swing back toward the building, acutely aware of the groan of tortured scaffolding above.

Finally, the heavy clamp swung back against the building. Using all of the strength in his powerful arms he tightened it into position on the concrete overhang with the scaffold spanner that hung in the steel ring on the back of his belt. Thirty minutes later, and after several more extremely dangerous maneuvers, Willard finally managed to secure most of the remaining steelwork that had not already collapsed, to the concrete overhang on either side of the breakaway. With his work now complete, he began a weary descent from the fourth-floor steelwork.

Every man on the worksite had watched in silence as the big Englishman climbed from one section of the scaffold to another, the heavy spanner swinging from his belt. At first most of them thought he was crazy to attempt something so obviously dangerous. But when they realised what he was trying to do they watched in silent admiration as he moved about above them, and when his feet finally touched the ground, a deafening cheer went up across the building site and continued for several minutes.

Mick Smythe was the first man to reach the Englishman, and when he did, he offered him his outstretched hand. 'You crazy bloody pom— that's the bravest thing I ever saw.'

'It had to be taken care of, Mick. There were men down below that weren't aware of what was going on. Anyway, I reckon I'd drawn meeself the short straw being so bloody close when it happened. But, you know, once I got up there, it wasn't so bad,' the big Englishman replied.

'Yeah righto, Will . . . Anyway, the big boss wants to see you over in the office, you crazy bugger. That is, as soon as you reckon you got your breath back, mate,' Mick said with relief and admiration showing on his face.

'Probably going to sack me for dangerous behavior, I would think,' Willard replied. He nodded to the site foreman and tied a handkerchief around his badly blistered left hand.

'He's waiting for you now mate. You better get yourself over there.'

Michael Montinari heard the knock on the door and asked the office woman at the main desk to open it for him.

Willard Burgess watched the door open. He smiled at the woman. 'Good morning, Betty.'

'Good morning, Will,' Betty Maloney gave the Englishman a smile and stood aside to let him enter.

'You wanted to see me, Mr Montinari?'

'Betty, would you mind stepping outside for a few minutes, my dear?' Michael asked the capable office woman.

'Of course, sir,' Betty Maloney replied. She hurried past the imposing figure of Willard Burgess and made her way outside, leaving the two men alone in the office.

'Yes, I wanted to see you all right. I'm Michael Montinari, the man you just crash-tackled into that overhang over there. You must be, Willard Burgess, the crazy Englishman that just went up and secured that scaffolding.' Michael offered his hand to the burly Englishman.

'Yep, that was me alright. Pretty jolly stupid I suppose.' Willard took Michael's outstretched hand and shook it respectfully.

'Safety is always our first priority on these jobs, Willard, and in doing what you did today; you may well have saved quite a few lives. I would like to thank you personally for that, and I would also like to thank you for saving my own life, and the lives of both the site supervisors with that not so gentle rugby tackle of yours. I owe you my life, Willard, a debt I will not forget.'

Michael still had hold of the Englishman's right hand and with his left; he took hold of the big man's shoulder and looked hard into his eyes. 'There are very few men in this world that I owe a damn thing to. But now it seems you are one of them.'

'Well, I just did what I thought had to be done, that's all.' Willard Burgess was suddenly quite embarrassed by Michael Montinari's gratitude.'

'How long have you been with us, Willard?'

'Call me, Will, sir. If you don't mind, that is.'

'Will it is, then. So, how long have you been with us, Will?'

'About six weeks, or thereabouts, I've been helping with the scaffolders work mainly.'

'Where are you living, if you don't mind me asking you?'

'I stay in an old guest house in the city, sir, 'The Digger's Rest.' Why do you ask?' Willard replied, wondering the point of the question.

'And let me ask you this, Will. What sort of a driver are you?' Michael enquired, a smile beginning to form on his face.

'If its cars that you're asking about, Mr Montinari, pretty fair I would say. I drove cabs in London for a spell a couple of years back.'

Michael Montinari's face took on a serious expression. 'Will, I need a driver to ferry me around to the different work sites and other engagements that I have to get to. I guess the job classification could be called, driver and personal assistant. I would like to offer you that position. It would mean a sizable rise in your wages, and if you take the position, your future accommodation would be taken care of as well.'

'I thank you for the offer, Mr Montinari. But you don't really know me at all. I'm sure there would be others more capable. And anyway, I'm not really that familiar with the city, for a start,' The Englishman replied, a serious expression on his grimy face.

'You let me worry about that. I've seen your file, Will and from what I have read, you are trustworthy, and from what I have been told, you're a damn good worker. I have also heard you were a pretty fair boxer back in the old country.'

'That's true sir. But those days are behind me now,' The Englishman replied with a grin.

Michael sat down at one of the site managers desks and pushed aside the pile of paperwork that was in his way and nodded for Willard to take a seat opposite.

'Let me get to the point, I have been on the lookout for someone I could trust for this job for quite a while now, and I always seem to come up empty. The position I am offering you would entail you being my driver and, as I said, my personal assistant as well. Over the years I seem to occasionally run into some fairly unsavoury characters if you know what I mean. Bully boys from the trade unions, irate sub-contractors, and the like. So I need a man that can handle himself when difficult situations arise. A man that understands what needs to be done, but knows how to be discrete, if need be. Do you understand my meaning?'

There was an uncomfortable silence for a short while, and then the big Englishman replied, 'I understand completely, Mr Montinari, and I am not without some experience in matters you have referred to.'

'If you decide to take up my offer, Will, your accommodation will be taken care of at my expense. I have a very comfortable flat annexed at the rear of my home. It is both private and well-appointed, and I am sure you will find it most adequate. This, I feel would be the most practical arrangement in regard to your position with me, and for your day to day work. Give it some serious thought, Will, and let Mick know your decision in the next day or so.'

Michael stood up to leave and offered the Englishman his hand again. 'I'd better get out of here. I have a meeting in the city shortly. I hope to hear from you soon, and thanks again for what you did today. You're a brave man, and I will not forget it.'

'No need for any serious thought, as far as I'm concerned. You've just hired yourself a diver and a personal assistant, Mr Montinari, and I would very much like to thank you for the opportunity to be of service.'

'That is what I was hoping for,' Michael replied with a smile. He shook Willard's hand again and then handed him one of his personal cards, given only to his most trusted acquaintances. 'My home address is on this card, Will. But please, show it to no-one. I place great value on my privacy. Take the next couple of days off, collect your gear and meet me at my home at six o'clock on Friday evening for dinner, if that is agreeable?'

'I'll be there sir. And thank you again for your generous offer I will endeavor to do my very best for you, Mr Montinari. Of that, you have my word.'

\* \* \*

The man in the rear of the big Packard sedan put the paperwork he'd been studying down on the top of heavy leather valise that sat on the seat next to him.

'I didn't really notice the traffic at all, Will.' Michael Montinari replied, as he took off his glasses. 'Did I tell you that, Isabella is heading home from Cockatoo Creek and should be here in a couple of weeks?'

'Yes you did, sir. Several times now at the very least, I would think. Would you like me to garage the car, or will we be going out again this evening?'

'I'll be staying in tonight, Will.' Michael slipped the paperwork back into his valise and waited for the car to come to a halt before stepping out and heading for the side portico. He was still fumbling with his house keys when the leadlight doors swung open and a portly middle-aged woman stepped outside.

'Good evening, Michael. I trust you have had a busy day as usual.'

'Thank you, Sofia. Yes too damn busy, if you ask me. By the way, there are too many damn keys on this key ring.'

'The key you want is the brass one, Michael. The one I scratched the S on. S for the side door if you remember,' the housekeeper explained with a patient smile.

'What would I do without you, Sofia?' Michael Montinari replied.

'I would imagine that you'd get by just fine, sir. But at the moment I'm quite sure you have far too much on your mind,' Sofia replied with a patient tone and stood aside to let her employer pass.

Michael put his arm around Sofia's shoulders and hugged her affectionately. 'Thank you, Sofia. I will be in the study for a while this evening, I have a few bits and pieces to catch up on. Just let me know when dinner is ready.'

'I have some good news for you, Michael.'

'And what would that be Sophia?'

'I managed to get some wonderfully fresh clams at the fish market this morning, so I will be preparing your favourite dish this evening, 'Clams and pancetta in white wine sauce with risotto,' the housekeeper said proudly.

'That sounds wonderful Sofia. You spoil me constantly,' Michael replied sincerely.

Sofia Moretti had been Michael Montinari's cook and housekeeper for more than 20 years. The portly Italian woman was a vital part of the Montinari family household, the very engine room of the beautiful federation home. She was an exceptional cook, a fastidious housekeeper, and the pillar that everyone leaned on when they needed support.

To Michael's daughter, Isabella, she had taken the place of her mother, after her mother had died quite suddenly when Isabella was just a young girl, and Isabella loved her unconditionally.

For Michael, she had been the very reason he had survived the tragic death of his wife, Rosa so many years before. Sofia had helped him through the painful months of loss, and then gently led him back toward the light from the darkness that had almost totally consumed the wealthy businessman. She had been patient and gentle with him at first. But eventually, she'd reminded him of the responsibility he had raising Isabella, and of setting an example to her, of love and guidance. She reminded him also that he had a very successful business to run, and that there were men in his employ whose very existence relied on him for their constant guidance.

Michael pushed open the study doors, entered the spacious room and closed them behind him. He loved this room. He had designed its refurbishment with great care a few years earlier. Originally, it had been a sitting room and was complete with a magnificent leadlight bay window that looked out toward the front of the house and its manicured gardens. Michael had several of his carpenters line the walls with mahogany panelling to a height of nine feet, and then had them fit a narrow shelf at its top so that he could display his many building achievement awards and various other personal paraphernalia from his regular trips overseas.

In pride of place on the shelf was a slightly yellowed photograph of Rosa and him on their wedding day. The photograph was taken in the Duomo di Santa Maria Assunta e di San Modestino, the Cathedral in his home town of Avellino. To Michael, the photograph, and its cheap oval frame constantly reminded him of how far he had come in his adopted country. While the love both he and Rosa had for each other was there for all to see. The crushing poverty they had endured in their home country was plainly evident as well. Rosa's beautiful face was partly covered with a faded ivory veil her grandmother had worn on her wedding day, and her dress, although lovingly crafted by her mother, showed obvious signs of her family's poor status in the community. Michael remembered only too well, the tight-fitting suit he'd borrowed from a married friend, its trousers too short and its brown colour not really suitable for a wedding. But regardless of all of that, it was still the happiest day of Michael Montinari's life.

On the wall to the left of the magnificent bay window, he had his joiners fit floor to ceiling bookshelves to accommodate his collection of fine books. On another wall, he'd had them build a mahogany bar, and a small wall niche that housed a custom made radiogram, so that when he desired he could listen to his collection of classical music.

Among his favourites were works by Giuseppe Verdi and Antonio Vivaldi. But his taste was varied, and at times he found great pleasure listening to more modern works. In particular, the talented guitar of Django Reinhardt, the famous Belgian born, Romani-French gypsy.

Michael sat at the mahogany desk in the well-lit space near the bay window and opened his leather valise. He was not a happy man. The financial depression that had almost completely crippled the Australian economy was once again biting into his business ventures. He had, for a short while, thought it was showing signs of easing, but now he knew he had been overly optimistic. The

Victorian government had recently decided to cut infrastructure spending again, and this had curtailed many of the projects that he had been counting on. For Michael, this would necessitate the unenviable task of putting off many of his construction workers, men whose very livelihood depended on his company. Some of whom had been with him for a very long time.

Fortunately, this would have little effect on his overall financial well-being as he had, over the years, invested wisely into offshore enterprises that were still quite profitable, although of course, not as profitable as they had once been. He had sizable holdings in several American companies that had managed to weather the current financial uncertainties well, companies such as *Campbell Soup, The American Tobacco Company, Wells Fargo*, and others. The astute businessman had also managed to keep a sizable amount of money as cash reserves. But for Michael, it was still of great concern, as he would have to lay off good hard working men. It would give him no pleasure at all confronting these men with what would be the sad realities of their immediate future.

Michael Montinari had for many years been a keen observer of international affairs, and he'd watched with great interest, the ever-changing political struggles now going on in Europe, and in particular Germany. He had been of the opinion for some time, that the allies, after the defeat of Germany, and the eventual signing of the armistice, had put impossible constrictions on that once proud country. Germany's ability to pay off the massive debt imposed on her as reparation for the war had led to great instability in that country. The continuing devaluation of the German Deutschmark, and then the eventual demands by the allies that the war debt is paid for in currency other than the Deutschmark had forced Germany to buy foreign currency at vastly inflated prices to meet the demands imposed on her. This, in turn, had devalued the German currency even more rapidly and had forced the general populace into crippling poverty, and there seemed to be no relief in sight for them.

Michael had newspapers sent to him regularly from London and Rome, and from these, he began to feel very uneasy about the future stability of Europe. Germany had begun to rebel against the impossible financial pressures put on her, and insurrection seemed inevitable. He had watched with growing unease as the Nationalist Socialist German Worker's Party: 'The Brown Shirts' had gained more and more popularity with the masses, and the seeming adoration of one of their leaders, an Austrian veteran of the previous war, a Mr Adolf Hitler. If this man were to be appointed chancellor of Germany by President Von Hindenburg, it could well lead Germany into another terrible conflict with those who had tried to crush her with their impossible demands. While many of his business associates did not agree with him, Michael Montinari could sense that another great conflict was imminent. He understood only too well that most people thought the war to end all wars would surely give the world a lasting, well-earned peace. But he was not so sure.

Michael slid the manila folder he had been studying back into his leather valise and latched its clasp. He got up and made his way across to the small mahogany bar and poured himself a large class of Ballantine's and returned to his desk. As he sat back down he looked at the photograph in pride of place next to the onyx Rolodex his daughter had given him for one of his birthdays. He could not remember which one. Isabella smiled back at him. His beautiful daughter was coming home. He got up and went across to the radiogram and put a record on the turntable and returned to his desk. Django Reinhardt's lilting guitar filled the room with a wonderful calmness. He sipped his Ballantine's and smiled at the photograph of his beautiful daughter.

# 40

# A Reunion

Captain James Hedley Bradford watched his men on the main deck begin the unloading of the small amount of cargo they had for the outback town of Derby. A single boom swung out attached to several containers of supplies and deposited them onto the rail carriages that were lined up along the jetty. His men were well practiced and it gave the old captain some satisfaction watching them work. But the captain was also aware that the unloading needed to be done without delay as there was a big tide running. They would need to depart Derby as it turned and make their way back out through the treacherous waters of King Sound with it.

Of the passengers that were due to board his ship, as yet there had been no sign of them. He watched the boom swing back over the ship's hold from its final load. Two of his men ran forward to secure it to its couplings. He looked back along the jetty and noticed three people step out from behind the small galvanized iron shed that served as the passenger's embarkation building. These were the passengers he had been waiting for. Jack Ballinger, Isabella Montinari and a tall coloured girl were making their way toward the Mindaroo's gangway. They were being followed by two men wearing shorts and singlets, carrying what appeared to be some of their luggage, more than likely staff from the Spinifex Hotel, the captain reasoned.

Isabella Montinari was dressed in a pair of off-white slacks with a wide black belt and a blouse of pale blue silk. The captain smiled, she was wearing the same white hat with the blue sash she wore the very first time he had seen her. Jack Ballinger was dressed in a pair of bone coloured trousers and a loose-fitting open-necked white shirt. He wore no hat and his sand coloured hair appeared a little longer than the captain remembered, and hung down over his shirt collar in an unruly tangle that suited the big man's easy manner. The tall Aboriginal girl walking with them was dressed in a simple blouse of bright green cotton and a pair of what looked to be home-made shorts of at least two different colours, she wore simple leather sandals on her feet and no hat, and her long dark hair was brushed and tied back in what looked to be an exact copy of Isabella's. Even from a distance, the captain could see the Aboriginal girl was beautiful. She was very tall, carried herself proudly, and walked with a sinuous, effortless grace that seemed to suit her. The captain hurried across to the head of the gangway to welcome his passengers. His crisp white uniform was, as usual, immaculate and freshly pressed. He adjusted his necktie and took off his cap just as Isabella Montinari appeared at the foot of the gangway.

'Ahoy there, my beautiful friend,' he called down. 'Welcome aboard my humble ship.'

'Ahoy there, yourself . . . !' Isabella called back and hurried up the gangway, followed closely by Jack, and the tall Aboriginal girl.

'G'day there Cap, me old mate.' Jack greeted the captain just as they reached the top of the gangway.

'Welcome aboard, Jack, my good friend.'

Isabella gave the captain an affectionate hug and turned back to the gangway just as Anna arrived at the top. 'Captain, I would like you to meet, Anna Cook, our young friend, and travelling companion.

'Good morning, Miss Cook. Welcome aboard the S.S. Mindaroo. I do hope you enjoy your trip south with us, my dear.'

'Please, Captain—Anna is not used to such formalities. I am sure she would prefer you just called her Anna,' Isabella added.

'Well then, Anna it is,' Captain Bradford replied. He took the young girl's hand, shook it lightly and gave her a courteous bow.

He turned back to Isabella. 'Isabella, a most warm welcome to you, my dear friend, although I must admit, I thought you were to have stayed at the station much longer than this. But of course, I am very happy to have you back on board once again.'

'There have been some unfortunate developments at the station. I hope to be able to discuss them with you a little later,' Isabella replied.

'I will look forward to it. But for now, let me get some porters to help with your luggage and get you to your cabins. After you are settled and have taken some rest, I would be pleased if you would join me for dinner this evening. I still have a good supply of that Chablis we enjoyed on your last voyage with us. Perhaps over a bottle or two, we could discuss your recent adventures at the station, if that is agreeable?'

'That sounds like a wonderful idea, Captain. We will be more than happy to accept,' Isabella replied and nodded her agreement with Jack.

The captain gave Isabella a polite bow and motioned to the porters who were standing nearby to pick up the luggage left by the Spinifex Hotel employees. Then he turned back to Isabella. 'If you would like to follow me, I will take you to your cabins.'

Less than an hour later, the *Mindaroo* was making her way along King Sound at a good pace, running fast with the outgoing tide and heading for the open sea beyond.

Standing at the stern watching Derby disappear slowly into the distance, were Jack, Isabella, and Anna.

'Well, Anna, you can say goodbye to your country now for a while. I do hope you enjoy our trip together. Tell me, my dear, do you like the captain?'

'Yes, he seems very nice,' Anna replied.

'I'm so glad you like him. He's a really sweet man.' Isabella took Jack's hand, smiled at him and the three of them watched the Derby jetty begin to slowly disappear into the dull green of the distant mangroves.

Suddenly, unexpectedly, two bottle-nosed dolphins broke through the surface, not more than thirty feet from where they stood. As they came up they jettisoned blasts of misty air from their blowholes and dived back beneath the surface again.

Anna laughed with sudden joy. 'Did you see them—did you see how big they were . . . !'

'I reckon they're trying to keep up with the ship. A couple of show-offs for sure,' Jack said with a laugh and put his arm around Isabella's shoulders.

'I hope they come back,' Anna replied excitedly. She leaned over the stern railing, hoping to see them again, should they resurface.

The three of them stood there looking down at the roiling swirl left by the ship's propeller, and the flattened wake beyond that trailed off into the distance. Anna reached for Isabella's hand for comfort. Isabella squeezed it in return. Isabella was glad she had convinced Anna to come with them on this trip. But she knew there would be times when it would overwhelm her, and when that happened, she would be there for her.

It was a little after six when Isabella, Jack, and Anna made their way into the *Mindaroo's* dining room. There were already a few diners seated, waiting patiently for stewards to take their orders. Isabella was the first to see the captain. He was sitting at a table in a quiet spot near the far end of the room. She gave him a wave and led them over to join him.

'It's really wonderful to be back on board again, Captain,' she declared as she reached for the captain's hand.

'And a great pleasure for me as well, my dear. A great pleasure indeed.' Captain Bradford stood up, took Isabella's hand and shook it lightly.

'Good evening, Cap. Good to see you again.' Jack reached for the captain's hand.

'Glad to have you aboard Jack,' the captain replied and went around the table to help Isabella with her chair.

Jack helped Anna with hers and sat down. 'So, Captain, have you been anywhere interesting?'

'Same old thing really, Jack. Although I did spend a couple of days in Singapore recently, had to get a few minor repairs done. It gave me the opportunity to have a look around the place. It's a beautiful city Singapore, lovely gardens and magnificent colonial buildings. I managed to spend a few hours shopping for a few bits and pieces on Orchard Road, while I was there, a wonderful place, but awfully busy.'

'Never been there myself, Cap. But I've heard it's worth the trip,' Jack replied.

'Perhaps one day you may like to join us for the complete voyage up the coast. I'm sure you would enjoy it.'

'I'm sure I would, Cap,' Jack replied.

'It's wonderful to be back on board, Captain. I've missed our stimulating discussions dearly,' Isabella said.

'I have most certainly missed them as well. But, here we are once again, my dear, and I look forward to catching up with all of your adventures.' Captain Bradford reached across the table, patted Isabella's hand and nodded a warm greeting to Anna.

'So, what is Henri cooking up for us tonight Cap,' Jack asked.

'Well now. It's Sunday, and we usually celebrate the Lord's Day with fish. That is if we are lucky enough to have any, and as luck would have it, we have some wonderfully fresh mackerel, which Henri usually bakes whole and then serves portions, along with his famous cucumber, mango, and sweetcorn salad. But if that is not suitable, he will certainly prepare something special for you at your request.'

They all agreed with the choice of the fish and salad, which they enjoyed immensely, and were later treated to a French version of a lime sorbet that the talented ship's chef had named '*Coulis Citron Vert et Pamplemousse.*'

'Well, I think I should go and get another couple of bottles of my Chablis. It seemed to agree nicely with our meal and I'm certain another one or two won't go astray,' the captain announced. He pushed back his chair and stood up.

'I'll come with you, Cap.' Jack got to his feet as well.

'No need, Jack.' The captain raised his hand to Jack.

'There's something I would like to discuss with you, Cap. It shouldn't take me more than a minute.'

Jack and the captain excused themselves from the table and headed for the ships main cool-room. The captain pushed open one of the glass-fronted doors and turned to Jack. 'So, what is it you need to discuss with me, my friend?'

'I wanted to get you aside for a bit so that I can tell you what happened out at the station.'

'It's all starting to sound a bit ominous, Jack,' the old captain declared as he slid a heavy wooden crate out from one of the cool-room shelves and opened it.

Jack went on to explain in detail the recent murder of Anna's people at the hand of the Cockatoo Creek station manager, and the later killing of the stockman, Beans. He told him how they had become concerned about Anna's well-being and of their decision to bring her with them on their trip. Jack related their meeting with the Kurdaitcha man, Pirramurar, and how the man had saved Anna's life. But he decided not to tell him about Anna being raped by Jan Muller. He felt it was not necessary, and that it should not be known by people other than those close to their young friend.

'Oh, how absolutely terrible—and how is Anna coping with it all?'

'She's been going through hell, Cap. She misses her people badly. We're hoping this trip will do her good.

'And, Isabella—how is she coping?'

'She's been a rock mate. But her main concern has been Anna.'

'And, I guess the reason for the trip south is to see Isabella's father and tell him the bad news.'

'He already knows about it, Cap. And of course, he is very concerned. He's asked Isabella and me to come down and see him as soon as possible, and that's what we are about to do, Cap, Jack replied.

'Poor, Anna, I feel so sorry for her.'

'Well, that's about all I wanted to tell you. I just wanted to let you know what happened and preferred to tell you in private, if you know what I mean.'

'Thanks, Jack. Well, I suppose we had better take this wine, and head on back to the table.'

'Oh, there is one other thing, Cap.'

'And what's that, Jack?'

'Isabella and I are an item. Just thought I'd let you know, mate.'

'An item . . . ?' The captain looked confused.

'I'm in love with her, Cap—that's what I mean, and I'm pretty sure she feels the same way about me, mate.'

'Well then, congratulations are in order, Jack. You're a very lucky man. Isabella is a wonderful and talented lady. You must look after her, my friend.'

'You have my word on that, Cap. Now, I guess we better get on back.'

Captain Bradford was stunned by the news of what had transpired since last he had seen his two friends. He could only imagine the suffering the young Aboriginal girl sitting at his table had gone through. He decided then that he would do his very best to help her in any way he could in the few days they had together. And later when Isabella asked if it was possible that Anna be shown around the ship, he was overjoyed and agreed to take care of it personally.

'Of course, my dear, I will see to it myself. Will tomorrow morning be okay for you, Anna?'

'Yes, that will be nice, Captain.' Anna replied shyly.

'Anna, don't forget. While we are on board we have your lessons each day,' Isabella interrupted. 'But I suppose there's no reason why we can't do them later in the day.'

'Thank you, Isabella. I won't forget,' Anna said with a wide smile.

'Alright, it's settled then. Anna, I will call at your cabin at nine in the morning, if that is agreeable.'

'Thank you, Captain. I will be ready.'

Jack, Isabella, and Anna thanked the captain for a delightful evening and left him to return to their rooms.

Captain Bradford bid them farewell and decided he would stay for a final glass of wine and a quiet reflection on the terrible news he had been told about the happenings out at Cockatoo Creek Station. When he finally stood to leave he overheard the end of a conversation from a nearby table of diners.

'. . . and, I do not care if they were dining with the captain. The shipping line should have a policy in regard to blacks coming into this dining room. It should not be allowed!'

'Shh, dear—someone will hear you!' A male voice interrupted.

Captain Bradford had heard enough. He straightened his tie, wiped away some imaginary crumbs from his jacket, and approached the table of diners. 'Good evening,' he began.

'Good evening, Captain,' one of the men at the table replied. He got up, nodded to the captain and sat back down.

'Tomorrow morning at around midday, we will be arriving in Broome for a short visit,' Captain Bradford announced, his voice a little louder than was necessary.

'We are well aware of that, Captain,' the woman that had been speaking earlier, interrupted.

'Please be kind enough to let me finish, Mrs Butler!'

The woman now realised by Captain Bradford's manner that he was not happy. 'Please, go ahead, Captain. But as I said, we are well aware that we will be calling at Broome in the morning.'

'I'm very pleased you are aware of it, Mrs Butler because it may be of some importance to you.'

'I'm sorry, Captain, but I don't quite understand your meaning,' Mrs Butler replied.

'Well now, let me clear it up for you. I have just overheard some of your earlier remarks in regard to my choice of dining companions. I suggest that, if you are not happy with my choice of dining companions, while we are in Broome, you make other arrangements for your passage south. I will not tolerate any bigoted, racial behavior by anyone while on board my ship, is that clear?'

'Well, I never . . . ! Mrs Butler replied.

'Do you understand my meaning, Mrs Butler?' The captain asked.

'Yes, I understand only too well, Captain. But I will insist when we return to Fremantle, that our party lodge a complaint about this, and about your rude behavior to your superiors!'

'Be quiet Edith before you get us all dumped in Broome!'

'You are free to do as you please when we reach Fremantle. But as of now, you will no longer be welcome in this dining room. For the remainder of this journey, you will use the second class dining room. I will instruct my crew accordingly. I bid you good evening.'

'Well really . . . !'

Captain Bradford gave the diners an abrupt bow, left the dining room and headed for the bridge.

The following morning at precisely nine o'clock, he tapped on Anna's door and was greeted warmly by the young Aboriginal girl.

'Good morning, my dear. Are you ready for your tour of the ship?'

'Yes, Captain,' Anna replied. She had been looking forward to her morning with the captain.

For Captain Bradford, getting to know the Aboriginal girl was an enormous pleasure. His great passion in life was his study of the northern Aboriginal tribes. Their early history and their interaction with the Makassar traders that he believed had regularly visited the Australian continent since ancient times. The Aboriginal girl was further proof of this interaction. She was indeed a rare beauty. She was as tall as the beautiful Isabella, slim and athletic, perhaps even boy-like. Her skin was as black as coal and yet her eyes were noticeably Asian. Proof enough for Captain Bradford that the northern Aboriginal people had had contact with people from the islands of what was once known as the Dutch East Indies.

Jack and Isabella spent their nights in the separate cabins that the captain had given them. Even though Jack had told the captain that he and Isabella were in love, he still thought it proper that they should not sleep together while on board. But as the days and nights wore on it was becoming more and more difficult for both of them. Jack knew the old captain thought the world of Isabella. It was obvious by the way he constantly fussed over her, and so, out of respect, he had made his decision.

For Captain James Hedley Bradford, the trip south to Fremantle went far too quickly. The time he spent with the beautiful Isabella Montinari and the fascinating Anna Cook, would, of course, never be enough. But the old captain was pleased to have been able to help in some way with the education of the young Aboriginal girl. To the captain; the time he spent with her each day was a furthering of his knowledge of the Aboriginal tribes of the Kimberley.

In the evenings his conversations with Jack and Isabella were equally stimulating. Their discussions covered subjects as diverse as the past war with Germany and their hopes for a peaceful future, Isabella's days in Europe, and Jack's colourful descriptions of his hunting exploits in Arnhem Land. While the captain thoroughly enjoyed the time he spent with Jack and Anna of even more importance to him was the very limited time he had to spend with Isabella Montinari. To Captain Bradford, Isabella was a treasure, and he loved every minute he spent with her. But as is the way, all good things must finally come to an end.

Jack, Isabella, and Anna departed the S.S *Mindaroo* in Fremantle, with Isabella making a solemn promise to the captain, that when they returned they would make every effort to sail with him again for their trip up the coast to Derby.

In Fremantle, Jack booked passage by train to the gold mining town of Kalgoorlie, where they were to spend a night at the Palace Hotel. In the morning, they would board the Indian-Pacific train bound for Adelaide, and then on to Melbourne.

After they had eaten that night Jack and Isabella showed Anna to her room, which, like theirs, was directly above the noisy front bar.

'Sorry about the noise, Anna. But they were the only rooms I could get, and we were probably lucky to get them. There's some sort of a miner's convention on in town at the moment, so I was told.' Jack unlocked Anna's door and handed her the key.

358

'The room looks nice, Jack. And thank you both for bringing me with you, I'm having a really wonderful time,' Anna replied with a smile.

'I'm glad you are enjoying yourself, my dear,' Isabella said. 'Get some sleep if you can with all that noise, and we'll see you in the morning for breakfast.'

'Goodnight,' Anna replied.

Jack took Isabella's hand, and they made their way along the creaking passage to their own room.

'Alone at last,' Jack whispered as he unlocked the door and stood aside to let Isabella enter.

'Why didn't you come to my cabin while we were on the ship? After all, you were supposed to be looking after me—remember.'

'I didn't think you'd want me to. You know, with the captain being so old fashioned and all. Anyway, it seemed the right thing to do, I suppose,' Jack replied

'Well, I've missed you.' Isabella put her arms around Jack, kissed him and pushed him back onto the bed.

'Anyway, right now Captain Bradford is the last thing on my mind,' Jack said as he slid off the bed and embraced Isabella.

Isabella walked back to the door and switched off the light. A faint reddish glow from the streetlight below filtered through the worn floral curtains into the room. A sudden peal of laughter rose up from the drinkers down in the bar.

Isabella took off her clothes and placed them in careful order on the wooden chair near the bed.

Jack watched, his heart hammering in his chest.

Another peal of laughter rose up from the bar. Isabella started to laugh as well.

'And just what is so funny, young lady?' Jack asked as he began taking off his clothes.

'By the sound of it everyone down there is having a good old time so I thought we may as well enjoy ourselves as well,' Isabella said mysteriously.

'Just what did you have in mind, Miss Montinari?'

Isabella smiled and walked across to the bed. 'Be patient my love,' she whispered.

'I know I keep telling you this. But you really are beautiful, my love.' Jack said softly, his naked readiness in plain sight of the woman he loved.

Isabella put both of her hands on Jack's shoulders for support, and with one lithe movement, she sat astride him. 'Lay back my darling and let me love you.'

Jack's body stiffened with the pleasure of her touch. 'My God Isabella, I do truly love you,' he whispered, as Isabella's warmth began to engulf him completely. He reached for her breasts and kissed her hardening nipples hungrily, and at the same time, pulled her down against him and held her there. He felt Isabella try to resist, but he held her down. He wanted to feel her warmth for as long as he could. Isabella fought hard against his strength. Jack was forced to let her go. She began to move above him, slowly, deliberately. He moved with her, driving up against each of her downward thrusts. Time seemed to stand still.

Finally, Isabella fell onto him. 'My God Jack, I've missed you so much!' she cried.

'Isabella—my Isabella,' Jack groaned and held her against him again, their bodies locked together in a rictus of passion. Just a moment, they were a single perfect being, wrapped together in a wondrous cocoon of love.

The following day as they travelled by train across the great Nullarbor Plain, Anna sat and watched in absolute awe of the vast tree-less, inhospitable desert that seemed to go on forever. The young girl now realized she had no true perception of the sheer size of the country she was born into. As she watched its vastness flicker past her window, she began to imagine that it could go on forever. She wondered if Melbourne sat at the edge of this great tree-less desert. She tried to imagine what it would be like.

Once, while she sat watching it go by, they passed a tiny railway siding, consisting of little more than a cluster of rusty, iron-clad buildings, huddled together along an off-ramp of the main rail line. Near one of these rusty iron dwellings, she noticed a group of Aboriginal people sheltering from the heat. She lifted her hand and waved, but they turned away. Anna felt a sudden rush of despair wash over her. She knew she was speeding toward a world she knew little about. A world made for white people. She looked across at the seat opposite, Isabella and Jack were sleeping. Jack had his head against the window and Isabella lay against him. She heard a distant, ding-ding as they rattled over a dusty crossing. She looked down at the book Isabella had given her in Fremantle, A Pictorial Guide to the City Of Melbourne. Loneliness gripped her young heart. She was afraid of what was to come, and for the first time since leaving the station, she wished she was back there, back in her country, back with her Dan. She closed her eyes and tried to sleep.

Three days, and three train changes later, they were on the outskirts of Isabella's hometown, the sprawling vibrant city of Melbourne.

# 41

# Max Crabbe

*Heavy scrub country*

*South-east of the Drysdale River*

Max Crabbe wiped the perspiration from his pockmarked face and smiled at his friend. 'Victor you are a lazy shit.'

Victor Bennett laughed. 'Well, it was all your bloody idea, you ugly bastard,' his partner replied. 'Easy money, you said. Round up a couple of hundred head of cattle and get them out of this godforsaken country and back to Wyndham. Sell 'em to that shifty froggy mate of yours, and we're home bloody free, you said.'

'Three quid a head, if they're in good nick by the time we get 'em there,' Crabbe replied and stuffed his dirty handkerchief back in his pocket. 'That's three hundred quid, Bennett, you lazy arsehole.'

'Yeah, yeah, but we have to get 'em there first,' Bennett grunted, and swung his horse back toward one of the slower moving steers on the left side of the mob and flicked at it with his stockwhip. 'Move damn you, we need to get you're stinkin red arses outa this country and into Wyndham sometime before the end of this bloody century.'

The two riders moved away from each other and took up their positions on either side of the slow-moving cattle.

'Move along there,' Crabbe grumbled at a steer in front of him and kicked his horse into a trot. As he moved forward he touched the brim of his hat and smiled a mock salute to his friend on the other side of the mob, and in a lowered voice, he whispered, 'Get your finger out of your lazy arse, you bastard or I'll put a bullet in your tiny brain and take them all in meself, and be all the bloody richer for it.'

\*   \*   \*

A few miles ahead of the slow-moving cattle, two Cockatoo Creek stockmen were working their way through the pindan and spinifex scrub on their old buckboard, heading for the windmill that was still a good hour's travel ahead of them. Both unaware of the drama that was unfolding behind them, and how it would inevitably involve them. Henry flicked the long wagon traces up and down as a gentle reminder to the old mare that plodded quietly ahead of them that they needed to get to windmill eleven before sunset. The two Aboriginal stockmen had been employed on Cockatoo Creek for several years and it had become their full-time job to look after the big simplex windmills that were strung out across the huge cattle station.

'Two more to check on, and then it's back to the station and back to some good tucker again,' Wooloo declared. He unhooked the canvas water bag that hung on the side of the buckboard, took a long swallow and offered it to his friend.

'Still, be a good day's ride yet, I reckon,' Henry answered, and took the canvas bag from his friend and lifted it to his lips.

An hour later, the two men pulled their buckboard into the sparse shade of a pair of twisted boab trees and began to unhitch the old mare. It was almost sundown and the nearby, creaking windmill was surrounded by more than fifty head of Cockatoo Creek cattle busy filling their bellies from the trough that ran a full sixty feet along its side. The recent wet season rains had nourished the country well, renewing it from the long dry season that had preceded it. Native grasses had sprung up here and there between the ever-present spinifex clumps and had given the harsh country a lush appearance. The stockmen set up their overnight camp and lit a fire with the few sticks and logs they carried on the buckboard for that purpose.

'We might get a bit of rain by the look of them clouds,' Wooloo remarked. He threw a handful of sticks on the fire and pointed one of the smaller twigs up at the overcast sky.

'Maybe better we sleep under the buckboard tonight,' his friend replied, just as a light rain began to fall.

'Yep, good idea I reckon. I hope it don't come down too heavy and bugger us gettin back to the station,' Wooloo commented. He got up and went across to the trough to fill their billy.

It wasn't long before the two men were sipping tea and eating their dried beef and the last of yesterday's damper under the cover of the buckboard. The sky above them had turned a dark purple, and the smell of rain filled their nostrils. When they had finished eating, they put their plate's aside and lounged back on their bedrolls and puffed contentedly on their cigarettes.

The following morning, while they sat under the buckboard sipping their tea mugs, it was still raining, but it had become quite heavy.

'I reckon we'll have to wait a bit longer before we can check that there mill,' Henry remarked, nodding toward the windmill, now barely visible through the rain. He picked up his mug and slid further under the buckboard, and was followed by his friend.

\* \* \*

Max Crabbe was dog tired. He'd spent the night in his saddle trying to keep his eyes on the stolen cattle. He'd tried to get some sleep while he sat on his horse but he was not a skilled stockman, and just before dawn, he fell from his saddle and landed in the mud next to his horse's hooves. He'd wiped some of the mud from his clothes, cursed his inept horsemanship, climbed back in the saddle, and tried to stay awake. During the night, his friend had been no use to him at all. As soon as the rain started, he had disregarded the cattle altogether. The fool had dismounted and curled up against the side of a fat boab tree. He'd threatened him, but it had been no use at all. Crabbe knew Bennett was as tired as he was, but at least he'd attempted to keep the cattle in a manageable mob. Crabbe made up his mind that, as soon as they were within a few miles of Wyndham, he would shoot his lazy friend, and take the herd in alone. He would get a tidy sum for the stolen cattle, and he would keep it all for himself.

When dawn finally came, Max Crabbe could see that the cattle were still in a fairly manageable mob. He breathed a sigh of relief, dismounted and prodded his friend with his boot. 'Wake up you lazy bastard, we've got work to do.'

'What about a billy of tea and a bit to eat before we head off, Max?' Bennett grumbled as he rolled out of his muddy swag.

'Fuck the tea, and fuck something to eat as well. We'll stop a bit later after we've covered a few miles. Come on, get 'em bloody moving.'

An hour later, with the rain still falling, they pushed the cattle through a heavy stand of paperbark trees and broke out into open ground. The cattle slowed and began to feed on the fresh grass around the edge of the trees.

'Hey, Max what's that up there? Looks like a buckboard,' Victor Bennett said and pointed to what he thought was an abandoned buckboard.

'There's a horse tied up over near those trees,' Crabbe replied in a low voice. 'Could be station fellas I reckon. You stay here and keep the cattle tight while I ride up and take a look.'

'What the hell are we gonna do if it is?' Victor Bennett asked nervously.

'Shut up, and stay here you lazy bugger. I'll look after this.'

Crabbe rode out of the paperbark thicket and made his way toward the distant buckboard. He could now see a windmill through the trees a short distance beyond the buckboard and more than fifty head of cattle milling about next to it. He smiled, adjusted his hat and whispered, 'Well now, a few more beasties for our little herd.' He'd almost reached the buckboard before he noticed the Aboriginal stockmen sheltering from the light rain beneath its board floor. The two men seemed oblivious to his approach, due probably to the wet ground and scrub he was riding through.

'Lazy bloody boongs,' he whispered. He undid the rusty stud on his pistol holster and urged his horse forward.

Suddenly, without any warning, the two Aboriginal stockmen jumped out from their shelter, surprise obvious on their dark faces. They'd finally heard the white man's horse as it plodded slowly toward their camp.

'Hey there, where'd you come from, Boss . . . ?' Henry, the taller of the two stockmen, asked nervously, as he got to his feet.

'Well now—just could just be hell, I reckon,' Crabbe replied. He smiled at the two men and looked around their untidy campsite for weapons, but there were none in clear sight.

'All this here land longas big boss, Cockatoo Creek,' Henry blurted. The Aboriginal stockman could sense something sinister about the rider approaching him.

'Any more of you black bastards around the place?' Crabbe grunted.

'No, Boss, just me and Wooloo here, all the rest probably back close to the station, I reckon,' Henry replied nervously.

'Well, now that's just what I wanted to hear.' Crabbe pulled the long-barrelled Colt revolver from the holster looped about his fat midriff and aimed it at the Aboriginal stockman.

'No—no, Boss, we ain't done nothin wrong. Me and Wooloo work for Cockatoo Creek. We look after them windmills there.' Henry pointed behind him to the windmill.

'Well now, I don't think there'll be too many of them where you're going,' Crabbe replied and shot the Aboriginal stockman in the face.

Henry jerked his hands up to his face and tried to scream, but made no sound at all. The heavy bullet had hit him in the right cheek, shattering his upper jaw and blasting a fist size hole through the back of his neck. He staggered back toward the buckboard, just as Crabbe fired again. The bullet hit him in the chest and he collapsed next to one of the front wheels of the buckboard. The old mare the stockmen used to pull their buckboard, alarmed by the gunshots, jerked hard at her tether, but found she couldn't free herself. She gave out a loud shriek, evacuated a sizable amount of her morning shit, pig-rooted a couple of times and then stood completely still.

Surprised by the sudden shriek from the old horse, Crabbe swung around and fired two shots at it, but his aiming was poor and he clean missed. The old mare started to pig root about again, pulling on her tether even harder, in a desperate attempt at escape. Crabbe's own mount began to move about beneath him, uncomfortable with the sudden gunshots. With his stirrups locked tight against the horse's belly to stop him getting thrown, and his hands tight on the reins, Crabbe looked back at the old horse he'd missed with his pistol. He shrugged with indifference. When his horse finally began to steady he looked down at the Aboriginal stockman lying near the buckboard.

'I thought we cleaned up most of you bastards with the poison bottle years ago.

After the shock of what he had just seen happen to his friend, Wooloo suddenly ducked under the big white man's horse, hoping as he did so that the sudden movement would upset it again. Then he ran as fast as he could toward the distant windmill and the protection he hoped it would give him.

Crabbe's horse reared up in sudden surprise from the ducking Aboriginal and almost threw its rider again. Crabbe dropped the long-barrelled Colt and pulled hard on the reins to steady his mount. Cattle started to rush past him, and then he heard Victor Bennett.

'Look out Max. The bloody cattle have stampeded.'

Crabbe looked back. He could see the stolen cattle were in wild disarray and charging off in all directions.

'Well—get on to them then, you lazy bastard,' He yelled back, still trying to bring his horse under control.

'It's those bloody pistol shots. You got 'em spooked and they took off.'

'Get after them then—go on, get fucking moving. I'll take care of this other bloody abo,' Crabbe yelled back.

Victor Bennett rushed past looking particularly unsteady in the saddle as he attempted to round up some of the cattle that were racing ahead of him.

'What the bloody hell did you need to shoot that poor bugger for?' he yelled back over his shoulder, and almost fell from his horse as it lurched to its left in an attempt to miss a steer that had decided to stop directly in its path.

'They've seen us, and that means they've seen too fucking much,' Crabbe snarled, as his horse finally stopped its antics and came to a momentary standstill.

'Whoa up there, fuck you,' he growled. He looked down at his pistol lying in the mud. Annoyed by the temporary inconvenience, he slid his Remington rifle out from behind his saddle and lifted it to his shoulder.

Wooloo had almost made it to the windmill when the bullet from Max Crabbe's rifle hit him low in the back. The stockman fell to the ground, just as dozens of cattle rushed past him.

'That's bloody murder, Crabbe, even if they are only blackfellas. They can hang us for that you know!' Bennett yelled back as he turned his horse off to his right and headed for a breakaway mob of steers that were crashing through a patch of spinifex.

'Stop your whining you lazy bastard. They're only blackfellas. Get after those bloody cattle if you know what's good for you,' Crabbe yelled back. He dismounted and reached down to pick up his pistol. Cursing, he shook loose a clod of mud that had stuck to the barrel, holstered it and climbed back in the saddle.

'Now let's get to it and round them up and get the fuck out of here,' he yelled after his friend and dug his spurs into his horse's flanks.

Crabbe swung away from the direction of the windmill, confident he'd killed the running Aboriginal, and galloped after the scattering herd of cattle. As he rode after them, he waved the Remington in the air. The adrenaline that rushed through his body from the killing of the Aboriginals had charged him with an energy that made him whoop with joy.

'Yee—harr,' he bellowed an ugly smile on his pockmarked face. 'I'm a fucking cattle baron.'

Wooloo lay still hoping he wouldn't be trampled by the cattle that were rushing past. Finally, after they'd raced off through the scrub with the two white men chasing after them, he tried to get up, but the pain in his back made him pass out. When he woke it was silent. He groaned and rolled to his left and stared back toward their campsite. Henry lay in the dirt next to the buckboard. There were black flies all over him. A couple of crows were hopping about near his dead friend's head. They were making bolder and bolder approaches, stopping occasionally, spinning about, and then hopping a little farther away, unsure whether the man was truly dead or only sleeping. The old roan mare was chewing quietly on a clump of fresh grass growing near the base of the tree where they had tied her the night before. Wooloo knew she'd be thirsty, as she always seemed to be each morning. He rolled onto his back, undid his belt and slowly removed his trousers. The effort caused him considerable pain, but he knew if he didn't wrap his back with something to staunch the flow of blood, he would soon bleed to death. He looked up at the sky. Rain clouds rolled overhead. He knew it wouldn't be long before it started to rain again.

# 42

# Bloody Crows

Santiago took his metal rod from its hook on the verandah post and swung it hard against the hollow pipe that hung next to it. *Clang–clang–clang.* 'Breakfast, come and get it,' he yelled across the muddy yard. Stockmen spilled out of the bunk-house and headed for the station dining room. The old cook hung the steel bar back on its rusty hook and turned to head back into the kitchen, just as someone yelled.

'Hey, that's the old buckboard coming into the yard. Looks like it's empty too. Where the bloody hell is Henry and Wooloo?'

'Whoa up there, old dear.' Famous Feet stepped in front of the old horse and managed to get her to stop.

'Have a look in the back, Famous. See if you can work out what's happened!' Santiago yelled.

'It's Wooloo—he's in here, and he don't look too good either!' Famous yelled back.

'Hold on, I'm coming over. Let me take a look at him.' The old cook ran across the yard and climbed into the buckboard.

Wooloo was lying on the floor in a scattered confusion of hessian bags, pipes, tools of all descriptions, some firewood, and a wooden extension ladder, his trousers had been removed

370

and wrapped around his lower body and held in place by the stockman's belt and were covered in blood.

Santiago put his fingers to the side of his neck. 'He's alive, poor bugger. Get him out and onto the veranda.'

Sam Belsen and Famous Feet lifted the blood-soaked stockman out of the buckboard and carried him across to the kitchen veranda. While they put him down on the floorboards, Santiago ran back into the kitchen to grab the small kitbag full of assorted bits and pieces that the old cook liked to call his medicine bag. When he got back, the two men had undone Wooloo's belt and carefully pulled away the blood-soaked trousers and were examining the wound in the stockman's back.

'Looks to me like the poor bugger's been shot, it don't look too bad though. But I reckon he's lost a hell of a lot of blood,' Sam declared and wiped his hands on his dungarees.

Santiago studied the small bullet hole on the stockman's lower back and then gently rolled the unconscious man onto his side to study the other, slightly larger, exit wound.

'Gone right through by the look of it Sam. It looks like his trousers stopped a fair bit of the bleeding. I'll sew him up and we'll see how he goes.'

Santiago cleaned the dried blood away with water from the kitchen sink and stitched up the bullet holes with the fine linen thread he found in the bottom of his medicine bag. When he was satisfied with his needlework, he swabbed the wounds with carbolic acid, dabbed them with iodine and wrapped a long cotton bandage around the stockman's lower back.

'Famous you sit here with him, and if he wakes up, try and dribble a bit of water into his mouth every now and then. It's important we get some liquid into him. I'll get Rosie to come and give you a hand shortly. We'll leave him where he is for a bit, and see how he goes. But I'll be surprised if he lives after the amount of blood he's lost. Anyway, the rest of you fellas, breakfast is ready, so you might as well go on in.' Santiago closed his old kit bag and got up. Before he left the veranda he looked back at the old Aboriginal tracker. 'I'll bring you out a bottle of water and some breakfast in a bit, Famous.'

'Can you bring me out a mug of tea too, and get Rosie to bring a blanket so I can cover him up and make him decent. We don't want her grabbing that big dick of his while the poor bugger's out to it.' The old tracker gave a bit of a chuckle, leaned back on the kitchen wall and started to roll a cigarette.

Billy Anders, the newly appointed station manager, decided to call a meeting in the dining room while the stockmen were still having their breakfast. If the wound that Wooloo had received was caused by a gunshot he knew there must have been some sort of trouble out bush.

'If I can have your attention for a minute,' he began. 'It appears Henry and Wooloo have run into some sort of trouble out bush. It looks like Wooloo's been shot by some bastard, and Henry's still out there somewhere. We've got no idea what's happened, but one thing's certain we'd better get out there and find out. I'll take Famous with me and we'll head on out straight away and see what we can find. We should be able to follow the buckboard tracks pretty easy and get to the bottom of it fairly quickly. The rest of you are to stick around here. I don't want anyone heading away from the station until we find out what's happened. Dan and Steve, you can check with Santiago to see if he has anything in the gardens for you do now that Anna's away. The rest of you, just do a bit of cleaning up around the place until we get back. Is that clear?'

'Yep, I reckon we understand alright. You better be bloody careful out there, Billy, if there's some silly bastard running about the place shooting people,' Bob Nugent warned. There was a murmur of agreement from the other stockmen in the room.

'We'll be careful alright, Bob,' Billy replied. He turned to Santiago. 'Santiago you better get someone to take over from Famous out there and get a bit of tucker put together for us just in case we're gone a bit longer than we'd like. We'll be off just as soon as I've got my rifle and a couple of horses ready.'

'I'll see to it straight away,' Santiago replied. The old cook had been leaning against the tea urn listening. He headed back into the kitchen.

Less than an hour later, Billy and Famous Feet had headed out on their mission to find out what had happened to Henry and Wooloo. The tracks left by the old buckboard were clear and easy to follow. But the two riders followed them cautiously, regularly checking the scrub ahead for any sign of strangers.

Not long after they rode out, Wooloo regained consciousness, but only for a short while. Rosie and Pearl had been sitting with him. Rosie wiped a wet cloth across the stockman's dusty face and smiled at him. 'Hush there, dearie—your back home now, thanks to that old mare of yours. I'm gonna give you a sip of water now.' She lifted a tin cup to the stockman's lips and dribbled some of it into his mouth. Wooloo swallowed it down and stared into Rosie's eyes.

'Where's Henry, Wooloo? Is he okay?' Rosie asked softly.

'He's dead Rosie! He's been shot!' Wooloo shut his eyes and lifted his hand to the wound on his side, as he remembered what had happened.

'You try and get some rest, and a bit later on we'll get you over to your bunk and you can try a bit of tucker if you feel like it.'

Just before sunset Billy Anders and Famous Feet reached mill eleven. The riders could see the surrounding scrub had been mostly knocked flat by a fair sized mob of cattle. They worked their way through the broken bushes carefully and when they reached a small stand of pindan trees that were still standing, they stopped.

'I reckon this must be the last mill the boys worked on, goin by the tracks, we better go quietly from here on, Famous.' Billy instructed.

'Okay, Boss. Maybe better we tie up the horses here in these trees and go ahead on foot,' Famous suggested nervously.

Billy swung down off his saddle and patted his horse's muzzle as stockmen do in the vain hope their mount will remain quiet. Famous did the same. The two men tied up their horses and Billy slid out his old Martini rifle. He loaded it quietly with one of the shells he had in his pocket and nodded to Famous. They moved forward carefully, working their way out of the last of the Pindan scrub and into the wide clearing of low spinifex and broken bushes that lay ahead of them.

'What's that, moving about over there near that twisted little boab tree, Famous?'

Looks like a big goanna to me. He's covered in mud and he looks kinda funny, I reckon. I never seen one look like that before.'

'Yep, I see him now.' Billy whispered. They continued forward.

The huge monitor lizard, more than seven feet long, its girth the size of man's waist seemed to be in some kind of feeding frenzy. Billy swung the Martini up onto his shoulder in an aiming position and they walked out of the trees and headed for the creaking windmill. When they got closer they could see the Goanna was feeding on something behind a broken clump of spinifex. As they watched, the big lizard jerked its mud-covered body about for leverage, as it tore at whatever it was feeding on, and it wasn't until they got closer that they realised the lizard was feeding on the body of their friend, Henry. The stockman's remains were covered with a constantly moving cloud of flies. Two crows were hopping about nearby, careful not to get too close to the massive lizard as it was feeding, and it wasn't until the mud covered goanna turned and snapped at one of them, that it saw the two men walking toward it. In a second it was gone, and in the same instant the crows, startled by the goanna's quick withdrawal, took to the air as well, their dark wings glinting like well-shone riding boots in the evening light. The stockmen, shocked by the scene in front of them, watched the birds settle in the high branches of a nearby tree.

'Fuckin dirty black bastards!' Famous snarled at them as they hopped about on the high branches and looked down at the two men.

'That's Henry alright, and that bloody lizard's been feeding on the poor bastard!' Billy pointed his old rifle at the spot where the goanna disappeared through the spinifex bushes and wished he could have got a shot at it.

'Don't seem to be anybody else around here anymore though.' Famous replied his voice not much more than a whisper.

'That's bullet holes right there in his face and another one in his chest, no doubt about that! Who the hell would do such a thing?' Billy said quietly.

'Looks like it alright—dirty fuckin bastards . . . !' Famous had got his voice back and grunted his reply.

The two men left the body where it lay. They were shocked and sickened by what they'd seen. They began to scout about looking for sign, both uneasy about looking at what remained of their friend for much longer. It didn't take them long to realise the whole area had been cut up badly by running cattle. Finally, they walked back through the clumps of spinifex to their dead friend's body.

'Jesus, Famous, the poor bastard's been chewed up awful bad by that fucking goanna. Anyway, it looks like he was shot though, that's for sure!'

The dead stockman's face was a terrible mess. His eyes had been pecked out by the hungry crows and most of the flesh of his cheeks had been ripped away as well. But the worst of the damage had been done by the big monitor lizard. The dead man's trousers had been torn away and his upper thighs ripped apart. Bits of half-eaten skin and bloody flesh hung out from the ripped material in long strands and lay in the mud.

'I saw a couple of shells lying over there by them horse tracks. I'm gonna go and pick 'em up, Boss.' Famous was feeling like he was going to be sick. He left the mutilated body of his friend and walked over to where he had seen the brass shells.

'Yeah, you go ahead and pick them up. Then have another walk around and try and work out what the fuck happened here. I'll go and get the horses.' Billy replied.

Famous walked over and picked up the empty shell casings and put them in his pocket. Sweat was trickling down his forehead. He felt sick. He swallowed down hard and started to walk around looking for sign.

When Billy returned with the horses the two men wrapped Henry's remains in one of Billy's swag blankets and then set about making a crude litter from saplings they found broken down by the stampeding cattle. When they finished they loaded the stockman's body onto it and dragged it across to the windmill. After a short discussion, they decided they'd camp for the night

375

near the windmill. In the morning they would attach the litter to one of their horses and head back to the station.

The following morning the two men decided against breakfast, drank a little sweet tea and started back for the station. The sky was dark with the promise of more rain as they rode away.

'So, Famous, you reckon it was two riders following a small mob of cattle eh?'

'It looks that way, Boss.'

'Well, they'd be the bastards that shot the boys I reckon.'

'Yep, that's what it looks like to me too,' Famous replied. The one time tracker had made his assumption from the mess of cattle tracks he'd followed, and those of the two horsemen following. The brass shell casings he'd picked up had puzzled him though. He could think of no good reason why anyone would want to shoot the two Cockatoo Creek stockmen.

'Could be they were stealing cattle, and they came across the boys just by accident,' Billy suggested.

'They must be bad bastards then,' Famous replied. He looked back at the litter dragging along behind his horse. The body of his friend jerked from side to side against the ropes they'd tied him with as the roughly made litter bounced over a small spinifex bush.

'Looks like it could be what happened alright. I wonder how Wooloo is getting on.' Billy let the reins lay on his horse's neck, while he rolled a cigarette.

'Dunno Boss,' Famous replied. 'Any chance I can get a smoke off you.'

'Alright—didn't you bring any baccy with you?'

'Yeah, Boss, but I only had a bit left.'

'Yeah righto,' Billy shook his head and handed Famous his tobacco pouch.

'Which way do you reckon the bastards were headed?'

'Looked to me like they was headin east, I reckon, Boss.'

'That'd mean they're making for Wyndham, by the look of it.' Billy said and spat on the ground. He was silent for a moment or two before he added, 'There's a couple of meatworks out that way.'

'Thanks, Boss.' Famous handed back the tobacco pouch.

A light rain started to fall. Both men adjusted their hats and hunkered down in their saddles preparing themselves for what was going to be a slow ride back to the station. A crow called out from somewhere behind them. The noise a melancholy reminder of what had happened to their friend on the litter.

'Dirty fuckin bastards,' Famous snarled. He took the cigarette out of his mouth and spat on the ground as well.

# 43

# Dinner at Avellino

Sofia Moretti was hard at work in her kitchen when she heard the front doorbell chime. She put down the knife she had been slicing cabbage with and went to the front door and opened it. 'Miss Isabella, your home!' She wiped her hands on her apron, reached for Isabella and hugged her for more than a minute. 'My darling, girl, it's so good to see you.'

'Sophie, it's good to see you too.' Isabella kissed both of Sophia's cheeks. 'Now, before I start to cry, I would like to introduce another couple of weary travellers. This is Jack Ballinger. I'm not sure whether Father has had him to the house or not?' Isabella looked at Jack and watched him shake his head.

'No, I don't think we have met before, but I have heard Michael speak of you,' Sophia replied and put out her hand for Jack to take.

Jack shook it lightly. 'Hello there, Sophia.'

'And this pretty girl is, Anna.' Isabella put her hand on Anna's shoulder and helped her forward. 'Anna is all the way from Cockatoo Creek. She will be staying with us as well.'

'Well, hello, Anna. You are very welcome here my dear.'

'Hello Sophia,' Anna said shyly.

'Is father home, or is he still at work Sophie?' Isabella looked past the housekeeper and along the hallway.

'Yes—yes. He's in the study, but still working, of course. Come with me.' Sophia led them along the hallway to the study door and knocked.

'Come in Sophie,' a voice from inside replied.

Sophia Moretti pushed the door open and smiled at the man sitting at the desk.

'We have visitors and a little earlier than we expected!'

Isabella stepped into the study. 'Hello, Father.'

'Isabella—my dear girl, we were not expecting you for another day or two.' Michael Montinari dropped the pen in his hand and got to his feet. 'My darling daughter, you are a sight for sore eyes!' Michael hurried across the room and embraced his beloved daughter. 'Welcome home sweetheart.'

'It's good to be home, Father.' Isabella whispered.

'Sophia, you said visitors. Who else is out there?'

The two people waiting in the hallway stepped inside.

'You've brought Jack with you—I hope he looked after you at the station, my dear.' Michael was a little surprised to see Jack at his home.

'G'day Michael, it's good to see you, my friend.' Jack took Michael Montinari's outstretched hand and shook it. 'I kept me eye on her just as you asked. She was no trouble at all, Michael.'

'Glad to hear it Jack—glad to hear it. I'm guessing this must be Anna?' Michael walked across to the shy girl standing near the doorway and put out his hand. 'You are very welcome here my dear. I am so sorry for your loss. I must tell you that I feel partly responsible for the horrible time you must have gone through. If only I had done a little more checking before I hired that monster, things may have been different.' Michael shook Anna's hand and looked into her eyes. Even though Anna was trying hard not to show her grief at losing her people, Michael could see it in her dark eyes. He had known that same terrible feeling of loss long ago. He reached for the Aboriginal girl and hugged her.

'Well, Sophie it looks like we will be having guests for dinner this evening. I hope you have enough in the larder.'

'Of course we do. But I had better get to it, it's already quite late.' Sophia kissed Isabella on the cheek and left the study.

'I am guessing you could all do with a bath and a little rest before dinner,' Michael suggested. 'Isabella, Anna could sleep with you in your room my dear.'

'That will be fine Father. Yes, we're all a bit weary and in need of a warm bath.'

'And, will Jack be staying with us, my dear?' Michael was still wondering why Jack had come to the house with his daughter. But he imagined that it was probably a matter of honour to his friend. After all, he had promised he would bring Isabella back unharmed, and that is what he had done.

'Yes Father, Jack will be staying with us as well. He has done a wonderful job looking after me. Even though at first I thought it wasn't at all necessary, and I told him so.'

'I'm so glad to hear it all went well for you, my dear, even though you have been through some terrible times, and seen things no woman should ever have to see.' Michael replied sincerely. He turned to Anna and smiled. 'Now that we have Anna here with us we must make her feel as welcome as we possibly can, and hope that she enjoys her stay.' He turned back to Jack. 'Jack, I must thank you for looking after Isabella through all the trouble that you must have endured out at the station. I am in your debt my friend we will talk of it again.'

Michael turned to his daughter. 'Isabella, what do you think? Jack, could have the bedroom across from mine, that way he could use my bathroom? Does that sound agreeable, my dear?' Michael watched Isabella's face. Something seemed different with his daughter's behavior, and he wondered what it could be.

'I think that would be very suitable father.' Isabella looked at Jack and nodded to him.

'That will suit me just fine, Michael—just fine.' Jack was now realizing just how close Michael and his daughter were. He had the greatest admiration for Michael Montinari, and he hoped that when it was time to talk to him about his feelings for Isabella, it did not ruin his relationship with him. He was starting to feel unsure of himself, perhaps even inadequate. He realised now, with sudden clarity that he would never be able to keep Isabella in the manner she had been kept by her father. He looked at Isabella. She smiled back at him. It was as if she knew what was going through his mind.

The dinner that night was a great success. Sophia had performed a miracle in the time she had available. They dined on a traditional Italian dish of, Arancini con ragu. Succulent balls containing rice, beef mince tomato paste, mozzarella, and a delicate mix of herbs, rolled in a peppery breadcrumb mix, deep fried, and then served with a béchamel sauce and a final dusting of pecorino. The talented cook complimented the dish with Bucatini pasta, and a crisp salad of lettuce, tomato, and cucumber. Followed later, with plates of her wonderful Tiramisu dessert, which Sophia remembered, was Isabella's favourite.

When she came to clear away the dishes Michael lifted his crystal glass of Nebbiolo, his favourite red wine reserved only for special occasions. 'Once again, Sophia you have performed a miracle in the time you had, a truly wonderful meal to welcome my, Isabella home. Thank you, my dear.' He took a sip of his wine and nodded his thanks to his housekeeper.

'Thank you, Sophia, it was really wonderful,' Isabella agreed and lifted her glass.

'You are surely spoilt, Michael. That's all I have to say,' Jack added and lifted his glass of wine to Sophia as well.

Anna sat quietly. She was enjoying herself immensely. Isabella's father seemed a wonderful man, and he had been so nice to her. But it was all an overwhelming experience for her.

'I hope you took a plate out to Will, Sophie,' Michael asked, just before Sophia left the room.

'Yes—yes of course I did. It's one of his favourites.

'Sophie, could you let him know that after he has taken me into the city in the morning, ask him to return to the house and take Isabella and Anna wherever they would like to go.'

Michael looked across the table to Jack, 'Jack would you like to join me in my study for a glass of scotch and a chat.'

'Certainly, Michael, it would be a pleasure.' Jack was suddenly feeling nervous. He stole a look at Isabella and noticed she looked nervous as well.

The two men wished Isabella and Anna goodnight and Jack followed Michael to his study. Michael pushed open the door and went across to his bar and poured two glasses of Ballantine's. 'Would you like a little soda with yours Jack?'

'Just a splash thanks, mate.'

Michael sat down at his desk and motioned for Jack to take the seat opposite. Jack was wondering what was about to happen. Had he done the right thing coming to his friend's house uninvited? He'd taken care of Isabella. He'd done what Michael had asked of him. He had tried his best. But for some strange reason, he felt a little guilty. He wanted desperately to tell Michael he was in love with his daughter, but he wasn't too sure what the outcome would be.

'Now Jack, I would like to hear your version of what happened out at the station. As you know, Isabella spoke to me about it on the phone from Derby. Is there anything else I should know?'

'Well, from what she told me after the call, I think you know most of it. I can tell you one thing though, Anna was lucky that spirit man or whatever you want to call him came along. The man saved her life, that's for certain. But by the time we got back to the station, he was gone. We'd met him a couple of days earlier out bush where Anna's people were shot. He was waiting there for Anna. It was a very strange experience. One that I don't think I will ever forget. He was the one that told her what had happened to her people.'

'A terrible business, all round, Jack.' Michael emptied his glass and waited while Jack drank the last of his. Then he went back to the bar and poured two more.

Jack waited until Michael sat back down and then he continued. 'That bastard Muller raped Anna sometime before we left the station to go bush. I think the poor girl was so ashamed, she kept it to herself. She told Isabella while we were out bush, and that's why we decided then to head on back. It was on the return trip that we met this, Pirramurar. I'll tell you this, Michael, if I had got near Muller I think I would have shot the bastard on the bloody spot.'

'Isabella told me about the rape, Jack. That poor girl has been to hell and back.'

'Anna took a knife from our camp and set off to kill the bastard, but it never went as she planned. Muller got hold of her and took her down to the dam. He was going to hide her body in the pump shed, and then poor Beans came along and that bastard cut his throat.'

'Terrible business all round. Tell me, Jack, what did you do with Muller's body? '

'Young Dan and I buried him out bush a few miles away from the station. I hope the mongrel rots in hell!'

'How's Isabella taken it all, Jack, She seems a little different to me?' Michael watched Jack's face.

'She's been just great. Her biggest concern has been Anna. The two of them have become quite close.'

'That's fine—just fine. It must have been a terrible experience for you all. But I still can't help but think there's a change in Isabella.'

'I'm not too sure how you are going to take this Michael, Isabella and I are in love, and I would like to ask you for her hand in marriage!'

'Stay here Jack, I'll be back shortly.' Michael got up from his desk and hurried out of the room. A short while later he returned with Isabella, dressed in her pyjamas, on his arm. He ushered her to a chair and went back behind his desk and drank down the last of his Ballantine's.

'Now, just what the hell has been going on out there at Cockatoo Creek?' He began with a solemn look on his face.

'What has Jack told you, father?' Isabella looked distraught.

'I've told your father about us. I thought it was the right thing to do, Isabella,' Jack interrupted. He could see the panic in Isabella's eyes.

'You told him already, Jack! It could have waited for a bit.'

383

'Look, Michael, I know you've done a hell of a lot for me, and the last thing I want you to think is that I would take advantage of your daughter. And please don't think badly of Isabella. We just got on so well, and it just seemed to happen, that's all.'

Michael got up and came around the desk and put his arms around Isabella. 'You have my blessing sweetheart.'

He turned back to Jack and took his hand. 'Congratulations, Jack, my friend. I must add that I was sort of hoping you two might get together, Isabella has been roaming around the world for far too long, and I can't wait forever for grandchildren.'

'Geez, Michael, you had me worried there for a bit.' Jack took Michael's hand and shook it vigorously.

'Thank you father—I love you, you know, even if you are a tease.' Isabella had tears in her eyes. She grabbed her father in a bear grip and hugged him.

'Just one thing my dear, there will be no monkey business while you're here in the house. You will just have to show a little patience—anyway, Sophia would have a fit. Now, my dear, I think you should get yourself off to bed. Jack and I have a bit of future planning to do.'

Michael picked up the empty glasses and went back to the bar. 'I don't know about you, Jack. But I think another drink is in order.'

'I'd have to agree with you on that,' Jack replied.

'Goodnight father.' Isabella hugged her father one last time and left the room.

The next few days were spent seeing the sights of Melbourne with Willard Burgess at the wheel of the big Packard 845. Anna was overwhelmed with the sheer size of the city and the crowds that seemed to be everywhere they visited. One of the highlights for her was their visit to Luna Park. She had never imagined that she could have so much fun. She and Isabella tried the merry-go-rounds, the ghost train, and finally the massive Big Dipper ride. When they crested the first hill of that particular ride and then paused for a split second before hurtling down the other side, she thought she was going to die. Something must have gone wrong—the tiny carriages couldn't possibly manage to stay on the tracks down an incline like that. She screamed along with everyone else on board as they hurtled down at frightening speed, only to then start to climb another massive mountain of steel. Anna had never enjoyed herself so much. As they strolled about, she tried fairy floss, and toffee apples, huge hot dogs, and brown paper bags filled to overflowing with salted popcorn.

One Sunday evening, Michael decided to join them for a late cruise and a meal along the Yarra River on board 'The River Lady.' Michael had insisted that the hard working Sophia join them, along with his driver, Will. While the meal that night was rather forgettable, it was a night thoroughly enjoyed by them all, and it wasn't until they returned home later, that things took a turn for the worse.

It was just as they walked through the front door that the phone rang. Sophia rushed to the hallstand and picked it up.

'Hello, this is the Montinari residence.' There was an extended pause, and then Sophia looked up at Michael. 'It's long distance, Michael, and it's not a very good line. I think it's someone from the Derby police in Western Australia!'

Michael took the handpiece. 'Yes, this is Michael Montinari. How can I help you?'

A somewhat unclear voice on the other end replied a moment later. 'Hello there. This is Sergeant Pat Collins of the Derby Police. By the sound of it, we don't have too good a line. Do I have Mr Michael Montinari there?'

'Yes you do, Pat, and just what seems to be the trouble?'

'I'm afraid I have some bad news for you. There have been a couple of shootings out at Cockatoo Creek. One of your stockmen, an Aboriginal fellow by the name of Henry, has been killed, and another chap, Wooloo, I believe his name is, was shot as well. But I believe he has survived, although, he is not too good at the moment.'

'How the hell did this happen?' Michael was stunned. They had just got through one shooting, and now there was another.

'I really can't say what happened as yet. I received a call on that pedal wireless you have out there from your new manager, a chap by the name of Billy Anders. He seems a nice enough fellow, by the way.'

Michael interrupted the sergeant. 'Would you mind getting to the point, sergeant?'

'I intend to head on out there tomorrow. There has been quite a bit of rain up this way recently, and I may have some trouble with the creeks. But I intend to give it a go in the morning. I'll be taking a tracker with me, but it will probably be of little use with the rains we've had. I intend to have a chat with Billy and this Wooloo fellow, and see where we go from there.'

'Do you have anything at all to go on at the moment, Pat?'

'Your man, Billy seems to think it may have something to do with cattle stealing. I won't know too much about that until I get there. I just thought I had better give you a ring and let you know, that was all.'

'Thank you, Pat. Can you keep me informed once you have something?'

'Will do Michael, will do. I'll be in touch.'

Michael hung the handpiece on its cradle and turned to the others and told them what the sergeant had told him.

'I can't believe it. Poor Henry, I remember him well. A damn good stockman, as I remember.' Michael said.

'Billy will be up to his neck in it at the moment, poor bugger, and new at the job as well,' Jack added.

'I might have to go up there myself and see what the hell is going on. It might be too much for Billy to handle along with all the station work as well,' Michael announced.

'I have a better idea, Michael. What if I went back up there and tried to sort it out for you. I'm sure you're too busy to even think about it,' Jack suggested.

'I am really. I have a big cutback with workers on the cards at the moment, and it is going to get a bit touchy with some of them. And on top of that, I'm in the throes of setting up a new truck assembly plant for an American company here in Melbourne, which I hope will enable me to retrain a lot of my construction workers for positions there. But it is going to take some doing.'

'Well, in that case, I can look after things up at the station for you,' Jack replied.

'Hell, you have just come back from up there. Are you quite sure about that, Jack?'

'If Jack is going, then so am I,' Isabella suddenly joined the conversation, 'and Anna might as well come with us.'

'That is not really necessary, my dear,' Michael replied.

'Father, we have been back here for more than a week, and we have had a wonderful time. But if Jack goes then both Anna and I may as well go back anyway. Anna will be expecting to get back to her work, and I would like to be near Jack should there be any trouble.'

'What a mess. I was just getting used to you all back here and now you're off again.'

'Anna, how do you feel about all this?' Isabella asked.

'I am worried about Dan. If there is trouble he may get involved, one way or another. I think I would like to go back as well.'

'Well, it seems you have all made up your minds to go, and I do appreciate it, I must add. So I guess it's up to me to sort out travel for you all. I will see to it in the morning.'

'Thank you, father,' Isabella kissed her father on the cheek.

'Anna, I would like to speak to you in my study after breakfast tomorrow morning. Please don't be concerned, my dear, it's just that I have a few things I would like to discuss with you,' Michael said.

'Yes, alright then, Mr Montinari.' Anna replied nervously.

'Thank you, my dear. You are a very sweet girl, and I hope I get to spend a lot more time with you at some later date.' Michael gave Anna a hug and wished them all goodnight.

The following morning Anna was woken by the chink of glass from somewhere outside. She looked across the room. Isabella was still asleep. She got up and went to the window and looked out in time to see the milkman quietly closing the front gate behind him. She knew there would be four one pint bottles of milk standing near the kitchen door ready for Sophia to take into her kitchen.

Anna was simply amazed at the vast difference in the way of life for people in the city. Her memories of her earlier life with her grandfather and her people were so different in every possible way.

Later, after they had eaten breakfast, Michael took Anna into his study and closed the door, so that he could speak to the young Aboriginal girl in private.

'Anna, please take a seat, my dear.' Michael went to his desk and sat down.

'Have I done something wrong, Mr Montinari?' Anna was feeling very nervous. She had no idea what this conversation was to be about.

'You have done nothing wrong, my dear. Let me explain. Anna, you have suffered greatly with the terrible loss of your people, and of the way you were treated by Jan Muller. Isabella has told me that he assaulted you in his wash-house at the station. It must have been a terrible experience for you. I am appalled by his disgraceful behavior toward you, and toward your people. Isabella has also told me in detail what happened while you were out bush, and of your meeting with this, Pirramurar fellow. While I would never condone violence of any sort, I am very glad that he came to your rescue when he did, and in doing so, saved your life. I am also aware that you and my daughter have grown very close, and I am sure this has helped you more than you imagine. Isabella is a very thoughtful person, and I am very proud of her.'

'Yes, it is true, Isabella is my friend. She is very wise, and she has a peaceful spirit. I hope we stay friends forever.' Anna smiled at Michael. She had begun to love this man in the very same way she felt about Santiago.

'Well, Anna I want you to know that your position at Cockatoo Creek will always be a permanent one. You will never have to worry about that detail as long as I own the place. I intend to set up a small trust for you, so that for as long as you live, you will be looked after, no matter what.

I consider you to be part of this family now, and you will be treated as such. I know your life is best spent in the country you understand and love, and I admire you for that. But I must add, in the short time you have been here, I have grown very fond of you myself, and I would like you to consider me your friend as well.'

'Thank you, Mr Montinari. You are a kind man and I would like to have you as my friend.'

'Now, there is just one more thing, my dear, have you learned how to write yet?'

'Not very well, but I am learning, thanks to Isabella,' Anna replied.

'My dear, when you are back at the station, should you ever feel like writing to me, please do. I will answer you promptly and tell you about all the boring things I have been doing here in the big city, and it will give me great pleasure to do so.'

'Yes, of course, I would love to write to you, Mr Montinari.'

'Well, that's all settled then.' Michael got up and took Anna by the hand and led her back to the kitchen where the others were chatting about their coming return to the station, and the planning that would need to be done.

\*   \*   \*

Six days later they were back in Derby. Isabella's father had performed miracles managing to find the quickest way for them to return. He had arranged for them to travel by rail to Brisbane and from there, he'd booked flights on the relatively new airline, Queensland and Northern Territory Airline Services to Darwin. In Darwin, he managed to locate a small company, Aerial Bush Charters and booked a charter for them on a small aircraft to take them on to Derby.

It had been quite an emotional time for them with their farewells to Isabella's father. Michael had not been happy that they were leaving him so soon, and he made Isabella promise that when they were done with their investigations at the stations, both she and Jack would return to the city. Michael announced that he still had much to discuss with Jack if he was to become his future son in law.

Even Sophia and Will were saddened to see them leave. Sophia had cried when Isabella explained to her their reason for returning.

'Shouldn't you be leaving that sort of thing for the police to handle, my dear. After all, it is their responsibility, and that is what they are trained for. But, more importantly, it could be very dangerous for you, and, I do not know how your father would survive if anything were to happen to you.' Sophia told her in the kitchen when they were alone together.

Isabella decided then that Sophia should know about her and Jack, and the love they had for each other, and so she told her. She explained that she would feel more comfortable being near Jack and that it seemed proper that she should represent the family interests by her presence at the station.

'Well now, I must say I approve of Jack, he seems a lovely man. But just make sure no harm comes to you, my dear,' She'd replied.

Anna had cried when she had said her farewell to Isabella's father. She had grown very fond of him and had enjoyed his company immensely. Just before they left, she had handed him a letter and assured him it would the first of many, and that she hoped he would notice her improved writing skill as time went by. After they had left for their return to the station Michael retired to his study. He poured himself a generous glass of Ballantine's, sat at his desk and opened the one-page letter Anna had given him as she climbed into the Packard just before they left. When he'd finished reading it there were tears in his eyes.

*Dear Mr Montinari,*

*Thank you very much for the wonderful time I have had while I stayed at your home. You are a very generous and thoughtful man. But you must not work so hard. I know you have known great sadness, for I have seen it in your eyes. You must find time to let your spirit find the peace it deserves.*

*I know from our discussions that you love my country as I do. So, when I return to the station I will sit among the boab trees and speak with you and hope that you hear me.*

*I should tell you, Isabella has helped me with this letter, for I still have so much to learn in regard to letter writing. But I am determined to improve, and I hope that you will notice it because the next time I write it shall be my very own words. Isabella is my best friend and I love her dearly. I will watch over her for you. Remember, you must not work so hard.*

*Goodbye kind man.*
*Love Anna*

# 44

# A Row of Seashells

Sergeant Pat Collins showed the weary travellers into his office. He invited the three of them to be seated and took his place behind his desk.

'Well now, how can I be of assistance?' He began his demeanor noticeably full of self-importance.

Jack, Isabella, and Anna had arrived back in Derby late that afternoon and had decided their first port of call should be the police station to find out if any progress had been made in regard to the shootings that had taken place out on Cockatoo Creek.

'Sergeant, it's been a good few days now. I would like to know if you have any news in regard to the incident out at the station.' Jack asked.

'Nothing of any great consequence, I'm afraid. I travelled out there last week and interviewed the stockman, Wooloo. It seems they were attacked by a couple of white men, who, he thinks, were stealing cattle. But that detail is not certain, as far as I am concerned. The stockman informed me, his friend, Henry was shot and murdered without reason, and that he himself was shot in the back by the same man and was lucky to have survived. His description of the two white men is very sketchy though, as I expected it would be. It seems that most white men look much the same to the Aboriginal. But he did say the man who shot him was quite a big fellow—not much help really.'

He shrugged, shook his head and continued. 'When we finally managed to travel out to the area in question, the rains had obliterated all sign, and so we couldn't gain much from that. As you would understand, without any tracks, there was little more I could do while I was out there.'

'And that's all you have for us at the moment?' Jack asked. He watched the Sergeant close the one-page file he had in front of him.

'That's about it, I'm afraid.'

'Thank you for the information Sergeant. I would like you to know that we will be travelling out to the station tomorrow morning. If there is anything we can do to help with your investigation, please let us know.' Isabella replied. Once again, Isabella was beginning to find the Sergeant's manner a little too casual and it annoyed her.

'Miss Montinari, I assure you I will continue my investigations as best I can from here. But I must add that I have very little to go on at the moment. In regard to the previous happenings out at your station, I would have liked to have interviewed young Anna here about that, as well. But it seems your father has been in touch with my superiors and asked that she be spared any embarrassment by reminding her of the things she endured at that particular time.'

'Tell me, Sergeant, are you not comfortable with the instructions you received from you're superiors? If so, I could have my father contact you personally to explain his actions in regard to Anna's welfare?' Isabella was starting to get quite annoyed.

'No, my dear that will most certainly not be necessary. Your father is highly regarded here in Derby. I'm not sure if you know this, but some time ago he helped the council with a generous donation toward a new fire truck which was most welcome. I have also been told that just recently he has made a sizable donation to the Catholic Church here in Derby. That donation, I have been told, is to be used to construct some sort of mission for wayward

Aboriginal people here in our town. From my point of view, I believe this will prove to be a total waste of money.'

'I find that a very cynical attitude, Sergeant.' Isabella replied.

'Well, be that as it may. But that is my belief on the matter.

'Thank you for your help Sergeant and please keep in touch.' Isabella rose to leave.

'Goodbye, for now, Miss Montinari, and you Jack. And of course you, Miss Anna—whatever your name is.' The Sergeant was having difficulty keeping his thoughts to himself.

'Her name is, Anna Cook, Sergeant. I must say, I find your demeaning manner rather difficult to bear. Let me suggest to you that in any future dealings we have you try a little harder to be civil. That way, I am sure you will remain in good stead with your superiors!'

'I meant no disrespect, Miss Montinari.' The sergeant decided to keep any future thoughts to himself. He watched Jack Ballinger get to his feet. He was suddenly aware of the big man's annoyance as well. Not someone to be trifled with, he imagined.

Jack took Isabella's hand and motioned for Anna to come closer. He put his arm around her and the three of them left the station.

'That man is a self-opinionated bore!' Isabella said as they crossed the road.

'I agree, and I'm fairly sure he knows how you feel about him as well. Anyway, let's get over to the Spini and see if we can get a drink before it's time for dinner,' Jack replied, and the three of them headed down the street in the direction of the Spinifex Hotel.

That evening after they had showered and changed into clean clothes, they went into the dining room to be greeted with a welcoming smile from the waitress, Teresa.

'Good evening, Jack and Isabella, and you Anna. I hope your holiday went well, and you enjoyed yourselves.' Teresa guided them to a quiet spot in the corner of the dining room.

'Thank you, Teresa. It's nice to see you again,' Isabella replied.

'I see young Tommy is back at his post over there.' Jack waved to the young boy working diligently on his rope.

'How are you, Anna?' Teresa asked with genuine concern on her face.

'I am alright thank you.'

'There has been more trouble out your way, I've been told. Although, all we know is that someone was shot out there. Don't count on Sergeant Collins being much help. He don't like us coloureds too much. Last week he locked up my young sister just for singing on her way home from the hotel. He's a real bugger, that one. Sorry about the language Isabella.'

'I can't say I'm too fond of the man myself,' Isabella replied with a smile.

After they had finished their meal and were about to leave, Teresa asked if she could bring Tommy over to say hello.

'Of course, you can, Teresa. Bring the lad over.' Jack replied.

The waitress waved to Tommy and he came over to their table. The young boy smiled self-consciously and waited for Teresa to speak.

'Tommy here is my older sister's boy and I love him dearly. But he says some really strange things at times.' Teresa patted the top of the young boy's head. 'He's had another of his silly dreams. He asked me to tell you to be very careful if you see a path that leads through some seashells.' Teresa patted Tommy's head again, and the boy returned to his post, and once again the ceiling panels began to swing in monotonous harmony above them.

'Take no notice. Sometimes he mixes things up terribly. But he is a good boy.' Teresa added.

'Tell him we will take special care. But what a strange thing for him to say,' Jack had no idea what Tommy was on about and decided to dismiss it as no more than a silly dream the boy had had. 'Tell me, Teresa. Does the lad go to school with the rest of the kids his age?'

'My older sister is not well, Jack. Tommy works here to keep food on the table. I help where I can. But it has become very difficult. We do our best with what we have.' Teresa gave them a smile, wished them goodnight and turned to leave.

'Hold on a minute.' Jack took a five-pound note from his wallet, folded it up so that any diners watching wouldn't know what it was, and handed it to the waitress, 'I hope it helps, I really do.'

'You are very kind, Jack. Thank you.'

After she had gone, Jack turned to his two companions. They were both smiling at him. 'It's a crook old world for some, that's for certain.'

'You're a real sweetheart Jack Ballinger.' Isabella said affectionately. They got up and went into the cocktail lounge for a quiet drink before bed.

The following morning, just after ten o'clock Billy Anders arrived at the hotel to pick them up for their journey back out to the station.

'So, Billy, you must have left early mate.' Jack said, as he helped the likable manager with the last of their bags into the back of the station truck, and covered them with a worn tarp.

'Yep, I left around five. I couldn't see too much for the first bit. The bloody road is still a hell of a mess. But the creeks are well down at the moment. It hasn't rained for a couple of days, which is a bit of a blessing. Glad to see you all back with us again though. But not what you planned on, I'll bet.'

'That's about the strength of it I reckon,' Jack replied as he helped Anna and Isabella into the rear seat of the truck and passed them a canvas tarp in case they needed it later.

'Good morning, Miss Isabella. Glad to have you back with us again.' Billy greeted Isabella and then turned to Anna. 'Hello there young, Anna. You might like to know, Dan's been a proper pain while you've been gone. He's been getting around the place like a steer with a busted hoof.'

'Hello Billy,' Anna replied with a wide smile as she helped Isabella fold the tarp.

Billy climbed into the driver's seat, started the truck and swung it into a dusty U-turn outside the entrance to the hotel. As they moved off, Isabella looked back in time to see Teresa and Tommy standing near the front door waving. She waved back, just before the dust from the rear wheels of the big truck made visibility totally impossible.

'What the hell has been going on out at the station while we've been gone, mate?' Jack asked as he shuffled about in the rudimentary confines of the truck trying to find enough room for his long legs and big frame.

Billy turned the truck onto the main road and started to work his way through the gears. 'Well, it's all been a bit of a mystery Jack,' he began. 'Wooloo came back to the station in the back of the old buckboard. He was out to it and almost dead from loss of blood. He must have hitched up their old horse, got in the back and hoped like hell it would take him home. If you ask me he was bloody lucky. Anyway, Santiago patched him up, and when he finally woke he told us what'd happened. I radioed through to the police in Derby, and a couple of days later they came out and interviewed him. I must say that Sergeant Collins didn't seem too concerned about the whole damn thing. Famous and a tracker he brought with him went out to the windmill where it happened. Anyway, because we'd had so much rain, they couldn't see too much at all.' Billy changed down a gear and turned the truck away from a deep washaway in the middle of the road.

'What has Wooloo told you, Billy?'

'Same story he told the copper. He reckons there were two white blokes, and he thinks they were pushing a mob of cattle with them. One of them, a big ugly bugger with a pock-marked face, shot and killed Henry, and then took a shot at him before they headed off. We buried Henry down there with Beans. It's been a bit it of a sad affair really if you ask me. The bastard that shot them must be a right mongrel, I reckon.'

'I intend to get to the bottom of it, Billy. You have my word on that. But I may need a bit of help along the way.'

'I'll help you anyway way I can, Jack.'

'How are things getting on at the station, apart from that, Billy?' Isabella joined in the conversation.

'Pretty good, Miss Isabella, we can't do a hell of a lot out on the station when it's wet. It's a seasonal thing really, but it's a good time to catch up on work around the homestead. We've still got yards to build down near the dam, and a hell of a lot of maintenance to be done as well,'

They hadn't travelled far before the road really began to deteriorate. Deep ruts filled with dried mud and sharp corrugations made the truck bounce and shudder from one side of the road to the other. Billy slowed the truck to a more manageable speed, and they continued on.

Anna sat quietly in the back seat. The Aboriginal girl was deeply upset by the news that there had been more trouble at the station. Henry was her friend. How could these white people do such things? It was not right and there was no reason for it. She looked out the window at the countryside rolling past. She was glad to be back. Dan would be waiting for her to arrive. He would have known Billy was picking them up in Derby. She remembered their last night together before they left for Melbourne. It had been warm and they'd gone down to the dam for a swim. They'd made love on the warm ground beneath their little tree. She could hardly wait to see him again.

Six hours later they pulled into the homestead grounds to a welcoming party of yapping station dogs. It had been an uncomfortable trip, but there had not been any more rain, and the creeks were well down and easy to cross. Jack had taken over the driving for the last two hours to give Billy a break, and they'd arrived just in time for dinner.

Isabella and Jack carried their bags across to the homestead while Anna took hers to her room behind the kitchen. She quickly changed into her work clothes and almost ran into the kitchen. She was in a hurry to see Santiago and tell him all about her wonderful trip. The old cook was busy carving a leg of pork when she pushed open the kitchen door.

'My sweet, Anna, you're back at last.' The old cook put down his carving knife and opened his arms just as Anna rushed into them. 'Was your trip wonderful, my dear?' he whispered as he held her tight.

Anna let go of her friend and took her apron from its hook near the bench. She was smiling when she put it on. 'Oh, Santiago, it was so much fun. We saw very important big buildings, and statues of famous white people, trams and big buses. We went to a place where we had rides on little trains that raced down hills. We had popcorn and apples covered in red toffee. Oh, Santiago it was such fun. Isabella bought me clothes to wear and new shoes, and we drove everywhere in a beautiful car.' Anna gushed with excitement as she continued. 'Isabella's father is a wonderful man, Santiago, and he has told me he wants to look after me. I am not sure what he meant. But he was very nice to me.'

'You are a very lucky girl, Anna.'

'Now, what would you like me to do?'

'Are you sure you want to come back to work so soon, my dear?'

'Yes—yes, I want to help. I really missed you and it's nice to be back.' Anna kissed the old cook on the cheek and finished tying her apron.

'You can go and fill the tea urns out in the dining room if you like.' Santiago picked up his carving knife, wiped it on his apron and started slicing the pork again. He watched Anna fill a large jug of water from the sink and take it out into the dining room. He was glad to have her back. There was a tap on the fly door behind him. The old cook knew who it would be. He looked back at the door.

'Is Anna here Santiago?' Dan was looking through the flywire, with a grin on his face.

'Anna, you'd better come back in here, my dear.' The old man was smiling with amusement when Anna came back into the kitchen with her empty jug. 'There's someone to see you.'

The following morning Isabella and Jack called for a meeting with all the hands employed on the station to discuss the events that had occurred while they had been away. After a few words of greeting from Isabella, she handed the meeting over to Jack.

'Good morning all. Sorry to drag you away from your work. But I have some news from the station owner, Mr Montinari. Firstly, he has asked me to forward his thanks in regard to the work you have carried on with while knowing of the killing of one of your fellow station workers, and the wounding of Wooloo. I have been instructed by Michael to try and get to the bottom of this brutal attack, and you have my word that I shall do my best, fellas. After breakfast tomorrow morning I intend to ride out to the windmill where the shooting took place and see what I can find. I know that, with the recent rains, there will probably be little hope of finding any clues. But I intend to look anyway. I will need to take Dan and Famous with me. So I hope you can spare them both for a day or two, Billy.' Jack looked across at Billy and saw him nod in agreement. 'Thanks, Billy. I've spoken to Wooloo and he's told me the shooting was done by a couple of men stealing cattle. Famous is of the same opinion and reckons they were heading for Wyndham. I will make a decision on that, and what we should do, when we return to the station. It's a nasty business all round, that's for sure. But I intend to find out what the hell happened, one way or another. Well, that's about it, fellas. I thank you for your attention, and now I will let you get back to your work.'

Jack turned to Isabella and indicated that he had said what he intended. Isabella smiled in agreement. Then, Jack heard someone in the back of the gathering of men say something. It was a voice he knew very well; it was Bob Nugent the station mechanic.

'Make sure you catch the bastards, Jack!'

'Bloody mongrels . . . !' Someone else hissed.

'You can count on it, Bob,' Jack said, to unexpected applause from everyone in the room.

Jack reached for Isabella with his left hand and lifted his right arm with a clenched fist in a firm salute to the gathering of angry stockmen.

Jack, Dan, and Famous arrived back at the station two days later. As expected, the trip had been a waste of time. Although they did manage to find another empty cartridge case lying not far from the area where the buckboard had been parked. Jack was now of the opinion that two weapons had been used during the shooting. One of them was a pistol of .44 calibre and the other, a rifle. The single shell casing he had found came from a not-so-common Remington rifle, of 25 calibre.

Famous had spent two hours wandering about the spinifex, but all he had found were broken bushes and smashed trees where a small herd of cattle had crashed through the scrub. They'd camped near the windmill on their first night out, and returned the following day. But they were all of the same opinion. It looked as if the two men and the cattle they were stealing, were heading in the general direction of Wyndham.

When they'd returned to the station, Jack had a long discussion with Billy about the feasibility of anyone selling branded cattle in Wyndham.

'Do you think it could be done, Billy, and if so, where?' Jack asked the station manager.

'Well firstly, I would think the mob they've got could well consist of more than just Cockatoo Creek stock. They would have most likely picked up other brands, possibly even unbranded stock as well. It's not always possible to brand every steer on a station, and some are often missed along the way.'

'So, they could have a bit of a mixed mob. Is that what you are saying?' Jack replied.

'Yes, and the other thing is, a lot of our stock is fairly wild and usually take a bit of handling, so I am guessing they probably managed to round up a fairly quiet mob, perhaps near one of the mills.'

'Do you think they could they sell them in Wyndham or not, Billy?'

'No, I do not think so, Jack. I am fairly sure there is only one meatworks there, and they would have standards to maintain. There is paperwork that must accompany all stock through a meatworks. No, I don't think that would be possible.'

'It doesn't seem to be worth the damn risk if you ask me.'

'I agree,' Billy replied with a puzzled expression.

'Well, I will have a talk with, Isabella, but I think the best thing for me to do is head to Wyndham and have a look around.'

'Will you be going on your own?'

'No, I think I'll take young Dan along with me for company unless you need him about the place.'

'That's fine with me, Jack. But I would be very careful if I were you though. These bastards sound like proper arseholes if you ask me.'

'The first thing I'll do when I get there is visit the police and hope I can get some help to get to the bottom of it. The thing is, Billy we don't have too much to go on at the moment. But I can assure you, we will be ready for trouble if any comes our way.'

# 45

# Wyndham

Try as he may, Jack could not convince Isabella that she should stay at the station while he and Dan headed to Wyndham.

'I'm sorry to disappoint you, Jack. But if you go, then I will be going as well,' she had insisted, with a wry smile.

'Is that really sensible though? It could get nasty, and I figure your father wouldn't be too happy with me getting you in harm's way.'

'How will we be getting there, Jack?'

'You're a headstrong woman, Isabella Montinari! In the station truck, I guess.' Jack shook his head with exasperation and shrugged his shoulders.

'We won't tell father that we expected any trouble. Anyway, it will be a job for the Wyndham police.'

'You win, my darling. Now then, I would like to head off tomorrow morning, if possible.'

'I'll be ready. But you had better go and tell Dan so he can say his goodbyes to Anna if that's the case.'

The following morning at dawn, they were on their way, and two days later they were on the outskirts of the town of Wyndham. The road had been a mess. The worst section was near the turnoff to Pago, a native mission further to the north run by a group of Benedictine monks.

The road at that particular spot was almost impassable, and if it hadn't been for the improvements made to the big Marmon Herrington truck by Bob Nugent in his workshop, they would not have got through at all. They had bogged down badly several times and had to resort to the powerful hand winch Bob had fitted to the bull bar at the front of the truck to get them out. Several of the creek crossings had proved difficult as well, but the extra ground clearance had made all the difference.

Wyndham, of course, was a cattle town, rough and ready. A town kept busy by its meatworks, a thriving enterprise started in 1919. The port at Wyndham had once been the stepping off point where fifteen thousand hopeful miners set off from on their way to the goldfields of nearby Halls Creek. During those heady days, the town had thrived, and at one time boasted six hotels. But when the gold at Halls Creek eventually petered out around the end of the nineteenth century, the town struggled for many years until the recently constructed meatworks gave it a new lease of life. Cattle slaughtered in the well-run meatworks was hung in chillers and later loaded onto state ships to be sent south to the port of Fremantle for distribution throughout Perth and the surrounding areas.

Jack turned the mud covered truck into the wide main street, and they set about finding accommodation for the next few days. A short while later he parked the truck outside the Wyndham Hotel. The three of them climbed down, stretched their weary bodies, and Jack headed in to see if he could book them rooms.

Two old men were sitting in the shade of the front veranda, smoking hand-rolled cigarettes. One of them grunted a greeting to Jack as he made his way up the wooden steps. 'Where're you from, mate?'

'Cockatoo Creek station,' Jack replied. He looked back at the two men.

The old man shrugged. 'Can't say I know the place, mate,'

Jack smiled. 'About a week's ride due north-west on a good horse, old friend.'

The old man took a drag on his thin cigarette, turned to his friend and laughed. The noise, a weary rasping sound that seemed to lack humour of any sort. 'Well now, me horse riding days are long gone, friend. So I won't be riding around lookin for the place any-time soon.'

'Just takin it easy and enjoying the shade is not too bad a bad pastime anyway.' Jack replied.

The old man looked at the burnt-down cigarette in his left hand and never replied. His friend shrugged, coughed and spat a good-sized dollop of brown spit onto the veranda floorboards and stared off into the distance.

'Well anyway, thanks for the welcome and the friendly chat, fellas. But right now I'm feelin a bit dry, so I'll leave you to it.' Jack touched his hat in an abbreviated military salute and pushed the door open. When he came outside he had a relieved smile on his face as he went over to the truck.

'We're in luck. Let's get our bags down and get in the cool.'

'I think a nice shower will be in order, Jack.' Isabella sounded relieved. She dusted herself down and started to help Dan undo the ropes that held their luggage in place.

'The lady in reception tells me they have just installed ceiling fans throughout the hotel, so it shouldn't be too bad,' Jack told them. He took the cases Dan offered him and headed back toward the front entrance again.

After they had showered and changed the three of them went into the lounge bar for a cold drink before dinner. The room was small, dark and smelled of stale beer and cigarette smoke. A brand new wooden-bladed ceiling fan whirred noisily on the discoloured pressed metal ceiling. The room was empty, apart from the barman, a portly older man who looked up from the book he was reading and watched them make their way toward him. His tired eyes suddenly fixed on Isabella. He closed his book and straightened up.

'What can I get you, love?' His craggy face erupted into a smile that displayed several gold teeth. He adjusted the flexible metal armbands on his shirtsleeves and leaned forward to study Isabella over the top of his glasses.

Isabella gave him a courteous smile and turned to Jack. 'I'm thirsty, Jack.'

'And what do you think you would like, Madam?' Jack asked.

'I think I fancy a gin and tonic with lots of ice thank you, Mr. Ballinger.'

Jack waited until the barman finally turned to face him. 'Now that I have your attention, friend—the lady fancies a gin and tonic with plenty of ice and two large glasses of cold beer for us gentlemen.'

'Gentlemen eh . . . ? We don't get too many of them in here these days. Come to think of it, we don't get too many ladies in here either.' The barman turned back to Isabella and nodded admiringly. When his attention returned to Jack, he gave him a somewhat less enthusiastic version of his gold-toothed smile and started on their order.

'So—where do you all hail from.'

'Cockatoo Creek Station,' Jack replied.

'I've heard of it, yeah. Owned by some big shot from down Melbourne way, I've been told.' The barman handed Isabella her drink and flashed her another of his gold-toothed smiles.

'The drink you just mixed is for his daughter,' Jack added with a grin.

'Is that so? Well now, no offense meant to the pretty lady here.' The barman placed the two glasses of beer on the bar. 'That'll be six and eight pence mate.'

Jack passed the barman a ten shilling note. 'How many meatworks are there here in Wyndham, if you don't mind me asking?'

'There is only the one, as far as I know. . . Hang on there a minute, there's two really. There's a small works and chiller a few miles out, on the King River. Not much of a setup really. It's owned by a rather shifty Frenchman, goes by the name of Pierre Bouchard. They call him Froggy Pete. He don't come into town too much and when he does, he usually causes trouble one way or another. It seems there's always someone after him for money.'

'Thanks for the info mate. By the way, I'm Jack Ballinger, my friend here is Dan Miller, and the lady is Isabella Montinari.'

'Glad to know you all. I'm Bob, Bob Jenkins, originally from Ballarat, down in the gold mining country.'

'You're a long way from home, Bob,' Jack replied and put out his hand. The barman shook it and reached across the bar for Isabella's. 'The pleasure's all mine, lovely lady.'

The three of them stayed at the bar enjoying a few more drinks and the company of the barman until the dinner gong rang.

'Time for a feed I reckon,' Jack announced and slid off his stool. The three of them thanked the barman for keeping them entertained and headed for the door.

'I'm off shortly. If you'd like to come back a bit later I'll buy you a drink.' The barman offered. He gave them his very best gold-toothed smile, adjusted his armbands once again, and bowed graciously to Isabella.

'There are a couple more things I wouldn't mind asking you anyway, Bob. So we'll see you after dinner then.' Jack pushed open the door and waited for Isabella and Dan to pass.

'You have an ardent admirer in our gold-toothed friend, Isabella,' Jack teased as they went through to the dining room.

'Well, I think he is a lovely man, Jack—so there!'

'What do you need to ask him, Jack?' Dan asked while they waited for the waitress.

'Well, I reckon if anyone knows who this mysterious rider is with the pock-marked face, it'd be our friend, Bob Jenkins.'

'Makes sense,' Dan replied, just as the waitress arrived to show them to their table.

'Our first port of call tomorrow will still be the police though,' Jack said as he pulled out Isabella's chair.

Their meal that night was a real surprise to the three of them. They feasted on freshly caught mangrove jack fillets that barely managed to fit on their plates. They had been pan-fried and basted lightly with a French mustard sauce, and accompanied by fresh vegetables grown out in the hotel's well-kept gardens.

An hour later they were back in the lounge bar chatting with their new friend, Bob Jenkins.

'The tucker's good here at the pub, Bob,' Jack announced, as he slid onto on one of the bar stools.

'They've got a bloody good cook, that's why. An old Chinese fella goes by the name of Zhang Wei,' Bob Jenkins replied, with a smile aimed directly at Isabella.

'So, how long have you been here in Wyndham, Bob,' Jack asked.

'Best part of three years now. I've been threatening to leave for just about as long as well, but I just never seem to get around to it,' he replied with his characteristic smile.

'So, you'd know most everyone around the place, I guess.'

'If they come into the pub, I certainly would, Jack, that's for certain.'

'I'm not really sure if this bloke comes from here. But anyway, do you know of a big fella with a badly pock-marked face?' Jack asked and watched the barman's face.

'Yep, I reckon I do. That sound a bit like Max Crabbe to me,' the barman replied. 'Steer clear of that bastard, Jack he's a nasty piece of work, that one.'

Jack smiled. If this Max Crabbe proved to be the man Wooloo spoke about, then it was beginning to look like they were on the right track. 'How do you mean, Bob?'

'He's a bad bugger that one, violent, unpredictable. Not a nice fellow at all. He's barred for life from this hotel for pulling a knife on a couple of drinkers a while back. Steer well clear of him, Jack.'

The following morning, Jack, Dan, and Isabella left the hotel and walked to the Wyndham police station. When the sergeant came to the desk Jack asked if it was possible to speak to him in private. The sergeant took them through to his office and pushed some chairs around to accommodate them.

'Now, what can I do for you folk,' he began.

'Well firstly, my name is Jack Ballinger. My friend here is Dan Miller, and the lady is Isabella Montinari. We've travelled here from Cockatoo Creek Station in the hope you may be able to help us?'

'What help did you have in mind, Jack?'

'We've had a shooting on the station. Two of our Aboriginal stockmen were shot. One was killed and the other was left for dead and was bloody lucky to survive. The stockman that survived was shot in the lower back with what appears to have been a high-power rifle. As I said, he was lucky to survive. If it wasn't for the fact that their carthorse carried the poor bugger back to the station, he most certainly wouldn't have. Now, I have spoken to this stockman to gather whatever information I could, and he has given me a description of one of the two men that rode into their camp.'

'And just what sort of description did this Aboriginal fellow give you, my friend. By the way, my name is Chris McCallum.'

'Well, Sergeant McCallum, he said it all happened very quickly. But he did tell me the shooter was a big fellow with a badly pock-marked face,' Jack explained.

'And just what makes you think he may have been from here?'

'We have an old fellow on the station that at one time was a tracker for the Derby police. An Aboriginal fellow goes by the name of, Famous Feet. He's quite handy with tracks and sign, and he seems to think that the two men that rode into the stockmen's camp were moving a small herd of cattle in front of them and were heading in this general direction. I know it's not much to go on, but that's all we have.'

'It seems to me that you have travelled quite a way on very sketchy information,' the sergeant replied. 'Wyndham is a pretty rough and ready town, Jack. We get a lot of undesirables drift in here chasing jobs at the works through most of the dry season. At the moment we're having quite a bit of trouble around the place from bored meatworkers trying to kill each other after a few drinks. I'm a one-man show here, and it keeps me fairly busy if you know what I mean.'

'I reckon I do,' Jack replied.

'Anyway, if I had to rush off and investigate every time some Abo gets himself killed, I'd never get anything done. From the information you've given me, I'm not too sure how I can help. I can't interview every bloke around the place on the description of his having a few pock-marks on his face. But, I'll tell you what I'll do. I'll look into it and see what I can come up with. In the meantime, what are your plans while you are here in Wyndham?'

'Not too much really. We're staying at the hotel for a couple more days, and then we'll be heading back to the station, I reckon.' Jack got up and reached for the sergeant's hand. 'Anyway, Chris thanks for talking to us.'

'I'll see what I can do in the next few days, and if I come up with anything I'll come down to the pub and see you.'

'Sergeant, I do hope you can help us. It has been a rather nasty turn of events for us all. While the two stockmen that were attacked at the station were Aboriginal, malicious wounding and murder are very serious crimes and should merit the full measure of the law. I'm not sure if you know my father, Michael Montinari, the owner of Cockatoo Creek Station, but I should tell you he is a man of some influence and he's very concerned that this matter is cleared up quickly. So I do hope we can look forward to hearing from you at some time in the very near future.' Isabella added. She was not impressed with the Sergeant's casual manner at all.

'I'm sorry, Miss Montinari, I can't say I have heard of him. But as I said, I will look into it. Now if you don't mind I have other business to take care of.'

Dan opened the door for Jack and Isabella and the three of them went outside and headed for the hotel

'Where do we go from here, Jack?' Dan asked.

'Well, for a start, I don't think the sergeant's in any hurry to do too much, that's for sure. But I've been thinking. If the stock has been brought into town on the quiet I don't reckon the Wyndham Meatworks would be too keen on putting them through their killing floor. This other smaller works could be in some way involved. I think our next port of call should be out there to see what we can find. Let's go and have a chat with our friendly barman and get some directions.'

'We'll need to be careful Jack,' Isabella added as they headed for the hotel, on their mission to talk to their new friend.

An hour later, with the directions given to them by Bob Jenkins, they were on their way to the King River Abattoir, owned by one, Pierre Bouchard.

# 46

## Pierre Bouchard

Max Crabbe had been back in Wyndham for a few days. He had delivered the stolen cattle out to the King River Abattoir before coming into the town itself. He'd been sorely tempted to shoot his partner, Victor Bennett before delivering the stolen stock, but he'd thought the better of it. Even though his friend had proved to be bone lazy, Crabbe knew he needed him to help drive the cattle. They'd lost quite a few of the steers in some of the heavy scrubland as they got closer to Wyndham. It had been a difficult task keeping them in a manageable mob through some of the country they had to push them through. When the stock was eventually counted at Bouchard's yard they had only managed to deliver one hundred and fifteen animals. It was a bitter disappointment to Crabbe he had hoped to bring in at least two hundred. But, be that as it may, the cattle he delivered to the stockyard were still worth a tidy sum.

Pierre Bouchard had paid Crabbe a hundred pounds the day he'd delivered them; with the promise, he would pay him the balance a few days later. The Frenchman told Crabbe he was waiting on a large payment from a group of butcher's he was contracted to supply in Perth. Crabbe had not been happy about waiting for his money but knew he had little choice in the matter. He'd paid off his friend from the money he'd received from the Frenchman. Victor Bennett was certainly not happy with the amount he received, but he knew better than to argue with Max Crabbe. He knew the man well, and he had watched him shoot the two Aboriginal stockmen near the windmill back on Cockatoo Creek. Crabbe had told him that he was involved with the shooting just as much as he was and warned him to keep his mouth shut about the whole thing if he knew what was good for him. Bennett grudgingly agreed, took his money and headed into town to spend the next few days in the Wyndham Hotel.

It had now been several days since he'd delivered the stock to Bouchard and Crabbe had waited long enough. He'd driven out in his old Ford buckboard to visit the Frenchman and collect the last of the money he was owed.

'You owe me, Bouchard, and I'm here to collect,' Crabbe grunted to the Frenchman when he entered the tin shed that served as his office.

'Yes—yes, I have it here for you,' Bouchard replied. He opened a drawer and took out the envelope with Crabbe's money. Pierre Bouchard would be pleased to see the last of Max Crabbe. The man was dangerous and unpredictable. He was sorry now that he'd had any dealings with him at all. He handed Crabbe the envelope and watched him pull out the money and count it.

'It had better all be here, you slimy little frog!' Crabbe grunted.

'It's all there,' Bouchard replied. Just then he heard a heavy vehicle, probably a truck, drive into the car park.

Crabbe closed the envelope and went over to the small louvre window and looked out. Two men were already out of the truck and heading over to the stock holding yard. He watched a woman climb down from the front passenger side and dust herself off.

'Looks like you got visitors Froggy.' Crabbe grunted and stuffed the envelope with the money in his pants pocket.

'You'd better stay here Max. I'll go and see what they want.'

Crabbe looked out again, just as the two men climbed onto the stockyard railing. 'What the fuck are they lookin at?'

'Just stay here and wait until they leave, Max,' Bouchard replied, with a lowered voice.

'Alright, but hurry it up, I have to get back into town,' Crabbe grunted.

* * *

Jack pulled the station truck to a stop in the muddy car park area near where a flattened piece of iron had been nailed to the side of one of the galvanized iron buildings. The sign read: *K.R.W, Office.* Below it, and leaning against the wall, was a small blackboard that read: *Boners wanted— Good rates.*

A narrow gravel path led from the car park to the office. It was raised slightly from the surrounding mud and lined on each side with large bleached, bailer seashells.

The King River Meatworks was located several miles out of town on a small rise not far from the banks of the King River from where they pumped water to use on their killing floor. The abattoir was little more than a series of galvanized iron sheds and lean-tos and a couple of poorly maintained stockyards partly full of shuffling cattle. A short line of rail tracks led from the main buildings to a more substantial, windowless building which was obviously the storage chiller. Two small sheds near this building housed a couple of noisy generators from where untidy bundles of electrical cables ran to the chiller.

'Isabella, would you mind staying near the truck for a bit while Dan and I check the cattle over there in the holding yard. I want to see if there is any Cockatoo Creek stock among them?'

'Alright, but be careful, Jack.'

Jack and Dan made their way across the muddy carpark to the stockyard and climbed up on the railing to look over the cattle. Just as a tall stooped man came out of the office.

'What can I do for you . . . *Mes amies?*' The man asked with a thick French accent.

Isabella joined Jack and Dan as they headed back from the stockyards.

'Would you be Mr Bouchard?' Jack inquired.

'Yes, that is my name,' Bouchard replied.

'My name is Jack Ballinger, and my friend here is Dan Miller, and the lady is, Isabella Montinari.'

414

Pierre Bouchard had been watching the two men approach him from the stockyard. He had taken no notice of the woman until then. He grinned. The woman was beautiful, stunningly beautiful. She was dressed casually in a pair of loose-fitting bone coloured linen slacks and a white cotton shirt that the humidity made cling revealingly to her ample breasts.

'Bonjour, jolie dame,' Pierre Bouchard greeted Isabella in French in an obvious attempt to impress her.

'Bonjour, Monsieur,' Isabella replied in a cultured Paris accent.

Pierre Bouchard's face broke into a wide smile. He was overjoyed. The beautiful woman spoke his language.

'Enchantée de vous connaître,' he said, with a wide smile and a nod of his head.

'Merci, Monsieur,' Isabella replied. 'Thank you, kind sir. But I think we should continue our conversation in English for the benefit of my friends.'

Pierre Bouchard's manner had now changed. At first, he'd not been happy. The two men looking over his stock had concerned him. He was a cautious man. In another two days, the cattle in the holding yard would be processed and then he could relax. But now the beautiful woman who spoke his native tongue had changed his mood altogether. The Frenchman reached for Jack's hand and shook it vigorously and then did the same with Dan.

'And now, gentlemen, how may I be of assistance?' He said, still smiling at Isabella.

'Like I said, the lady here is, Isabella Montinari. She is one of the owners of Cockatoo Creek Station, a cattle station back towards Derby from here.' Jack began.

Yes—yes, I have heard of the place!' Bouchard interrupted. The Frenchman suddenly began to look quite nervous.

'Well now, if I can finish.' Jack said.

'Yes—yes, please go ahead!'

'We have had a bit of serious trouble out our way. Two of our stockmen were attacked on the station, and one of them was murdered.'

'How terrible for you, Miss Montinari,' Bouchard interrupted again.

'The stockman that survived was badly wounded, and when he recovered he has given us some details of what had happened. It seems they were attacked by two men on horseback driving a small herd of stolen cattle through Cockatoo Creek country. We have since taken an experienced tracker out to where the attack happened and he followed the tracks for quite a distance and was of the opinion that the two men and the stolen cattle were probably heading in this general direction,' Jack continued to explain.

'That's terrible, and I am certainly sorry to hear it. But how do you think I can help?' the Frenchman asked nervously.

'We are wondering if any of the cattle have been sold to you.'

'No—no, all the stock I buy here at the works come from reputable sources, I can assure you.'

'The Cockatoo Creek brand is quite unique. I am sure if you had seen it you would have remembered it. It consists of a circle with the letter C doubled inside the circle.' Jack turned and looked back at the cattle yard. 'I see you have a good number of them in your holding yard. Can you explain that Mr Bouchard.'

'The cattle in the yard are all accounted for. I purchased them from a stock buyer that assured me they were his to sell.' Pierre Bouchard was in trouble, and he knew it.

'And you would have the paperwork in your office if that is the case, I take it?' Jack could see the Frenchman was beginning to panic.

'It was a cash sale—yes a cash sale. I don't usually bother with the paperwork in such cases,' he replied and coughed to clear his throat.

'Tell me, who was this man you bought the cattle from?' Jack asked. 'Because it seems you have purchased stolen cattle, and if I might add, from a murdering bastard as well!'

'Well now—how was I to know about any of that?' the Frenchman replied. He was trying desperately to remove any blame from himself.

'What was this man's name?' Jack asked.

'Max Crabbe—His name is Max Crabbe . . . !'

Jack was angry. He didn't like the Frenchman at all, the man reminded him of a ferret. 'So let me get this straight. You say you purchased the stock over in that yard from a bloke by the name of Max Crabbe, is that correct?'

'Look, I thought the stock were his. He told me that he'd paid for them. I had no reason not to believe him.' Bouchard knew the stock was most probably stolen. He'd bought stolen cattle from Crabbe in the past. But he certainly didn't know about any blacks getting shot. He was in trouble, big trouble, and he knew it.

'Thank you, Mr Bouchard. And while we're talking names, the name of the man this Crabbe bastard murdered was Henry, a good man that never did a soul any harm. I have to inform you that this is now a matter for the Wyndham police to handle.' Jack knew instinctively the Frenchman was lying through his teeth.

'Would it be possible to offer you some sort of financial compensation for the cattle in the yard? I am truly sorry. But as I said, I believed Crabbe's story, and I can assure you I knew nothing of any shooting taking place.'

'You can shove your compensation mate. And I'll tell you this—I don't believe a single word you've told me. As far as I'm concerned you bought stolen cattle, and you damn well knew it.'

'No—no, that is not so!' the Frenchman replied. He turned to Isabella with a pleading look in his eyes. 'I would never do such a thing! Mademoiselle s'il vous plaît croyez-moi!'

'Au revoir Monsieur.' Isabella headed for the truck.

'Goodbye, Mr Bouchard.' Jack said and followed Isabella.

Dan had been silent through all the conversations that had taken place. Instead of following Jack and Isabella, he stepped forward to confront the Frenchman.

'I reckon you're a lying bastard as well, and I hope they hang you along with the other bastard that killed our Henry!' Dan kept his voice hushed so Isabella wouldn't hear him. When he'd finished he turned for the truck as well.

'No—no, I did not know I assure you!'

'It's time to go, Dan,' Jack yelled across the muddy yard. He opened the truck's passenger side door and helped Isabella inside and waited for Dan to join them.

Max Crabbe had been listening to the heated conversation going on outside very carefully. He knew he was in trouble, big trouble! He decided he must do something to stop the three outside from going to the police.

The fool, Bouchard had told them his name and everything they needed to know to convict him of murder. He'd not bothered to tell the Frenchman about the shooting of the Aboriginals back on Cockatoo Creek station, there had been no need to. But Crabbe was worried. He had come out to the works without a weapon. He began to panic. He had to stop them from leaving somehow. He looked around the Frenchman's office. He noticed a tall storage cupboard against one wall and opened it. Inside, behind a couple of brooms was an old Winchester lever action rifle. Crabbe pulled it out and checked to see if it was loaded, but it was not. He heard the truck start. They were about to leave.

He reached up to the shelf above and wiped his hand along it. He felt a cardboard box. He pulled it down. It was open and there were several .44 cartridges lying in it, along with some pencils and a couple of boxes of matches. Crabbe grabbed the cartridges and loaded the Winchester as quickly as he could.

Jack put the truck into reverse and began to ease out the clutch, and then all hell broke loose . . . ! A rifle bullet smashed through the windscreen missing Isabella by mere inches. Jack hit the throttle down hard, and they tore backward for several yards. He rammed the gear lever into first and let out the clutch, and at the same time, he yelled. 'Get down Isabella! Get on the bloody floor! Some crazy bastard's shooting at us!'

Dan was already on the floor in the back. But he wasn't trying to take cover; he was reaching for the .303 rifle that lay at his feet. Another shot rang out and the windscreen exploded inwards. Dan heard Isabella scream. The sound sent a chill through him. It was a sound the young stockman would remember for the rest of his days. The truck stalled, jerked forward a couple of times and stopped. Dan finally managed to get hold of the .303. He sat up and looked out the side window. Pierre Bouchard was screaming something in French that Dan couldn't understand. Another rifle shot smashed into the truck, this time blasting a fist-sized hole through the side door where he sat, missing him by just inches.

Isabella began to scream again. The sound was terrible! 'Jack's been shot . . . ! He's been shot, Dan . . . !'

Dan yelled back, 'Stay down—get down on the floor!'

'Oh, my God, I think he's dead. There's blood everywhere!' Isabella started to scream again.

Dan felt sick. He shook his head to clear his thoughts. He must protect Isabella at all costs—he must! He crawled across the back seat and reached for the door handle just as another bullet tore through the windscreen sending shards of glass all over the front seat and Isabella's back as she crouched on the front floor. He eased the door open. He could hear someone arguing. He climbed down and crawled back to the protection of the rear wheel. Then he heard a different sound—a creak. It was the office door opening. Whoever had been shooting at them must have been doing it from inside the office. Dan worked a cartridge into the chamber of the .303. He had made up his mind, he would protect Isabella or he'd die trying. He stood up and stepped away from the protection of the truck. There was a man at the office door with a rifle in his hand. He was arguing with the Frenchman.

'You can't just shoot people, you mad fool.' Bouchard's voice was hysterical. '*Vous êtes fou.*'

'Get out of my fucking way you stupid French cunt,' the man with the rifle yelled back.

Dan watched him hit the Frenchman with the butt of his rifle, in an attempt to get him to move aside.

When Crabbe finally had Bouchard out of his way he turned back to the truck. He saw a young lad step away from the protection of the heavy vehicle. The lad had a rifle in his hands, but he looked uncomfortable with it. He grinned, ejected the empty shell from the Winchester and closed the chamber. He would finish it now.

Dan watched the shooter work the lever of the Winchester. He remembered Jack's instruction at the black billabong. 'Lean forward a little, take careful aim and squeeze the trigger.' The man had the rifle to his shoulder now—he was going to fire. Suddenly everything seemed to slow down for Dan. He was calm, unafraid and determined. He aimed the .303 at the middle of the man's chest and squeezed the trigger!

Max Crabbe was about to fire when the heavy bullet from the .303 smashed into his chest. The shock of the impact knocked him back through the doorway and into the office. The bullet had torn through his heart and killed him instantly.

The Frenchman screamed and put up his hands. 'Don't shoot—don't shoot *Monsieur* . . . !'

Dan leaned the heavy rifle against the side of the truck. He began to shake uncontrollably. He could hear Isabella crying in the front seat. He made his way to the front of the truck and pulled open the driver side door.

# Epilogue

Sister Murphy stopped writing. The old woman was sobbing quietly in the bed next to her. 'Oh no—how terrible it must have been for you all. Poor Isabella,' The Sister had not expected to learn what she had just heard. Jack was dead, murdered senselessly by a madman. She waited for Anna to gather her thoughts.

'Yes, Jack had been shot, killed by that monster, Max Crabbe. It was just so awful for Isabella. I wish I could have been there for her.' Anna wiped her eyes with the handkerchief the Sister handed to her.

'How terribly sad for Isabella, and can you tell me what happened after that?' Sister Murphy asked respectfully.

'Dan and Isabella had Jack's body prepared by the funeral director in Wyndham, and, even though he advised against it, they carried him back with them to Cockatoo Creek Station,' Anna said sadly.

'It must have been such an awful experience for both of them,' Sister Murphy whispered and stroked the old woman's arm.

'I think it was during those terrible times that Dan became a man. When he arrived back at the station he was different. He was no longer the gentle boy I knew before he left me. The innocence was gone from him forever. It was a long time before I heard him laugh again.' Anna was fighting back tears.

'Tell me, Anna, what happened to the others that were involved with the cattle stealing, and the shooting of the two stockmen?'

'They were arrested, and later faced trial, and then prison. I was told that the Frenchman, Pierre Bouchard spent several years in jail for his involvement. I believe his meatworks was eventually condemned and pulled down as well.

'And, my dear, what became of poor Isabella?'

'We buried Jack in our little cemetery among the boab trees at the station. It was a sad time for us all. Jack was loved by everyone. He was a wonderful man. Isabella was never the same after that. She stayed at the station for a few more days and then moved into Derby to wait for passage on the Mindaroo for Fremantle. From there she travelled to Perth, and then on to her father's home in Melbourne,' Anna explained.

'Did you ever see her again, my dear?'

'No I did not, although we did keep in touch over the years regularly by letter. Jack's death changed her though. It changed us all really. She stayed with her father in their beautiful home in Melbourne and helped him with his business. She told me in one of her letters that she dearly missed the wonderful times we had when we went out into the bush together. She told me she remembered us swimming together in the crystal pool we found near the falls on the Drysdale River. She said that if she closed her eyes she could still remember the tiny birds chasing insects in the grottos above us while we swam together. In another letter, she told me she would never forget my stories about the Milky Way, and that sometimes she would go out into the garden alone at night and sit and look along the edges of the Milky Way and imagine she could see Jack sitting near a campfire and smiling at her.' Anna dabbed at her eyes and tried to smile.

'How terribly sad for you, my dear, Isabella must have been a wonderful person, by the sounds of it.'

'Isabella was my best friend, and I loved her so much. I wished I could have helped her with her sadness, but it was not possible.'

'Such a shame—such an awful shame and you say she stayed with her father, and never returned to the station at all? You must have missed her so much.'

'Yes, I did,' Anna replied. 'Isabella stayed with her father until he died several years later. He had a stroke and never recovered.

He died at home with Isabella by his side. The doctors told Isabella they had warned him about working too hard. But he had taken no notice.'

'Poor Isabella, alone after all that she had gone through,' Sister Murphy was close to tears herself when she replied.

'Isabella took over her father's business, and with the help of her father's man, Willard, she managed quite well, I believe. She never married, although, in later years she and Willard became very close. Eventually, when it became too difficult for her to continue she stepped down and spent the rest of her days in retirement at 'Avellino' with Willard.

Isabella died in the winter of 1972. She was buried beside her father and her mother. Willard contacted me and told me the sad news. He arranged for me to travel across to Melbourne for the funeral. It was a very small affair, and so very sad. I remember feeling so alone while I was there. But Willard was kind to me and I stayed with him at 'Avellino' for several days before returning to the station. There are other things I could tell you Sister, private things about Isabella. But I have decided to keep them secret. As I am sure Isabella would have wished.'

'I have no wish to pry into anything private, my dear. But tell me, Anna, were you and Dan ever married?'

'No we were not. We were planning to, but two years after Dan brought Jack's body back to the station he was killed.'

'How—how did that happen, my dear?' Sister Murphy felt tears begin to run down her cheeks.

'It was a long, long time ago, Sister. He was kicked in the chest by a stock horse. It was a terrible accident. He was caught with his body against the stockyard railing. He died almost instantly. He is buried out there among the trees next to his good friend Jack. I wanted more than anything to be married to Dan, to have had his children, and have them sit with me and listen to my stories. But it was not meant to be.'

'You have endured some truly difficult times in your long life, Anna.'

Yes, that is true Sister. But, I have so many wonderful memories, and it is those memories that have kept me going all this time. The world has changed so much from those days. There are roads through my country now that carry white people to the remote and sacred places that were hidden for so long. I have seen pictures in the newspaper of our cave paintings, of the Wandjina, of the sailing ships that once visited our country. I hope the spirit people are not annoyed by these visitors. But there are still secret places hidden in the wild country where it is too difficult to travel comfortably, and I hope it stays that way so that the spirits of my people can live in peace.'

It was a little over a month later that Anna Cook died peacefully in her sleep at the Derby District Hospital. There were no relatives for the hospital to notify and until then, no contact had been made with the hospital from outside of the small cattle town, so her body was transferred to the morgue to await collection by the local undertaker.

On the day that Anna's body was collected from the hospital by the undertaker, Sister Murphy received a letter. She had just come from Morning Prayer when she was handed the mysterious letter. Wondering what it contained, she went directly to her small bedroom at the rear of the school and sat on her bed, cut open the envelope and read the contents.

*Dear Sister Kathleen,*

*I have not been well these last few days, and I feel I am not long for this world. But please do not be concerned. I am not afraid, for I have lived a long and mostly happy life. If your God is as true as I have grown to believe he is, I will soon be in his heaven with my Dan, and with my dear friend, Isabella and her Jack. I have been told that your God is kind and that he welcomes the Aboriginal people into his heaven, so when I arrive I will search for my grandfather and hope that I can find him.*

*I was so glad you visited me and listened to my stories, Kathleen. You are a kind and gentle person. I have made some arrangements with the hospital staff in regard to what is to happen should I pass away, and if it were to happen, my dear, then you will receive this short letter. Within a day or so of my passing, you will receive a phone call. The caller will tell you that he has made arrangements for my remains to be carried out to Cockatoo Creek where I am to be buried among the boab trees with all of my dear friends. The caller will invite you to attend the small service that will be held there. It is my last wish that you can find the time to attend, and so I hope you can do so. May your God bless and keep you safe, my dear.*

*Yours Sincerely*

*Anna Cook*

The following morning Sister Kathleen Murphy received her phone call as promised. The call came from a solicitor's office in Melbourne, and the caller told her that Anna Cook's body was to be transferred by the Derby funeral director out to Cockatoo Creek Station where it was to be interred in the small private cemetery there. The caller also told her that transport would be arranged for her should she decide to travel out to the station for the burial of the old lady, and the small service that would follow.

Sister Murphy thanked the caller and informed him that she would be more than happy to take up their offer and travel to the station for the funeral. After the Sister put down the phone she burst into tears. She had grown to love the old Aboriginal woman.

Two days later, as promised, Sister Murphy was picked up at the Holy Rosary School by a man in a four-wheel-drive vehicle and was driven out to Cockatoo Creek Station to attend the funeral of the Aboriginal woman, Anna Cook. Cockatoo Creek Station had been sold by Isabella Montinari many years before. It had been said that it held difficult memories for her. There had been an agreement made during the sale that the tiny cemetery would be maintained in reasonable condition and that if any of the original staff that worked for the Montinari family wished to be buried there it would be agreed upon.

For Sister Murphy, the trip to the station was something she would remember always. For the first part of the journey, they travelled on the upgraded Gibb River road which passed through open scrubland and occasional ramparts of multi-coloured sandstone. Two hours later her driver turned north onto the Kalumbaru road, and the going became more difficult. Even though it was nearing the end of the dry season, the road was badly corrugated and several times the Sister found herself holding on for dear life as her experienced driver navigated badly eroded creek crossings and massive ruts of dried mud. For the Sister, it was the first time she had travelled into the wild Kimberley country and she found herself enjoying it immensely. It was so very different from the rolling green hills of her native Ireland.

When her driver's four-wheel drive finally pulled through the trees and up onto the low plateau where the Cockatoo Creek homestead and station buildings were, the Sister found herself remembering Anna's descriptions of where she had lived for so long. The low plateau was surrounded by a circle of massive boab trees, some with girths so huge they reminded the Sister of laughing Buddhas. The station itself was, as Anna had described it, with its shady trees and pleasant lawns that meandered among them. But of course, there had been changes. Several blocks of gleaming white transportable buildings had been placed in and about the shady trees. A couple of dust-covered four-wheel drive vehicles were parked near them, along with an assortment of motorcycles, some with four wheels and some with two.

The magnificent station homestead, built so long ago by Michael Montinari, was exactly as Anna had described it to the Sister. Its wide verandas that shaded its massive, multi-coloured stone walls gave it a cool and inviting appearance. The corrugated iron roof was showing signs of its age, with many of its sheets partly rusted, as were some of the gutters.

White cockatoos flew in and about the treetops squawking noisily, heralding the arrival of the alien four wheel drive that had carried the young Sister out from Derby.

'Well, here we are Sister. I hope you enjoy your day my dear. I'm going to head over to the kitchen and get myself a feed. When you're ready to head back to town just come over and give me a yell. I know a couple of the fellas here so I'll spend the day with them. I may even come over for the funeral a bit later to see how it goes,' her driver announced as he got out of his vehicle and brushed his clothes of the imaginary dust he'd got from the interior of his air-conditioned four-wheel drive.

'Thank you for a wonderful trip, Max,' The Sister said as she climbed out.

Max gave her a nod and started toward one of the transportable buildings.

Sister Murphy could see several people milling about beneath the shady trees. In the distance, she caught a mirror glint of water. Death Adder Dam she imagined and smiled as she remembered Anna's stories. Just then she saw a man making his way down the homestead steps and heading toward her. She waited next to the vehicle.

'Hi, there—you would be, Sister Murphy, I take it?'

Sister Murphy smiled and shook the man's outstretched hand. 'Yes I am,' she replied.

'My name is Derick Jacob; I'm the manager of Cockatoo Creek these days. I hope your trip out wasn't too rough?'

'It was very enjoyable, Mr Jacob, very enjoyable indeed.'

'There is someone over in the house that is waiting to meet you, Sister. He would have come across himself, but he was still dressing when you arrived,' Derick Jacob said with a warm smile.

'I wonder who that could be. I wasn't aware there would be anyone to meet me. I have just travelled out to pay my respects at the funeral that is to be held here, and that is all,' she replied.

'If you would like to accompany me I'll take you across to the house,' Derick Jacob said with a friendly tone.

Sister Murphy followed the station manager across the well-maintained lawns and up the steps of the magnificent homestead, just as one of the glass panelled entrance doors swung open. A tall well-built man stepped out onto the veranda.

The Sister studied him carefully. He would have been around forty years of age or possibly a little more, she guessed. He wore an expensive, off-white linen suit, and an open-necked green shirt which seemed to accentuate his disarmingly pale-green eyes. He wore no hat, and his hair was the colour of beach sand and hung down over his shirt collar in an unruly tangle, that seemed to compliment his easy manner.

'Hello, Sister, I am very pleased to meet you. I hope your trip out was not too uncomfortable,' the man with the pale green eyes said.

'Most enjoyable, sir—most enjoyable indeed,' Sister Murphy replied. There was something about this man's appearance that seemed familiar. She took the outstretched hand he offered.

'My name is Michael Montinari, Sister. I am very glad to finally meet you and very happy you could join us here at the station for our dear friend, Anna's funeral.' I myself arrived here yesterday, having travelled from Melbourne so that I could pay my respects to an old woman who has meant a great deal to my family.

Sister Murphy was suddenly speechless. How could this be, it was if she was looking at a man who had risen from the grave! A man so clearly described in Anna's stories, the same pale green eyes—the same sand coloured hair. But his name had been Ballinger—Jack Ballinger, and not, Montinari. The Sister was confused. She started to feel light-headed and reached for the veranda railing for support.

'I—I am very pleased to meet you, Michael! Please excuse my manner. It's just that I'm a little taken aback by your appearance sir,' the Sister replied, 'If you could just give me a moment.' She tried to compose herself.

'Are you sure you are alright, Sister?' Michael Montinari asked with a concerned expression.

'I'm sure I will be in a moment, Michael. Let me try to explain, I have spent some considerable time with, Anna listening to her stories—stories that I have been trying to document over the last few months. It all started as a project my students were doing at the school about the early days of the cattle industry here in the Kimberley. One of my students told me that Anna worked out here at Cockatoo Creek and suggested I visit her at the hospital. As time went by, I grew very fond of Anna and intrigued by her colourful tales of her days out here at the station. Her descriptions of her friends from those days were so vivid, and explained so wonderfully well, that I found myself visualizing them so clearly, and you sir, seemed to have stepped out from those very pages and into reality.'

'I'm sorry if I have startled you, Sister. Yes, I know the stories of which you speak so very well myself, and I loved them dearly. I sat with my grandmother and listened to them so many times that

I feel I also know most of the characters off by heart,' Michael Montinari said with a gentle understanding expression.

'Your grandmother—Isabella was your grandmother?'

'Yes, that is correct,' Michael replied.

'And your father's name . . . ?'

'My father's name was, Jack Montinari, named after his father, Jack Ballinger. It was decided that because my grandmother and grandfather had never married, and that my grandfather had been murdered, they would keep the name Montinari as a way of continuing our bloodline. A little unusual I suppose. But it was decided long ago by my dear Grandmother. But, be that as it may, I should also tell you that I am the managing director of 'Montinari Incorporated' our family company, and have been for some considerable period. And now, to clarify some of the more recent happenings that may have been somewhat of a puzzle to you. Many years ago my great-grandfather, Michael, made Anna a promise that she would be looked after and would never have to suffer financial hardship for the remainder of her days. I was told that he felt partly responsible for the murder of her people at the hands of the then station manager, a Mr Jan Muller. It was a promise that he took very seriously, and over the years he assisted Anna in any way he could, and this tradition has continued over the years by my father, and by me. Anna has lived for many years in a small cottage in Derby, paid for long ago by my great grandfather and she has been paid a modest pension by our company ever since. The home Anna lived in, while hers in most respects has been kept in our companies name so that we could cover all expenses that occurred with it over the years. But now that Anna has passed away, the cottage will be sold, and to comply with her last wishes, the proceeds are to go to your school, The Holy Rosary School in Derby.' Michael stopped to catch his breath.

'My goodness—how generous, it will be most welcome,' Sister Murphy replied. She was still having difficulty coming to terms with Michael Montinari's appearance, and with his familiarity with the events in Anna's life.

'It was Anna's wish, my dear,' Michael said humbly.

'Thank you, and can you tell me, Michael, was Anna aware that your grandmother, Isabella had a child to Jack Ballinger?'

'Yes, Isabella wrote and told her when she realised she was pregnant. She knew all about it, and she knew that it was a great joy to my grandmother.'

'She never mentioned it at all, and I suppose that is why I was so surprised when I first saw you and was introduced to you, and then told your name,' Sister Murphy explained.

'Well, Sister, I am pleased that I have been able to clear up some of the details of my families earlier days for you. I should also tell you that my grandmother and I were very close. Isabella was certainly a fascinating woman and quite an accomplished artist in her day. I still live at *'Avellino,'* our family home in Melbourne and my study walls proudly display some of her works. As a young boy, I spent many hours studying them. My favourite, I suppose is one she painted of two Aboriginal women sitting on a veranda smoking cigarettes. I quite often spend time admiring it. There are many others as well. Some of waterfalls, one of ducks landing on what I imagine to be the dam here at the station and another quite remarkable scene of a dry waterhole with several boab trees lining its banks.'

'How nice for you, Michael, Isabella must have been a wonderful person. Thank you for telling me about her,' the Sister said politely.

'Well, my dear I suppose we should get on with the funeral, and the celebrations of a life well lived by a woman that has been loved by so many,' Michael Montinari replied. He took the Sisters hand and they made their way down the steps toward the group of mourners waiting near the little cemetery among the trees.

Anna's open gravesite was surrounded by a small group of people that the Sister didn't know. Probably station hands, she thought, that decided, because they worked at the station they should attend to make up the numbers for the old Aboriginal woman that none of them knew.

Michael led her past a row of well-tended graves, each with different headstones and grave markers. One of which was a simple wooden cross with a hammered brass nameplate that the

# 46 Epilogue

sister recognized as the grave of Anna's friend, the stockman, Beans. They walked on, past several more graves with names the Sister remembered from Anna's wonderful stories. They passed the headstones of Santiago Mendoza, the old Filipino cook and Anna's dear friend, the stockman Golly, and the one-time station manager Billy Anders and a little further on, the grave of Famous Feet, the old Aboriginal tracker. Next to Anna's freshly dug grave was the grave of the stockman, Dan Miller, Anna's great love. On the other side of the Aboriginal woman's final resting place was the last of them, the grave of Jack Ballinger. The headstone on this grave was a little larger than the others and had been cut from a beautiful piece of red and ivory sandstone. More than likely, the Sister thought, quarried from somewhere nearby. The words inscribed on this irregular piece of coloured stone had been carved by a careful hand and were a poignant reminder to the Sister of the sad happenings of those days.

John Arthur (Jack) Ballinger
Died 1933. Age 35 Years
Fought bravely in the war to end all wars
A good friend to all who knew him.
Wait for me, my love,
Isabella.

The gravestones listed the year each of them died, and some of them carried short lines of touching verse. Bunches of flowers taken from the station's gardens had been heaped against all of the headstones earlier that morning as a mark of respect to those who lay there among the trees.

Michael Montinari took the bible he'd found in the homestead library and made his way to the head of Anna's open grave. He began; 'We are gathered here today to celebrate the life and times of Anna Cook, a dearly loved friend to all who knew her. Anna worked here at Cockatoo Creek Station many years ago, and it was her final wish that she be buried out here next to her friends from those long ago days. Anna was a Ngarinyin Aboriginal, who, with her people, wandered into this station to beg for food almost eighty years ago.

Most of you wouldn't have heard this story, as it was so long ago. Anna's people were given food in exchange for the young Anna being left here at the station to work in the kitchen. Sometime later Anna's people were brutally murdered for having speared a station steer for food. The man that committed this unspeakable act was the Cockatoo Creek manager of that time, a man who would eventually pay dearly for his terrible crimes. Jan Muller, the station manager, was speared to death by a mysterious Aboriginal spirit man. A man the Derby police attempted briefly to bring to justice but failed in their endeavors.

That man, Pirramurar, disappeared into the bush and was never seen again. Some say his country is the wild lands near the coast to the north of here, and local legend has it that he still lives and roams there today. A fanciful story without much truth to it, I would imagine. I have been told the stories about him are many. My grandmother, Isabella met this man long ago and told me it was an experience she would never forget. The stories my grandmother told me were many, and much of what I heard from those days I have forgotten, or perhaps found a little too difficult to believe. But one thing is certain, Anna and my grandmother became very close friends during those times, and even though my grandmother never visited the station again, they remained best friends and kept in touch by letter for the rest of my grandmother's life. Anna spent the last years of her life in Derby and . . . '

Tears began to run down the young Irish Sister's cheeks as she listened to Michael Montinari deliver his eulogy. She had to turn away. She looked up into the tree-tops. Hundreds of white cockatoos were sitting quietly along the uppermost branches of the massive boab trees looking down at the sombre gathering. Some were lazily nodding their heads and shuffling about for better position on the high branches, while others were as still as alabaster statues.

Far above them all, she watched a huge wedge-tailed eagle begin a lazy circle of the station buildings.

A strange feeling suddenly tugged at the Sister's mind. A feeling that made her look beyond the handsome Michael Montinari and off into the distance. Something had caught her eye, a dark movement in the shade of the distant trees. She looked along the edges of a straggly stand of paperbarks away in the distance. The afternoon's heat seemed to distort them and make them shimmer and move about. Then, just for a second, she thought she caught a glimpse of a dark figure standing in the shade of one of the paperbarks, the figure of a tall bush native. The man held a spear in one hand and a long killer boomerang in the other and seemed to be watching them.

The sun flickered through the trees again, sending mirrored shafts of light dancing back toward the Sister. She blinked to clear her vision, and stared hard at the trees again, searching for the dark man she thought she had seen, but he'd disappeared. A mirage, she reasoned, a trick of the light. Perhaps Anna's stories were playing on her mind a little too much. She turned her attention back to Michael Montinari.

*The End*

# About The Author

The author's life experiences have included time as a construction supervisor, general builder, cabinetmaker, a painter, baker and pastry cook, and a salesman. He has traveled widely around Australia and New Zealand and spent a considerable part of his life in remote areas, which include the Kimberley, Arnhem Land, and islands off the northern coast. This is his second book. His first 'Here and There' was written as a keepsake for his children, Shannon and John and relates his travels during his days in the construction industry. The author has drawn on these experiences and his passion for early Australian history as a background for this work of fiction. Baden and his wife, Judy are recently retired and living in Renmark on the mighty Murray River.

Printed in Australia
AUHW010213181119
320073AU00008B/17

9 780648 50895